I Surrender

Monica James

Copyrighted Material
I Surrender (Book 1 in the I Surrender Series)

This book is a work of fiction. Names, characters, places and incidents are the product of the author's imagination, or are used fictitiously. Any resemblance to actual events, locales, or persons living or dead, is coincidental. Any trademarks, service marks, product names or named features are assumed to be the property of their respective owners and are used only for reference.

Copyright © 2016 by Monica James

All rights reserved. No part of this work may be reproduced, scanned or distributed in any printed or electronic form without the express, written consent of the author.

Cover Design by Marisa-Rose Shor, Cover Me Darling
Editing by Toni Rakestraw of Rakestraw Book Design
Formatted by Tianne Samson from E.M. Tippetts Book Designs

CreateSpace Independent Publishing platform

Follow me on:
Facebook: https://www.facebook.com/authormonicajames

I Surrender

Other Books by Monica James

Surrender Series

I Surrender
Surrender to Me
Surrendered
White

Something Like Normal Series

Something Like Normal
Something like Redemption
Something like Love

The Sinful Pleasures Series

Addicted to Sin

Dedication

Daniel... na na nah na nah!
I heart you...even though you drive me crazy

Chapter 1
Up, Up and Away

"Ladies and gentlemen, the Captain has turned off the Fasten Seat Belt sign so you may now move around the cabin.

"In a few moments, the flight attendants will be offering you hot or cold beverages. Now, sit back, relax, and enjoy the flight. Thank you."

Glancing at the reflection staring back at me from the window, I wonder, is this how others see me? A girl whose eyes are too big for her melancholy face. A girl whose frame is so small, her feet barely reach the sticky floor. A girl that laughs at everyone's jokes, even when she doesn't see the point of laughing at mindless nothingness. A girl whose heart has been crushed, chewed on, spat out, set on fire—and put on repeat just for fun.

Wow, when did I get so serious?

Oh, probably around the time my stupid boyfriend told me, with his stupid blue eyes, that he no longer sees a future with me. And stupid me, stares dumbfounded, thinking this is some sick joke, right? And surely he must be kidding when he leaves me standing in the bar, getting inappropriately touched by stupid strangers, pushing me out of their way to get to their destination—

the stupid bar!

Stupid! Stupid! Stupid!

Replaying our last moments over and over, the impact is still the same. I still ache. And I'm not sure if it'll ever stop.

"I don't love you anymore, Ava."

I stare, speechless, because I've surely misunderstood him. However, judging by that cold look, I know I've heard him correctly.

"What do you mean? How can you just stop loving someone?" I reply after finally finding my voice.

"It happens all the time."

That's it? That's all he has to offer me?

"Yeah, to other people, but not to us."

This can't be happening, I'm surely dreaming. How can he be so calm while I'm dying inside? But I know this is no dream when his only response to my utter desolation is a carefree shrug.

I can't believe that after four years of dating, he's going to end it with a simple shrug, and a lame ass explanation. He's got to be joking, because this person who looks like my boyfriend clearly isn't him. My boyfriend of four years would never stand in front of me, so distant, breaking my heart into a million tiny pieces.

He leans down to give me a quick, cold, dismissive kiss on the forehead.

"Goodbye, Ava."

"Goodbye? What! You're doing this now? Here?" I ask, stunned, looking around our surroundings. "In a karaoke bar? You're not coming home with me to try and sort this out?"

"I don't know what coming home with you would achieve. There's nothing to sort out. I can't be with someone who has no life goals."

He is so matter of fact. His perfect face with his perfect hair just insulted me in a not so perfect manner.

No life goals. Is he serious? I had life goals, but I gave them up for him because I love him.

"B-but…" I stutter.

He cuts me off before I can finish pleading with him to change his mind.

"Go home and forget we ever existed."

That's it? Those are really his parting words?

He turns his back on me, walking away so easily, like I never mattered to him, while I feel like I'm about to die.

I stare around the fluorescent lit bar in a catatonic stupor, questioning what just happened. He just broke up with me in a freakin' karaoke bar! I am drowning in endless tears and I'm afraid they will never stop.

I vaguely hear a song in the background being sung by a happy patron. It's Amy Winehouse's "Back to Black," and I can't help but crumble, listening to the lyrics. The irony of life has just slapped me silly, as I feel like 'I died a hundred times.'

The memory is still so fresh and I wonder how did I get here? Well, I have seventeen hours and twenty minutes of hell to endure, and by hell I am referring to myself being piled into a plane full of screaming kids, whining teenagers, and sullen-faced adults. I look at the crying baby, propped over his mother's shoulder in front of me. He is staring wide-eyed and confused as to where he is—You and me both, kid.

His mother is rubbing his little back, consoling him. I wish someone would give me the same confirmation that everything will, in fact, be okay, because this is hell.

But the worse part of that hell is being trapped with me, with my brain, and my thoughts, with nowhere to go. No escape. No place to run, or hide, or cry, or oh God help me…I raise my hand quickly, alerting an attendant to my seat.

"What can I get you, Miss?" she asks offhandedly while eye-fucking a man two rows in front of me.

Taking a closer look at her, I wonder why she cakes on so much makeup. But as I glance around the aircraft, they all seem to be wearing thick layers of gunk, like fake is the new black. But what would I know. I'm no fashion guru. I hardly wear any makeup, and when I do, it's light and natural. Only on the rare occasions when I did go all out with the foundation, mascara and eye shadow, it was because I knew he liked it. He liked it when I dressed up for him, dressed like all the wives and girlfriends of the hotshots he strived to become. I did a lot of things to please him. Too bad he never returned the favor.

"Miss?"

Oh shit, there I go again, to a happy place where stupid blue eyes and I never met.

"Um… sorry. I'll have a lemon-lime and bitter."

Then his stupid blue eyes make yet another unwanted appearance, and I recall it was his favorite drink. And now I realize, I HATE that drink, just as much as I hate his stupid blue eyes.

Before I look like a total moron, I correct myself, "Sorry, can I please make that vodka?"

"With?" the talking Barbie asks abruptly.

"With?" I reply confused, as I don't speak Barbie.

She sees my confusion and asks, "With what, Miss? Raspberry? Orange juice?" She motions with her hands to imply there is an endless list of beverages that would accompany my vodka.

I stare once again at my sad, deflated reflection in the window. Wow, I look like death—correction, death run over by a steamroller.

"Just the vodka, thanks. Make it a double."

She walks off, unimpressed by my obvious alcoholism at 7:30a.m. But hey lady, don't judge me, you'd also be drowning your sorrows if you had your heart ripped to teeny tiny pieces only hours earlier.

Yeah…this was going to be a lonnnng flight.

"Ladies and gentlemen, we have started our descent in preparation for landing, please make sure your tray tables are up and your seats are in their full upright position. Make sure your seat belt is securely fastened, and all carry-on luggage is stowed underneath the seat in front of you or in the overhead bins. Please turn off all electronic devices until we are safely parked at the gate. Thank you."

Jolting out of a semi-coma, I look sleepily down at my tray. Holy crap, I didn't drink all that, did I? Looking at the array of plastic cups, I sigh. Yup, I did.

Hands up—who's a big, fat, pathetic loser?

Barbie flight attendant clears her throat for the thousandth time. "Your rubbish please, Miss." The word rubbish really implying, "give me the proof of your raging alcoholism and get the fuck off my plane, as I need to remove my makeup with a chisel!"

I shamefully hand her my numerous empty cups.

"Welcome to Los Angeles, where the local time is 9:00a.m. On behalf of your crew, we thank you for flying with us today."

After an eternity of people shuffling off the plane, I finally set foot on home soil. I've been living in Singapore with HIM for over a year, following him to pursue his dream of becoming a corporate hotshot at a multimillion dollar globally recognized company.

I will not think about him. I will not think about him, I repeat my mantra. I am home now. Goodbye big blue eyes, goodbye laugh that made me smile every time, goodbye sculptured six pack. Ugh! Goddamned goodbye, already! And good riddance!

I am lost in thought after a grueling flight and just want to collapse into a heap and hibernate for a week.

"Ava!" I hear my name very faintly as I look around the terminal. "Ava!"

Then I see a bouncing chestnut head pushing her way through the crowd, like her 5'5" frame can wrestle any man in her path to welcome her best friend home.

Sadly, it looks like my hibernation will be put on hiatus for the time being.

"Ava! Oh my God!" she shrieks, charging into me while laughing, wrapping her tiny tattooed arms around my neck.

I awkwardly hug her back as my hands are fully engaged with my luggage. I have missed my best friend dearly, but I know I'll dread her next sentence. Why does my best friend have to be so nosey? But let's face facts—if she wasn't nosey, then she wouldn't be my Veronica. This is one of the many reasons why I love this girl to the stars and back.

"Ah, Ava, not that I'm overly concerned, but aren't you traveling a little light?"

Cocking my eyebrow, I play dumb, because maybe if I pretend like he never existed, she'll stop with the questions I'm so not ready to answer.

Of course I'm mistaken.

Laughing, she looks behind me, then back at me. "Looks like I'm going to have to be blunt. Where is your annoying, egotistical boyfriend, Harper?"

Oh man, even his name is stupid!

"Um, well about that…" I falter uncomfortably.

You'd think I could tell my best friend of ten years that my boyfriend, the man I left my home for, the man I traveled to a foreign country for, has dumped my ass a mere forty-eight hours ago.

Shit, word vomit is coming with a vengeance.

Swallowing and sighing, I give her the best explanation I can after a taxing plane ride, doused with a double dose of vodka. "He's not coming."

She stares at me, frowning, and then her mouth forms a prefect O.

Yup, she gets it. It didn't take her long, and this is why I love this girl—she can read me without words. However, the death mask I'm currently wearing might be a dead giveaway as to why Harper the asshole isn't with me.

She opens her mouth to ask me a million and one questions, which I don't want to answer.

Before I get quizzed, I hold up a finger to silence her. "V, seriously, I just want to go home. I promise to tell you all about it when I'm not in tear-soaked, vodka-stained clothes."

V nods, understanding that my story isn't one to be shared in a noisy, crowded airport. She grabs my bag and throws it over her shoulder, offering me a smile that's worth a million words.

Fuck, I love this woman.

Chapter 2
No Place Like Home

Looking at the familiar streets, I sigh, contented for the first time in forever.

V looks over, chewing on the corner of her lip. Oh man, here she goes. I look at my watch. It's been six minutes and thirty-five seconds. That's a record for little Miss Nosey Pants. She chews her lip ring anxiously while brushing strands of hair that have escaped her pigtails behind her pierced ears.

"Sooo…" she asks, looking over at me apprehensively.

And here comes the inquisition.

"I know you probably don't want to talk about it, but dude, you look like shit."

"Gee thanks, good to see you're in fine form today," I reply, tapping my navy Chucks absentmindedly on the floor.

I really don't want to talk about this. I've had enough thinking time on the plane to last me a lifetime.

"I mean that in a good way, babe. Well, not really, but I just meant you look upset and sad, and angry, and um… kind of homicidal. I'm worried, that's all. What kind of best friend would I be if I wasn't concerned?"

Even after the shitty few days I've had, my best friend knows how to make me feel better. I knew this conversation had to take place. But she wants to do this now? I really am not ready to share. But will I ever be?

"Hello? Earth to Ava!" she yells, snapping me into reality.

I know if I don't spill the beans, V won't let this go, and I have no energy to argue with her.

"V, look, Harper is a jerk. He's a lying, manipulative ass who can fall off the face of this earth, and I would thank the stars another asshole has been eradicated from this world so he can no longer hurt, betray, or break one's heart in a bar—a fucking karaoke bar I might add—as he tells his loyal partner of four years he no longer loves her and can't be with someone who has no life goals and leaves her staring at his receding form while she drowns in her tears surrounded by people singing Amy Winehouse off key!"

I take a deep breath. Oh God, there it was—word vomit.

V takes a minute to digest my ramblings, and then, all of a sudden, I see her face turn a deep shade of red.

Uh oh—she's about to explode.

"I take it you're not talking in the rhetorical sense. That motherfucker! I always hated his ass, but now…now I want him skinned and barbequed filet mignon style!"

I let out a tiny chuckle at my friend's reaction because V is a firecracker. She may be slender, but she is far from fragile. I've seen a grown man cower in fear when a famous 'Veronica Donovan Death Stare' was shot his way.

I look at my best friend, taking in her beautiful appearance. She hasn't changed much over the past year. Her long chestnut hair is tied into two messy pigtails and loose tendrils frame her heart-shaped face. Her striking green eyes are forever bright, always ready for the next adventure. She has added a second set of studs in her ears, which complement her existing piercings in her nose and lip.

"So Harper did that to you? What does he mean he no longer sees a future with you? You moved to Singapore to support his future and he feeds you that bullshit? I didn't think it was possible, but I actually hate him more than ever."

V has calmed down enough to construct a sentence without it involving too much profanity.

"Your guess is as good as mine. Maybe he woke up one day and turned into a giant ass," I answer miserably, because I seriously did not see this coming.

V peers over at me, sees my glum expression, and lets another string of profanities rip. "No honey, he was always a jackass, you were just too blinded by love. Well, you're better off without him. Why, out of 100,000 sperm, was he the one that got there first? He's a good for nothing, sonofabitch dog!" she yells, honking her horn to emphasize her frustration.

I take it back—she's just as angry as before.

Frowning, I bite my lip to stop myself from crying. I feel so lost and alone, and I think revisiting my decision to hibernate for a week is a fantastic idea.

V notices my misery and calms down, trying to make me feel better. "Hey babe, don't beat yourself up, okay? Men are all asses in their own way. I heard it was in their DNA or something." She laughs hysterically at her own joke, slapping the steering wheel in delight.

I let out a soft chuckle because it's either that or cry…again.

I stare at my reflection in the window as I vaguely hear V talking about trivial topics to try and steer my mind off Harper.

My reflection looks no better than when I saw it last, I still look lost and abandoned. I lean my head back and close my eyes, wondering when this pain will go away.

"Thanks for letting me stay here. I honestly cannot face my parents right now. I can do without the whole 'I told you so' speech."

"Mi casa es su casa." V smiles happily while making up the spare bed for me.

V's home is a modest two bedroom apartment in California, and we've had many good times in this little abode. I'm looking forward to spending some time chilling in a place I would proudly call home.

V is blessed with brains as well as beauty. She runs, and is co-owner of, a tattoo studio, Ink of Queens, downtown. I'm so proud of V, as her life could have taken a destructive turn when her parents were killed in a car accident when she was twelve. She went to live with her Aunt Mary, who just happened to be our next door neighbor. Mary treated V like her own child, and I believe her influence on V's life is the reason why my friend has such a good head on her shoulders.

When V and I met, we were two very awkward, shy teenagers, with a love for big hair bands and tacky romance films—it goes without saying we were BFF.

"So enough about me, tell me about Lucas," I coo, teasing V about her new lover.

He hasn't been given the official boyfriend title just yet, but the poor guy didn't realize what he was getting himself into when he said hello to my little friend.

Tugging on her silver bracelets, she beams, "Oh, Ava. He. Is. The. One. I just know it this time."

"Uh huh," I murmur while unpacking my underwear into the top drawer.

"Oh shush you, he is. When you meet him tonight, you'll know exactly what I mean."

"Huh? What? Tonight? Where am I exactly meeting Mr. Multiple Orgasmic Pants?" I tease.

We may not have been living in the same country, but that didn't stop my friend from spilling all the nasty details of her sex life—God bless her honesty.

"Passengers of Ego," she replies, like I should know what that means.

I cock my eyebrow at her with a 'have you lost your mind' look.

She giggles. "Lucas' band, silly. They're playing Little Sisters tonight."

Looking at the wall clock she squeals, "Oh my God, I can't wait for you to meet him. He gives me a tickle."

"I'm sure he does," I laugh, teasing my now blushing best friend.

"Oh, be quiet. You're going to have so much fun tonight!"

"Yeah, I really don't think that's a great idea," I reply, squashing my t-shirts into the dresser.

"And why not?" V asks, hands on hips, unimpressed with my response.

"Um, are we really going to start this?" I sigh, too tired to talk.

Looking over at the bed and picturing myself snuggled under the covers has my body itching to make that a reality. However, judging by the irate look on V's face, me snuggling into anything won't be happening anytime soon.

"Yeah, we really are. I'm all ears," demands V, who obviously has a bee in her bonnet today.

"Because I'm in no mood to make meaningless conversations with people I will never see again. And I really don't want strangers rubbing up against me in heat, hoping to score with the damsel in clear distress." Raising my hand in the air, I sarcastically add, "In case you're wondering, I'm that damsel in distress!"

"Ava, you need to take a chill pill. No one will be rubbing up against you, as you so elegantly put it, unless you want them to. And judging by how uptight you are, some inappropriate rubbing is exactly what you need!"

I stare open mouthed. Oh no, she didn't! Before I can rebuke, she laughs that musical laugh that automatically makes me forgive her. I'm a sucker, I know.

"Babe, look, what Harper did to you, it sucks, and I get it. But I knew this would happen eventually." She shrugs like it's common knowledge, while I stare, shell shocked.

"You what?" I ask, dumbfounded. Am I blinded by some unseen 'Harper is a douche' smoke screen?

"Harper has always been an asshole, Ava. You were just blinded by his bullshit. I hated him from the first moment you guys met. I wish we never went to that party where he sweet talked you into dancing with him, because we wouldn't be having this conversation if we had just stayed home and watched Brad Pitt like we were supposed to. You were oblivious to his controlling streak. I tried to tell you, but you wouldn't listen. Love is blind and all that crap. Harper is the past, and you came home to start afresh without that muppet in a meat suit!"

I laugh hysterically as my friend is on a rampage. Veronica never ceases to amaze me with her analogies. And no matter how politically incorrect they are, they seem to fit perfectly.

"So, you're going to unpack and unwind, and maybe have a nap, because the bags under your eyes are damn well frightening." I cringe at her comment because I know she's right, but she ignores me. "Once you're well rested and looking less corpse-like, you are totally going to go put on those gorgeous, second-skin black jeans, which make that butt look bootylicious, that red and white stripy top that reveals just enough cleavage, and your dancing shoes, 'cause my girl, we are going to paint this town red—Veronica Donovan style!"

I smile, never shocked at her bossiness. We're in for an interesting night, but I'm still unsure.

V senses my apprehension as I chew away at my lip nervously. "Don't be giving me that look, Ms. Thompson. You're going and that's final."

There's no point arguing with her because I would just be wasting my breath. She kisses the top of my head and sweeps out of my room to give me a minute to process everything that's just happened.

I collapse onto the queen bed and spread my arms out wide. My tiny arms and legs barely reach the edge of the mattress, and I feel like I'm swimming in sheets and blankets. It feels nice and comforting, and I wish I could stay hidden for the next week or… month.

What am I going to do now? I jumped onto the plane without giving my future a second thought. But now that I'm here, that future is pending for a decision.

I count the glow in the dark stars on my ceiling, wishing I was faceless just like them. I remember reading a quote that strikes a chord with me as I'm studying the illuminated stars: "Shoot for the moon, even if you miss, you'll land among the stars."

At the moment, I'd give anything to land anywhere, on the proviso that I'm free of this ache.

I can smell the rich aroma of the coffee V is percolating in the kitchen downstairs, and I can hear her shuffling around, banging doors preparing crockery for our coffee. I decide going down there is better than sulking up here.

In the words of Clarke Gable: "I never laugh till I have my coffee." I'm hoping he's right.

Although, I think it's going to take a lot more than a cup of coffee to make me laugh again.

Chapter 3
Put Your Arms Around Me

Looking at my reflection in the full-length mirror in the tiny cluttered bathroom, I sigh, utterly disheartened. I don't want to go against V's wardrobe selection for me, because that girl has style, so I pass—but only just.

With big brown eyes and long lashes that frame my face, I barely look twenty-two. The light dusting of freckles which spread across my cheeks doesn't really help my case, and I've always seen myself as cute, but not gorgeous or 'hot.'

I look semi-presentable, but I can't shake the look like I haven't slept for weeks. And no matter how many coats of mascara I apply, I still have that slight murderous glare in my eye which won't dissolve.

A night out will be good, I convince myself, while restraightening my long brown hair, which falls down my back. My dark brown eyes are covered in a deep grey shimmer with dark kohl, and my lashes are enhanced by my faithful blackest black mascara. A light dusting of foundation covers my freckles, and a sheer pink lip gloss makes me look human—well, almost. When will this hole in my chest close over? I haven't spoken to Harper since that fateful night, and I wonder, is he thinking of me?

Thinking back to happier times, Harper knew how much I was missing my friends and family, so he surprised me by buying us tickets to fly back home for a short vacation with what little holiday pay he had. I was over the moon, but look how that turned out. Yes, I am home, but I'm alone.

I moved to Singapore with Harper to support him while he pursued his dreams, but by doing this, I put *my* dreams and *my* life goals on hold. However, I didn't mind because I knew how important it was to him, and relationships are all about sacrifice. How could I have been so naïve? It was never *my* dream to move halfway across the world. But I loved him so much, and he convinced me his life goals were in turn mine, as it would benefit our future together.

So I gave up my dreams of becoming a renowned chef when I dropped out of the Culinary Institute of America at Greystone in St. Helena, California to follow Harper to Singapore where I knew no one and had no friends. But Harper made it sound like we would be living the dream. He'd lined up the perfect job for himself, a cute apartment in the CBD, and had gotten me a secretarial job at his office.

When we arrived, it most certainly was not what I thought it would be. The apartment was actually a one bedroom dwelling, above a twenty-four hour laundromat, which was put to good use all of those twenty-four hours. The job that Harper lined up for me was something a monkey in a polka dot hat could do, while smoking a cigar. It was mindless filing and running errands for everyone. But I didn't mind, as it meant I could see Harper every day. He was following his dreams, and what kind of girlfriend would I be not to support him?

After a few months, the constant hum of dryers lulled me to sleep, and I eventually liked the monotonous routine of work. And after six months, Harper was promoted to a senior role in the company. He was excelling, and the company could see he had potential.

He always looked impeccable with his pressed suits and ties, and his cocky smile, slicked back sandy hair, and strong jaw made him a favorite amongst the female population. Those big blue eyes, wow, they could encourage a vegetarian to devour a steak—raw, because what Harper wanted, Harper got. It never concerned him that being eye candy got him favors. If it meant Harper got his way, he'd sell his own mom out.

But I loved him. I loved his drive and determination. Now looking back, I realize Harper was a control freak. And not in a good, sexy way, either. He chose the places we ate, the new friends I made, and on occasion, what I wore. He would manipulate the situation and behave like it was my idea all along.

In hindsight, I should have spoken up, but with Harper, there was no such thing as a disagreement. If I was to raise a question about anything, it would end up in a huge argument, which I didn't want to have. So to prevent fighting, I would submit, which is against my nature, as I'm not a passive person when it comes to my beliefs. But to save arguing with Harper, I would give in. Man, love really is blind!

"Stop with the pity party and get your ass out here!" I swear the woman has ESP!

Enough with the depressing thoughts, I check my reflection one last time, sighing.

"Stop with the sighing already, your shoes are fine," V mutters through the door.

"Here goes nothing, Ava," I whisper to myself.

If only I knew how wrong I was.

"Would it kill you to smile?" V grins at me as we hit the pavement.

My monster stilettos make us the same height, and now I can watch the world as V sees it. I sometimes wish I could wear her rose-tinted glasses because maybe this freakin' feeling of despair, loneliness, and longing will go away.

I need to snap the fuck out of this mood, as I should be happy and excited for my friend. She animatedly bounced up and down in the twenty minute cab ride, explaining how Lucas was now acceptable boyfriend material.

I force my best attempt at a smile, considering my insides are certainly not in a smiling mood.

"There you go. You now only look a quarter homicidal, mixed with a shot of crazy."

"Ha ha. I didn't know you were a comedian. Must be all that lip locking with Lucas that's changed you," I reply, while we walk down a derelict street to reach our destination.

This part of town used to be thriving in the 60s. It was filled with touristy trinkets and unusual boutiques. Now it's packed with Chinese takeaway, pawn shops and thankfully, a few of the original, unusual boutiques from the 60s, which V and I frequent regularly. What other people consider weird or fashionably unacceptable, V and I consider vintage.

Looking down at her awesome dress, I ask, "Where did you buy that, young lady? It's amazing and I need to visit its purchase place like yesterday."

V spins around like a glamor model, flaunting her leopard print dress. "I got it at a cute store right next door to my studio. Can you believe it? I can tattoo AND go shopping all on the same block. A girl's life is complete with that kind of fashion accessibility at her disposal."

I laugh and make a mental note to visit this store. A little retail therapy cures everything, right? Rounding a corner, I see our destination illuminated by a noisy, buzzing neon sign of a cute sailor girl holding a martini glass. This venue has changed owners more times than I can count. From punk to goth to rock, now it's just a hot spot for local bands to play gigs, drink cheap booze, and eat hearty counter meals. The building has been painted black since I was last here, and it has changed its name, and surprise surprise, its ownership. I love this place. It brings back so many memories of V and me sneaking in when we were barely sixteen to enjoy the goth scene. Oh yeah, we were hardcore.

Standing in the tiny doorway are two humongous security

guards, and I thank my lucky stars these two giants weren't on guard when we were kids, as we wouldn't have stood a chance.

Now at the ripe old age of twenty-two, I have nothing to hide, however both V and I get carded. This is a common occurrence we frequently run into when we're out, and it does feel nice to know that I still look underage. With a curt nod, the security guard gives us the go ahead to enter, I smile while looking around the venue. It looks and smells the same, although due to the stifling summer we've apparently had, maybe with a hint of B.O. Gross!

The massive dance floor is identical. It's still scuffed, and no doubt it's seen many individuals bust a move over the years. The stage is now set upon a little podium against the far back wall, and on one side, off to the left of the stage, is a silhouette of a lady holding an umbrella, and on the other side, is a silhouetted man holding a golf club, indicating where the bathrooms are.

To the right, the huge neon bar is filled with many thirsty patrons waiting impatiently, while bopping away to "Arms" by Christina Perri, which is blaring over the speakers. Liquor is stored in shelves along the wall behind the bar. Tables and barstools are scattered randomly around the rest of the venue.

It's small but cozy, and with so many people packed in together, it looks excessively full.

There's one thing that's changed about Little Sisters besides management, and that's the bar staff. Now I can see that this place was appropriately named as it looks like management went out and hired all the little sisters they could find, and then the 'little sisters' raided THEIR little sisters' closets! Wow, I've never seen so much flesh on a bartender before. I bet her tips are off the scale!

V suddenly jolts me out of my prudish thoughts with the highest pitch squeal I have EVER heard.

"What the hell?" I ask, looking at her, but she's no longer by my side.

I catch a glimpse of her back as she charges over to a very tall, jock-looking guy near the stage. Who the hell is that, I question myself silently, as Mr. Random seems absolutely thrilled to see my friend. He's wearing baggy skater pants and a basketball tank with a huge number twelve on it, which exposes his intimidating biceps. His hair is slightly longish—shaggy, I guess you could call it—and is a deep brown color, mixed with a hint of copper.

Again I question myself, who is this strange man, because holy crap, V just hurdled onto his waist. This can't be? Is it? No way… Lucas?

Judging by the way they're mauling each other's faces off, I think it's safe to assume it's him. Wow, I never would have pictured my slightly alternative, Bettie Page-inspired friend finding someone like Lucas, her 'type.' Oh yeah, nice thinking, Ava, because you aren't exactly a winner with your choice of men.

I look away, uncomfortable with their blazing PDA when V bites his taut neck.

"AVA!" I hear. Maybe if I continue to look at the wall and pretend these posters have all the answers to my problems, she'll leave me alone.

"AVA!" Damn, this woman is like a pit bull.

I turn and see V waving wildly for me to join her and Lucas (I hope that's Lucas!) Sighing, as I feel they have exchanged enough saliva and the coast is clear for a repeat performance, I walk over. My heels are too high and it takes a while for me to get to them. Why does this feel like the walk of shame? I know V has told Lucas all about me, and I suddenly feel self-conscious.

However, before I can process another thought, my breath catches in my throat as I look past the doting couple and see the biggest pair of cerulean eyes observing me curiously. With a strong angled jaw lined with light stubble, he is gazing at me with his head cocked to the side, amused. But OH MY GOD with that face, which is undoubtedly out of this world, his dark brown, almost black hair sits in a frenzied, wild mess. It's longer on top with shorter sides, and as he's running his long fingers through his messy bangs, tousling it further, I nearly gag on my saliva.

Holy Fuck! Who is this person that has my heart kicking against my ribcage in excitement?

While trying not to stare and be too obvious, I trip (damn these heels), luckily catching onto the bar for support. OhMyGod!

Seriously, kill me, like now!

Timidly looking up, I see he's actually risen out of his chair to help me find my footing. Thankfully V is there to offer her shoulder before I face plant and embarrass myself further. Laughing, she says, "Lucas, may I present my best friend in the whole wide world, who surely knows how to make an entrance, this is Ava."

I nod, vaguely acknowledging Lucas while still holding onto the bar with a death grip. I scan the vicinity. I know I'm being tremendously rude to Lucas, but I can't focus. Where did bed head go?

V clears her throat like I've totally lost the plot, but I can't talk as my mouth has gone dry. I know there's an uncomfortable silence because of my reaction, or should I say my non-reaction to meeting my best friend's boyfriend.

After I hear V clearing her throat again, at full volume this time, I mentally slap myself and refocus. "Oh hey, Lucas, it's really nice to meet you."

I extend my hand for the universal greeting of hello, but Lucas' huge hand, which swallows mine whole, pulls me towards him. He traps me into a huge bear hug. I'm startled and kind of choking as I pat his back awkwardly. Man, I suck at introductions. Can this get any more awkward?

Finally after being held hostage by Lucas' arms of steel, he lets me go, and I subtly search the area for my mystery man…who is now standing directly beside V.

I can't help but stare like I'm mentally handicapped—what the hell is wrong with me?

V looks up at my object of fascination and smirks. Oh no, I know that look.

"Hey Jasper, what's up?" I look from my friend to Jasper (the cerulean phantom has a name!).

Jasper half smiles at me and replies with a shrug, "Ah, not much, just chilling before the show. Who's this?" he questions, nodding his head in my direction, his soft hair tumbling into his eyes.

He's asking who *I* am. Floor, please swallow me before I die of embarrassment.

V smirks again, and I'm going to kill her! "Oh Jasper, this is my best friend. She recently moved back from Singapore after a bad break-up, and is currently single. This is Ava."

And I'm officially going to jail for murder.

Glaring at a smiling V, I make a mental note to pay her back good and proper. I half smile, half choke in embarrassment. Judging by the huge grin plastered on Jasper's face, he seems to find watching me squirm quite hilarious.

I can't help but notice his eyes. Wow, they are the color of the deepest blue sea. Blue. Oh God, no, no, no! And here comes hysterical Ava. It's bad enough I nearly face planted in front of him, but now he surely can see the crumbling mess my face has transformed into. Okay great, Jasper most likely thinks I escaped from a mental asylum in Singapore, hitching a ride on a shrimp boat!

I let out an obvious, calming breath—better than tears I remind myself—and attempt a half smile. Who cares what gorgeous big blue eyes thinks, as I am officially D O N E with men. And in my experience, blue eyes are nothing but trouble. I try to convince myself unsuccessfully, while looking into Jasper's orbs of beauty.

"Well, it's a pleasure meeting you, Ava, I'm Jasper. I have heard a lot about you." Jasper nods politely, while the tip of his tongue quickly sweeps out to brush his upper lip.

I tell myself to breathe and calm the fuck down because as his deep voice resonates into me, I shiver in desire. Why is this stranger making me feel like I'm twelve years old again?

"Hi Jasper, I'm Ava," I reply a little too loudly, and cringe when I realize my response. Yes, Ava, we have established who everyone is—I liked myself better when he thought I was mute.

Jasper smiles, a genuine, full tooth, dimples proudly on display smile. I melt, and then berate myself. As the uncomfortable silence stretches, Jasper is looking at me attentively, leaving no part of me unexplored.

His intense gaze blushes my cheeks a bright scarlet, but I can't stop staring at him and am so conflicted with my reaction to him.

The connection between us is instant, and the air is charged with a sexual static, which makes no sense.

"Sooo…who wants a drink?" Lucas asks, sensing the tension between us.

Jasper continues his observation of me with that mystifying smirk, while I'm trying desperately not to hyperventilate.

V answers as Jasper and I continue on with our staring match. "I will, baby, a gin and tonic, please. Ava?"

Hearing my name, I tear my eyes away from Jasper and reply, "Um, no, I'm good, thanks."

How far from the truth that really is.

"J?"

Jasper's still giving me that sultry look. He finally replies, "Nah, man, all's good, I have to warm up for the show, anyway. It was a pleasure meeting you, Ava. I hope to see you around soon." Jasper stares into my eyes and time freezes.

I can only nod, as I am incapable of speech, and I watch him fixedly as he throws me an unreadable look over his shoulder before he disappears out back. Finally I can concentrate, and I remind myself to swallow. What is wrong with me? I must be getting a fever because all of a sudden, I'm heated from head to toe.

At last I feel like I can breathe again, and my brain has stopped with the fog, enabling words. "Why is Jasper going backstage?" I squeak.

"'Cause he's in the band, silly, he's the singer," V replies, and as I turn to look at her, she has the look of someone up to no good plastered all over her scheming face.

I am going to kill her, the little so and so.

Chapter 4
Bitch Claws

"Mind explaining what that was back there?" V asks, indicating with her head to where the awkwardness of mine and Jasper's encounter occurred.

"I have no idea what you're talking about," I reply, twisting my pink umbrella in some strawberry mocktail I blindly ordered.

"Oh pleeease, that was so awkward I wanted to gouge my own eyeballs out." V is sitting on her barstool, swinging her legs happily, totally oblivious to the fact that I am literally puzzled over what happened between Jasper and I. What was that? I rotate my head from side to side, feeling an impending headache approaching.

Before I can question myself further, the lights dim and the crowd roars in delight. Suddenly, out strut three very confident men, walking to their instruments like they are their weapons of mass destruction. I can see Lucas is the drummer as he gives a wave to V, who beams back an adoring smile.

My eyes flick over to a handsome, surfy looking dude with long blond hair, cut off shorts, and a white t-shirt as he picks up his blazing red guitar and places the strap over his shoulder. To the right of the stage, another member, who totally looks like he stepped off the runway, picks up his bass guitar. Lucas kicks off with a beat, and then the other two boys join in with their instruments. The crowd is cheering, holding up their beers, saluting the loud, assaulting music.

I know I'm holding my breath, along with a few other girls, who I can see are highly anticipating Jasper's arrival. The bellow of screams alerts me to his presence even before I see him hit the stage. I don't want to look up, and suddenly my pink umbrella is the best thing in the world.

V kicks me and nods her head toward the stage. Fine, I'll look; although I wish I didn't, because I'll never be the same after witnessing Jasper smolder under the bright lights, highlighting his epic hotness.

He's shielding his eyes from the blinding light, trying to catch sight of his fans, and the huge, dimpled smile on his face indicates how at home he is on that stage. I tilt my head to the side, taking in all things Jasper, and almost fall off my seat at the sight before me.

He's wearing a navy short sleeved shirt over a tight white t-shirt, ripped, snug black jeans, which ride low on his narrow hips, and scuffed combat boots. And even thought his attire is simple and plain, he looks fucking gorgeous, as I can clearly see the defined shape of his muscles under the stage lights. Jasper may not be big, but he's lean, and he has muscles in all the right places. And under that well-fitted shirt, I know, lays a well defined, well looked after physique. He isn't overly tall, maybe 5'11", but on that stage he's a giant, and he knows it, if that smirk is anything to go by.

Finally, he holds onto that microphone like it's his lifeline and sings his first note. Wow. He's not only beautiful, he is beautifully talented.

His muscled forearms are taut while playing the guitar, and I let out a breath I didn't realize I was holding. I can't stop looking at him as he is simply mesmerizing.

V is singing along to the words while I smile at her excitement. I can tell she only has eyes for Lucas, and it looks like she might be right. He may just be THE one.

Deep in thought, staring at the stage, I catch Jasper's eye. He sings a deep melody about broken dreams and lies, and stares at me intensely. I turn around to look behind me, because surely he's not looking at me that way. I turn back and catch him smirk, shaking his scruffy locks, which are sticking out in all directions. He *is* looking at me, and suddenly I am extremely self-conscious.

V catches our weird looks and kicks me hard to get my attention. I turn to look at her as she mouths, "OMG."

I roll my eyes, but internally, I am mimicking her statement.

The show is fantastic, and the boys are actually pretty good.

We're waiting for Lucas to come join us, as a DJ is programmed to play some tunes till 5a.m. It's about 1a.m., and my brain is in overdrive. I haven't slept after my grueling flight, but I'm not tired. I wonder why, then stupid blue eyes pop into my head. Oh yes, that's the reason why. He knows I'm here. And he knows I've left Singapore. But news flash, Ava, he doesn't care. He never did.

I sullenly wipe my exhausted face and I need some fresh air. I quickly push off my seat and motion to V that I'm going outside for a minute. I think she can tell by the grim look on my face why I need a breather.

The fresh air hits me and it's a relief. It's like a slap in the face, something I need to make me feel anything besides this anguish. I sidestep a bunch of squealing drunken girls, and turn to cross the road, as I see a park not too far away. I just want to sit and recollect what the hell my life is. The feeling of being back home is overwhelming, but it's the happiest I've been in a while. But there's something missing, and I know what, or should I say who, that is.

Deep in thought as I take a seat, I fail to notice a puff of smoke in my peripheral vision. I jump up in alarm, totally paranoid I have been followed by a deranged stalker. However, the street lamps illuminate a familiar face, and it's not one of a madman, it's Jasper. He quickly steps out from under the tree, concern in his eyes when he notices my reaction as he removes his hood, uncloaking his face. "Sorry, I didn't mean to scare you."

Peering up at him from under my lashes, I attempt a half smile. He's just as handsome as before, and suddenly I wonder… did he follow me here? Secretly, my insides are fist pumping in excitement, but my heart barely registers a response. Am I that dead inside? After this one breakup? Has Harper broken me forever?

"Are you okay?" he asks softly. If only I could answer that question and feel I was being truthful to myself.

"Not really, but I'll live. What doesn't break you makes you stronger and all that." Why did I just say that? I hate all those cheesy clichés.

Jasper only nods, puffing on his cigarette, and I feel ridiculous sitting while he towers over me.

"You're most welcome to sit. My moodiness isn't contagious." I earn a chuckle from him as he puts out his cigarette and takes a seat.

He leaves a gap between us and I turn to face him, tucking a leg under my knee. Under these lights, his eyes blow my mind. They're not only the deepest blue I have ever seen, they are so big, giving him an innocent, doe eyed appearance. We just sit and look intently at one another, but not in a creepy, awkward way like earlier. There's something about him, something deeper to him, and I find myself inching forward to bask in his presence.

He clears his throat. "So, V said you lived in Singapore. How did you like that?"

I shrug because even the word Singapore hurts my heart.

"It was okay. The food was great, which was right up my alley, because before I left I was in the middle of getting my degree in Culinary Art."

Jasper nods, watching me closely, eager for me to go on.

"The people are really lovely, so respectful of one another. It was a nice change from living in L.A., where you don't know who to trust." Trust, even that word makes me want to puke.

Jasper chuckles, and the sound drives my flesh into a frenzy. "Yeah, I know what you mean. What did you do for a job over there?"

"I worked as a file clerk—correction, it was office bitch."

Smiling sincerely for the first time in a long time, I'm so pleased at myself for being able to string a sentence together, as it's nice talking to Jasper. He's a really good listener and being in his presence is strangely soothing.

My eyes can't help but stray and I notice Jasper has a scar above his right eyebrow, like one would have after sporting a piercing. His top lip is perfectly bow shaped, and his bottom lip is deliciously full. Looking at his mouth, the only thing that mars that perfection is a small scar, running along the corner of his bottom lip. Staring at it, I realize that makes him all the more attractive. I marvel at the smoothness of it, and just stop myself from behaving like a madwoman and creepily reaching out and touching it.

"So, what about you?" I ask, surprised at my ability to voice a coherent remark after mentally undressing Jasper.

He shrugs, looking straight ahead, deep in thought. After a while he turns to look at me, his head tilted slightly. He looks baffled, like he's attempting to figure out an ambiguous puzzle. I have a feeling that puzzle is me, which makes zero sense, as I only met this man like five seconds ago. I mean, it would be absolutely no sense if there was some weird chemistry happening between us, right?

Snapping me out of my daze he says, "I was born and raised in Chicago, and I have an older brother who is thirty-one. But I don't see much of him, as he lives in Texas. My mom is still in Chicago, and she remarried like two years ago." He takes a deep breath before he quietly adds, "My dad died last year in a house fire."

I gasp, as losing a parent is simply awful. I open my mouth to offer my condolences, but Jasper shakes his head, and quickly continues, not wanting to acknowledge his comment. "Music is my life, and so…" However, before he can finish his sentence, a loud wailing can be heard from across the street.

"JASPER! Are you out here? JASPER!"

We both look at the culprit assaulting our eardrums, and I see the biggest blonde bimbo, waving frantically at Jasper. I consider this female a threat, but ignore the reasoning behind that impractical response.

She is tall, probably 5'9", and has the silkiest blonde hair I've ever seen. It runs down her back, almost touching her tiny waist. And as she rushes toward us, I try not to notice her bountiful assets, which bounce with each step she takes. A female with such a small frame and boobs like hers can only mean one thing—there is no way they're real.

Her skintight black jeans and turquoise silk halter shape her slender frame, and as she approaches in her monster wedges, I see Jasper tense up. Curious about his reaction, I look between the two, interested.

"Jasper, I'm so sorry I'm late. Work ran late, traffic was hell getting here, but here I am," she declares, spreading her hands like she has solved some riddle.

"That's okay, Indie, I knew you'd make it if you could," Jasper replies evenly, clearing his throat.

Indie? Seriously, that's her name?

Indie looks at me, and then at Jasper, then back at me, and the hatred between us is instantaneous. She raises a suspicious sculptured eyebrow, and rudely sticks her hand into my face without a word. I think she wants to shake my hand, but I can't be too certain. Does she want me to shake her hand, high five her, or play patty cake?

I glance down at her limb like it's an offending object, and pull back slightly. Who the hell introduces themselves by sticking their hand into someone's face, expecting a handshake without a verbal introduction? Crazy people, that's who!

"I'm not too sure what you're expecting me to do with your hand, but would you kindly remove it from my personal space?"

She looks at me, clearly irritated, so I continue. "Normal people don't go around waving their claws in someone's face. Civilized people usually use language to express their hellos. But I guess you don't fall into that category."

Wow...hello, bitch claws! Where did that come from?

Indie opens her mouth, attempting to answer, but my uncalled for insolence has obviously pissed her off, and she storms away while glaring at me—oops, I've clearly pissed off the princess. But suddenly, I remember Jasper is sitting next to me, and my manners have obviously taken a holiday to insult a total stranger. No matter how annoying she is, it gives me no right to be rude to her, even though she totally deserved it, the impolite tramp. *Okay, Ava, enough*, I scold myself.

I then question, who is this person to Jasper? Have I just insulted his friend, or *girlfriend*?

I turn steadily, not sure what I'll see. Fortunately he's hiding a dimpled smile and biting his lip to contain his laughter.

Kudos to me.

Chapter 5
Home Sweet Home

It has been three days since I've been home and I can't put off the inevitable, I have to go see my parents. Don't get me wrong, I love my parents, but they are sometimes too overbearing and treat me like I'm five years old. As you can imagine, when I up and left with Harper, they nearly had a coronary.

Walking up the driveway of my childhood home brings back so many welcome memories. When I lived here, I always thought it was so big and welcoming. But now when I look up at the window of my old bedroom, I see my hopes and dreams of marrying my Prince Charming shattering all around me onto the perfect lawn.

Snapping out of my funk, I knock on the front door and am greeted by my mother. "Oh, honey, you don't have to knock. This will always be your home. I've missed you, come in. I baked us cookies." And it's like Groundhog Day all over again. Things in the Thompson house will never change.

I enter my old home—it's exactly how I remembered it. The living room has the same black leather sofa, two recliners, and a huge flat screen. My mom has added a few paintings and knickknacks, but the place even smells the same. Dad is watching a football game, and he rises when he sees me.

"Princess, it's so good to see you," he says into my hair while I wrap my arms tightly around his chubby frame.

He pulls me back to get a good look at me. "Wow, princess, have you grown?"

I laugh cheerfully. "No, Dad, I'm twenty-two, I think I missed that train long ago."

Teasing me, he pulls me in for another hug, while Mom ushers us into the kitchen.

"Sit, sweetheart. It's been so long since we've seen you," my mom says, pulling out a seat for me.

I oblige, and she serves up a few cut sandwiches and pours me a glass of juice. We all sit, politely chewing for a few minutes, all too afraid to address the huge elephant in the room. But as my mom clears her throat, I know she's about to set that elephant free.

"Honey, where's Harper?"

His name still tears a hole right through me, and I pick at my lunch, suddenly not very hungry as I blankly stare out the window.

There's a long, awkward silence before I confess, "Harper and I broke up, Mom. He broke up with me the day before we were scheduled to come visit. He said he didn't love me anymore, and judging by the way he broke up with me, he hadn't for a long while. He couldn't see a future with me because I had no life goals. He told me to go back home and forget what we had. I exchanged my ticket for a one way trip, and I am officially back for good." I say, sniffing back a tear.

That was the first time I repeated Harper's actual words out loud, and God, it still hurt like he only had said it seconds ago. My parents' faces mirror my shock and disbelief, and all of a sudden, my dad's face tightens.

"How dare that sonofabitch! How dare he!"

"Calm down, Paul," my mother coos.

"I most certainly will not calm down, Maggie. How dare he speak to our daughter that way. I'll fly myself over to Singapore and teach him a thing or two about life goals." Now I see where I get my temper from.

Mom soothes a hand over Dad's clenched fist while I sigh. Harper is like a disease, and I'm infected with his sickness, and now, so are my parents.

"So, honey, are you coming back home?" Mom asks hopefully.

I honestly haven't even thought about that. What am I going to do?

"I'm not sure, Mom. I'm staying with V at the moment until I decide what to do."

"You will return to CIA, won't you? You dropped out when your grades were exceptional, and your teachers were singing your praises. You were top of your class, then you just left… to become an office worker." So this is my life, according to my mom.

"It wasn't that simple, Mom."

"You were going places, honey. I just know you would have become a world famous chef with your dishes."

"You don't know that, Mom. You weren't in my classes," I reply, pissed.

"That's true, but your father and I saw and tasted the dishes you created. Your creativity and your interest to try new recipes made you unique and special. Unlike other parents who can't appreciate their child's chosen career path while they learn, your father and I were lucky enough to actually see what you were creating. And that's what you were doing, Ava, you weren't just cooking, it was an art for you."

I sigh because my mother is right. I loved creating dishes that were different. They were my work of art on a plate. It was my way of expressing myself through food.

I feel like I'm suffocating with all this deep talk, and Dad sees my mood change as he clutches my hand. "Whatever *you* decide, princess, we will support you. We have your old car in the garage. You take that, stay with Veronica for a while, and see what happens. Culinary school isn't going anywhere. You take a breather and decide what's best for you." I love my dad, as we're always on the same page.

My mother however, doesn't look impressed with my father's comment, but doesn't say a word. Wow, another awkward silence.

I seem to be having a lot of them lately.

After lunch, my dad leads me to the garage out back, where my little white Honda sits. It looks exactly the way I left it, down to the bobbling skeleton head hanging from the rearview mirror. Dad hands me the keys, and as I sit inside my car, the feeling is surreal. I have good memories in this car. Of Harper and I being happy, driving around like we didn't have a care in the world. And back then, we didn't. But now, man, it even hurts to breathe.

Waving goodbye to my parents, I head back to Veronica's studio to watch her work and kill some time. Any distraction is better than being alone.

Chapter 6
Closure is the Key

The tattoo gun is buzzing loudly when I enter Ink of Queens. V looks up from the back room through her little window, her hair bundled up in a bandana to keep it off her face.

"Hey, bestie," she yells while tattooing.

"Hey, babe," I reply, and collapse onto the sofa next to her.

I have no tattoos, and don't think I ever will. But never say never. V has quite a few covering her arms. They are colorful tattoos of cartoon characters she loved as a kid. But being the playful artist that she is, she designed them to be a little more adult friendly. Snow White now looks like she's had a makeover: A Hugh Hefner makeover.

"What did you get up to today?" she asks while working away.

"Saw my parents, and yes, it went how you think it did—awful. On the plus side, I got my car back."

"Oh my God, you got Harriet back?"

"Yes, V, I got my car back, and its name is not Harriet," I reply, giggling at the imagination on this girl.

"And why not?" V asks, bunching up her nose in query.

"'Cause it just isn't. And besides, Harriet sounds like an old lady's name," I reply, picking at a loose cushion thread.

"Harriet the Honda is a great car name. Don't you think, Henry?" Her client grunts in agreement, as I think he's too afraid to argue with Veronica while she's wielding a tattoo gun so close to his privates.

"Sooo…You coming with me tonight?" V playfully asks.

"That depends on where you're going." I laugh at my friend's randomness. I never know what to expect from her, so I always like to clarify *where* she's thinking of going before I blindly agree.

"It's Andy's birthday party," V says, like I should know who Andy is.

I lift my eyebrow in query. "Who is Andy?"

"Oh sorry, I always forget. I talk about you to the guys so much, I feel like you know them, too. Andy is the bassist, who looks like he's just walked off a runway in Milan."

Oh, Mr. Model has a name.

I shrug. "Yeah, why the hell not. It'll be fun, and I can drive my car that has no name."

She throws her gloves at me as she finishes with her client, who pays, then hobbles out the door with a freshly inked, bandaged thigh.

"I know why you really want to go. Eh? Eh?" She smiles, nudging me and wiggling her eyebrows up and down.

"Oh, yeah? Please enlighten me, oh wise one." I smirk sarcastically at her.

"Duh,' cause of Jasper. I saw the way you two were eye-fucking each other. You go, girl. Jasper is…" she trails off, and I wait for her to continue. She looks deep in thought to find a word to best describe Jasper, but only shrugs. "It'll be so much fun tonight. I'm so happy you're back for good."

I look at her suspiciously—what is my friend plotting?

V locks up and I follow her in my car. Driving always clears my head, and I love my car, as we've been through a lot. I look at the heating vents where Harper accidently dropped his spare car key. I can still hear the rattle and my stomach drops. I must remember to remove that key and burn any evidence of it existing. I take a calming breath and let my mind think about Jasper.

I've been kind of avoiding thinking about him after our weird but nice chat a couple of nights ago. After I insulted Indie (who the hell names a kid that!), we both went back inside and I didn't see him for the rest of the evening. I didn't want to think we had a weird moment outside, but it kind of felt like we did. There was definitely some kind of strange chemistry in the air. But I shouldn't, and wouldn't be having any "moments" with him or anyone else for a long time, as I was going to focus on me.

Pulling up at V's, she races into the shower while I look through my clothes, wondering what the dress code will be. I decide, seeing as the temperature is still stifling, to wear a simple, but stylish blue silk dress that flows out to the knee. When choosing shoes, I find myself wondering which ones would make me the perfect height to peer into someone's beautiful blue eyes. Shaking that thought out of my head, I settle for the lowest heel.

When I'm ready and waiting on V, who has changed five times, I look at my phone. He hasn't called or even texted me. Why? What have I done that he can't even be civil towards me? I need closure, damn him, and in my pretty dress, standing in V's kitchen, looking at my phone, I decide that's what I need to do to move on. That's what I need to ease this ache—even just a fraction.

I feel happy, well, maybe the word is relieved that after all this, there may be light for me, when all I have been surrounded in is darkness.

~

"Why are you so smiley?" V asks suspiciously.

Cruising down some very ritzy houses by the beach, I breathe in the ocean breeze. "I have made a decision. I'm going to get closure with Harper. That's what I need to do to move on." I am scared to look at V, as she is quiet, which is never a good sign.

"What do you mean by closure? Oh, Av, you're not thinking of going all *Basic Instinct* on his ass, are you?"

"No, V, even though the bastard does deserve it. I think I'm going to send an email. Seeing as he's chained to his desk all day long, he's certain to get it. I'll explain how I feel and that I need closure to move on. I respect his decision, wish him a happy life, and so long, etcetera," I say quickly, hoping to convince her, and myself, that this ingenious plan will work.

V doesn't look convinced and sighs. "Babe, I get you need closure, but I don't want you to get your hopes up that this tool will actually contact you. He's made no effort to contact you so far, and he knows you're back home. What makes you think he'll respond to an email? He's a jerk, and jerks like him don't respond to anything unless it benefits them, or their dicks."

She's right, but I just can't go on like this. "I know, V, but I have to at least try. Maybe if I try, that'll be enough. I can tell myself I did all I could, and maybe, just maybe…" I pause on the verge of tears, "I'll believe it."

V throws her arms around my waist while I swerve. "V!"

"Sorry, you just looked so sad. It was a knee-jerk reaction. Anyway, enough with this depressing talk, because that's where our party is." Pointing to a huge, three story mansion on the beachfront, she raises an eyebrow excitedly. "For tonight, just forget about it all, okay? Have a good night, let your hair down, and forget Harper Holden ever crossed your path."

I smile half heartedly—if only it was that simple.

Chapter 7
Quiet Company

This house is a freaking castle, a modern chic castle, that is. We peer up at the towering white building, which is mostly made of glass, and can see that the party is in full swing.

"Whose house is this?" It's a palace. A very modern, I can see right through the house kind of palace, but it's gorgeous.

"It's Andy's girlfriend, Mariah's, house. Her dad is a senator, and this is their beach house. They come here on vacation and rent it out when it's unoccupied. Mariah is a doll. She and Andy are meant for one another. I can't wait for us to all hang out and be best friends." She smiles breathlessly while we scale the long driveway.

When we finally reach the open front door, I can hear music blaring from inside. The sudden sensation of running back to the car and high tailing it back home to hide under my blanket overcomes me. V senses my shift and stands behind me, pushing me into the door. There are so many people here, and I'm glad I picked one of the best dresses I own. The guys are dressed in jeans and shirts, and the girls are dressed in very couture looking outfits. These people look like they have too much time and money to play with. With their whitened teeth and fake-tanned skin, I cringe, astounded that people like this exist.

"Wow," is all I say to V, who's looking around for Lucas.

"Oh quit it with the sarcasm. Most of them are lovely people who look like they—"

"Belong in a Beverly Hills 90210 rerun," I finish. She just smirks at my smartness, and we locate Lucas, playfully slapping Andy on the back. We walk over; well, I walk, while V practically sprints.

"Hey, baby." Lucas smiles, wrapping his strong arms around her tiny frame and lifting her feet off the ground, while she squeals in excitement. I stand a few steps back as I remember the last time I encountered a famous Lucas hug.

"Hi, Ava." Lucas waves, sensing my apprehension.

"Hi, Lucas. It's really good to see you again," I say, and I'm so proud of myself for constructing a sentence this time around.

I look around the happy group and give Andy a small smile.

"Hi Ava, I'm Andy. We haven't been officially introduced, but I know a lot about you from V. This is my girlfriend, Mariah," he says, nodding to the pretty girl to his left.

I extend my hand out first to Andy, and then to Mariah, who laughs, and pulls me in for a hug. "I feel like I know you already, so no handshaking, okay?"

I nod, smiling at her slight country twang—she must be from Mississippi.

"Happy birthday, Andy, by the way." I smile politely.

"Hey, thanks, Ava, much appreciated." Mariah passes me a glass of something bubbly, which I accept gratefully.

"Hey, is Shooter coming?" Lucas questions.

I look over at V, who is staring affectionately up at Lucas. She must feel my stare and mouths "guitarist" to me. Oh, okay, Shooter is the other guitarist.

"What about J?" asks Lucas. Just the mere mention of his name, correction, just his initial, is enough to make my stomach drop for some stupid reason. I look casually at Andy, waiting for a reply.

"I'm not sure, man. You know Jasper, moody artist and all. Never know which Jasper you'll get." I try to act nonchalant, but V can see straight through me.

I'm convinced this girl was a detective in her former life.

~

The night passes smoothly, but as the drinks flow freely and the alcohol kicks in, the amorous couples start to get very affectionate and I feel like I'm intruding on their private moments. I am an outsider, wishing I was a part of their love and devotion. I would give anything to feel that love again. Isn't that what everyone wants, to find their soul mate in life? Scoffing at my juvenile ideals of romance and love, I retreat to the balcony, overlooking the water. There are a few drunken couples cradling each other, but they are far enough away that I can't hear or see their tender, private exchanges of love.

It's a beautiful, clear night, and the breeze from the water brushes my cheeks like a lovers caress. I look out at the ocean, contemplating my life. How did I become that girl? Why did destiny select me to pass Harper's path four years ago? What was the point of it all if our fate was headed for a collision course all along? Looking at a sea bird flapping its wings against the full moon, I wish I could grow wings and fly away from everything and be free. I wish I could lose myself in the vast ocean and float away from all this pain in my heart.

I bow my head onto the railing and let the tears roll freely. This is the first time I've let it all out and allowed myself to think about how he broke me. I will never be the same Ava Thompson ever again. And that's because I fell in love. What was the point of loving if it ended this way?

"Hey," a voice whispers, startling me.

I whip my head around, quickly wiping away my betrayal of the ache in my chest. I see Jasper standing with his back against the railing, looking concerned. I didn't even hear him approach, and I wonder how long he's been standing here.

I can't even verbalize a hello, or pretend like everything inside me doesn't want to break down. This time it's not because I'm silenced by his beauty, no, it's because I can't pretend that I'm going to be okay. I can't guarantee my parents that I'm going to go back to school, or promise V I'll be the happy, adventurous friend she once knew. But most importantly, I can't promise myself I'll get through this and come out on top. It just hurts, it hurts to breathe.

Jasper, sensing my despair, unexpectedly pulls me into his warm embrace, and I do all that feels natural in this situation, I cry.

Chapter 8
Fly Away

I don't know how long I stay in Jasper's arms crying. He says nothing, only rubs my back, trying to sooth me. He rests his chin on my head and takes a deep breath. Totally self-conscious that I am blubbering all over his black t-shirt, I slowly pull away when I think all my tears have dried up.

Jasper gazes at me with curious, worried eyes, and I'm taken by surprise as he slowly reaches forward, running a knuckle over my cheek to wipe away my runaway tears. I stare at him and heave a sigh. I just have no words.

He smiles down at me, raising a mischievous eyebrow. "The party isn't that bad, is it?" I half laugh, half sniffle. Good, laughing is better than being an emotional ball of tears.

I peer out over the railing, feeling comforted by Jasper's presence. "So, do you make a habit of consoling melodramatic crybabies?" I ask, attempting to make light of my embarrassing meltdown.

Jasper lets out a deep, throaty laugh. "Only the pretty ones." His comment throws me off guard, and I chew my lip nervously.

To break the silence, I whisper, "I didn't see you arrive. Have you been here long?"

"Not that long. I came out here when I couldn't see you inside."

Again I am taken aback by his admission. "Sorry that you came out here when I was such a mess." I decide then and there I need to stop being an emotional pariah in public, especially when Jasper is likely to walk in on my tears.

"Never apologize for being you, Ava. True feelings that are raw, no matter how messy they may be, I will gladly take over superficial, insincere actions. You told me so much about yourself—about your vulnerability and your heartache, and you didn't even utter a single word. Your tears told me everything. Sometimes those cheesy metaphors hold some truth."

Wow, I'm speechless. This guy is beautiful AND smart. Jasper, I've decided, is a conundrum, one with millions of pieces.

"So, count back two minutes before I arrived, what were you doing?" he asks quietly. I think back, hmm… okay, before I wanted to jump off the balcony, oh yeah, that's right, the bird.

Brushing my hair out my eyes, I murmur, "I was wishing I was a bird. That I could fly away and never have to land. I don't want to plant my feet into anything permanent, I just want to fly away when things get tough."

"A bird, huh?" Jasper asks politely, ignoring my emotional outburst.

"Yup, a bird."

"I can see how being a bird would rock. I like your animal choice." He smiles, leaning over the railing.

He stares out into the ocean, deep in thought. His tousled hair is blowing slightly in the wind, and as he runs his fingers through it, I realize this is a nervous habit of his, and I wonder what he has to be nervous about.

"So, apart from being a rock star," I ask, "want else do you do?"

Rewarding me with a full smile, he replies, "Rock star, that's funny. Music is my passion and I feel so privileged people come see us play. But when I'm not a rock star, as you so sophisticatedly suggested, I work at an animal shelter. It's downtown, a twenty-four hour clinic where people bring in hurt or lost animals. I work most nights, as I'm a night person. Sleeping is overrated, anyway." I stare, stunned, because I was not expecting that.

When I don't speak, Jasper chuckles and asks, "Oh no, please don't tell me you're an animal hater?"

"God no!" I answer too quickly. "I was just taken aback…Your job is so important, so fundamental, and I admire that."

Jasper is now the one that looks taken aback and I apologize quickly. "I'm sorry, that came out kind of creepy, and semi-stalkerish."

Jasper throws his head back in laughter. "No, please, not at all. I just don't get too many people admiring what I do, seeing as it's below minimal wage and the hours suck. But I like it, the animals are cool, and they don't mind me playing my music loudly—well, they haven't told me otherwise." He smirks with two big dimples hugging his cheeks.

Even with his lame jokes, this boy makes me forget I was crying my eyes out five minutes earlier.

"So, Ava, I know this is really personal and you can tell me to go screw myself, but are you okay? I walked into some heavy shit, and well, I now feel like I'm involved, and I want to help, if I can. What can I do to make it better?"

If only it was that simple and I could take a miracle pill that would subside these emotions. "It's not your problem, Jasper. I really appreciate your kindness and concern, but this something *I* don't even know how to fix."

"Fair enough. But all I know is that guy is a jerk. He will realize what he's done, and that he's made a horrible mistake. He'll come running back, begging for forgiveness, and I hope you kick his request, along with his ass, to the curb."

I laugh a proper full-throated, genuine laugh. I really couldn't have phrased it any better. But deep down, I'm scared to think what would actually happen if Harper did come back to me. Would I kick his forgiveness to the curb? I hate that I can't commit to an answer when I know what it should be.

"Judging by your silence and plagued expression, kicking one to the curb may not happen?" He looks at me curiously, like he authentically wants to know.

Talking with Jasper eases some pain, if only temporally, and I answer honestly, "I know what the answer should be, but love doesn't make sense, right? The harder it is, the more a person tries to make it work and would do anything, sacrifice anything, to have their happy ending. I thought I knew the end of my story, and it was with Harper. But now, I'm not so sure of anything."

Jasper looks at me with inquisitive blue eyes, and cautiously reaches out to barely graze my cheek with his fingertips, startling me. "Ava, no one is sure of anything. Life throws us challenges and we have to either embrace them, or turn our backs in fear. In my personal experience, what doesn't break you, make you crazy or homicidal, are experiences to be learned from. I'm not pretending to know what Harper did to you, or how you feel. But judging by the way you are now, he broke you. Don't let someone who doesn't give a shit dictate how you plan your future. Because, babe, it's just that, it's yours to plan. You can't live your life for someone else, as you will fade and become a shadow of your former self."

I gasp at his honesty, and take a closer look at the astounding enigma in front of me. His skin looks a smooth, creamy white, set against the contrast of his dark messy hair. His perfect, strong, angled jaw is covered in heavier stubble from when I last saw him, and his simple nose is slightly peaked at the tip, giving him an almost arrogant look, but it complements his face. His cupid bow mouth is sensual, and with that tiny scar, that one imperfection, I can't help but shiver at its beauty. But there is so much more to him than just his appearance. I stare, just stare into his eyes, those blue, endless pools of wisdom, and for the first time, I really look past his beauty because his mind, his beliefs, are what I find more appealing that his stature.

I don't know why, but I turn my cheek deeper into his palm, as his warm fingertips are still softly stroking my face. It feels like the natural thing to do, which is ridiculous, because I don't know him well enough to be behaving so forward, but I can't help it. I couldn't have stopped myself, even if I tried to. The scene to anyone looking in on us is intimate, but not sordid. It's kind, it's supportive, and it's just magnetic.

Jasper's blue, sultry eyes are searching mine closely, and as I peer up at him through my lashes, a heat scorches throughout my entire body. Where has this come from? I was mourning my ex-boyfriend not long ago, but now, now I feel something, as little as that may be, but that something isn't painful. No matter how small it may be, it gives me hope that maybe, just maybe, things will get better.

"What the fuck do you think you're doing with my boyfriend?"

And then that hope shatters, along with my heart.

Chapter 9
Girlfriend

My cheek feels cool as Jasper quickly removes his fingers, resembling a child being caught with his hand in the cookie jar, and the look on his face is one I cannot read. His mouth is hanging open, ready to speak, but then he closes it quickly, changing his mind. He looks slightly annoyed and frustrated, like he is unhappy with Indie, and I have a feeling he doesn't agree with the title she just loosely threw around.

"Well… I'm waiting," Indie spits, tapping her stiletto-shod foot impatiently. I am shocked. All I can hear on repeat is the word, boyfriend. I shouldn't be upset, but I am.

"Indie, calm down. We were just talking, there's no need to overreact," Jasper says, rubbing his forehead.

"Overreact? So you're telling me a girl dribbling all over you doesn't merit a reaction?" Indie is glaring daggers at me, and all I can think is wow, merit, that's a big word for the Barbie doll.

"Look, there's nothing to be mad about, okay? There's nothing to explain because there was nothing going on. Right, Ava?" Jasper asks me coolly.

There was indeed nothing going on per se, but then again, I

felt like we were sharing another moment. Am I totally that out of touch with the male species?

Clearing my throat, I affirm his statement. "Jasper is right, Indie, we were just talking. I just broke up with my boyfriend, a bad breakup, and Jasper was lending an ear, that's all."

Indie, still seething, flicks back her hair. "Fine, but next time you want to *talk*, keep your hands to yourself." I don't dare clarify my hands were indeed to myself, but it was *her* boyfriend whose hands were not. Yes, I know I wasn't innocent, but it was my cheek, technically my *hands* were not involved.

"Okay, yeah sure, sorry," I mumble uncomfortably.

Jasper clears his throat, obviously ill at ease with the situation. "Indie, Ava, do you want something to drink?"

Indie, still glaring at me, crosses her arms. "Yeah, sure, thanks. You know how I take it." I cringe at the obvious sexual innuendo, and Jasper blanches.

Declining, I silently shake my head no.

"Well, I'll catch you around soon, Ava," he whispers quickly, taking off and leaving me alone with the queen of all bitches.

Pushing back off the railing, I'm desperate to make an escape, but she steps forward, her hand slapping down on the banister in front of me, foiling my plans to retreat.

Stepping inches from my face, she hisses, "Listen here, *bitch,* whatever sob story you have fed Jasper, you'll quit it with the innocent eyes and leave him the fuck alone. He's mine, and he will NEVER leave me for you, got it? You will not talk to him, look at him, or talk to him via your annoying little friend. Forget you ever met him and go back to the depressing place you crawled out from. If I ever, EVER, see you talking to Jasper again, I will personally make your life a living hell. You think your breakup was bad? I'll make that pain seem like a picnic. So stay the fuck away."

My chest is rising in panicked breaths as my temper is about to boil over. I am picturing tossing Indie over the railing, while doing a victory dance. Taking several calming breaths, I close my eyes and slowly cool down.

What can I say? She's right; if the tables were turned and I saw Harper touching another woman in such a way, I would be behaving like Indie. Maybe not as crazed, but I understand. Love makes you do crazy things. So I do all I can do, I nod, deflated, and walk away.

Walking into the living room, I see V sitting on the armrest of the chair Lucas is occupying. Seeing my face, which I can imagine looks confused and hurt, she reads me instantly. Hopping up quickly, she races over to my side.

"Are you okay? What's happened? You look like you've been crying."

Attempting to muster the bravest smile, I reply, "I'm okay, V, just tired. Would it be okay if Lucas took you home?"

V raises an eyebrow. "Of course he can. I'm worried about you, though. I can leave with you," she offers, nodding.

"No, it's okay. You stay. You're having a good night. Don't let me ruin it. I just want to go to bed." V looks at me, unconvinced. "I'm sure, V." I am defeated and just want to go home.

She sighs and nods. "Okay. But you need me for anything, you call."

Looking around, she attempts to attract Lucas' attention so I can say goodbye, but he seems to be in a deep conversation with Andy. Casually peering around the room, I see those cerulean eyes, looking at me regretfully.

I give Jasper a look filled with disappointment and finality. I will respect Indie's request and leave Jasper alone. I convince myself that's why I'll no longer talk to him, or even look his way. Not because Jasper disregarded our moment as nothing. I don't know why I expected anything more. I couldn't rely on Harper, so why would I expect anything more from Jasper, a complete stranger?

Jasper's face is one of concern, his brow crinkling. It appears he's about to walk over to me, but Indie saunters to his side, whispering God knows what into his ear, while smiling like a cat that got the cream. I look away, disgusted. I'm done.

But I don't understand why this is upsetting me so. I've only spoken to this guy twice, but yet I feel somewhat envious of Indie salivating all over him.

V notices our exchange and looks at me suspiciously. "What's going on with you and Jasper? Is he the reason you're leaving early?"

Unable to lie to my best friend, I shake my head, indicating I don't want to talk about it. I know I'm in for an inquisition when she comes home, but I don't want to talk about this with so many people around.

"We'll talk about this later."

Jadedly nodding, I pull her into a tight hug and wave my goodbyes to everyone.

I allow myself one last glance at Jasper, who is still looking at me with a look of pure defeat marring his troubled features. I memorize those eyes and close the door on everything Jasper.

Driving home, I let a single tear escape, but I wipe it away furiously. Why the hell am I crying? Why should I care if Jasper disregarded what happened between us? I've sworn to myself I won't let another be the center of my universe, and the next relationship I'm focusing on is with myself. I'm going to heal myself, heal my heart, because how can I make another happy when I'm not happy with myself?

Chapter 10
Save Me

"Okay, spill it." Obviously no small talk with V this morning. Staring at my soy chai latte, I puff out an exhausted sigh. It's Sunday, and I really don't want to talk about last night. However, I know V won't let this go, and I might feel better after I share.

After tossing and turning all night, I was wide awake before the morning sun peeked through my blinds. I'm so tired of being tired and wanting to cry all the time, but I can't sleep. And adding to my insomnia is not one, but two pairs of blue eyes, haunting my dreams—like I didn't have enough problems to deal with.

"V, I really don't know what you want to hear," I reply honestly.

"How about the truth, Ava? You need to talk about this. I don't know what the fuck is going on with you. You've told me *what* happened with Harper, but you haven't told me what's important, how you feel. And what is up with you and Jasper? Don't you dare deny it. I can feel the sexual charge bouncing between the two of you."

There's no point arguing because she's right. I'm woman enough to admit that there *is* some weird, sexual charge between Jasper and I, which makes no sense considering I only just met him. I don't know what it is, and I'm too afraid to question it further. I haven't even fully faced the whole Harper issue yet. So dealing with whatever 'this' is between Jasper and me, is something I'm in no hurry to explore.

V is looking at me, waiting for an answer, so I shrug, overwhelmed. "V, the Harper thing, it hurts. It hurts every day. Waking up and getting out of bed is a chore. I want to cry most of the time, and if I don't want to cry, I want to scream. I want to scale the tallest building and scream at the top of my lungs, scream and scream into the wind, 'why did this happen to me? What did I do to deserve this?' But then I question, what's the point? How's that going to make me feel any better? It's not. It's just going to keep this awful cycle of Harper hurt on repeat. I want it to end. I want out. And the Jasper thing, V, I don't even want to go there, because I seriously don't know. It must just be my hormones in overdrive because he's smoking hot. And anyway, I'm not prepared to do anything with him, or anyone else, because I broke up with Harper like five minutes ago. I'm just a fucking mess." I sigh, rubbing my temples.

V stares at me, like she's only really seen me for the first time since my return. Tears form in her bright eyes, and her hand covers her mouth in sympathy.

"Ava, I'm so sorry. I didn't realize you were feeling this way. I knew you were hurting, but babe, these feelings you have, they're serious."

I only nod because I'm out of words, and I'm afraid V is going to look at me differently. Like she finally understands that endless hugs and support aren't going to be enough this time.

"What happened last night with Jasper?" she asks me hesitantly, like I might crumble at any moment.

"Indie happened," I reply bluntly.

"Oh fuck, what did that bitch do?"

"She warned me off Jasper in a not so subtle way." V narrows her eyes angrily—this Indie reaction must be contagious.

"I don't know what the fuck Jasper is doing with her. She's a right royal pain in the ass. They make up and break up so much it gives me whiplash. I don't know what he sees in her. He's such a great guy and she's—she's just a Botox injection away from being Barbie's big sister. What they have in common is a mystery to everyone." And once again with the accurate analogies.

"What's their story? Are they dating or not?" I need to find out their history, because Jasper's reaction to him being called her boyfriend was not a pleasant one.

"Oh, don't get me started. They've been together since high school, on and off, of course. They break up for months at a time, and then she comes crawling back, legs spread, and he forgives her."

But that doesn't answer my question. All it does is leave a nasty visual I wish I could singe from my brain.

Cringing, I ask, "Since high school? Sheesh, that's a long time. Has he seen anyone in between?"

"Av, Jasper is different. I've never seen him with a girlfriend. Lucas said Indie is the closest thing to a "normal" relationship he's ever had. He sleeps around because he certainly doesn't lack female suitors, but honestly, since I've known him, I haven't seen him with a steady partner, apart from Indie, which doesn't really count. I don't think he really knows what it's like to be in a faithful, loving relationship."

I am really confused, but more so, I'm humiliated that I shared an emotionally charged moment with an emotional reject! So my wires *were* obviously crossed. What I thought was pure, heartfelt, and just sweet, Jasper probably viewed in the same light as discussing the weather. I am such an idiot. I internally criticize myself for thinking we shared 'something.'

"Av, what are you thinking?" If only she knew.

"Nothing, V. I don't want to talk about Jasper or Harper anymore. I need to focus on me and decide what's next. I don't think I can go back to school, not yet. I need a job, though. I've decided something unchallenging and brainless is right up my alley."

"Wow, sounds rewarding," V jokes.

"That's what I need to do. It's the only thing that makes sense right now. Throw my ass into a boring job and hope my answers to life miraculously appear while earning minimum wage."

V laughs. "I love you, Ava. You're my best friend, my sister, and I know how strong, determined and wise you are. You'll figure this out. You always do."

I wish I had her confidence.

"Are you coming to Little Sisters for dinner and some tunes tonight? Everyone is going."

I shake my head. "No. I want to start checking out jobs online. No time like the present to change the world with my dazzling resume."

V smiles at me lovingly. "Ava Thompson, things will work out, you'll see. You've had your share of bad luck, seriously, what else could go wrong?

Life has been unpredictable thus far. I don't even want to think about what could happen next.

~

I'm so glad I stayed home. V tried numerous plea bargains to get me to join her at dinner, but she finally gave up, and I, at last, have the house to myself. I put on my well loved blue jeans and casual tank top while my microwave lasagna reheats.

Sitting up on the kitchen counter and dangling my feet over the edge, I ponder where I go from here. I know that throwing myself into work is a plausible idea, but for how long? I still want to send that email to Harper and try for closure, but what would I say? Fuck you for breaking my heart? Why did you do it? Are you happy? I love you? I groan at my stupidity for thinking the latter thought. I need to get over Harper, as that ship sailed long ago, and I've missed the maiden journey. I knew this breakup was going to hurt, but for how long?

While my meal cooks, I sit down at the kitchen table, attempting to start my resume. Staring at the blank screen with the black cursor flashing at me, I close the lid irritably. How do I sugar coat 'drop out'?

I thump my head lightly on the table as if that will give me the answers I seek, when the doorbell chimes. I look up at the clock. It's nine p.m. It's early for V to be home, because dinner was at seven. Then another thought registers, why would V ring her own doorbell?

I walk through the living room to answer the door and groan. It looks like a tornado has ripped through our house, leaving debris everywhere in its destructive path. While processing the disorder strewn around the room, I lose my footing and stub my toe on a lone dumbbell. Cursing as I tumble while opening the door, I luckily fall into a set of arms, as I would have face planted onto the cement otherwise. My stomach drops as I glance up at my knight in shining armor, his cerulean eyes assessing me cautiously.

Fuck…it's Jasper.

Chapter 11
Friends and Fire

"Uh-what are you doing here?" I stutter while staring into Jasper's eyes.

He has a tight hold around me, and I squirm to stand on my own two feet. I can't be having this conversation with him while he's holding me like we're about to tango.

He lets go reluctantly and replies low, "I came to see you." That's it? He offers me no other explanation.

"Okay, well, you saw me. Mission accomplished, see ya," I say, retreating into the safety of the house, away from Jasper and those eyes.

He plants his foot in the way as I attempt to shut the door in his face. Rude, I know, but I can't deal with this right now… or ever.

"Why didn't you come to dinner?" he asks, his eyes peering at me through the wedge of the door, the door I'm still trying to close.

"I'm not hungry." At that precise moment, the traitorous microwave dings.

The corners of Jasper's sinful mouth tip up in amusement.

"I wasn't hungry before, but I am now." Not that my appetite is any of his business. "So, please move your foot so I can go enjoy my meal…alone." Nice try, Ava. No way is that foot moving an inch.

"I want to talk to you, Ava…about last night." Jasper's words halt my actions.

"There's nothing to discuss." I shrug dismissively, attempting to hide my discomfort.

"There most definitely is. I know you and Indie had words after I left." Getting a verbal slaying from Indie is far more than 'words.'

"Yes, we had words, and…?" I leave the question hanging.

"She had no right to say anything to you. I know she can be harsh, but she felt threatened," Jasper replies, his face blank, giving nothing away.

My temper flares, and that rage is evident in the sudden color flushing my cheeks. "What? How the hell did I threaten her?" She was the one that threatened to give me a beat down, UFC style.

"You threatened her figuratively." He senses my fury and averts his eyes, avoiding eye contact.

"Jasper, quit with the vagueness. I have absolutely no idea what you're talking about." This conversation is going nowhere and my dinner is getting cold.

Jasper looks uncomfortable, but I make my intentions clear by giving him a pointed look. He has ten seconds to explain himself before I slam this door shut.

Thankfully, he gets the message loud and clear. "She feels threatened about you… and me," he replies awkwardly, scratching the back of his neck.

"You and me?"

I can't deal with the emotional turmoil of being around Jasper, but I need to clarify what he meant by 'you and me.'

"What exactly about you and me is there for her to feel threatened about?" I question, suddenly very interested in his answer.

He only clears his throat, looking everywhere but at me. Could it be Jasper actually felt *something* during our moment? Maybe I wasn't imagining things.

Meeting my eyes, he gives me an ambiguous smile. "Can I

please come in? I really don't want an audience," he says, nodding his chin towards Mrs. Carmichael, whose nosey head can be seen through her kitchen window, watching our unusual exchange.

He's right. This spectacle is one I don't want the whole neighborhood gossiping about, so reluctantly, I open the door. As he steps inside and peers around the living area, I'm suddenly very aware of the messy state my house is in, and most importantly, my attire. While this man stands before me looking like God's gift to women, I look like I've ransacked a homeless person.

I try desperately to collect magazines, lip glosses, and clothes off the sofa so Jasper can sit down. But with my hands full and with nowhere to put anything neatly, I toss the items behind the couch, giving Jasper a small smile.

Jasper returns the gesture, and his left dimple is more pronounced than I have ever seen it as he displays his obvious entertainment at my nervousness. Well, I'm pleased one of us is amused.

"Please sit, sorry about the mess," I say, slightly embarrassed.

He sits on one end of the sofa, while I'm pushed up against the other end with nowhere to go, because the armrest obstructs an escape. I feel embarrassed around him, on edge even. I feel like a frightened animal, assessing the threat presented before her. Jasper, on the other hand, looks quite relaxed and calm. With his right hand leaning causally against the back of the sofa, he turns to look at me. I subtly move back and curse the damn armrest.

"Ava, why are you so nervous?" he asks calmly, almost smug.

Yeah, Ava, why *are* you so nervous? That's the million dollar question.

"I'm not nervous," I reply lamely, looking around the room for the quickest escape route.

"Then why do you look like you're about to scream bloody murder if I breathe the wrong way?" He smirks.

His smile is infectious, but I am pissed off with his smugness, so I abruptly answer, "Ha ha. So you wanted to talk, talk. I don't have time for your ambiguity."

That wipes that arrogant look off his face. Win for Ava!

"I just wanted to apologize for what Indie said to you," Jasper whispers, giving nothing away.

"You know what she said?" I ask, surprised she would tell him.

"I don't know details, but I know she said something to you. And I wanted to correct what she said in regards to me being her boyfriend."

That has my attention and I look at him, crossing my arms over my chest, waiting for him to continue.

He clears his throat, obviously uncomfortable with what he is about to confess. "I've known Indie since she was fourteen, and we have been… on and off for longer than I can remember."

Calling an obvious unstable relationship 'on and off' is not the phrase I would have chosen, but I bite my tongue to correct his oversight.

"I appreciate the sentiment, but you have nothing to apologize for. Indie is the one who should be apologizing for being such a gigantic bitch." Oh crap, I said that out loud.

Jasper laughs. Did he not hear me call his girlfriend an enormous bitch? Where is his loyalty? Yes, Indie is a bitch, but if someone else dared cuss out Harper when we were together, they would be in for an ear bashing.

Jasper must see my alarm at his treachery as he quickly explains, "I just wanted to make it clear. Indie and I are *not* together."

I sit and stare. Well God damn, I *was* right. But I remind myself it doesn't matter either way because I am staying away from men. But of course, curiosity gets the better of me. "What do you mean? You didn't seem to correct her when she all but sky wrote the fact she was your girlfriend!"

Jasper chuckles, but he bites his lip when he sees I mean business.

He has a big hole ripped in the knee of his faded blue jeans, and an 'AC/DC' t-shirt is hugging his taut chest. He looks younger today because he's clean shaven, and with that huge grin plastered all over his face, he appears all the more delinquent. Why does he find this so amusing? I am beyond frustrated, but he looks like he's heard the funniest joke.

"Things with Indie and me, they're complicated," he replies, like that's meant to answer my question.

"Oh God, quit it with your Facebook phrases. You're either together, or you're not. Black and white. Judging by Indie's reaction to us *talking* last night, I think it's safe to assume she thinks you guys are together." Very together, I add silently, remembering her promise to make my life a living hell if I even looked in Jasper's direction.

"Nothing in a relationship is ever black and white, Ava," Jasper sadly replies, avoiding my eyes.

"I disagree. When you make the decision to spend your life with someone, that is black and white." My views on relationships won't change just because Harper didn't know the first thing about loyalty.

"Is that why you're here now and not in Singapore?" Jasper retorts, crooking an eyebrow at me.

That jerk! I see red…again. I'm starting to realize this is a common occurrence with Jasper.

I throw my hands out in exasperation. "This isn't about me. This is about why your *girlfriend* has an issue with us talking. I was quite happy to respect her wishes, but then you show up on my doorstep, an enigma. Please explain, as I think I've missed the memo."

Jasper takes a visible breath before he explains. "She got jealous when she saw us together, and she wanted to stake her claim. But let me clarify, Indie and I are NOT together. We don't do the conventional 'dating' thing."

Seriously, am I meant to understand what that means? I am so confused. So, coming to a conclusion, I blurt out, "Oh okay, so you just use each other for sex." Crap, again with the Tourette's.

Jasper half smiles. "Something like that."

Is that meant to explain anything, and should I just disregard the thought that's currently going through my mind that Jasper is a manwhore?

"It's not just sex, Ava," Jasper says intensely as he sees me mulling over his revelation.

"Holy shit, can you be any more cryptic?" I roll my eyes, annoyed with his games. He looks deliciously sinful as he tongues his upper lip, like he is contemplating his next comment.

"I've known Indie forever, and we understand each other. We know where we stand on the relationship front, and I've made it clear that our future will not end in three kids, a white picket fence, and a minivan. We comfort each other emotionally and physically," he replies calmly, while running his hand through his tangled hair.

I, however, flush when thinking about Jasper comforting Indie physically. I know a twenty-two year old shouldn't be blushing, but taking in Jasper's messy hair, which is now sticking up in rebellious spikes, his perfect bow lips, and that devilish body—which would look perfect naked—a girl can't help but redden, no matter her age.

Judging by the verbal bashing I received, I think Jasper needs to have another talk with Indie, because her perception of their relationship differs vastly from his.

"Okay great, glad we've cleared that up, but why did you come here tonight to tell me this?" I want to know the answer, but I'm afraid of his response.

Jasper blows a breath through his wicked lips as he weighs his answer. "I wanted to explain this to you because I…I just wanted things to be clear between us." And again with the ambiguity.

I roll my eyes at him yet again, because this conversation is wasting my time. As I attempt to get off the couch, putting an end to this pointless discussion, Jasper quickly recovers.

"Ava, I know you don't know me, but when I want something, I get it. I feel like there's something between us. I know you've gone through a messy breakup, and I'm, well, complicated…" He smirks before continuing. "But I really don't want to pass up this opportunity of getting to know you better. Wherever that leads, no one knows." He shrugs. "But if we don't pursue it, I think we'll both look back with regrets."

If someone told me Jasper would be sitting on my couch, telling me he wants to uncover our 'something,' I would have laughed hysterically in their face. But here's Jasper, in my living room, telling me just that.

Jasper's head is cocked to the side, his eyes searching mine, awaiting my response to his honesty. I haven't really appreciated how blue his eyes really are until now, and that's because they're focused so intently on me. "Please tell me you feel the same, and I haven't just made an ass of myself."

I take two deep breaths, overcome with emotion. "Yes, you're right, but I can't offer you anything more than friendship—you get that, right?" I reply, stressing the fact that I am in no way looking for a relationship with him, or anybody, for a while.

Jasper nods, his hair flicking over his brow. "I understand, and I'm happy with whatever you want to give. I just want to know what this 'thing' is between us," he replies, motioning between the two of us with his fingers.

This is the first lick of sense my life has made since Harper broke my heart. I can do this, I can be Jasper's friend.

"One problem though, and that is Indie. She won't like us being friends, believe me. She made that point quite clear."

He frowns. "You let me handle Indie."

"Okay." I can do that. "So…what do we do now?"

Jasper laughs deeply, and I disregard the way my body reacts to the sound. "Well, what do friends normally do? Go get coffee, hang out, that kind of stuff. That's all I'm asking, Ava. I'm an artist and I like to explore, then write about it. You never know, if you turn out to be as interesting as I think you are, there just may be a hit song about you."

I throw a pillow at him jokingly. "You most definitely won't be singing about me, or our friendship."

Looking across the sofa at one another, Jasper extends his hand out for a handshake. His eyes are unreadable, but I can see he's just as intrigued with me as I am with him.

"Friends?" he asks.

As I hesitantly move closer and slip my palm into his, a sudden, unexpected warmth pools in my belly, which throws me off guard. But I ignore it and smile. "Friends."

Our hands stay entwined for a second longer than a friendly handshake should, but being friends should be easy, right?

Chapter 12
My Heart is Beating Like a Jungle Drum

I hate Mondays, especially after tossing and turning for most of the night, thinking about my new friend. I don't even know why I'm thinking about him—my brain has officially been fired.

Getting out of bed frustrated and exhausted, I head downstairs for a cup of my morning pick-me-up. V is scrambling eggs before she heads off to work, and I sit down at the kitchen table, resting my head on the table top.

I can feel V staring at me, but I don't move. "What's up with you?" she asks.

Most days I can deal with her inquiries, but today my brain is fried, and I really need to conserve brain power to write my resume.

"Don't give me the silent treatment. You know that doesn't work with me," V states, scrambling her eggs happily. Looking at her breakfast pensively, I realize my brain actually feels like V's eggs. I let out a random chuckle, and V knows it has nothing to do with her comment.

"Ava, you're scaring me right now. Are you going to cut down my door with an axe and scream 'HERE'S AVA' in the middle of the night?"

I giggle at her reference to the movie *The Shining*.

"Sorry, V. I was comparing your breakfast to my brain, and well, it sounded a lot funnier in my head."

"Ah ha," V replies, puzzled. "You need to go out and get some fresh air, and get the hell out of the house. Go for a walk and enjoy the sunshine, it'll help unscramble your brain." I wish it was that simple. If that was the solution, then I would be out there from dawn till dusk.

"It's not that simple, V."

"I know, but it's better than moping around here all day, waiting for Harper to call." V adds salt and pepper to her breakfast, ignoring the fact she's just offended me.

"I'm not waiting for Harper," *oh God, even saying his name makes me ill*, "to call. I know that's not going to happen. I just need time." I feel the need to clarify this to V because it'll help me believe it, also.

"Time for what? To become a crazy old cat lady? Seriously, babe, the sooner you get back on the horse, the better. Go forth and prosper," she says, sitting at the kitchen table with me.

Taking a sip of her coffee, I decide to ask her what she thinks about Jasper and I being friends.

"So, Jasper came over last night."

If I told V I'm actually considering a sex change, she would have taken the news better than me telling her about Jasper. She inhales her toast and chokes, her eyes watering as she tries to breathe.

After clearing her throat, she wheezes, "Why?"

"He wanted to know why I wasn't at dinner, and to tell me he and Indie are only friends. Apparently she feels threatened by me."

"I'm so confused right now." V looks at me with a puzzled expression, her fork paused in front of her open, gobsmacked mouth.

I know the feeling.

"Please explain in English," V says after a minute of processing my sentence.

"Jasper explained he and Indie aren't dating. He said he feels there's something between us, and wants to get to know me better. I told him I can only offer him friendship and he is fine with that." But am I? I don't want to think about why my insides soften whenever I think about him.

"And he came all the way over here to tell you this?" I nod.

"I really don't know what to say. I've never seen Jasper try hard with a girl. This is an effort for him." V looks as astonished as I was when Jasper came to visit, but her comment ticks me off.

"Going over to someone's house is an effort for him? That's just ridiculous. Just because he's blessed with good looks doesn't mean he can check his manners at the door." I fail to mention I was the one whose manners were left at the door while I was slamming it into his face.

"No, I'm not saying that. It's just… different. Do you like him?" V corrects herself quickly.

"Like him? I hardly know him."

"Well, from what you do know about him, do you think you *could* like him?" V probes, up to no good as usual.

"V, there's no way I'll be pursuing a relationship with Jasper, or anyone else for that matter, for a very long time. I admit I find Jasper…interesting, but we're just friends."

"Yeah, for now." V laughs while gobbling up her breakfast.

"Oh Veronica, shut it. Look, I find Jasper attractive, and he's right, there is some chemistry between us, but it's purely of a friendly nature." My reply feels false, like I'm lying to her, and also to myself. I choose to ignore the reasoning behind those feelings.

V is quiet, which is never a good sign. Before she can interrogate me further, I steal her coffee and head upstairs to work on getting my life back on track.

I have cleaned my room, straightening everything—twice—but I can't put off the unavoidable any longer. I have to start on my resume. Actually sitting down and committing to paper my life failures is a depressing thought, hence the procrastination. I never thought I would be sitting here, writing my resume without a diploma to add to my credentials. When did my life become so backward?

I finally succumb and make a start on getting my life back, and things are going well, until I am glaring at the heading, 'EDUCATION.' It may as well be screaming at me in big, bold letters that I am a failure. Exhaling a frustrated sigh, I wonder when will this feeling go away? The ache I felt when I first returned is slowly fading bit by bit, but I still feel unsettled. I want to establish myself again without being so afraid of living my life without Harper.

Giving up, I head downstairs to make myself some lunch. As I open the fridge, I'm taken aback by all the bright colors of the produce inside, and suddenly, I feel inspired to create a meal. This is the first time in a long time I have felt motivated to cook, and that gives me hope that things might actually be okay.

As I finely slice my seared tuna to accompany my Salad Nicoise, my mind is at complete peace. This is why I decided to pursue a career in the culinary world. I always feel at home in the kitchen, and whenever I have a bad day, I create my best dishes. Judging by the colorful creation I just produced, my day totally sucks.

With Florence and the Machine, "Dog Days are Over" blaring over my speakers, I can't help but relate to the lyrics. I am singing very loudly and off-key, freely shaking my booty embarrassingly around the room, and I don't know if it's getting back into the kitchen, or the song striking a chord with me, but whatever it is, I feel alive.

I am clapping away with enthusiasm and am halfway through butchering the chorus, when I hear another voice huskily singing along with me. This voice, unlike mine, has rhythm, and heats me from the inside out. And this voice belongs to the male who is currently sitting in my kitchen. And that male is Jasper.

Spinning around surprised, I'm totally mortified he witnessed me wailing and shuffling around the kitchen like a lunatic. I feel my cheeks redden to match the color of the tomatoes sitting in front of me, ready for slicing. He's toying with his bottom lip, and his smoldering eyes are not so discreetly exploring me from head to toe. I redden even further under his examination.

I wasn't expecting company, and am currently in my short jean shorts and stripy red and white cut-off shirt that stops above my navel. My long brown hair is piled messily into a loose ponytail, and due to my uncoordinated boogying, most of it has come undone. I am also barefoot. Peering down, I thank the heavens my toenails are still painted a devilish red. I am wearing my silver toe ring and anklet, but apart from that, I have on no other jewelry. Luckily I coated on a little foundation and mascara, but I still look a mess. However, disregarding my appearance, I wonder why Jasper is sitting in my kitchen. How did he get in? And more importantly, why is he liquefying my insides with that heated look.

"Jungle Drum" by Emiliana Torrini is the next song on my playlist—how appropriate.

Jasper is slouching casually, his legs parted with his fingers interlaced behind his head. He's wearing a black baseball cap, which is turned backwards, covering his drool worthy hair. Dressed in tight black jeans and a grey tank, I can clearly see his impressive physique. The low sides on the tank reveal his toned oblique muscles, and with his hands propped up that way, his collarbones and upper shoulders look menacing. The curve of his chest is taunting me with all that solidity and I visibly gulp. He looks stunning.

Jasper is absolutely aware that I'm mentally molesting him, but he doesn't seem to care. If his smirk is anything to go by, I dare say he's actually enjoying it. I shake the wicked thoughts from my head, as friends don't mentally undress their friends as inappropriately as I am right now.

Warily peering into his eyes, I can see he's as affected by me as I am by him, which makes zero sense. I clear my throat as the tension between us can be cut with a knife.

"Hi," I lamely croak.

"Hi." He doesn't say anything else, but his look is worth a thousand confusing words, and I need to say something to distract myself from all those muscles on display for my viewing pleasure.

"Are you hungry?" In hindsight, probably not the best thing to say with the way Jasper is looking at me.

"You bet," he replies. His voice is so suggestive, my pulse starts racing like I have just run a marathon.

I cower at the fact that I'm pretty certain he's referring to being hungry...for me. I feel self-conscious and bashful, but more than anything, it terrifies me, because at the moment, I would happily let him devour me.

"Do you eat porn... oh God, I meant prawns. Do you eat prawns? Because I was going to make a prawn cocktail to go with my Salad Nicoise," I quickly correct myself. Mother of God, what the hell? If that wasn't a Freudian slip, then I don't know what it was.

Jasper lets out a confident chuckle as he doesn't seem to be fazed by this embarrassing exchange. I, on the other hand, want to run upstairs and hide.

"That sounds good," he finally replies after sensing my uneasiness.

I quickly turn around to complete our lunch, thankful for the distraction. Reaching for a tomato, I begin slicing quickly and scatter the pieces throughout the salad, arranging everything onto the plate to make it look appetizing. The last addition is the hard boiled eggs, which will add that vibrant dash of color, enhancing the presentation. I'm lost in thought peeling the eggs, but am suddenly distracted by the most delicious scent. It's a deep, masculine fragrance which is unlike anything I have ever smelled before. My breath hitches in my throat, as I know Jasper is standing right behind me.

I continue peeling the eggs, because this I can do. Processing why my heart is beating out of my chest, I cannot.

"Wow, you're really good at that," he says over my shoulder, while I'm arranging everything to sit just the way I want.

His breath tickles my neck and I shiver, realizing he must be a lot closer than I originally thought. *What is wrong with me*, I question myself. *Why am I suddenly so nervous with Jasper being so near?*

Taking calming breath, I reply, "Thanks, it comes naturally to me."

I mix the ingredients together for the cocktail sauce, adding a dash of Tabasco. I like my sauce to be a little spicy. Although, judging by how I'm currently burning up, I don't think I need any extra spice.

Arranging the prawns so they're sitting neatly on a bed of shredded lettuce in martini glasses, I pour the cocktail sauce over each one, and looking at the colorful salad, I'm proud of my creation.

"That looks amazing."

Turning around, I nearly bump into Jasper, and I grab the bench behind me for support, as we are standing so close.

"Thanks." It's all I can say, because as I peer up at him, this close, I'm winded by his beauty. He is the epitome of masculinity. I can feel my breath quicken in response to him being so near.

I realize I'm staring and should look away, but I can't. However, as I'm gaping at his luscious lips, appreciating their kiss-worthiness, that thought brings me back down to earth, as I know I shouldn't be kissing anyone. I haven't even figured out where my life is headed, and Jasper's lips are not going to solve my dilemma. If anything, they're going to confuse me further.

But the thing that confuses me the most about Jasper is that he doesn't seem to mind me mentally stripping him. This connection between us has been evident from the first moment we met, and the air is electric whenever we're in the same room as one another. And *that* is what I find most puzzling. I should be mourning my breakup with Harper, but Harper is the furthest thing from my mind when I'm with Jasper.

But Jasper is my friend, and I need to get over this sexual tension and remember that—no matter how tempting he looks.

My head hurts and my stomach is grumbling, which is as good a distraction as any not to think about this further. I grin with enthusiasm, because I'm excited for Jasper to try my food.

"Take a seat. It's ready."

Jasper takes a step back slowly and heads to his seat while I place our lunch and silverware on the table. He takes a bite of the salad and I suddenly feel nervous. What if he hates it? Biting my lip and reevaluating my lunch choice, Jasper quickly puts my mind at ease.

"It's fucking awesome," he says between mouthfuls.

I giggle and take a bite. I'm proud to say it *is* fucking awesome.

After we have taken a few silent bites, I bravely ask, "So how long were you subjected to my lack of coordination?"

"Not long enough," he replies, grinning broadly. I am beyond mortified and lower my eyes.

"V let me in on her way to work," he continues quickly, sensing my mortification and attempting to change the subject.

This is the thing I like the most about Jasper. He always seems to know what to say to make things less awkward. I, on the other hand, do not.

Wondering why he is here, I am far from disappointed that he's sitting in my kitchen, eating my food, but I think back to V's comment about Jasper not trying with anyone. But this doesn't feel like he's trying, this feels natural.

"Have you always been so talented in the kitchen?" Jasper questions.

Looking up at him, I sadly realize this is a conversation I never had with Harper. He constantly mocked me, and never really saw my career choice as going anywhere further than a school canteen.

"I never really considered myself to be gifted or talented, because I loved being in the kitchen so much, and it just came effortlessly to me. I just figured everyone could cook, but then I witnessed V in the kitchen and realized that wasn't true." I chuckle at the memory of my friend trying to make pasta, which ended in a fiery disaster.

Jasper laughs, appearing genuinely interested, and I feel at ease with him—well, apart from when I'm envisioning him naked, that is. He's chewing his meal and looks to be enjoying it immensely, which warms my heart. It's the best compliment he could give me without even knowing it.

Wanting to return the favor, I say, "Just like you and your music. As you witnessed earlier, I'm not so talented in the music and dance department, but your voice—I know that comes effortlessly to you. I mean, it's breathtaking."

I cringe as Jasper looks up at me with a look I can't decipher and quickly stuff my mouth before I can embarrass myself further. Courageously looking at him after a minute of silence, he looks taken aback, like he doesn't believe me. His self-doubt saddens me, so once again, I'm all for the over share as I add, "You know that, right? You have something special."

Okay, well that definitely didn't make me sound like a stalker, or even worse, a groupie.

I need to shut my mouth as I'm obviously embarrassing myself, and by the look on Jasper's face, him as well. Putting down his fork gently and clearing his throat, he rubs the back of his neck, and I can't help but melt at the sight of his biceps flexing.

I need to cut this out—like now.

"Thank you. That means a lot because I know you actually mean it." By the look on his face, I know I have unintentionally touched on a personal topic.

He continues, "I'm not used to hearing I'm anything special. It's just hard to take in when it's been drummed into your head that you'll be a failure forever." I look into Jasper's eyes, and they seem focused on a not so pleasant time for him. I wonder what's happened for him to look so melancholy.

Trying to make up for my comment, I say the most stupid thing, and it's out before I can stop myself.

"Well, I think you're special." Great, now I definitely sound like a stalker!

I shove a forkful of salad into my mouth till my cheeks are bursting with food—this is good. This will stop the verbal diarrhea.

I can't even look at Jasper because I know the minute I do, I'll die of embarrassment.

"Well, I think you're special, too," I hear him reply kindly after a moment of uncomfortable silence. Holy crap. I swallow my food before I choke.

On the outside I may look totally stunned, but within, I'm on cloud nine.

Over the next few weeks, Jasper and I do all the normal things friends usually do. Go for coffee, see a movie, and he even helps me find a job waiting tables and occasionally helping out at the register, which is perfect. The place is cleverly named The Bean Bag, as we stock every coffee bean known to mankind.

Most mornings while I was busy taking orders, a familiar pair of cerulean eyes would stroll into the shop. Jasper loves coffee, hence him being in my shop so often. I dare not assume he was there for any other reason. He would quietly sit on a stool overlooking the busy street corner and write in his scruffy notebook. V is right, the brooding artist he is. But he looked most peaceful and in his comfort zone when writing.

One day while the shop is quiet after the morning rush, I take a quick break and sit next to Jasper. He doesn't even realize I'm there, and I suddenly feel like I'm intruding on a private moment. I'm about to get up and leave him to his creativity, but his hand reaches out to stop my departure. I'm stunned he knew I was there in the first place, as he looked so deep in thought and lost in his writing. I look at his hand wrapped around my arm, and he lets go quickly.

"Sorry, I didn't mean to scare you," he says with a dimpled smile.

"You didn't scare me. I just didn't want to interrupt an obvious artistic moment," I joke.

Jasper smirks as he runs his fingers through his damp hair, and I my mind runs rampant with images of him in the shower, in all of his naked glory. I can't help but admire him—he really is breathtaking. He looks older than twenty-four, and I believe those blue eyes have seen enough grief over his short lifetime. We don't talk about his past, but whenever he asks about mine, I'm happy to share as long as it doesn't involve Harper.

"So, what were you writing?" I ask, realizing I'm staring at him openly.

He shrugs, once again brushing his hair out of his eyes. I know he's nervous. I wonder why.

"Nothing really."

"That didn't look like nothing. That looked like you were trying to find a cure for some obscure medical disease."

Jasper rewards me with a playful smirk. "Well, yes, you caught me out, that's exactly what it was." I smile, as I love when he's so playful and carefree. Being Jasper's friend has been easy, natural even. He makes me feel at ease, and the hole in my chest closes over a fraction every day.

"How do you keep a track of everything you write in there?" I question, looking at his ratty notebook.

Jasper taps his forehead. "It's all in here. I only write stuff down to see what it looks like on paper. Thinking something and actually seeing something are two totally different things. What I think in my head makes perfect sense, may make no sense at all when I see it."

"Are you always this vague?" I laugh, jokingly bumping him with my shoulder.

His voice is intense, almost coarse due to smoking too many cigarettes and screaming high notes.

"Ava, just because something may seem like a good idea, doesn't mean it is when you act it out."

I look at him nervously, and feel like we're not talking about his writing anymore.

Chapter 13
Royal Flush

Do I think going to the movies with Lucas, V, and Jasper is a good idea? No. Do I have a choice? No.

V has emphasized this most certainly is not a double date, but somehow, I think she's just humoring me. I really don't want to see the new action movie everyone is raving about, but V said I have no choice. It's Lucas' turn to pick a movie for their date night, and he has opted for the testosterone-filled flick, much to V's dismay. So I have to go with her to 'save her from dying of boredom.' It just happens Jasper is also coming. This is so wrong for so many reasons, but I start with the obvious.

"I'm not comfortable going out with you guys on 'date night.'"

"Oh, please. I told you a gory, bloodthirsty movie doesn't count as a date night. You're coming to save me from dying of boredom. You know how much I hate those movies. Something with a hunky, dreamy-eyed lead is more my scene, but I think Lucas would get a little offended if I sat there ignoring him, while drooling into my popcorn over Mr. Dreamboat."

"V, you know you can't die of boredom." I chuckle at her melodramatics.

"There is a first for everything, especially with Lucas living out his Rambo dreams." I laugh lightly as I feel uncomfortable addressing the next issue.

"I also don't feel comfortable going to the movies…just us four. It feels like a double date," I press once again.

"Ava, Jasper is Lucas' best friend, and you are my best friend. You and Jasper are friends, so what's wrong with us friends going out all together?" She knows perfectly well what the problem is.

Jasper has turned out to be an amazingly good friend. I honestly didn't think we would get along as well as we do. We have similar interests, and he really listens to me when I talk incessantly. But the problem is, I feel an unexplainable pull to Jasper and it scares me. I have caught him looking at me when he believes I'm unaware of his glances. But the reason I've noticed these exchanges is because I'm stealing looks his way, too. I can't help it. Not only is he the most attractive man I've ever seen, he makes me feel… something. He makes me feel something other than being afraid. He gives me hope.

And that's the problem, the problem that V knows all too well.

I swore to myself that when I returned, I would focus on myself and not let anything or anyone stand in the way of getting my life back on track. Jasper is a big someone that would shatter my goals of independence. And V knows this, just by being in the same room as us. I didn't think anyone noticed our exchanges, but I was wrong. So, this is my reason for doubting us four going to the movies is a good idea. Jasper and I, alone together in a dark room, sitting shoulder to shoulder, equates to an uncomfortable awkwardness which I can do without. Our friendship I can deal with, but the weird chemistry, I cannot.

Every time I feel we have established an uncomplicated friendship, my hormones take control, and the line blurs between friendship, and something…else.

~

Halfway through the movie, I think V would gladly volunteer

to be involved in any of the flaming explosions playing out on screen to put her out of her misery. I stand corrected as I think my friend might actually be the first person to die of boredom.

I made sure the seating arrangements were boy, boy, girl, girl. Me, being the girl furthest from Jasper. He looks exceptional tonight in black jeans, boots, and a white v-neck t-shirt. His hair is styled messily, slipping into his dazzling eyes ever so often.

As I convince myself that it's okay to stare, as we're in a dark theatre, and no one can see me, I'm proven wrong. V and Lucas are making out in between Jasper and I, and I foolishly believe this is enough of a veil to protect me from my blatant eye-fucking. As I'm peering at him in a not so subtle manner, he turns to look at me. I'm stunned, and I should be looking away, or dying of embarrassment, but surprisingly, I'm not, and neither is he.

We're staring at one another, and a small grin pulls at his sinful lips. His strong jaw line emphasizes that grin—a grin that should be illegal. As he bites his bottom lip, his scar disappears into that wicked mouth. I can't turn away, and this is exactly the weird chemistry that confuses me. Whenever I'm around Jasper, it's like no one else exists. And here in the dark, I can almost convince myself that no one actually does. That is until I see Lucas' hand wander up V's skirt. I turn away quickly, not quite comfortable with seeing *that* much of my best friend's skin on show.

I have no idea what the storyline of this movie is, and even if I did, it still wouldn't make it any more interesting. I sigh and decide being in the bathroom for twenty minutes would be more exciting than being in here. And it looks like V and Lucas are on their way towards making their own R rated movie. That is something I most definitely do not want to see.

Quietly excusing myself, I slip past a few patrons and run to the sanctuary of the bathroom. What was *that* between Jasper and I? It was like he felt my eyes devouring him, and the worst part is when I was caught, I wasn't embarrassed like usual. Nothing about Jasper and me makes sense.

My heartache always takes a back seat when I'm with Jasper, which is something enormous for me. The pain I felt when I came back from Singapore, it was something I never thought I would recover from. But being Jasper White's friend has changed that. I still feel that pain, but it isn't as hard for me to smile and laugh and be happy with Jasper as my friend. I feel almost guilty, like I should be mourning my break up, but around Jasper, I don't.

Sadly I have exhausted my bathroom stay, and if I stay in here any longer, Jasper may think I'm hiding, or God forbid, I have a nervous bladder. I walk regretfully back to the cinema, but for some unknown reason I turn around and see Jasper outside. He's leaning against a street sign having a cigarette and blowing smoke rings, and he looks absolutely gorgeous. He has no idea I've spotted him, so I decide to sneak up on him. Attempting to be as quiet as possible, I creep toward him, but it's like we have some invisible connection and he turns around at the last second.

"Boo," I say lamely.

He smirks at me, his left dimple standing out. The streetlights cast a shadow over his face, his skin looking milky white and smooth.

"What are you doing out here?" I ask before I drool all over myself.

He shrugs while puffing on his cigarette. "V and Lucas were kinda getting hot and heavy, and I felt like I paid my $12 to see them make out, and that's just weird. Besides, the movie blows, so I'd prefer to sit out here. What's your excuse for running off?"

I'm elated he saw me leave, as he must have been watching me. Or he could have noticed I wasn't there a minute before he left. This questioning myself is what I don't like. It confuses me, and I don't want this uncertainty because that's what I had when I was with Harper. Doubting myself and feeling insecure is why things with Jasper leave me on edge at times.

"Yeah, they were getting a little heated. I think that was V's answer to not being bored shitless."

Jasper laughs, and it's a nice sound because he doesn't laugh often. He smiles, but I can tell he guards himself from being too exposed, and I can't help but think Jasper has a tainted past. I can see it sometimes when he's writing and deep in thought. That's the only time I can really watch him, not in a heated way, but just really look at him, and see there's more than meets the eye.

"Are you happy?" he asks unexpectedly.

Right now…I'm happy being here with him.

But he must see my hesitation and corrects, "Sorry, I meant, are you happier than you were before?" He leaves the question hanging, not clarifying what he means by 'before.' But I know he means before Harper.

"Yes, I am," I say with conviction, because I am.

He nods, contemplating my response.

"Are you?" Maybe he'll be in a sharing mood and tell me a bit about his past, although the timing is totally inappropriate.

"I don't know. I've never really been perfectly happy. You know, like over the moon, I fucking love life, happy," he answers honestly, staring off into the distance.

"No one is perfectly happy, Jasper. We have to play with the cards we're dealt with in life, and try to turn them into a winning hand."

He looks at me, reflecting on my words. "Most of the time, I feel like I've been dealt a really bad hand, and I'm bluffing my way through life."

"Then you just have to turn that hand into a royal flush," I answer quickly, without even thinking about my response. I'm not one to preach, but I'm trying my best to turn my luck around.

"You astound me," he replies, full of emotion.

With his jaw clenched, I wonder what he's thinking about to make him look so somber. His comment baffles me, but I don't know why I'm so surprised, because Jasper does this to me often, as I never know what he's going to say next.

"Me? Why?" I ask.

"Because, when I think I have you all figured out, you go and say something that throws me on my ass."

He earnestly looks at me as he takes a drag of his cigarette. All the while, I work my lip anxiously as his intense gaze sets me alight.

"I'm sorry, I didn't mean for it to come out so preachy," I

answer, averting my eyes.

"Don't apologize, I like it. I like that you keep me guessing."

I look at him quickly, stunned by his admission. He half smiles while rolling a stone under his boot. He looks nervous, like he's said too much and doesn't know how I'll respond to his confession.

"Well, in that case, I better make sure I don't disappoint you and become predicable," I reply playfully, relieved I'm able to make a joke.

The breeze blows Jasper's windswept bangs off his brow, allowing me to see the heavy look in his eyes. These looks between us are driving me insane, because under his scrutinizing gaze, I feel naked.

Jasper puts out his cigarette and does something that most definitely cannot be considered predicable. He pulls me into his strong, warm arms, and surprisingly hugs me with such care and longing. His smell is so masculine, so refined, and being this close to him, I am saturated in his signature fragrance.

Losing myself in his embrace, I melt into his firm arms. Resting my head against his chest, I can feel his heartbeat, which is pounding as fast as mine. Being enfolded in his strong embrace, a little voice whispers how natural this feels.

Every nerve ending in my body is tingling with anticipation, and this just adds to the list of uncertainties of how my feelings for Jasper really lie.

Chapter 14
I Surrender

There's more to Jasper than his ridiculously good looks, and that is his love for animals. I saw a different side to Jasper when he tended to the neglected, injured, and unwanted animals at the shelter. A side that has me wondering, what other sides does Jasper White have? The gentle, almost personal care he shows towards the animals that are neglected has me speculating that he too was once just as wounded and unloved as these creatures.

Life has a rhythmic pattern which suits me just fine. Work is going great, keeping me busy. When I have the motivation (which rarely happens), I go for a jog with V. After dinner, I usually head over to the shelter to see Jasper. I tell myself it's helping at the shelter that I'm looking forward to all day, not seeing him.

The feelings of heartache are still nearby, but when I'm with Jasper, they don't consume every part of me. He keeps my mind busy, and yes, he's very attractive to look at with his black torn jeans, combat boots, and some ratty band t-shirt being his outfit for the shelter, but it's his company, just hanging out, I find most comforting.

So, on a warm Thursday evening, while I was brushing my hair into a high ponytail, V asks, "So, what's going on with Jasper?"

Cringing at her question, I can acknowledge that we have a connection, but there's nothing going on, per se.

"Nothing," I reply, fastening my hair.

V scoffs, totally unbelieving, and I smile. "Sorry to disappoint you, but we're friends. No one seems to have a problem with us being friends, and constantly asking what's going on with us. Why is it any different with Jasper? Cause he's a guy?"

"No, because he's Jasper. Jasper doesn't do friends. I've never even seen him be friends with his so called friends, but with you, he's different. He's happy."

"And that's a bad thing, why?" I question, secretly high fiving myself, elated that I make him happy.

"It's not a bad thing, if you guys are just friends, then that's great. I'm happy for you, as you're both less moody when you're together." V laughs as I throw my hairbrush at her, narrowly missing her head. "But I don't want you to get hurt."

"How am I going to get hurt by being friends with Jasper?" I inquire, but I know the answer.

"Because I know there's more going on than just being friends. Deny it all you want, but there will come a time when you both won't be able to keep up with this friendship façade. And then, there's the Indie situation. Jasper is still seeing Indie for some unknown reason. If you have feelings for him, and he's still seeing Indie, I'm just concerned you'll get hurt. I see the way you look at each other when you think no one is looking."

"What?" I blanch, wishing I wasn't so transparent.

"Calm down. I just think there's something more going on, and you're both too scared to act on it. Whether it's because you think it'll ruin your friendship, or maybe you guys are too afraid of what would happen if things actually worked out, who knows. But hey, I could be totally wrong. You guys could pursue things and it might lead to a dead end."

"Dead end?" I ask, irritated. "Why would it be a dead end? We seem to be doing just fine as friends."

"Ava, c'mon, we both know being in a friendship and being

in a relationship are two totally different ball games. Let's say, for argument's sake, if you and Jasper hooked up and it did end in a messy, emotional fiery ball of pain, which is quite likely seeing as you're both the most stubborn, determined people I have ever met—do you think you could go back to just being friends?"

I ponder her question and choose to disregard it, but address her comment regarding my stubbornness. "I'm not stubborn. Look at what I did for Harper. I left everything for him, to please him. I can make compromises in a relationship."

"That's because Harper was a control freak with mommy issues. If you didn't do what he wanted, it would end in a fight. He squashed your spirit and you accepted it because you loved him. We all make sacrifices for our first love, but you've grown since Harper. You know you won't be that girl anymore, that girl that Harper turned you into because he's a spineless, narcissist asshole."

V's name calling doesn't affect me as much as it used to, and I'm proud of myself. I stare at my reflection—is she right? Have I really grow into the stronger person I strived to become? I don't think I'm totally there yet, but I'm trying, and it feels good.

I have decided emailing Harper would accomplish nothing, and I'm happy to move on and learn from my Harper experience. And V is right, I will never change who I am just to please another ever again.

Smiling sweetly at my intuitive best friend, I casually reply, "V, I love you, but really, you have nothing to be worried about. Jasper and I are just friends."

V looks at me, unbelieving. "Don't say I didn't warn you."

In the car ride over to the shelter, V's words play on my mind. Would Jasper and I really end in a messy, emotional ball of pain? The thought scares me, as I really couldn't handle any more pain. The ache in my chest seems to be getting a little more bearable every day, and that in part, is thanks to Jasper. His cheeky smile, compassionate nature, and unique views on life have helped me heal. But I don't know if I'm ready to explore anything further than friendship with Jasper, or anyone else for a while. If it ain't broke, don't fix it. And mine and Jasper's friendship is definitely not broke.

Pulling into the dark parking lot at 12:20a.m. always creeps me out, but Jasper, forever the gentleman, waits outside for me, having a cigarette. He waves when he sees my car, rewarding me with a breathtaking smile. He looks just as attractive as ever in his customary ripped black jeans, combat boots, and tonight a One Direction t-shirt. I love the humor of this guy.

Taking a deep, calming breath, I wipe my sweaty palms on my jeans. I always get this way when I see him, and I tell myself it's perfectly normal, as I have no doubt every hot blooded woman has this reaction towards him.

"Hey, Ava." He smiles as I quickly walk over to him, my body humming in excitement.

He pulls me in for a warm hug, and I hug him back, inhaling his unique, mouth-watering scent. I know Jasper doesn't wear any fancy aftershaves. He doesn't need to, because his fragrance is something that can't be bottled.

"Hey, friend. Busy night?" I reply, hoping I don't sound as breathless as I feel.

With one arm still slung around my waist, he puts out his smoke with his boot and then runs his hand through his hair. I have come to realize this indeed is a habit of his when he's nervous or angry.

"Yeah, a bit. I want you to meet somebody." I tense up and Jasper can sense my nervousness. "Relax, it's a good somebody. I know you'll get along famously."

I'm on edge even more so when he doesn't mention *who* this somebody is. My mind involuntarily screams that Indie is inside, wielding an arsenal with my name written on it. She may be okay with us being friends, but she most definitely would not be okay if she knew how much time Jasper and I spent together. Especially at 12:25a.m.

Jasper leads me inside, all the while smirking with that damn dimple on parade. What is he up to?

Following him out back to where the stray animals are detained, I look around the room and my heart goes out to these poor abandoned animals. How can people just discard these creatures like trash? Jasper takes extra care with the strays, another reason why I think he's an amazing person with a huge heart.

Jasper heads to the last cage and stops in front of it.

"Surprise." He smiles, his broad back blocking the cage.

Looking behind him, totally confused, I bite my lip.

His eyes are lit up like a Christmas tree. "Take a closer look," he says, taking a step to the left.

Pressing my face inches away from the cage proves to be a big mistake as a tiny hiss startles me, and when a little paw comes swiping out at my face, I jump back, bumping into Jasper, who supports me with his warm hands.

My back is pressed to his chiseled chest as he whispers lightly into my ear, "I would like you to meet Oscar."

My eyes widen when I see a tiny black face with big green eyes staring at me, frightened. It is the smallest kitten I have ever laid eyes on, and I cautiously approach the cage, sticking my finger into the small space. The kitten apprehensively approaches, smelling my finger and then surprisingly, allows me to pat him under the chin. He begins purring like a lawn mower, and I'm in love.

"I knew you two would get along." Jasper smiles as I turn my head, looking at him while still stroking Oscar.

"And how did you know that? What are you, the animal whisperer?"

"Well, apart from that, I knew the little guy had spirit when I found him behind the clinic, hunting for food in the dumpster. I took him inside and within ten minutes, he picked a fight with a pit-bull, stole my dinner, crapped everywhere but his litter tray, but most importantly, he's a grumpy shit, just like you."

I laugh, and Oscar seems to like the sound as his purring increases an octave.

"Hence the name. He's grouchy like you are most days," Jasper explains with a chuckle as I glare at him and attempt to punch him playfully on the arm.

He's too fast and darts out of my path, but he is *so* going down.

"You're in so much trouble, White." I laugh, giving Oscar one last pat, before turning around to face him, hands on hips.

"Oh yeah?" he taunts with a smirk, "whatcha gonna do?"

"I don't know yet, but when I do, you'll be begging me to stop," I reply, and he chuckles, raising his brow.

"That's really not much of a threat," he says, his lips pulling up into a lopsided smirk.

"Oh yeah?" I ask breathlessly, as the heated look in his eyes has my body responding in a way it shouldn't. "And why not?"

Jasper's dimple appears as he replies, "Because you're going to have to catch me first." He catches me unaware as he quickly dashes around the room, using the gurney as his barricade.

Giggling, I swiftly take chase, knocking over some supplies, but I'm determined to make him pay for that comment.

"I am not grouchy, and if I am, it's because I have to put up with you." I chuckle, while we dance around the table.

"Oh please, you make Oscar the Grouch look like Mary Poppins." He snorts with laughter, a devilish gleam in his eyes.

I can't help but laugh. I know I'm moody, but I'll be damned if I ever admit that to Jasper.

"Surrender."

"Never. Face facts, you and Oscar are a perfect grouchy pair." He's thoroughly enjoying his taunting, and a big smile lights up his self-righteous face.

That's it, no more Mr. Nice Guy! I make a mad dash towards him, as we are on opposite ends of the gurney, but he easily darts out of the way. Looking to my right, I see a saline bottle. I reach for it and blindly throw it—somehow it explodes on impact when it hits him, square in the jaw.

I know this is my opportunity to entrap him as he's momentarily distracted, and I race towards him, attempting to pull him into a tackle. I didn't, however, take into consideration the spilled saline. I slip, colliding into him, sending us both to the floor. Jasper breaks our tumble by falling onto his back. I end up lying on top of his chest.

Both our chests are rising with the adrenalin of our chase, but as I comprehend the position we're in, I'm breathing uneasy for another reason. His entire body is pressed against mine, and as he gazes at me with a partial smile, his dimples on show, I am suddenly aware of how close we are. Suddenly, I can't move.

My cheeks unexpectedly heat, and my heart begins to beat madly. I know what Jasper wants. The gentle warmth of his skin against mine has me gasping at the delicious contact, and slowly, his smile disappears and his eyes drop to my trembling lips. When he looks at me with such intensity, the butterflies in my stomach begin to flutter uncontrollably. As he reaches up to brush a runaway hair from my face, his fingers passing gently over my cheek, I involuntarily liquefy.

I stare into those cerulean depths and I feel it. That tickle you usually feel in your belly right before something big is about to happen.

"I surrender," he whispers huskily, his fingers lingering on my cheek. Why do I feel there is a hidden message behind those two little words?

With his fierce jaw, piercing blue eyes, and unruly bedroom hair, he looks perfect. But that's not what knocks me flat. I know Jasper wants to kiss me.

I'm torn. The sexual chemistry between us is palpable, and I shouldn't want this for so many reasons, but why does it feel so right, so intrinsic? I feel like a fool for convincing myself I didn't want to explore anything other than friendship with Jasper, because right now, looking at him, looking at his perfect lips, I can think of nothing else.

He reaches up, closing the agonizing distance between us, and I replicate his movements. He smells like Jasper, that fresh, comforting smell to which I have become so accustomed. As our mouths are inches away, I can feel his warm breath on my cheeks. His breathing is so heavy and full of desire, a pool of yearning hits me with such force, a soft moan escapes me. He bites his lip, sensing my desire for him and takes two steadying breaths.

His eyes are the deepest blue, and being this close to him, I feel like I could stare into those orbs and get lost for an eternity. His eyes burn deeper and he licks his lips, leaving them wet and inviting. I am breathing deeply, in frantic need to kiss him, and I realize I've wanted this to happen for a very long time.

Closing my eyes, I know we're just a breath away from kissing. Opening my mouth, I'm ready to feel his lips on mine, but unexpectedly, the front doorbell chimes, ruining the moment.

Pulling back, startled, I look into Jasper's hungry eyes. He looks…disappointed and annoyed. Has he wanted something like this to happen all along? Have I? Our breathing has quickened to a frenzied rate, and I immediately become very embarrassed at my obvious arousal. I push off him quickly, very aware of what we were about to do.

Jasper, however, is far from being bashful. He lies unmoving on the floor, eyes raised to the ceiling. His hands are interlaced across his abdomen and he exhales a frustrated sigh, while lightly thumping his head against the floor.

I look at him apprehensively, but turn to pat Oscar, needing to calm down my nerves.

Jasper sighs again, but doesn't speak as I hear him get up and attend to whoever walked in on something that could have been amazing.

Oscar is purring away and I'm glad for the distraction. That was so intense. I have never felt that electricity, that spark before, not even with Harper. What does that mean? I felt terrified, but excited at the same time. It was like every inch of my body was on fire, and we hadn't even kissed!

Did I want to find out where that fire led?

Abso-fucking-lutely.

Chapter 15
Needs

It has been a couple of months since I've been back home, and I am somewhat resembling my former self. Jasper and I never discussed what nearly happened the night I got Oscar, as it seemed easier for us to both pretend it never took place. But by the hidden glances we've been giving each other when we believed the other wasn't looking, we both know what happened.

That night has been singed into me, body and soul. And no matter how hard I tried to look at Jasper as just a friend, I couldn't stop thinking about our intimate moment and where it would have led if not for the interruption. This whole situation makes no sense. How can one man affect me so? We hadn't even kissed, so this obsession is ridiculous. But I knew that if we had, there would have been fireworks—corny, but true.

So, our denial has suited us both fine, both too afraid to face the truth. We continue on like nothing happened, but when an accidental touch occurred, or the other was caught staring, the denial wasn't so easy to ignore. I don't want to stop seeing him as often because he makes me happy. Jasper makes me feel alive again. And he makes me feel like I'm worth something.

But there is one troubling reason why kissing Jasper would have been a bad idea, and that would be Indie. I'm not sure if he's still seeing her—in the naked sense, that is. Why does that thought make my skin crawl?

I am at work, and Jasper is sitting in a small brown booth, not his usual spot near the window. I can't stop thinking about Indie. I could ask him, or I could drop not so subtle hints, because I need to know what's going on between them.

As I pass by his seat, he reaches out to grab my arm and I freeze like an electric current has passed through me. I look down at his perfect, long fingers, which are setting my skin ablaze, while trying to ignore the galloping of my heart.

Jasper senses my yearning, and a mysterious grin passes over his lips. He's so confusing, and damned hot. This is why I swore off men. But Jasper isn't just any man.

"When you get off work, come have a coffee with me, okay?" I beam happily that he wants to spend time with me.

"Okay sure, I'm done in fifteen minutes." Jasper nods, running his hands through his thick hair nervously.

I suddenly feel tense. What does he have to say that would make him nervous? I look at my watch—only fourteen minutes and thirty-five seconds till I find out.

~

Feeling gross in my coffee-stained white t-shirt and black jeans, I wish we had a work bathroom so I could freshen up, as Jasper looks immaculate, as usual. But I can't help but notice the preoccupied look on his face, which has been there all morning, and I can't help but wonder what's up.

Nervously fiddling with the different sugars stacked messily in the canister next to me, I can feel Jasper examining me, which makes me all the more anxious. I decide color coding the sugar packets will be a great distraction. Why is he acting so strange?

"Indie and I stopped seeing one another," he blurts out suddenly.

Okay, that wasn't what I was expecting. Is this the reason he seemed so lost in thought?

I casually nod, but secretly, his confession has sent euphoric shivers down my spine. I convince myself the reason for that happiness is because Indie is a tramp and he deserves better.

"I thought you would have something to say, seeing as you're her biggest fan." Jasper is looking at me, his eyebrow raised in question.

"Jasper, my mother taught me if I didn't have anything nice to say, then it was best not to say anything at all. So in this instance, my lips are sealed," I reply smartly. I take a sip of my scalding coffee, burning my lip in the process. Serves me right for being a smart ass.

Pulling away quickly, I run my tongue over my burned lower lip and look over at Jasper, who is casually gazing at my mouth. A slow, sexy smile spreads across his luscious lips, and as I'm openly staring at him, I wonder if he's thinking the same thing I am. Oh, Ava Thompson, get your mind out of the gutter!

After a few hot moments of undressing him in my mind and liking what I see, he interrupts my thoughts.

"So, now it's your turn," he says, his mouth pulling into a lopsided smile.

What were we talking about before I was envisioning his lips on mine? Oh yeah, Indie.

The stern look on his face indicates that the Indie topic is no longer up for discussion, which is a shame, as I have a hundred questions I want to ask. I wonder when exactly he stopped seeing her. Was it before, or after our almost kiss? A heat creeps up my face when I think about the memory, and I quickly clear my head. "My turn for what?"

"To tell me something interesting. Have you heard from Harper?" He half smiles, while I nearly choke on my lemon tart.

When I think of the word 'interesting,' Harper isn't the first thing that pops into my head.

After attempting to dislodge my dessert, I reply, "You and I don't share the same opinion on what we consider interesting.

Harper is on the opposite end of interesting. Way, way down the opposite end."

"Fair enough, but I find your reaction to him interesting," he replies calmly, his arms folded casually over his broad chest.

I, on the other hand, am far from calm. "Why?"

"Because he still gets to you. I thought you would be over him by now," he says honestly with a shrug.

Suddenly angered by his insensitivity, I snap. "What the hell does that mean? He does not."

"Yeah, I think he does. It's okay, Ava, I'm not having a go at you. I'm just surprised you still have feelings for him." Jasper looks relaxed, almost contemplative.

Did I just hear him correctly? He surely didn't say I have *feelings* for the man who smashed my heart into a billion smithereens.

"I do not have feelings for him. The only feelings I have for him are when I imagine he's beaten into a bloody pulp," I bark. I can't help it…I see red.

When I calm down enough to look at him, he has his hands up in surrender. "I'm just trying to understand you better, that's all. I mean, he must have been some guy if you still get so worked up talking about him." Is he deliberately trying to piss me off?

Oh, I take it back, I am absolutely livid.

"I'm getting worked up because Harper is an asshole. When I think about how stupid I was to please him, it makes me furious." I feel my cheeks heat in annoyance, and I hate how my body still constricts whenever I think about him.

"Yeah, I can see that," Jasper replies with a smirk.

This whole thing is obviously entertaining. This man is so irritating, but I can't stay mad at him for long, as his look turns to one of dejection.

"Why do you want to talk about Harper?" I question, suddenly very interested.

"Why not?" Jasper shrugs.

A nagging thought occurs to me. Is he trying to gauge my response to Harper? Is he happy that I'm fuming at the mere mention of his name? Is Jasper fishing for information to find out if I still have romantic feelings for Harper?

Do I really want to go there? No.

Calming down, I reply as sincerely as I can, "I don't want to talk about Harper. You saw how I was when I came back from Singapore. Do you really want to be friends with that emotional mess of a person?"

I berate myself for asking such a stupid question, as there is an uncomfortable silence that I can do without.

"Ava, I'll take you any way I can have you," Jasper softly replies.

"In that case, I don't want you to have the emotional, unstable blubbering Ava I once was. I like this Ava. This is me, after Harper," I breathlessly reply.

"Well in that case, I like this Ava. I like this Ava a lot," he declares with a wink before he takes a sip of coffee.

Holy crap, someone just turned the heating up, right?

After my coffee date with Jasper, I feel even more confused. The almost kiss and hidden innuendos are driving me crazy. I need to talk to V, but I know I'm going to get an, 'I told you so,' speech. But I need some advice, and I need it now, no matter how hard it may be to digest.

As I walk into the living room, I see my friend lying on the sofa, watching some trashy reality show. I take a seat and look at her seriously. She turns to look at me.

"What the fuck has happened with you two now?"

How does she know?

I stare at the TV for a while, avoiding V's gaze. I know once I say this, there will be no going back.

Taking a deep breath, I let it all out before I chicken out. "We almost kissed, and now there is this weird flirting, but not flirting going on between us. I'm so confused, V. I never meant for this to happen. I never thought I would have… feelings for someone else after Harper." This is the first time I've admitted I have feelings for Jasper. Of what nature I am unsure, but I definitely feel something for him.

V looks at me like I have lost my mind. "So, what are you going to do about it?"

That's it? No gloating? I'm extremely surprised by her response, but nothing should surprise me these days.

"I don't know. That's why I'm talking to you." I'm hoping she has the answers I so desperately seek, as V has a way of making things seem less complicated. But by the way she's looking at me, I have a feeling she'll confuse me further.

"Ava, how do you feel?" she responds while sipping her root beer.

"I don't know, V. I don't want to feel anything more for Jasper other than friendship, but I just can't help it. There's something between us, and it's been there since the first minute we met. I should be turning away, but I'm drawn to him." I put my head in my hands, confused and frustrated.

"Why should you be turning away? Just because you broke up with Harper doesn't mean you have to live your life like a nun. You've found someone you have an amazing connection with, so why deny it?"

When V explains things, everything seems so simple. But I know nothing about me and Jasper will ever be simple. But she's right, and I know it all comes down to being terrified of the unknown with Jasper. I'm scared to give him my all, just in case I get hurt again.

"I just can't put myself out there again and get hurt, V." I know I couldn't handle my heart getting broken a second time, not so soon after Harper.

"What's worse, Ava? Not trying and getting hurt because you aren't with him the way you want, or trying something more than friendship, maybe getting hurt, but at least giving it an honest shot?"

My friend is so clever. I wish I could see things as clearly as her.

I sigh, blowing my bangs out of my eyes. "Why are you always right?"

V just shrugs, not seeing my predicament as an issue. Maybe

I'm the only one who can see the danger in jeopardizing my friendship with Jasper by taking things further.

Great, I'm no better off than I was before talking to V.

"Stop with the sulking. Lucas is coming over soon and we can all hang out. He'll cheer you up. He has an amazing ability to make anyone smile." V beams, thinking about her boyfriend.

I doubt Lucas can lift my mood, and besides, the last time we hung out, V and Lucas snuck upstairs to have some alone time, and that alone time ended in loud, earth shattering moans that I wish I could erase from my memory forever.

And I'm in no mood for a repeat performance.

~

I'm lying on the sofa with my iPod and TV volume turned up to a ridiculous level to drown out the unspeakable moans coming from V's room. I knew this would happen, even though V promised I wasn't going to be subjected to V and Lucas: The Sex Musical—Part Two!

I look at my watch—wow, Lucas has stamina. Surely he can't go on for much longer.

I think back to the last time I had sex.

Sex with Harper was good—I think. I have nothing to compare it to. Harper was my first, and it was nothing like what you see in the movies, or what you read about in those romance novels. I didn't see the proverbial stars, or collapse into an orgasmic ball of bliss. It was nice and it was familiar because it was with Harper. We weren't really a sexual couple, and he would make up for his lack of affection by purchasing me lavish, unnecessary gifts. Little did he know telling me he loved me every day was gift enough.

Bravely pulling out an earbud, I listen intently, and the coast seems to be clear. I mute the TV before the neighbors begin banging down the door, demanding I keep the noise level down. However, I wonder which racket they would be referring to.

As I'm about to arise, I hear my friend calling out to a divine entity to help her. Her impassioned plea, combined with some very enthusiastic moans, has me reinserting my earbuds. God help us both. I sigh, and I decide sleeping through this very public display of affection is my only option.

Twenty minutes later, I'm half asleep, but unexpectedly, I feel the sofa dip beside me. I figure it's just Oscar snuggling up to me to escape the sexing happening upstairs. Sleepily, I reach down to pat him, but shrink back petrified when I feel skin, not fur. My eyes pop open, and as I'm about to throw the remote at the intruder, I'm greeted by Jasper's amused face.

Sitting up and pushing my sleep-ridden hair off my brow, I notice Jasper is looking extremely entertained by scaring the bejesus out of me.

"Sorry." He grins, holding up his hands in surrender, as I must look like I'm about to attack.

"What are you doing here? How did you get in?" I ask, lowering my feeble weapon.

"The door was unlocked," he explains. With a smirk, he continues, "You girls really need to be more careful. I mean, I could have been a pervert, wanting to get a front row seat to the orchestra you have going on upstairs."

My face instantly blushes when he warmly laughs, as he's actually finding this funny. I, on the other hand, want to escape for another reason now. I'm sitting with Jasper, while my best friend is getting screwed six ways till Sunday. Can this get any more embarrassing? As I hear a squeaky bed squeak rapidly, leaving nothing to the imagination, I feel my cheeks heat promptly.

"Are you blushing, Ava?" Jasper asks, the corners of his mouth turned up. Correction, this just got a whole lot more uncomfortable.

"No, I am not." I so am. I have never been good at hiding my emotions, and I wish in this instance I could at least sound semi-convincing.

"You so are. You're adorable," he says, laughing uncontrollably.

Crossing my arms over my chest, I'm annoyed at how immaturely I'm reacting, but I can't help it. After our almost kiss, Jasper brings out my bashful side, especially when we can hear what's happening quite loudly upstairs.

"If you can't talk about it, Ava, then you shouldn't be doing it." Jasper winks, detecting my thoughts.

"I'm not," I retort before I can stop myself.

My inept response wipes the smirk off his face, and he looks sincere as he asks, "Why not?"

Did he just ask me why I'm not currently having sex? My blush puts the brightest sunset to shame.

"Sorry, I didn't mean for it to come out so blunt," he apologizes, scratching his head. "I just meant you can, if you wanted."

Was Jasper giving me permission to sleep around if I wanted? This conversation is getting worse by the minute, and to make matters even worse, V and Lucas are starting round two!

I clear my throat. "Um… thanks?" I phrase my comment as a question because I don't really know how to respond.

Jasper looks slightly uncomfortable with our exchange, which has me rethinking my initial reaction. I don't want there to be any embarrassment between us because friends talk about this stuff, and Jasper is my friend.

"I've never been one to sleep around," I confess. "Harper was my…um, first, so when I do… that again, it'll be with someone I care about. I don't think I can ever be aone night stand kind of girl." There, that wasn't so bad. I exhale in relief that I phrased it the way I intended.

"That's really noble, Ava," Jasper replies with a smile. "You've got morals and I respect that. Not many people believe in monogamy anymore." Jasper looks at me, his messy hair shadowing his eyes. He's gazing at me like I'm a riddle he can't seem to solve, and as I think about his female friends, I guess Indie wouldn't know what monogamy was if it bitch slapped her in the face. Maybe I'm abnormal and old-fashioned with my relationship beliefs. Either way, I don't care. This is who I am, and I doubt my views on monogamy will ever change.

"I do. I won't let one asshole ruin my chance of finding that with someone, someday." I realize this is the first time I am openly discussing Harper with Jasper. When he asked me earlier about Harper, I jumped down his throat, but now, I'm doing this for me.

Saying the words aloud helps me believe that one day, I will get my happily ever after.

"Well, that someone is a lucky sonofabitch," Jasper replies with poise.

Beyond stunned at his confession, my breath hitches in my throat, because I know if I was to be totally honest with myself, I want that lucky sonofabitch to be him. And all of a sudden, I want to kiss him like yesterday.

We sit, facing each other motionlessly because I'm too afraid to move, not trusting my heated body. However, Jasper shifts closer, leaning slightly into me with his arm wrapped around the sofa behind me. With a look I instantly recognize on his face, my body warms and I bite the inside of my cheek in anticipation. He watches closely, attempting to gauge my reaction to us sitting so close, so intimately. He lightly grazes my shoulder with his fingertips and I shiver at the contact, sending goose-pimples all over my body. Licking his bottom lip, he moves even closer and his fragrance punches me in the face. I gulp with desire.

Our faces are inches apart and I'm still sitting submissively, too afraid to make the first move. Jasper rests his forehead against mine, inhaling softly. He slides his nose against mine, backwards and forwards, and I take a steady breath before I pass out.

"You smell like lilacs," he whispers hoarsely, his mouth fluttering over my chin.

He unhurriedly moves to my neck, his nose gliding over my skin, inhaling my scent. I detonate as the tip of his tongue slowly sashays along my collarbone, but before I can demand more, his tongue retreats and he begins kissing my cheeks delicately. I wish in this moment I looked nicer or had on more makeup. But under his passionate gaze, I feel like a queen. His tranquil blue eyes take in my impassioned face and he rewards me with a dimpled smirk.

"You look so beautiful, looking at me with those big brown eyes," he says, and a low moan escapes me as he passes his thumb softly along my bottom lip. I purr with desire and close my eyes involuntarily, because the scene playing out before me is too much.

"Open your eyes," Jasper whispers. I oblige.

As I take in the man before me, I gasp at what I see. Jasper is sitting before me, inches away from my face, his eyes consumed in a blistering stare. As he slowly leans in to kiss me, I'm waiting with bated breath to feel his lips on mine. But sadly, the only thing I feel is disappointment as the moment is rudely interrupted by Veronica.

"HOLY FUCKKKKK!" she screams at an octave which could burst an eardrum.

I quickly pull back, cursing my friend and her lousy timing. What a way to shatter a moment.

Jasper laughs a deep, throaty laugh, while I exhale an irritated breath.

"Looks like someone is well spent." He grins, hiding his smile behind his hand.

I flop back onto the couch, slightly cheesed off and whisper, "Yeah, well, that makes one of us."

Chapter 16
Fight! Fight! Fight!

I don't want to overanalyze why I have on my best black jeans and lacy pink boob tube just to see Passengers of Ego perform tonight. The reason, I tell myself as I curl my long hair, is because I enjoy their music. I also tell myself, as I apply my pink lip gloss to enhance my already full lips, that I like hanging at the bar that has become our local retreat. But as I really look at myself in the bathroom mirror, I see the face of a liar.

There is no denying I'm going to all this effort because of Jasper. After our almost kiss, I have been feeling self-conscious around him, and I also want to look my best tonight, as I know Indie will be there. Staring at my reflection, which three months ago was gazing back at me deflated, bruised, and broken, it now looks almost healed, almost back to my former self. I have rose-colored cheeks and a sparkle is returning to my eyes. It's dim, but it's there, and that's a start.

V whistles as I enter the kitchen. "Just friends? Yeah, right."

I don't question to whom she is referring because after our talk, I have endeavored to steer clear of all Jasper talk. My best friend is way too smart for her own good, and I don't want to deal with some of the valid points she raised.

As the cab drops us off two blocks away from Little Sisters, V smiles, "You look hot, by the way."

"Thanks, V," I reply as we hit the sidewalk, shrugging off her compliment.

"Seriously, babe, you are so much better now, and if that's Jasper's doing, then so be it. Whatever you guys are doing in your 'friendship', it's obviously good for you. But I just don't want you to get hurt. What kind of friend wouldn't look out for her BFF?" she asks with a smile.

I just want to live in my world of denial where Jasper and I are friends, because with Indie being here tonight, I'm already on edge.

"I appreciate you looking out for me, V, but everything is fine, and no one is getting hurt," I reply, cringing at how bogus I sound.

She gives me a disbelieving look as we head into an extremely busy, filled to the brim Little Sisters, but doesn't push, which I'm thankful for.

We head straight to the bar, as she no doubt knows I need some Dutch Courage before I face Indie. Ordering two Saint Balls to start the night off, we quickly follow them with a Fruity Tingle cocktail, which we down enthusiastically

As I'm twirling my little yellow umbrella, I suddenly feel *his* eyes on me. Before I can stop myself, I eagerly peer around and find his cerulean eyes locked with mine, accompanied with an amused grin. He's sitting at the end of the bar nursing a beer and looking absolutely drool worthy wearing a white Little Sisters Bar t-shirt. Wow, white brings out the color of those intense eyes, and with all that tousled hair, it looks like he's had a tumble in the hay only minutes prior. My stomach suddenly rolls with that thought, as I know Indie would be more than happy to take a tumble with him.

His curious smirk brings me back down to earth, and as he waves, I timidly smile and wave back with my pointer finger. In a room filled with hundreds of people, I feel like it's only us. Like no one else exists, and that feeling is surreal and daunting. The sexual chemistry winds me and I take a steady breath.

However, that breath gets knocked out of me when Indie shatters my trance-like stare as she appears out of nowhere, passionately kissing Jasper on his sinful lips. She adds tongue just in case I didn't quite grasp her claim on him. I can see he's taken aback and hesitates to return the affection. But as she shoves her manicured fingers into his wild hair, forcing his mouth to hers to deepen the kiss, he surrenders.

I'm shell shocked. So much for not seeing her anymore.

My heart drops into my stomach alongside my cocktail, and suddenly feeling extremely nauseous, I make a bolt for the bathroom, my hand covering my mouth to stop myself from being sick. Barely making it in time, I push open the toiler door and lose my drinks, which don't taste as nice coming back up as they did going down. Taking a steady breath, I flush the toilet and shudder in dejection. What the fuck just happened?

Washing my hands, I splash some water on my cheeks, trying to calm down. However, as I look at my reflection, I sneer to myself, *so much for being happy with my reflection*.

"Ava, are you okay?" V asks, frantically running into the bathroom.

Seeing me braced over the basin, she knows the answer. "It's Indie, isn't it? The minute you saw her pissing contest, you looked like you were going to puke up your cocktail."

I wanted to lie because the truth was too painful to confess, but it was pointless lying. No point being dishonest with V, and more importantly, with myself.

"Yes, it was Indie. But more so Jasper's reaction to her. I can deal with her kissing him to prove a point to me, but he kissed her back. He told me they weren't seeing each other anymore, but that's obviously untrue. I have no right to be mad, but I am. He lied to me." I sigh, depressed, and doubt I can go back out there to face him.

V nods, understanding my sudden dash to the bathroom. She had predicted this happening from the beginning.

"I feel so stupid, V. I tried pretending there was nothing between us, but seeing him kiss her that way makes me physically ill. What does that mean? I'm attracted to him, but is it only physical?"

I'm too afraid to admit that the attraction I feel for Jasper is something more than just being attracted to his good looks. I'm afraid of making myself emotionally available to him.

"I don't have the answers, babe, but I see the way you guys are around each other. Those guarded glances you give one another when you think no one is looking, it's mutual. I think he's in the same position you are. Stop being so stubborn and punishing yourself for having feelings. Have you spoken to him about it?"

I scoff. "No. What am I going to say? I'm scared it'll ruin our friendship. I won't risk our friendship if it's just a physical attraction." I'm so perplexed and scared of my feelings for Jasper.

V tucks a stray hair behind my ear, attempting to console me, but I feel like I'm an inconsolable mess at the moment.

Her beautiful hazel eyes assess me cautiously. "Be honest with yourself, Ava. Do you think it's just physical, or can you see something more happening?" I look at her guiltily. I don't need to reply, we both know the answer.

"Then tell him." V huffs in frustration, while I recoil, thinking how that conversation will go down.

If I had anything left to throw up, I would have. The thought of telling Jasper I have feelings for him is terrifying. But V is right; I have to tell him, I can't go on like this. I'm going to end up in a padded cell, otherwise. I just don't know how to blurt it out. What's the right protocol for a situation like this?

"You're right. I just don't know how, or when." I look at my best friend, searching her face for the answers I seek.

"I don't think there's ever a right time to tell someone you have feelings for them. You and Jasper, you discuss everything, don't let this be any different," V says, giving me a tight hug.

She's absolutely right, and talking to her has calmed me down somewhat. "Okay, I'll do it when it feels right," I mumble into her shoulder.

V breaks our embrace, and smiles. "It'll never feel right. You'll find every excuse why it's not the right time. Do it sooner rather than later, that's my advice. Now, get your ass out there. No time like the present."

With that, she drags me out to face the music, literally, as Passengers of Ego have started. I watch V smile and wave lovingly at Lucas, her official boyfriend of two months. Their love looks so simple, so easy. My eyes drift up to Jasper, who is lost in his music. I am so mad and confused right now.

He told me he and Indie were over, so what the hell was that back there then? If they're still friends and just saying hello, then I got the short end of the friendship stick, as he never kisses me hello that way…or at all! On that note, I need a drink, or maybe ten.

While I'm waiting in line for my drink, I make a conscious effort to ignore Jasper as his husky voice is a major distraction, and totally not helping me sift through my feelings for him.

Finally, it's my turn to be served and I cheer internally because at long last, I can drown my sorrows. I order a Tequila Sunrise and two fancy shots, which cost way too much, but the tasty alcoholic content makes up for the steep price. I reach into my bag, searching for my purse, but it's not there. I know I haven't left it at home as I paid for my drinks earlier.

After a minute of futile searching, I apologize to the annoyed bartender and patrons who are giving me severe stink eye because my frantic hunt has produced lip gloss, gum, a hair tie, pens, an empty bag of M & M's, but sadly, no wallet. I'm seriously contemplating emptying my belongings on the bar as I really, *really* need a drink, but I guess I'll have to go find V, or my wallet.

Giving up, I mutter yet another apology to the customers and turn to leave. However, I'm stopped in my tracks when I see a hand pass the bartender a hundred dollar note. I look over at the mysterious saint—the mysterious, *handsome* saint. My eyes take in his blue jeans, white shirt, and brown shaggy hair.

"Let me get that for you." He grins broadly, and I can't help but return his warm smile.

"No, I can't let you do that," I stammer, bowled over by his kindness.

The bartender, however, has other ideas, handing my mystery saint his change and moving onto the next thirsty patron.

"Too late," he shouts loudly, and salutes me with his beer.

"Thank you. That was really nice of you," I say, looking over shyly while attempting to move my drinks out of the way so the people behind me can place their order.

"Don't mention it. You looked like you needed a drink," he replies, and I instantly hear his South African accent.

As I'm trying, but failing miserably, in moving my three drinks without spilling them all over my hands, I do what any reasonable person would, I throw back a shot while making a pained face as it burns my throat. My mysterious saint looks at me, shaking his head, laughing at my reaction to the potent beverage.

"Would you have a drink with me?" he timidly asks, while I almost fall over my feet in shock.

His question has thrown me off guard, so I quickly reach for another shot, which I toss back quickly, relishing in the sting. Feeling a small, but much needed buzz, I give him a quick once over and I'm not sure if it's the twenty-two dollar shot talking or not, but I quickly reply, "Sure, why not."

He smirks and leads the way to the only vacant table in the venue. As I take a seat on the barstool, I ensure I sit with my back facing the stage, as I can't face Jasper while consorting with another, which is ridiculous.

"So, what's your name?" I shout to be heard over Jasper's melodic voice.

"Brandon," he replies with a smile. "I've been in America for about three years. I am originally from South Africa, if you couldn't tell," he teases, referring to his strong accent.

"Well, it's a pleasure meeting you, Brandon. I'm Ava." I extend my hand over the table and he grips it, giving it a gentle shake.

The contact is light and warm, but it certainly doesn't send me into a spiral of desire like someone else I'm trying very hard not to think about.

"What brings you to America?" I ask quickly, trying to drown out Jasper.

"I'm studying Economics at the University of California. I'm in my second year," he replies.

That would mean he's about my age. I should be getting to know him better, but deep down, I can't stop thinking about Jasper. And it doesn't help that his hoarse voice is blaring over the speakers, reminding me of his presence.

I gulp down my tequila, hoping to get ridiculously drunk in record time, as I want to kill some brain cells, hopefully the ones that constantly remind me of Jasper.

"Can I get you another drink?" Brandon asks, nodding his head towards my empty glass with a smile.

I can do this. It's just a drink with a handsome stranger, I reason with myself.

Looking at him sheepishly, I reply, "I will totally pay you back. I just need to find my friend, or my wallet. Whatever I find first, I promise paying you back is my first priority. Cross my heart," I reply, crossing my heart.

Brandon snorts a laugh, and I giggle, feeling a little intoxicated.

"Don't worry about it. You can pay me back by having another drink with me," he says with a wink as he heads to the bar.

I wipe my sweaty palms on my jeans and I don't know if I'm nervous because I'm in the company of a polite, not to mention hot guy, or if the one singing about hidden desires is the cause of my trepidation. Either way I'm going to enjoy myself and forget the galloping of my heart.

I like Brandon. He makes me laugh and I feel at ease with him. Our conversation is light, but I'm actually enjoying myself, as Brandon has some very entertaining stories from back home.

He insists on buying me drinks, and after a while, I lose count of how many I've had. It might be my beer (tequila) goggles, but Brandon is looking hotter as the night progresses. But could I make out with the hot, emerald-eyed South African sitting next to me? I heave a sigh at the answer. He may be all the things I should be looking for in a mate, but his emerald eyes are not the eyes I want.

I shake off those depressing thoughts because Brandon is making me giggle while telling me a story of a cheeky monkey back home who stalked his town. I'm having a ball and the alcohol is really helping me unwind, so I tell myself to enjoy the moment. I've totally lost track of time, engrossed in his storytelling and it's not until I hear a barstool scraping across the floor, that I become very aware of the time—it's Jasper time.

Positioning the barstool to my left, Jasper looks at us with an unreadable glare. As I turn to look at him, I can smell cigarettes mixed with the mint gum he's chewing, and I am suddenly panting in need.

I visibly swallow, as the hard look he's giving me is one of absolute possession and anger. But I can't figure out why. Why is he mad at me? Judging by the way he's glaring at Brandon, it has something to do with him.

Is he…jealous? That's just ludicrous, as he was the one all but sexing Indie on this very same dance floor an hour ago.

Whatever it is, this situation is suffocating, and I shift slightly, my shoulder brushing Brandon's. It's only then do I realize Brandon has his hand resting lightly on my leg, which makes me wonder, when did I get so close that I'm basically sitting in his lap? This is why I shouldn't drink unsupervised. But why should I care if I am sitting in his, or anyone else's lap? As I take in Jasper's enraged expression, I realize, yeah, that's the reason why.

Looking over at him nervously, I honestly can't gauge his reaction to this situation. The space between us is mere inches, and this close to him, his even breath hits me square in the face.

"Having fun?" he whispers, leaning in close, his hair tickling the side of my face.

I don't know how to respond, as I can feel the rage seeping out of his pores, and again, I'm so turned on, I dare not move.

As I sit immobile, biting my bottom lip, he leans into my neck, nuzzling me softly. I let out a deep, steady breath before I pass out because the contact feels wonderful. I'm staring straight ahead, too afraid to meet Jasper's hungry gaze. Brandon, however, snaps me out of my erotic dream as he awkwardly reaches his hand around my front to offer a hello, in the form of a handshake to Jasper.

"Hi, I'm Brandon. Great show, man," he offers uncomfortably to Jasper, who stares at his hand like it's a diseased limb.

Being stuck in the middle of Jasper and Brandon is as uncomfortable as it sounds, and I suddenly feel dizzy.

Jasper is being rude, my rational side pipes up. Who gives a damn, he's jealous, my harlot side whispers. I'm uncertain how to behave right now, but my rational side finally wins out because the way Jasper is looking at Brandon is not cool. He's looking at him like a predator. His eyes are narrowed in unspoken challenge, and that pisses me off. I'm not a piece of meat they can fight over—this is not the jungle, my inner self screams.

Shaking my head, I decide attempting to diffuse the situation is the best option for everyone. Brandon still has his hand extended towards Jasper, but Jasper rudely slaps his peace offering away and pulls on my upper arm, shoving me off the barstool.

"I need to talk to you in private," he snarls in my ear.

What the *hell*?

His abrupt action surprises me, and as I am half off the barstool, the alcohol hits me and I almost fall flat on my face. Both Jasper and Brandon lunge to stop my descent, but Jasper is there first. I feel like a damsel in distress, and really wish I didn't.

Jasper's voice is hard, and I'm shocked at the venom behind his words as he spits, "I've got her. Keep your hands to yourself!"

Brandon raises his hands in defeat, as he doesn't want to fight. He looks over at me with a confused look, and I shrug, matching his puzzlement. Why is Jasper behaving so unrestrained? As I look at him, I notice his disheveled hair is sticking out in angry peaks, matching his mood, and his usual calm, blue eyes are filled with fury, and I'm afraid to see that anger detonate.

Jasper pulls me toward him, but I'm still half-sitting, half-standing, and have no balance. I feel like a child being reprimanded by their parent for doing something naughty. How dare he treat me this way? I am not his to boss around. And even if we were together, I wouldn't stand for this obvious testosterone-filled performance.

Shaking his hand violently off my arm, I yell, "Let me go, Jasper! Stop treating me like I'm a child." However, I didn't realize how tight his vise-like grip is and my efforts are fruitless.

"Then stop acting like one!" he yells back, glaring at me sharply. Luckily, the rowdy patrons around us mask our heated exchange.

I should resolve the situation, but I am beside myself, shaking with rage. Slowly standing, I try to put some space between Jasper and I, but his fingers won't budge from my arm. He pulls me toward him and we are standing inches apart, our faces nearly touching. This close, his smell is enhanced to a zillion percent, and I shake my head to clear my thoughts because I won't allow his hotness to sway me.

Jamming my finger into his firm chest, I question, "How am I acting like a child? We were just having a drink, not that it's any of your business." Probably not the best thing to say seeing as I was basically giving Brandon his own private lap dance before Jasper interrupted us.

Jasper tips his head toward the ceiling, letting out a sarcastic laugh. As he turns those blue, infuriated eyes towards me, I gasp.

"If you call that," he says, flicking his fingers toward the offending table I was sitting at, "just a drink, then I must be blind. But I'm pretty certain me and everyone in here can vouch for the fact you were practically riding his lap!" Jasper runs a hand through his hair, gripping it tightly in frustration.

My mouth drops open. I'm hurt that Jasper would imply such a thing. Yes, to outsiders it may have appeared that way, but it was harmless.

I can't let this slide, as he isn't exactly innocent. "Excuse me? You're not fucking serious, are you? *You* were the one shoving your tongue down Indie's throat earlier!" I snarl, glaring at him, challenging him to explain himself.

Jasper leans down, peering profoundly into my eyes. "That's because she's my girlfriend."

His curt words feel like a sharp slap to my face, and I know that was his intention all along. Gasping, I take a small step away from him, my blank face reflecting my hurt. I instantly see he regrets his comment, as the remorse shines brightly in his eyes. However, I, on the other hand, want him and his 'girlfriend,' to go to hell!

I muster all the fight I have left in me and snarl on the verge of tears, "Girlfriend? Oh so she's your *girlfriend* now? Well, you and *your girlfriend* can go to hell!"

I attempt to storm off, but he still has his hand wrapped firmly around my bicep. Damn, there goes my smooth exit.

His thumb is rubbing my upper arm softly in an attempt to calm me down, as he knows he has wounded me deeply with his girlfriend comment.

"I'm sorry. I don't know why the fuck I said that. Please, please forgive me," he begs.

But it's too late. I need to get out of here. I can feel the heavy stream of tears steadily building.

"Let me go!"

I bite the inside of my cheek to stop myself from crying while violently shaking my arm to break free. It's ineffective as Jasper pulls me toward him, pressing me against his chiseled front. We're staring at one another, our faces inches apart, but there are no words in this moment, as we are both speechless.

Brandon chooses this moment to step in. "Hey, man, let her go, okay? You're hurting her."

Looking down at my arm, I realize that Jasper's fingertips are pinching into me. He must realize it too, because he immediately loosens his grip, but he never lets go. He knows that if he does, I'll be out of here in a heartbeat.

As Brandon witnesses Jasper's grip slacken, he quickly latches onto my arm, attempting to pull me toward him.

I feel like a freakin' ragdoll being pulled in different directions, and Jasper senses my annoyance.

"Back off and leave her alone," he says, overcome with emotion.

His tone has thankfully calmed, but Brandon doesn't care.

"No. You let her go!" he snarls, and forcibly pulls me toward him.

I stumble, and as I feel Brandon's hands secure around my

waist, I attempt to break free as his hands feel so wrong on me. I shrug him off, but before I can process another thought, Jasper launches forward and punches Brandon in the face. And suddenly, it's like everything is in slow motion.

Brandon falls backward onto some inquisitive patrons and Jasper dives head first to continue his assault. He hits him repeatedly, and Brandon drops to the ground with an audible thud, never standing a chance.

Jasper looks so fierce, so feral, and as his fists are raised high in the air, connecting with Brandon's face, I know I have to stop him. But by the time I can move, Brandon has flipped Jasper over and is punching him over and over again with no hint of mercy. The sickening thuds now give life to Jasper being beaten into a bloody pulp, and I can't just stand here and watch this happening. I mentally slap myself to stop this—now.

I scream for Brandon to stop hurting Jasper, but it falls on deaf ears. My eyes dive to Jasper, who is lying still and not fighting back. He's accepting his punishment, like he deserves it. He looks up at me sadly, and I know he indeed feels this beating is justified.

Processing everything that has happened, I know that nothing merits this kind of abuse, and I can't let this continue for a second longer.

So, I shriek at the top of my lungs, "LEAVE HIM ALONE!"

Brandon stills, looking up at me like I'm a raving banshee and backs off slowly, hands up, bloody palms facing me in surrender.

Running over to Jasper, all my anger fades. He's bleeding from his nose and a deep gash on his chin is pouring blood. I think he'll need stitches. One beautiful eye has swollen shut and my heart breaks at the beaten sight of him. I bend down to tend to his wounds, but he turns his face away.

"No, I don't deserve your sympathy. You shouldn't have stopped him."

It pains me to see him so miserable. "What? Are you crazy? He would have killed you."

"Good," he replies, not meeting my eyes.

"Jasper," I beseech. "Let me know how to help you." He

keeps pulling away as I attempt to assess the damage. However, I stubbornly grasp his face and turn his chin toward me.

"Let me help you," I press, "you're bleeding badly." Instead, he bites his bloodied lip and shakes his head.

Lucas, V, and Andy run over to see what all the commotion is, and as V sees me crouched over Jasper, tears in my eyes, she yells, "What did he do to you?"

Lucas latches onto her arm to stop her from finishing what Brandon started.

"Nothing, V. He did nothing. It was all a misunderstanding." I look up at her, eyes wide, attempting to calm her down.

"Bullshit!" she screams, looking at Jasper, ready to pounce if he has so much touched a hair on my head.

"V, calm down," coos Lucas. "Everything okay, man?" he asks Jasper, who miserably nods, eyes shut tight.

I run my hand across his forehead, gently brushing away the sweaty, bloody hair plastered to his brow. "Let me clean you up."

"No," he responds stubbornly.

The hard resolve of his chin makes clear he won't listen. Bending down so no one else can hear, I whisper into his ear, "You have nothing to be sorry for, Jasper."

He turns to look at me, his eyes tortured, and my heart hitches in my throat. "I hurt you. I fucking put my hands on you and I had no right." Jasper looks so upset and angry, but I can't back off. I have to reassure him I'm not mad at him.

"It's okay," I press, because it really is.

"No, it most definitely is not okay," he spits, finally getting up and limping outside.

As I attempt to follow him, V latches onto my arm.

"Did he hurt you?" she asks, looking at the door Jasper just exited. The door I should be following him through to make sure he's okay.

"No, V, I told you, it was all a misunderstanding," I reply quickly, then I try to make a mad dash toward the exit, but she stops me with her stern look.

"You better not be making excuses for him. Sort your shit

out, Ava. Do yourself a favor, okay, because this is unhealthy for everyone."

She's right-again.

Chapter 17
Fireworks

After I calm V down, and assure her for the hundredth time Jasper didn't hurt me, I finally make an escape and see him seated on a bench in the park across the road. He looks so deflated, head hung low, and I approach him like I would a wounded animal—slow and steady. He must hear my rapid breathing because he raises his head to see who's there. Gosh, his face is a mess.

When he sees it's me, he rakes his hands through his hair. Closing his eyes, he whispers, "Go back inside, Ava, you don't want to be around me right now."

I stop a few feet away from him, my heart stinging at his words. "Why are you so angry at me? What have I done?"

As he opens his eyes, I see he's wiped the majority of blood off his face, but deep purple bruising is starting to materialize everywhere. "Don't you get it? I'm angry at myself, not you. You've done nothing wrong, it's all me," he replies with a sigh.

Leaving a gap between us, I slowly sit down, needing to know what's going on. "Wh-why did you get so mad when you saw me with that guy?"

"Because I'm a fucking idiot, that's why," he replies, rubbing his temples.

"That doesn't answer my question." I know I'm like a dog with a bone, but I can't let this slide.

Jasper turns to look at me briefly before he softly replies, "Because I was jealous."

My eyes widen in disbelief.

"Why?" I probe quietly, afraid of his answer.

"Isn't it obvious?" he asks, giving me a heartbreaking smile.

I shake my head. I need to hear him say it.

"Because of what you make me feel, in here," he says, pointing to his heart. "I can't control it, and it scares me. I don't understand these feelings I have for you. They're irrational, and when I saw you with that guy, with his hands all over you, that feeling turned to rage."

"Rage? Why?"

"Because he was making you laugh and smile, and I wanted to be him."

I don't reply, as the emotions I feel cannot be expressed into words.

"Ava, I'm falling for you," he whispers, and those four simple words have my heart kicking against my ribcage. "I don't normally do that. It's never happened to me before. I distance myself from people, I always have. But then you came into my life and it was like you opened my eyes to everything. I know you don't want a relationship because you're still trying to find your feet, and I'm trying so hard to respect your decision. But these feelings you evoke in me, they leave me breathless. I can't stop myself. I have no control when I'm around you."

I am speechless.

After a minute of silence, Jasper begs, "Please tell me you feel the same way."

I open my mouth, attempting to speak, but the words get caught in my throat. Instead, I just sit and stare at this beautiful creature before me. He has the most frightened look in his eyes, like he's afraid his feelings are not reciprocated.

I know I need to say something, anything, but I need a minute or two to digest his confession. He, however, mistakes my silence for something else, and he stands up quickly, looking down at me sadly.

"I was stupid to think you felt the same. I'm nothing." He sighs and turns to leave.

I'm so scared to confess the truth to him. What if we give this a go and it goes south? What if he leaves a big, gaping hole in my chest? How am I to ever recover from that again? But then I recall all the times he's made me smile and laugh. How being with him has made me feel whole again.

It's only then do I realize that Jasper has helped me without even realizing it. He has helped me become human again. I can't let him leave like this. I have to get over my fear of being hurt again, because this pain of Jasper walking away from me is far worse than Harper breaking my heart. He said he's nothing—he's so wrong. He's everything.

"WAIT!" I yell, quickly chasing after him.

He turns with haunted eyes, and looks taken aback, like he wasn't expecting me to follow him.

As I stand a few feet away, I take a deep, courageous breath, because this is it. This is the moment that will change everything.

"You're everything, Jasper," I whisper, a tear slipping down my cheek. "You leave me speechless. I don't know what this is between us, but I feel it, too."

He stands still, watching me closely, and appears incredulous. But as another tear rolls down my cheek, he walks toward me slowly and gently wipes it away.

We look intently at one another and a surge of confidence overcomes me as I reach up and do something I've wanted to do from the first moment I met him—I grab fistfuls of his messy hair and pull his face toward me, resting our foreheads together. All of a sudden, he's wiping away my flood of tears, and my body is utterly awakened being this close to him.

Everything in this moment is heightened—the smell of him, his harsh breath on my face, and the loud thumping of my heart.

This is Jasper, being vulnerable, and in this moment I realize I have healed him as much as he has healed me. I have showed him that it's okay to let someone in.

As he inches his lips towards mine, I have no more apprehensions, no more what if's. He stops millimeters away, asking me to meet him halfway, and finally, I do. I close the gap that has been between us for months, and at long last, we kiss.

It's just as predicated. I hear, feel, see and taste fireworks.

Jasper gently places a hand on my lower back while the other sweeps up into my hair, running it lightly through my curls. His hand descends to my ear, stroking it softly, and I can't help but whimper in response.

I can't get close enough to him, so I push my body into his so we are pressed, chest to chest, but it's still not close enough. He increases the tempo of the kiss, gliding his tongue into my willing mouth. I let out a soft moan. As he sucks my lower lip tenderly, I can't help but want more. As I stand on tippy toes, angling my head for better access, our fireworks can be heard three states over.

We kiss passionately with Jasper's fingers caressing the back of my neck. His other hand touches my face, hair, and jaw, never once breaking contact. He dips his head to gain better access to my mouth when the height difference between us grows, because I can no longer hold myself up on my toes. He lifts me effortlessly with one arm so I'm higher, and we deepen the kiss further.

He holds me like I weigh nothing, and in his strong arms, I feel tiny. As his breath hitches slightly, I know he is as into this as I am, but I need more. And judging by the way he's intensifying the kiss, our needs are on the same page.

Taking my passion a little too far, I foolishly bite his lip a little too forcibly and he suddenly pulls away, wincing in pain.

"Shit, sorry," I apologize breathlessly.

Jasper sets me on my feet, but thankfully, he doesn't let go, as I would have collapsed into a ball of goo.

"Sorry," I mumble again, embarrassed when I see him tonguing his lip.

Shaking his head, he chuckles. "Sorry for what? You most

definitely have nothing to be sorry for. I should be thanking you."

I peek up at him from under my lashes, feeling a blush creep up my neck.

"What is it about you? You make me feel like a better man," Jasper says seriously, clutching my hand.

"You *are* a good man, Jasper," I reply, squeezing his fingers.

Lifting my chin towards his mouth, he places a soft kiss onto my greedy lips, but pulls away too quickly. He laughs at my disappointed expression, but I can't help it. After tasting Jasper, I want more. More. More.

"So, where do we take this?" he asks, peering into my eyes, searching my face for answers.

"Where do you want to take it?" I ask, still a little afraid of rejection.

Jasper senses my worry and softly cradles my face in his warm palms. "Ava, we will take this wherever, however, you want it to go. I'm here for the ride, and at the moment, I don't want to get off. I want to hold your hand and follow you. You decide what path we take. I'm your passenger."

This man blows my mind, and again, I'm speechless.

One thought, however, ruins the moment.

"Indie," I whisper. "I won't do this with you, whatever it is, if you're seeing someone else."

"I know." He nods firmly. "I'll tell her it's over between us, and I mean it this time. I'm not going to pretend that she'll understand, because she won't. She'll bitch and moan, but eventually, she'll get over it and move onto the next guy."

He pulls me into a tight embrace. "I promise you, she won't be an issue between us. If we're going to try this, we have to do it right."

Pulling back, I stare up at him, and he rewards me with an infectious smile. "What?"

"Did you know this would happen? When we first met?" I ask.

Jasper smirks, those blue eyes hiding an unknown secret. "Ava, I told you. I get what I want…and I want you."

Well, God damn.

I rouse the next morning when I feel a pair of eyes willing me awake. I crack open an eye and see V sitting on my bed, arms crossed angrily over her chest. Maybe if I pretend to go back to sleep, she'll leave me alone.

"Don't even think about it," she says abruptly.

I haven't even been awake for thirty seconds, and she's already grilling me.

"What the hell went down last night?"

Craning my head back and staring at the ceiling, deep in thought, a huge smile assaults my face. Jasper and I shared the most mind-blowing kiss known to mankind. Just thinking about it leaves me panting in eagerness for a repeat performance.

"You two kissed!" V leaps off my bed, pointing her finger at me.

Am I that obvious?

"Don't even answer that, it's written all over your face. How did you guys go from Jasper looking like he went ten rounds with Mike Tyson, to you blinding me with that despicably happy grin?"

I run my fingertips over my lips, remembering the feel of Jasper's mouth on mine.

It was nothing short of amazing, and I would be a liar if I didn't confess I wanted to do it again. And again. But it wasn't only the physical response that has me reeling, it was his words. The honesty and sincerity in them have melted my heart. Where does that leave me? Screwed, that's where.

I'm vaguely aware of V snapping her fingers in front of my face to get my attention. "Earth to Ava!" I shake my head and throw my friend a dazed look.

"Holy shit, you've got it bad!"

Her comment snaps me out of my daydream. Is she right? It was never my intention to have it 'bad' for anyone after Harper, but Jasper isn't just anyone.

In your lifetime, there are a small handful of people you'll meet and have an instant connection with. You may read about it, or watch it play out on TV, but actually experiencing it, that's a whole different story. No movie or book can prepare you for that feeling of completeness with another. I was never a believer in kismet, but meeting Jasper White has altered that belief. Suffering the loss of Harper is something I'll never fully recover from, but what if it was my destiny to experience that defeat to become victorious? What if Jasper is my victory prize?

It's way too early for these philosophic thoughts, and I'm not ready to face them, just yet. I don't even know what this means for Jasper and I. Yes, we kissed, but that doesn't mean he wants to be my boyfriend.

The word boyfriend and Jasper in the same sentence knocks the winds out of my sails, and I really need to talk to him before I go planning our future wedding.

"Ava, are you even listening to me?" V asks, throwing a pillow at my head.

"No," I reply with a sleepy, happy smile.

V looks at me and sighs. "Well, you should. There's no smoke without fire," she plainly replies.

"What? Are you trying to say I'm a pyromaniac?" I half smile, but I know where she's headed with this. She raises an eyebrow at me, and I heave a sigh. "Yes, okay, enough with the third degree. I get it, loud and clear."

"Just be careful, that's all I'm saying. The way you guys were last night, that shit turns into crazy love. I just want you to be sure this is what you want."

"You were totally Team Jasper last night, cheering me on, encouraging me to tell him how I felt."

"That's not what I'm saying, Av. I just want you be careful, okay? I don't want you to get hurt, that's all." Before I can question what exactly about Jasper and I being together would result in me getting hurt, the doorbell chimes.

V smirks and pulls me in for a quick hug. "Saved by the bell, Missy."

She heads downstairs while I make a short trip to the bathroom.

I have a quick shower, the water clearing my head. V is right. I do need to be careful with Jasper. Not because I think he'll break my heart, but because I think *I* might break his heart unintentionally. I still harbor all this Harper baggage, which weighs me down with silly insecurities. I need to take this slow and steady because hurting Jasper is the last thing I want to do.

Wrapping a white, fluffy towel around my torso, I step out into my room and unexpectedly come face to face with Jasper, who's sitting on the edge of my bed, legs crossed comfortably at the ankles.

I let out a small yelp while crossing my legs and pulling down the towel to cover up my bits and pieces. Jasper gives me a look filled with mischief, and I really wish I wasn't standing here in a towel.

"Hi." He smirks, his left dimple on show.

His face is battered and bruised, but not as bad as I thought it would be. He has a thin strip of gauze taped under his chin, and his eye looks slightly swollen with a small cut above it. I feel awful that he looks this way because of me.

"Hi," I reply, lowering my eyes.

I know I'm wrapped in a towel, but under his penetrating gaze, I may as well be naked.

Jasper senses my anxiety and lets out a soft chuckle. "Would you like me to give you a minute to get dressed? Although, your current attire is—" he pauses as I feel my cheeks redden "—fucking amazing." His eyes take in every inch of my very exposed flesh.

My body heats at his choice of words, and as he pulls on his bottom lip, a small whimper escapes me, betraying how much I want him. A surge of embarrassment overwhelms me, and while he appears as cool as a cucumber, I'm seconds away from charging back into the bathroom and having a very cold shower.

Jasper chuckles once again, obviously enjoying watching me writhe in embarrassment.

Luckily, I know the antidote for that smugness. "No, it's fine, I'll only take a second," I casually reply while pretending to unhook the towel from under my arms.

Jasper's eyes widen in shock and he jumps up off the bed, turning his back to me.

Win for me!

As he rubs the back of his neck uneasily, I let out a giggle. Jasper is embarrassed. Wow, that's a first.

Creeping around to my closest, I quickly pull on my underwear, a pair of blue jeans, and a plain t-shirt. I try fluffing my hair, but decide on tying it back because I need more than a minute to tame that beast.

Speaking of beasts, I take a break from my frantic dressing to examine the one standing before me. A tight fitting shirt hugs his broad back tightly, and his perfect butt is screaming for a quick smack. I stare hungrily at his back profile for a little longer than I intended when I hear Jasper clear his throat. "Are you staring at my butt? I feel so objectified."

A smile spreads from cheek to cheek, and as he turns around, his features match my amusement.

Finally catching my breath, I take a seat on the edge of the bed, waiting for him to speak. He looks down at me, a look of uncertainty on his face, and decides to prop up against my dresser instead. I look at him curiously, and realize Jasper and I sitting together on my bed would probably lead to a whole lotta not talking. I feel a blush spread across my cheeks and fiddle with my amethyst ring to distract myself.

We're silent for a short while, and I can feel Jasper's intense gaze penetrating me. For this reason alone I keep my eyes down, focused on anything but Jasper's eyes.

"I'm sorry I came here unannounced. I had to see you after last night," he says, breaking the silence.

However, the silence between us is not uncomfortable. It's more like we're walking on eggshells, not knowing the right set of rules. But Jasper has made the effort, and now it's my turn to meet him halfway.

I nervously peek up at him. "I want you to be here."

"Yeah?" he questions.

"Of course I do. I think we should talk…" I leave the comment hanging, too afraid to elaborate as I search his unreadable face.

"I think we should talk, too. I'm so sorry for the way I behaved last night. The things I said to you were wrong. I don't know why I said that thing about Indie being my…you know."

I flinch at the memory and he continues quickly as he senses my discomfort. "And I never should have put my fucking hands on you." He looks downs at my arm and clenches his jaw. "I never meant for any of that to happen. I'm not making excuses because I know I fucked up." He rubs his hands down his face, looking beaten, and I gasp when I see his knuckles are grazed and red raw.

"Are you okay?" I ask quickly.

Jasper looks at me, his hands frozen midstride. He looks puzzled, so I point to his hands.

"Oh. Yeah, totally fine. Don't worry about it."

His disregard for his injuries upsets me, so I slowly stand and walk over to him. He looks down at me, breathing steadily. In trepidation, I reach forward and lightly rest my palm on his cheek. I can feel his scratchy stubble underneath my fingers and I remember the way it felt against my mouth last night. I shiver at the delicious memory.

"Of course I worry," I whisper, my fingers leading into his hair to toy with the tresses at his temples. Jasper closes his eyes and exhales softly. The air is thick and heavy with our mutual chemistry. I want to drown in it.

As he slowly opens his blue eyes, I'm engulfed in his ardor. He is my own personal drug and I am addicted. He rubs his thumb over my bottom lip and I mewl in response.

"I like you worrying about me," he whispers.

I don't know how to reply, so I merely stand frozen under his hands.

"Ava, when I kissed you last night, I've wanted that to happen for a long time. I've wanted *you* for a long time. I meant everything I said to you, I won't push you. You decide where you want this to go."

I stare, stunned, and I lick my lips nervously. I can't deny my feelings for Jasper, no matter how hard I try not to acknowledge them. Jasper is patiently allowing me to digest my thoughts and not pushing for an answer, but he deserves one.

He was right when he once told me we would look back with regret if we didn't get to know one another better. Well, I have come to know the Friendship Jasper quite well. And now, I really want to know what Relationship Jasper is like. I have a sneaking suspicion I'm going to be devoted to both.

"Jasper, I've wanted to kiss you for a long time, too. I've just been afraid, and I still am. But I'm more afraid of not living than living in fear. I can't promise you anything, but I'd like to give it a go. With you. If you want to."

Okay, I need to stop rambling now.

Jasper smiles a sexy smirk as he runs his index finger down the middle of my lips, toying with my bottom lip.

"Yeah, I want to. I really want to," he replies.

I blush instantly at the heated undertone of his words.

"Do you blush so easily everywhere on your body?"

I attempt to stop blushing, but fail terribly. Jasper tilts my chin up towards his face, and a little sigh escapes me at the gentleness of his touch.

"Looks like I'm going to have to be creative and find out."

Holy freakin' hell!

My skin instantly betrays me as I feel my neck and chest gleam a crimson red. I don't want to think about the color of my skin when Jasper dips his head and consumes my mouth with his.

Chapter 18
Flames

The next month, Jasper and I take things to the next level. We don't put any labels on what we have because it's nice, it's chaste, and it feels natural. Our routine hasn't changed much. I still visit every night at the shelter and he visits me at work. The only thing that has changed is the physical aspect to our relationship, and it's safe to say, Jasper is driving me crazy.

We make out for hours, he being the perfect gentlemen, sticking to kissing and over the clothes touching because he doesn't want to start our relationship based on sex. Judging by the amazing make out sessions we've had, sex with Jasper is going to be *something*. I don't know when I'm going to be ready for that, but Jasper never pushes.

What he does push however, are his beliefs and opinions on topics that are important to him. We fight incessantly because we're both stubborn, hot tempered, and proud, but we always make up without delay. It's nice to be able to voice an honest opinion, something I could never do with Harper.

I'm still coming to terms with seeing someone who isn't Harper, and I'm trying my best, but I know Jasper can sense my detachment at times. But he never questions or makes me feel uncomfortable about it.

Jasper said being together meant we should be doing 'datey' things, which warm's my heart. And nothing says date better than seeing a band.

Flames is a local band that has recently been signed. They're playing at a big venue downtown before they commence their European tour. Jasper has known these guys for years, and when the members asked Jasper and Lucas to attend their last local show, the boys gladly accepted. V and Lucas are meeting us at the club, so I guess this is our *real* first double date.

Parking his truck, he comes around to open my door before I even have a chance to unbuckle my seatbelt. He's always such a gentleman, another reason I adore him. Lifting me down to meet his lips, he kisses me passionately, and of course, I happily comply. He walks me backward, pressing my back up against the cold truck door to continue his kissing assault. Dueling with his tongue and pulling softly at his messy hair, I reach behind me, attempting to open the door to lead us somewhere more private, but he pulls away.

He smirks, biting his lip. "Come on, we're going to miss the set."

"And whose fault would that be?" I pout, blowing my bangs off my face.

"Yours, for wearing that outfit." I look down at my simple blue jeans, Chucks, and cute cardigan.

"Outfit? You call this an outfit? Wait till you see what I'm wearing underneath," I tease.

He gives me a pained look, and just when I think he may take me up on the offer, I hear a wolf whistle and see Lucas and V strolling towards us, hand in hand.

Failing to hide my disappointment, and trying my hardest not to pout, Jasper pulls me into his hard chest and murmurs, "If you don't pull in that bottom lip, I'm going to take you into my truck and do unspeakable things to you." I glance up at him, mouth agape.

"Don't look so surprised, Ava. Being around you requires a lot of will power, and you make that difficult when you give me that look."

"What look?" I question before I can stop myself.

Jasper leans forward, giving me a sultry peck on the lips. "The look that tells me you want me as much as I want you."

Again my mouth is agape. How is it possible that this man can turn me on with his voice alone?

Before I can reply, V rushes forward and tackles me into a bear hug. Jasper and Lucas fist bump, and we head toward the club.

V links her arm through mine and whispers so the boys can't hear. "What did we just walk into?" She raises her eyebrows and I grin happily. "Ugh, I don't even want to know. You two are nauseatingly cute together."

And she's absolutely right.

~

The band is fantastic, and I can see why they're going overseas on tour. During their whole performance, Jasper holds my hand and pulls me possessively into his hip, which is nice. This feels so effortless, like we've been here before, and I realize Jasper and I had established a solid friendship before we decided to take it to the next level. Maybe, just maybe, we can make this relationship work.

Jasper reaches down, kissing my cheek, his stubble brushing my face.

"Do you want a drink?" he asks into my ear, yelling over the music.

Giving him a thumbs up, he gives me a swift peck on the cheek before heading to the bar. I see most girls looking at him hungrily, nudging their friends to check him out. But Jasper has no idea how his looks effect other women. He doesn't notice other girls looking his way because he only has eyes for me, and that thought humbles me.

As he walks back with our drinks, a bold girl latches onto him, whispering something into his ear. I look over protectively, crossing my arms over my chest, not liking someone talking to him so closely. Jasper smiles, looking flattered, but motions my way with his head. The girl glares my way, disappointed that he has a date.

"Don't worry about her," V shouts, glaring at the tramp molesting him.

I shrug offhandedly, but V knows me too well, rubbing my arm compassionately.

I know I'm not much to look at, as I'm not sexy or seductive. I barely wear any makeup, and am more comfortable in my Chucks and jeans, but as I look around the bar at all the girls Jasper could have, I wince and think, maybe I should try and make more of an effort.

Jasper returns, handing me my beer while kissing the top of my head. He must see my apprehension and brings me in for a hug. I snuggle into his warm chest, surrounded by his smell and try to forget my insecurities.

After a few minutes of being lost in all things Jasper, I feel his grip stiffen around my waist. Gazing curiously around the room to find what, or should I say *who,* has caught his attention, I see Indie throwing herself onto some poor chump, who is none the wiser to her ruse. I casually peer up at Jasper, who has an indecipherable look on his face and my stomach drops.

I wish I could read him better, as he gives nothing away. Is he jealous? The thought saddens me, and I wish he didn't have such a firm hold on me so I could slip away undetected. I can feel V staring at me, picking up on my discomfort. Risking a quick glance her way, she nods a look of compassion, because she gets it.

Jasper is still observing Indie, and I feel vulnerable standing here, watching this exchange with his ex. I consider making some lame ass excuse to make a mad dash to the bathroom, but the band concludes their set.

Clapping half-heartedly, I'm thankful when I see Indie saunter off with her new boy-toy. However, I gasp when I see her flick an arrogant look over her shoulder towards Jasper and I. She knew he was watching her, but more importantly, she knew *I* witnessed the way he reacted. But how was he reacting? I'm so confused, but more so, I'm furious at that scheming whore.

Jasper's gaze follows them out the door and when she's finally gone, he returns his attentions to me. He's utterly oblivious and unaware I saw him react the way he did as he kisses my forehead quickly.

"Did you like them?"

Nodding, I try my best to appear cheerful. "They were great."

But I don't want to be talking about the band. I want to know what the hell was going on with Indie.

Before I can ask him, Lucas wraps his arm around Jasper's shoulders. "We should go wish them good luck before they get big heads and forget who we are." Jasper nods, smiling at Lucas' sarcasm.

"Baby, I'll be back in a minute."

"Okay, I'll stay right here. I don't want to impose on your bromance." Jasper laughs, kissing my lips way too briefly before heading over to his friends, who are being swarmed by screaming fans.

"What the fuck?" V whispers, dragging me into a booth the moment the boys are gone. We slide in quickly before they come back.

"You saw that, right?" I ask, hands out in annoyance.

"I sure did," V replies, putting her hand on mine to calm me down.

I'm looking over her shoulder, keeping an eye out so we don't get caught gossiping. "What am I to make of that? Was he jealous? He was giving that guy serious stink eye." I frown, slouching in my seat.

"It didn't look like he was jealous. And he wasn't giving that guy stink eye."

I scoff, not believing a word.

"I promise. I wouldn't lie to you. It looked like he was more intrigued, or just curious. He didn't look envious or resentful. He just looked like he was thinking…whatever." She shrugs her shoulders.

"What the hell does that mean?" I ask, biting my fingernail nervously.

"I don't know. But I do know he's crazy about you. He can't keep his eyes or hands off you. He really likes you, Ava. Don't doubt yourself over this, and don't question your relationship."

I wish I had her confidence, but then I ask myself, how would I react if I saw Harper consorting with another? Probably the same way Jasper behaved. V's right, he didn't look envious he just looked…curious. Whatever look he gave her, I would prefer that he didn't look at her at all.

Taking a deep breath, I sigh. "You're right, V. I know he likes me, and I need to stop over analyzing everything."

"That's my girl!" V smiles, clapping lightly in encouragement.

And then all my positivity gets flushed down the toilet when I see the same girl who approached Jasper earlier stroll over to him as he's talking to his friends. I feel even more insecure when I witness her flaunting her 'assets' into Jasper's face because I realize I'll never have her confidence. Jasper looks at her bulging bust and subtly takes a step backward. But I still feel awkward, sitting here and watching as he gets molested by this tramp. Unfortunately, I don't have the balls to confront her.

V looks over her shoulder to catch a glimpse of Jasper getting all but dry humped by his admirer. Before she can stop me, I quickly make a run for the exit, as I can't handle seeing his reaction. What if he flirts back?

Pushing open the door, I'm thankful to be out here, as the cool breeze is exactly what I need to clear my head. I'm sitting on the stairs, biting my nails when Jasper comes outside, looking for me. He sees me and I cower, as I may have overreacted just a tad to that girl, but I can't help it. It irritates me; Jasper is mine, and I don't want some hussy flaunting her bits anywhere near him.

I'm shocked at my jealousy because I was never this way with Harper. The feelings I have for Jasper seem to grow each day, and they are also getting stronger—hence the green-eyed Ava. But I still doubt myself, and this thing with Indie hasn't helped.

As much as I hate to admit it, my relationship with Harper

plays on my mind from time to time. Will Jasper hurt me like Harper? Could I really love someone as much as I did him? Do I want to fall in love like that again? Am I ready to let someone in? Will I ever?

I know I'm reserved with Jasper, but I'm trying my best. Damn these stupid insecurities. And it doesn't help when Jasper has random girls and a devious ex stalking him frequently.

"What are you doing out here?" Jasper asks, interrupting my depressing thoughts.

I shrug, not wanting to divulge my jealousy, or let him in on my Harper thoughts.

"You weren't jealous over that girl, were you?" He smiles, placing his hand on my leg.

"What girl?" I lamely reply, because we both know I am.

Jasper only smirks, pulling me in for an embrace, and I happily comply, needing the reassurance that he still wants me.

"Ava, what's wrong? Are you mad at me?" he asks after a moment of silence.

Not able to meet his eyes, I berate myself for being such an idiot because Jasper has done nothing wrong. My own insecurities are the problem.

"No, I'm just being silly," I reply with a sigh.

"About?" he questions when I don't continue.

Taking a deep breath, I pull out of his embrace and confess, "About that girl. About *every* girl. About Indie," I conclude on a whisper.

Jasper only cocks a confused eyebrow at my admission, so I elaborate. "I saw the way you were looking at her." I hold in a deep breath, afraid of what he will tell me.

"I'm sorry. I didn't realize you saw her. I was looking at her obvious attempt to make me jealous," he says with a sigh.

"And did it work?" I whisper sheepishly, biting my lip.

"What do you think?" he asks me honestly.

I ponder his question and shake my head in defeat. I wish I could be more confident, but at the moment I feel like the ugly duckling amongst all the supermodel lookalikes throwing themselves at Jasper.

Jasper reaches forward, his blue eyes searching mine. "You need to trust me, Ava. I want you and only you."

But that's not the problem. I trust him. It's the girls, especially Indie, that I don't trust. "I don't like the way other girls look at you," I own up, turning away from his gaze, as it sounds even more pathetic aloud.

He pulls my chin towards him, kissing the tip of my nose. "How do they look at me?" Gosh, this boy can be daft sometimes.

"They look like they want to devour you," I reply, sticking out my bottom lip unhappily.

Brushing my hair off my brow, he asks, "And how do I look at them?"

"You don't," I reply softly, feeling like an even bigger idiot.

Jasper looks at me with a 'then what's the problem' look.

He's totally missing the point, and I run a hand down my weary face. "That's not the point. I will never be like those girls or Indie. I will only be just me. I will never be…sexy or daring." Expressing my fears out loud sounds petty and I should have kept my mouth shut because I sound like a whiny schoolgirl.

Jasper looks like I've slapped him. "Are you serious?" he asks, placing a hand to my cheek.

When I lower my eyes, he continues. "You don't realize how sexy and daring and beautiful you are to me, Ava. You're perfect. All those other girls, they don't know me, they just see this," he says, motioning to his face and body. "It's all superficial. But with you, you see *me*, you really see me, and that to me, is more attractive than you will ever know."

My eyes widen, shocked at his admission.

"So, stop worrying about stupid stuff, okay? Just be with me because that's all I want." He bends forward, claiming my mouth as his own.

The way he kisses me, I know he speaks the truth. He worships every part of me, no matter what I am wearing or how I look. He likes me for *me*, and I most certainly like *him* for him. My silly insecurities clouded that, and I feel like I can breathe for the first time all night.

Intensifying our kiss, I lean over to straddle him, pushing his back into the step behind him. He is vulnerable to me, me being above him, but he braces his hands on the step below him, letting me direct where I want this to go. He knows I need to assert some dominance over him, and he's more than willing to submit.

My lips trail down his taut neck and I can feel his muscles tensing under my lips, aroused by my control. As I bite him softly, he hisses a quick breath through his teeth. My harlot side has reared her wicked head because I boldly run my hands down his jeans, stopping at the top button. However, he stops me.

Biting my lip in disappointment, I peer up at him and wonder, why did he stop me? Yes, I know we're in public, but what a perfect sight for little Miss Flirty Pants or Indie to walk into.

"Not here," he says with a smirk. "As much as I want to, if we start, I'm not going to be able to say no."

"Then don't," I reply valiantly; I'm shocked by my courage. Must be my rampant hormones talking.

He chuckles hoarsely, kissing my chin. "And you said you're not daring, Ms. Thompson."

"Well, Mr. White, you must bring out my brave side," I reply, melting under his skilful mouth.

Kissing my forehead, he whispers, "You're the bravest person I know. I just wish you knew how fearless you really are."

I can hear the echo of P!nk's "Try" playing faintly in the background, mingled in with happy patrons in high spirits, cheerfully singing along. I can smell an earthy, metal overtone, and I distinguish the smell as someone smoking a joint around the corner. And I can feel the cool breeze whip my hair around my face so it catches on my sticky lip gloss. All my senses are on high alert, but it's my sight that's most aware.

Looking down at Jasper as he expresses his feelings for me renders everything else void. He's searching my eyes for a response to his confessions, and in this moment, I don't feel brave. I feel quite the opposite, dodging his gaze. I wish I was courageous enough to express my affections, but yet again, my nerves tie a knot in my stomach and tongue. Sadly, I know why that is.

I wish I could make myself more emotionally available to Jasper, but Harper has squashed my spirit, and at times, I forget how to breathe without him. I know I'm emotionally damaged goods, and I criticize myself for letting him effect me this way. When will I be able to move on without always associating my future experiences with my past?

Jasper is aware of my uncertainty and releases my teeth, that are unintentionally biting my bottom lip, with his thumb.

Giving me a sincere smile, he says with conviction, "One day, you will."

I hope he's right. And I also hope he's with me when that day arrives.

Chapter 19
Have Faith

I don't know why I'm here, but I just ended up at this juncture. As I sit staring at the familiar building before me, a feeling of longing kicks me in the guts. What most people consider a prison, or hard labor, I consider my second home. I am looking at The Culinary Institute of America.

I haven't been back here since my return, and sitting out in front in my beat up Honda brings back many happy memories. I was happy here, and I was on my way of achieving my dreams.

I gaze enviously at the students laughing with their peers on their way to class, because I would have graduated by now. That thought is a hard one to process.

Could I go back to being that person? Should I go back? And would I be happy?

Coulda/shoulda/woulda!

My phone beeps, thankfully snapping me out of my slump, and as I glance down, my iPhone indicates I have a text from Jasper.

Good morning. You? Me? Pancakes?

I let out a small smile. It's like he knows I need a sugar fix to mend my sour mood.

> **You buying?** *I type out cheekily.*
>
> **Depends.**
>
> **On?** *This text war will help steer my mind away from my education dilemma.*
>
> **What do I get in return for treating you to a nutritious breakfast? :)**
>
> **What do you want?** *I giggle and realize I must look like a loon, sitting in the car, smirking to myself.*
>
> **You know what I want ;)**
>
> **I do?**
>
> **Yeah I want it all the time.**

I feel my skin prickle at his suggestive words.

> **Give me a hint**, *I text, just in case I misunderstood.*
>
> **Y**
>
> **What kind of clue is that :)**
>
> **A good one. Okay here's another, O**

Staring at that singular letter, a shiver creeps up my spine.

> **U guessed it yet? I'm starving btw**

What Jasper wants is staring at me in big, bold letters.

Y O U

He wants *me*.
I bite my lip happily and tap out, only too happy to oblige.

C u in 10 xx

Parking my car into a tight fitting parking space, I quickly check my reflection in the rear view mirror. Cringing when I see my wild hair, I secure a bobby pin into my bangs to sweep them off my face.

I love how our meeting place remains unspoken between us. That's because we had gotten into the routine of knowing each other's drink preference, what TV channels were the other's favorite, and where to meet for pancakes, without uttering a single word. It was comforting, but it was also a little daunting that we had fallen into a comfortable routine so quickly. I exit the car hurriedly before I start over-analyzing-again.

The bell above the door chimes, announcing my arrival. The appetizing scent of maple syrup and coffee assaults my nose. I scan the diner to find Jasper sitting in a corner booth, perusing the menu. A backwards baseball cap sits snugly on his head and is complimented by a blue and white checkered shirt. He is a sight for sore eyes. As I look at him, totally unaware of my observation, I can't believe how lucky I am to know someone like him. And even luckier to hold his affections.

I'm totally busted as Jasper catches me dribbling all over myself. He half smiles and places the menu on the table while intertwining his fingers behind his head. What a show off! Rolling my eyes mockingly, I make my way over to him. As I approach the booth, I lean in to give him a quick kiss, but Jasper has other ideas as he lightly grips the back of my head, holding my mouth prisoner to his probing lips. I liquefy as I brace my hands on the table to stop myself from tumbling over in passion. He pulls away coolly while I stumble slightly with a giddy head rush.

He squeezes my hand tightly as I sit across the table from him. "Good morning, baby."

I love hearing him use that term of endearment for me.

As I peer up at him, I melt looking into his crystal clear, blue eyes.

"Good morning," I reply happily.

"I ordered you a soy chai latte," he says while nodding his head to the steaming mug in front of me.

Inhaling the mouth-watering cinnamon, I smile. "Thanks."

"No worries." Jasper grins while rubbing the pad of his thumb over the top of my hand. He assess me inquisitively, head tipped to the side. "What's wrong?"

How can anything be wrong with Jasper caressing my hand the way he is? But he knows something's up. "Wrong? Nothing's wrong." I'm such a terrible liar.

He looks at me incredulously. "What were you up to this morning when I messaged you?"

How does he know? Averting my eyes, I nervously pick up the menu to screen myself from Jasper's inquisitive eyes.

"Wow, I'm starved. What are you going to have?" I pathetically mumble in hopes of changing the subject.

Jasper places his hand on the menu, bringing it back down onto the table top. I shyly peer up at him. Damn, he's not falling for it.

"For someone who was starving, you sure want to do a whole lotta talking, and not a whole lotta eating," I playfully tease with a smile.

Jasper smirks, running his fingers along my forearm. "I'd rather know what's eating you."

This man is infuriating. "At the moment, you are."

Jasper lets out a soft chuckle while sipping his coffee.

Heaving a sigh, I finally give in as I know he won't let this slide. "I was parked outside my school."

Jasper looks slightly amused. "Why?"

"Because I'm going crazy, that's why." I huff, covering my face with my hands to hide my beet red complexion.

Parting my fingers, I steal a look at Jasper and see he's biting back a smirk. He brushes my fingers back down to the table, but doesn't let go of my hands.

"You miss it?"

That's the million dollar question, and I shrug, unsure of the right answer.

"Well, I hate to state the obvious, but if you're revisiting your old school, I think the safe answer here is yes. Have you thought about going back?"

I move around in my seat uncomfortably because suddenly, I feel like I'm getting the third degree from my mom.

"I've thought about it."

"And?" he asks, sensing my apprehension.

"And…I don't know," I confess sadly.

"Ava, its okay to be unsure of what you want to do. The answer will become clear to you," he says with a firm shake of his head.

"Yeah, clear as mud," I reply grumpily, while fiddling with the spoon in my latte.

"Stop doubting yourself. This self-doubt is the reason you're so confused. You know you're amazing, and I have faith in you, even if you don't."

I peer up at Jasper, surprised by his confidence in me.

"What if I go back and I hate it? What if I go back and I'm not any good?" I really don't know why I'm so confused because I know I won't hate it, nor will I suck at it. I want to hide my face again, but Jasper has a strong grip on my hands.

"Ava, we're not given a roadmap for success. Life's a gamble—be brave and take a chance. Just like you did with us."

My eyes snap up to meet his, as I was so not expecting his comment.

"I know you were torn giving me a go, but you did. And I'm really happy you made that choice."

I gulp nervously, my palms suddenly becoming clammy and

my skin heating to a thousand degrees.

Aware of my discomfort, he chuckles. "'Cause if you didn't, who would I be sharing my breakfast with?"

He is so good at diffusing a situation before it can get too uncomfortable.

I squeeze his fingers lightly. "Thank you for believing in me."

"Always," he says with conviction.

Again, I question myself, how did I get so lucky? And I thought I was happy when I was with Harper. He never showed me the support Jasper has.

"We're not all bastards." He smiles, looking intently into my eyes.

I don't have to question to whom he is referring. I must be easy to read, my face giving me away.

Glancing up at him and working my lip, I murmur, "I know."

He's on the verge of saying something when our busty, blonde waitress interrupts us with an annoying southern drawl. "Y'all ready to order?" she asks happily, while infuriatingly tapping the top of her pen on the notepad she's holding, poised, ready to take our orders.

I feel my shoulders drop in relief as I really wasn't hungry for a side order of Harper with my pancakes this morning.

Jasper smiles up at our waitress and I see her gasp as she rakes over Jasper's face.

"I'll have the buttermilk pancakes, the large stack, with the cinnamon apples, please."

"Would you like an extra helping of maple syrup or whipped butter?" she asks, pulling in her bottom lip.

"No thanks, I'm good," he replies while handing her his menu.

"Yeah, I bet y'all just sweet enough."

Jasper smiles politely, while I'm about to jam that pen she's running seductively along her lips down her throat.

"Ahem." I cough loudly.

She glances my way viciously, like she only just realized he has company.

"I'll have the whole wheat and honey pancakes with the

whipped butter and maple syrup, thanks." Dismissing me like I'm a parasite, she quickly writes down my order.

She leans down in her low cut top to arrange Jasper's cutlery and turns her face up to his. "If I can help you with anything else, and I mean *anything,* please give me a holler."

Jasper leans back uncomfortably, his hands braced on the edge of the table, attempting to evade her flirtations. She slowly backs away, licking her lips lavishly, not getting the hint.

If I were a cartoon character, steam would be coming out of my ears right about now.

"Nancy, is it?" I spit, reading her nametag.

She tilts an annoyed eyebrow at me, waiting for me to continue.

"How about less talk, more work?" I say, smiling sarcastically.

Jasper chokes on his coffee from laughter as Nancy's mouth opens and closes, surprised by my comment. Giving her a daring look, I lean back into my booth smugly while she openly glares at me for a moment, but when she senses I mean business, she storms off in a huff.

Meanwhile, I frown at Jasper.

"What?" he asks complacently.

"You know what," I reply, crooking my thumb over my shoulder to where little Miss Helpful went.

Strangely, unlike the other times Jasper has been hit on, I am feeling less insecure. He never asked for her flirtations, and I witnessed his obvious discomfort.

Deep in thought, Jasper leans over the table, applying a soft kiss on the tip on my nose. "You have nothing to worry about." He sits back down and takes a sip of his coffee.

"Yeah, why's that?" I ask, curious to hear his response.

Jasper rewards me with a ghost of a smile. "Because it's *you* I want. No one else. Only you."

I gulp in desire, and also in fear. I should be returning the sentiment because I know I feel it, but why is it so hard to voice my feelings? I know why.

Looks like I will be having a side order of Harper with my pancakes after all.

Chapter 20
Piece by Piece I'm Taking Back What's Mine

On a cool Wednesday evening, I am snuggled up in Jasper's bed. He has the night off, so he asked me over to watch a movie.

Jasper's house is a little two bedroom town house, about twenty minutes from V's place, which is perfect. It's very outdated, built in the 70s, but it's a bachelor pad, and it suits Jasper perfectly. The house is a mess, but Jasper's bedroom is neat, well, apart from his desk. The little desk is situated in a corner with piles of books, scraps of paper, and pens, scattered everywhere. I have no idea how he finds anything in that chaos, but he says his 'chaos' has order.

As I sit with my back pressed up against the headboard, waiting for Jasper to return with snacks for our movie, I spot a photograph, tucked away on his shelving along the wall. It looks as if it slipped out of a CD case accidently. Curiosity gets the better of me and I silently get up to have a look. Standing on tippy toes, I can just reach it.

When I look at the photograph, I know immediately this is Jasper's family. His mom and dad look young, and Jasper is only about five or six, and I would say his brother is eleven or twelve.

His mom stares with melancholy eyes, looking slightly over the camera man's shoulder, and I wonder what she's looking at. His dad looks as if he has had a hard life, and has a firm hand on each of his son's shoulders. Looking in on the White family, they look like any other family, but I know that's not the case. Jasper's family isn't something he'll discuss with me, and I know it's because it's something he doesn't want to revisit.

"What are you doing?" Jasper asks as I turn to look at him over my shoulder with the most innocent look I can muster.

It's now or never. "Tell me about them?" I ask, showing him the photo in my hands.

"Where did you get that?" he asks, stunned, like he had forgotten he owned the picture.

"I saw it tucked behind your CDs. I'm sorry, I shouldn't have raided your stuff," I apologize, realizing what I did was quite disrespectful.

He walks over to me, dumping our snacks onto his bed and removes the picture from my hands. He stares at the photograph for the longest time, his scruffy hair falling into his blue eyes. I can't read the emotions behind his eyes, but I know he's thinking back to when the photo was snapped.

"This was taken at some shitty park my parents would take me and my brother Stephen to on a Sunday afternoon. The park was so derelict, filled with syringes and broken beer bottles. But we were kids and we loved it. It's the only happy family memory I can remember."

"Why did you guys only get to go on a Sunday?" I question softly, not wanting to push him.

"That was the only day the bar my dad frequented was closed. He had no choice but to spend time with his family. Stephen and I would count how many sleeps till Sunday. It was the best day of the week for us. Mom and Dad would act like parents, and Stephen could be a kid, and not be forced to look after his bratty younger brother."

"What were your parents doing during the week that forced Stephen to look after you?" I know I'm pushing, but this is the first time he's openly discussing his family with me.

"My mom was too busy popping prescription pills, and Dad was getting drunk, chasing tail. We were an inconvenience to them, and they never failed to mention this daily. Dad would come home in fits of anger, drunk as a skunk at night, and take that anger out on Stephen and me."

It pains me to see him drop his guard about his family, but I persist gently. "Is that how you got this?" I ask, reaching over to rub my finger over the scar on his bottom lip.

He kisses my finger and softly fondles the back of my hand.

"Yes. I had enough of Dad beating up Stephen, so I tried to stop him, yanking on his arms, biting his legs, whatever I could do to make him stop. But that just wound him up further. He turned around and knocked me out cold. All I remember is waking up in bed with Stephen nursing my bottom lip. When Dad punched me, the corner of the kitchen table broke my fall. The wood split my lip right open. I needed stitches, but never went to the hospital."

I cover my mouth, horrified that someone could do that to their child. "How old were you?"

"Eight," he replies quietly, fiddling with the corner of the photograph.

My heart is aching for him. My heart is aching for the eight year old Jasper being treated like no eight-year-old should.

When I finally find my voice, I ask, "You mentioned your dad died in a house, what about your mom? And Stephen? How could your mom just stand there and let your dad hit you boys?"

"My mom didn't want to deal with her abusive husband. If she did, she knew she would be next in line for his punishing fists. Stephen left Chicago when he was eighteen and moved to Texas. I was twelve at the time and begged him to take me with him. He wanted to, but my parents needed a child to live with them to receive their child support payments. Dad threatened Stephen with the biggest beat down of his life if he took me, so he left, and I was my parents' emotional and physical punching bag for the next six years. I left as soon as I turned eighteen, followed a girl to sunny L.A. and haven't looked back. Stephen is still in Texas. He's married, but we don't see each other, or speak. I think I remind him too much of a past he wants to escape. Mom has moved into a new house and remarried some loser. Now that she has a new house and husband, she's trying to make up for being a shitty mother. I don't talk to her often, and when I do, it usually ends in a, 'fuck you' and me feeling like I'm twelve years old again."

Now I know why Jasper never wanted to talk about his past. It's one I have a hard time listening to, so I couldn't imagine living it. No matter how overbearing my parents are, they never once lifted a finger against me. I had a happy, normal childhood. No wonder Jasper has never wanted to get close to anyone with an upbringing like his. I'm surprised he isn't an alcoholic, in prison, or in a psych ward.

There is one question I have been dying to ask him for a while.

"How did you and Indie get together? You're total opposites, and I don't understand how you could…"

"Could what? Be involved with her?" I only nod, as I'm too afraid I've overstepped some line.

"Indie, she saved me."

What? Now I've heard it all.

Jasper half smiles as he senses my disbelief.

"I know it's hard to believe, but she did. When I was a kid, I was withdrawn and awkward. She was just the opposite. She was loud and she was liked by everyone. One day, we were paired up in biology and she was nice to me. Genuinely nice. She was my only friend. I couldn't believe someone, especially a girl as popular as Indie, would care about a shy, weird kid like me. As we grew up, things got more involved, but it was for comfort, and curiosity. She was the first girl I kissed, and the first girl I ever had sex with."

I suddenly wish I'd kept my mouth shut, as I feel uncomfortable with the over share.

"But she's… not a good person," I say, and that's the nicest way I can phrase it without blurting out what a huge bitch she is.

Jasper nods, and I'm relieved he agrees. "She's changed now. When we were kids, fake boobs and Botox weren't important to her. I know who the real Indie is, and that's why she's still in my life. She gave me a chance when no one else did. It's the least I can do for her now."

I understand Jasper is holding onto the memory of a younger, kinder Indie, but it's hard to believe she was ever a good person, judging by the soulless individual she has become.

Silence passes between us. He sadly looks at the picture of his family. I feel his grief and my hand covers his, wanting to comfort him. "It wasn't your fault. Your mom and dad, they were horrible people, who didn't deserve such good kids. Considering your role models, I think you turned out extraordinary."

"Really?" he asks, taken aback, meeting my eyes.

"Yes, really. You work at an animal shelter, caring for animals that have been disregarded and forgotten, but you give them a second chance. Not to mention you're a talented musician. Your words are real because you have lived that life…You are an inspiration just by breathing." I bite my cheek to keep myself from saying anything further, as I think I've said too much.

Jasper's blue eyes are so big and expressive, I feel lost looking into them. He places the photograph onto his bed, and slowly takes a hold of the back of my neck, pulling me in for a deep kiss. I am drowning in all things Jasper, and I match his passion, kiss for kiss, because I want him so badly it hurts.

Walking me backward, my knees hit the edge of the bed and he nudges me down onto my back. As his arm settles underneath me, embracing my waist, I am on fire. Wherever he touches and kisses, I am scorching.

When he slides his hand under my t-shirt, brushing over my bra, I'm internally fist pumping in excitement because this is uncharacteristic for Jasper. Wrapping my arms tightly around his neck and trapping him close to my body, he happily complies and allows me to close the distance between us. As he descends to my neck, kissing and biting softly, I writhe underneath him, yearning for more.

He raises my t-shirt, exposing my belly button as his lips travel down my body. Stopping at my uncovered tummy he looks up, his eyes requesting permission to explore further. I shyly nod, and without delay he unbuttons my jeans, slowly pulling down the zipper. He hooks his fingers inside my jeans and slips them past my knees. I accommodate by lifting my hips, and hey presto, my jeans are thrown off the side of the bed.

I'm grateful I've worn some appropriate black lacy underwear, as this scenario would have been embarrassing otherwise. But there's nothing embarrassing about this moment with Jasper. The look he awards me with as he gazes down at me while resting back on his heels, is one of worship and adoration. I feel like a goddess.

"Tell me to stop if I'm going too far." He swallows, the passion in his voice clearly evident.

"Okay," I whisper.

As he leans down, giving me one of his heart-stopping kisses, I need to feel his warm skin against mine. I urge his t-shirt off, and when I do, I'm stunned by his beauty. I was right, he's all lean muscle. I examine his sharp collarbones, the hard planes of his chest, and my eyes feast on the dark snail trail that is sprinkled down past his navel, leading into the waistband of his jeans. His abdominals are perfectly ripped, and his V muscle is so defined, I am freakin' panting in need to run my tongue over it. My breath hitches in my throat and he smiles at me modestly.

Reaching up with apprehensive fingers, I slowly place my hand over his beating heart, feeling it racing a million miles an hour. Not able to help myself, I lean up, kissing his firm stomach. He groans, leaning his head back.

He pushes me back down and within moments, his bare chest is pressed to mine. I detonate in longing because he feels so good. As Jasper's kisses travel down my stomach and over my underwear, his stubble tickling my most intimate area, I suddenly freeze as the realization of what we are about to do hits home.

I haven't been intimate with anyone since Harper, and just the thought of Harper turns my mood sour. I hate that after six months of being apart; he still has the ability to evoke this insecurity in me.

What if I'm not good enough for Jasper? I've only ever been with Harper, and I'm sure Jasper has had an endless list of sexual partners. What if this changes things between us for the worse, and not the better? I thought I was ready, but obviously, I was mistaken.

I feel like I might throw up.

"Hey, where did you go?" Jasper whispers, an intense look in his eyes. "Come back to me, Ava."

Looking down at his face, which is planted between my legs, I know I just can't do this, not now. Harper has destroyed a moment of innocence between Jasper and I.

I cover my eyes in embarrassment, and also, in frustration. "I'm sorry, I can't do this now. I'm sorry." I scramble up the bed with my knees pressed to my chest.

"It's okay, don't apologize," he replies softly.

Feeling beyond stupid, I press my face into my knees to hide my approaching tears. I have wanted this to happen for months, and now I've ruined it.

"Did I do something wrong?" he asks, concerned, when I remain silent.

"No, God no, it's me, or Harper." Jasper cocks a confused eyebrow at my reply.

"I didn't mean it like that," I quickly reply, realizing how insensitive my response was.

"Well, how did you mean it?" he asks, staring at me, waiting for an explanation.

This is going to embarrass me further, but I owe him this. "I haven't been intimate with anyone since Harper, and thinking about him just ruined my mood. I'm sorry." I'm so mad at myself. I berate myself further when a hard, unreadable look sweeps over Jasper's features.

He looks offended, and I mentally kick my own butt for being such an idiot. "Have I hurt your feelings?"

Jasper shakes his head and sits up, covering his glorious body with his t-shirt. But I know that I have.

Placing my hand on his shoulder, attempting to stop him from leaping off the bed, I say, "No, tell me, Jasper," but I wish I didn't persist.

"Well, it's a blow to a guy's ego if his girl is thinking about her ex while he's trying to get into her pants. My ex was the furthest thing from my mind when I was in between your legs."

I cringe at the crudeness of his comment, but I know he's offended. His words are spoken out of spite, but I totally deserve it.

"It's not like that, Jasper. It came out all wrong. I'm sorry, just give me a minute and we can try again." Seriously, my mouth is not attached to my brain right now.

Jasper jumps off the bed, looking absolutely enraged.

Massaging his temples, he states, "This isn't a science project, Ava. This was meant to feel natural, and it was, until your fucking ex somehow ended up in bed with us!"

I look up at him guiltily because he's right. "I'm sorry."

"Please stop apologizing," he spits out.

He is giving nothing away, but as I see him mull over his next question, I suddenly feel faint.

"Is it always going to be him?" he asks dejectedly, pulling his hair in frustration.

"What?" I reply, my breath caught in my throat.

"Will Harper always be the wedge between us? Are you still in love with him?" He spins around to determine my reaction.

"What?" I say, horrified. "No, of course not. How can you even ask me that?" I suddenly feel nauseous because I knew this talk was imminent.

"Because I always feel second best. I'm trying to give you everything, but I feel it's not good enough for you. What more can I do? I'm trying my best here, but you won't meet me halfway." Jasper's comment punches me in the guts, and my guards go up.

"How dare you?" I cry, lunging off the bed to get dressed, as I suddenly feel very naked in front of him.

"I *am* trying. You have no idea what it was like when I came back home. I was broken, and the thought of facing another day alone, without him, was like getting my heart broken all over again." I'm fumbling with my zipper, my hands shaking in anger, and an unexpected tear slides down my cheek.

"I know what you were like. I found you, remember? Crying your eyes out on that balcony while that motherfucker didn't give you a second thought. But here you are, still shedding tears for this asshole, who hasn't made a single effort to contact you. Why are you still giving this guy a second of your time, Ava, why?" Jasper is furious, his hands braced behind his head, pacing the room.

I feel so hollow inside, and I clutch my stomach in grief. I know why, but I don't want to say it, not now, not like this when we are both so heated.

"Tell me," Jasper perseveres, sensing my thoughts.

Shaking my head, I make a dash for the door before I'm sick, but Jasper grabs my arm. "Tell me. For once in your life, be honest and let me in. I'm trying here. Meet me halfway. Please."

I know my words will hurt Jasper, and I don't want to wound him. He's been my savior, but this thing with Harper, it's complicated.

"Tell me…please," Jasper begs, his gaze softening slightly.

Guiltily looking up at him, I know I owe him the truth. I also know he won't let up until I tell him the truth.

"I don't know if I will be able to love anyone ever again. When Harper broke up with me, he took a piece of me with him. I don't know how to get that back. I don't know if I want it back. It hurts too much to love someone that much. I'm just so scared to try again," I whisper, lowering my eyes at my confession.

And there it is—the truth. The truth I have been trying so hard to escape. I thought I could forget all my insecurities—I thought wrong.

But I do have feelings for Jasper. And those feelings terrify me. What if he breaks my heart, too? This is the reason I never wanted to pursue anything further with Jasper, because deep down, I knew he would make me feel…too much.

Jasper's expression breaks my heart and I quickly attempt to explain, but he won't let me, as he lets me go.

"So what am I? Just something to occupy your time with until someone better comes along? I don't get it, Ava." He looks defeated, and with each step, he's breaking my heart further.

"That's not what I meant and you know it," I reply, desperately trying to fix this. Fix my fuck up.

"No, I don't, actually. You go nuts when another girl looks my way, but when you have me, you act like you don't want me. What *do* you want?" he demands. "You need to take risks in life to grow, and you are so afraid that we *would* work, you would rather not let me in. You're so afraid I'm going to hurt you like Harper, and because of that, you won't give me everything. Why won't you let me in? Let me prove to you I'm different. Prove to you that I'm not him," he begs. A silent sob wracks my body as I'm struggling to hold back my tears.

"It's easy to blame Harper for making you so detached, but deep down, you know you're the one that's stopping yourself from being happy. You think you don't deserve to be happy again. And you're too scared to try. Break-ups suck, but if you don't move on, they'll haunt you the rest of your life."

His words hit home, and I'm afraid to acknowledge the truth because he's right.

But I can't deal with this—I feel vulnerable and hurt, and Jasper riding in on his high, perfect horse, pisses me off.

I regret the words as soon as they leave my mouth. "How would you know? You haven't been in a meaningful relationship. I doubt you've ever been in love! The only affection you know is from dysfunctional, crazy people!"

He stares at me, stunned, while working his jaw angrily, and I'm afraid to speak in case I say something else I'll regret. But I have to make amends for my comment.

"Jasper, I—"

He silences me by holding up his hand. "It's good to know what you really think of me. After everything I just told you, Ava, how could you say that? I think you should leave," he spits, shaking his head in disgust.

"No, please, let me explain," I cry, desperate to correct myself.

I grab onto his arm, but as he shrugs me away, my heart breaks with his formality.

"I think you've done enough explaining, Ava." Jasper is fuming, taking deep breaths and sidestepping me when I attempt to touch him.

"Let me—" I beg.

How the hell did this spiral out of control so quickly? I know the answer, but I can't face the truth right now.

"Just. Leave," he sneers with such venom, I'm taken aback.

He won't even listen to me, and I'm wounded he won't give me the opportunity to explain myself. If he won't let me defend myself, then there's nothing left to say.

"Fine, I'm outta here," I spit angrily, but more importantly, I'm angry at myself.

Tears of rage are threatening to burst free any moment, so I quickly grab my keys and storm down the stairs, running to the front door. I can't get out of his house fast enough as I don't want him to see me cry over this—I'm embarrassed enough.

But before I can escape this car wreck, Jasper rushes after me, holding onto my arm, attempting to stop my retreat. I barely choke back a snivel because I'm coming apart at the seams.

"Did I mean anything to you? Or did you just want him back the whole time we were together?" I turn around, his tormented expression giving me insight into his emotions. I did this to him. With my cruel words.

The longer I stand here, the louder the silence, so I voice the only thing I can without breaking down.

"I don't want him back. I just want to take back what he took from me. Good-bye, Jasper."

Storming out the front door, I charge down the stairs, but before I hit the bottom step, I hear a pleading, barely audible whisper slip through Jasper's lips. "Please don't go."

But I keep walking, my avalanche of tears spilling down my cheeks.

Chapter 21
Hit and Run

I come home after our argument and collapse as soon I close my bedroom door. Luckily V isn't home and I can mourn alone. I have blown things with Jasper, and I doubt he'll ever forgive me. He's right in what he said to me. I am too afraid that things would work for us. The attraction between us was instant and growing every day, and I should have been embracing it, not running away. Jasper deserves better than an emotional, fucked up mess like me.

I'll miss Jasper, because I know after tonight he probably won't want to see me for a while. That thought tears another deep sob from my chest, and I cry myself to sleep.

The next day, I can't dodge V any longer, as I've slept in long enough. I try my hardest to smile, but she isn't fooled when I shakily pour myself a cup of coffee.

"What the fuck happened?" I shake my head, not wanting to talk about it.

"Is everything okay?" I shake my head again, and a tear slides down my cheek.

V rushes over, giving me a tight hug.

"What's happened, Ava?" she asks, firmer this time.

"We had a fight." I'm still caught up in her arms, and I can feel myself about to breakdown.

"Over?" I don't even have to clarify who I fought with because she knows who.

I stifle a sob. "Over Harper. Over my stupid insecurities. Over me being a big ol' scaredycat."

"Harper?" V asks, clearly confused.

I really don't want to repeat what happened, but V will keep harassing me till I budge.

"We were getting heated, and at a time when I shouldn't have been thinking about Harper, I was, and I told Jasper."

"You what?" V shrieks, pulling me out of her embrace and staring at me wildly.

"Okay, it wasn't exactly like that." I cringe under her scrutiny.

"Then how was it? Because if you called out Harper's name mid-orgasm, Jasper has every right to be mad at you."

"We didn't even get that far." I lower my eyes, embarrassed.

V looks baffled and says, "You've been hanging around Jasper for too long. You're starting to become ambiguous like him."

Exhaling in defeat, I peer out the window, wishing I was anywhere but here. "We were making out and Jasper was headed… south, and I just froze."

"You froze? I thought that's what you wanted."

"I did. I do. I just thought about how the only guy I've ever been with is Harper, and I'm sure Jasper has been with loads of girls. Then I started thinking what if I'm not good enough, and this changes things for the worse." As I vocalize what happened, I realize how foolish I was to behave the way I did.

"And you told him this?" V tries to piece together how I ended up the emotional wreckage I currently am.

"Not exactly," I mumble, feeling faint.

"What do you mean, 'not exactly,'" V asks, raising her eyebrow.

"It just got out of hand. Jasper asked if I still loved Harper, and it went downhill from there."

V's eyes widen in disbelief. "How did you address the Harper issue?"

"Like an idiot, that's how," I reply quickly, groaning.

"Oh God, what did you do?" V braces herself for my response while chewing on her lip ring.

"Thanks for the vote of confidence." I sigh.

She only shrugs. "I know what you're like when confronted with Harper talk. You babble on, and anger replaces your common sense."

She's right. I put my head in my hands and groan again. "I'm such an idiot."

"Talk to him."

"No. I'm embarrassed, and he has every right to hate me." I can still remember the anger behind his words, and I bury my head deeper within my hands.

"Just explain to him your feelings regarding Harper, he'll understand." If only it was that simple.

"It wasn't only the Harper thing," I reply, biting my lip guiltily as I raise my head.

"Oh, Ava, what did you do?" V has her head tilted to the side, and takes a deep breath.

"I kind of told him he's never been in love, and he only knows affection from crazy people," I confess.

V stares at me, her mouth agape. I am such an A-hole!

"He opened up to me about his family, about Indie, and I just threw it back in his face because I was confronted with the truth, and I didn't want to hear it."

V shakes her head. "You need to talk to him. He's crazy about you, he'll listen to you."

I sigh dismally. "I don't think he will. He told me to leave, and he meant it. I saw the hurt in his eyes. The hurt I put there."

V, for the first time, looks speechless, and I know I'm in trouble. I have fucked up royally with Jasper, and I have no one to blame but myself.

So, for the next few weeks, I mope and ghost around like a nobody. I work, eat, and sleep. My routine sadly didn't stop my thoughts from wandering to Jasper every five seconds. I would call people Jasper by accident at work, and even slipped by calling myself Jasper when I left my name to reserve a DVD at the video store. I wish I would man up and call him, but what would I say? I'm sorry for insulting you. I'm sorry for being such an emotional retard. I'm sorry I've given you mixed signals with my bi-polar behavior. Whatever I say, I know it wouldn't be good enough.

So it goes without saying it has been the saddest few weeks of my life. I feel sick, empty and guilty. What I did, what I said to Jasper was wrong. We both said things in the heat of the moment, and I know my words burned him, but that wasn't my intention. I was just so angry. It was Harper and his poison seeping into my common sense. Jasper and I had a good thing, and now I've ruined it with my insecurities.

The only comfort I take is sitting in my favorite armchair, staring out the window, overlooking the street. I watch the neighbors mow their lawns, the dogs chase the neighborhood cats, and the children play happily, none the wiser. Little do they know, a girl with a broken heart is watching their actions, wishing she could be them. I would have given anything to partake in their ordinary tasks, because it looked so easy. It looked so easy for them to live. It looked like it didn't hurt to breathe.

But the most comforting pastime of being a recluse is my observation of a common raven, perched on a tall, blue oak tree branch. He would balance on that branch for hours, looking down at the world with a bird's eye view. I wonder what he could see, and why he chose that particular tree to sit upon daily. If he sensed danger, he would spread his wings and take to the air. I was envious, because I wanted to learn how to fly, to spread my wings and fly away.

Fly away from this torture of being me.

It's now early November, and the dreary weather is worsening my mood. V is the most tolerant friend but she has warned me, if I play my depressing Emo music once more, she's going to break all my CDs, and I know she'll make good on her word. I don't know how long I've been staring at the ceiling of my bedroom, counting the trillions of glow in the dark stars. Each day now blends into one, and I'm sinking in regrets.

"Ava, get up!" I squint as V turns on my bedroom light.

Ugh, it's so bright. I liked it better when my glow in the dark stars was my only light source.

"I'm getting you out of this room because quite frankly, it smells like something died in here."

Yeah…me. I attempt to crawl under the covers, but V has other ideas and rips off my blankets.

"Hey!" I protest, which falls on deaf ears as V raids my closet, pulling out garment after garment.

I shield my eyes with my hands as the light is still burning my corneas, trying to decipher what she's up to.

"You're coming with me to Little Sisters tonight, and no, this is not optional. This is an intervention."

"Are you crazy? I'm not going anywhere." I look down at my pasta splattered sweater, and can only imagine what my hair looks like.

"Yes, you are. You need fresh air, and Jasper won't be there, so you can hang with me and Lucas."

Just the mere mention of his name hurts my head and heart. But what hurts even more is that I know Jasper won't be there, because I've memorized his work schedule. I think I'm border-lining on being a stalker.

"No." I sigh.

"Yes. Don't make me drag you out this room, kicking and screaming, because you know I will." I look at my best friend and see that determined gleam in her eye—I'm screwed.

Dragging myself out of bed because I don't have the energy to fight a losing battle, I give in with a sigh. "Fine, let's go!"

"You may want to put on something that doesn't resemble a homeless person." V makes a face at my clothes.

"No, I'm good, let's go." V shrugs, also not wanting to fight a losing battle.

~

Feeling depressed and wanting to hide under my blankets for a year, I glance around the bar and see Lucas and Andy.

The boy's heads snap up when they hear V calling out to Lucas. "Hey, papa bear."

V beams when she sees her handsome boyfriend give her a small wave. I, on the other hand, cringe. Papa bear? Seriously? I never thought I'd hear V use a term of endearment for a boyfriend, let alone one that consisted of the words 'papa' and 'bear.' And here comes the bitterness.

However, I won't let my sour mood get in the way of V's love fest with Lucas. We take a seat with V perching on Lucas' lap.

"Good to see you, Ava, how've you been?" Lucas asks, laying a soft kiss on V's temple.

I can see why my friend is head over heels for this guy. He's polite, genuine, and totally adores her. What's not to love about papa bear? However, his next question has me quickly changing my tune.

"So, have you spoken to Jasper?" he asks uncomfortably.

And there goes my laundry list of why papa bear is a good guy. I squirm uneasily because although Jasper may not be here, his presence is everywhere—it's haunting me. Hanging out at the place where we first met suddenly feels like a horrible idea.

"He's really upset," Lucas says when I don't reply. "And won't tell me what's going on. He's being really weird and private. J and I have known each other for years, ever since he came to L.A., and I've seen him get into his moods where he shuts people out, but I've never seen him like this. He won't even come to band practice, and that's saying a lot. Jasper never misses practice. Ava, what's going on? I can't get jack outta him, so maybe you can shed some light on what the hell is going on. We're all really worried about him," he concludes, and I close my eyes, depression overtaking me.

I'm startled to hear he's missing band rehearsal, as Lucas is right, that's very uncharacteristic of him. "Why isn't he going to practice?" I ask, finally able to speak without breaking down.

"I don't know. That's why I'm asking you. I'm worried about him. He looks like shit, and is even moodier than usual, which is saying a lot for him." V rubs Lucas' shoulder in concern. Ugh. This is all my fault.

"We had a fight, and I haven't spoken to him since," I blurt out before I can stop myself.

"Must have been some fight if you guys aren't talking. I see the way he is around you, you challenge that bastard, and I don't think he knows how to handle that. He's accustomed to girls being what they think he wants them to be, and then you come along and screw that up." Lucas smiles at me, pulling a label off his beer bottle.

I wipe that smug look off his face, however, when I retort, "And how did I exactly screw anything up? I'm not going to throw my morals and beliefs to the curb just because he's pretty to look at." Poor Lucas, he looks like he's about ready to wield his bottle as a weapon.

But he smiles in response, not concerned with my sarcasm. "That's what I mean. J isn't just a pretty face to you, you see him for what's inside. He hasn't had that before. The girls he's been with use him as a status fuck because he's that singer outta some band. They use him just as much as he uses them."

Lucas' words slap me hard. When Jasper and I were getting hot and heavy, he never pushed me, it was always what I wanted, how far I wanted to go. When it happened between us, he said he wanted it to be perfect. And I never pushed because I knew he was right.

Of course he was right, look what happened the one and only time our clothes came off. We stopped talking—after I did too much talking, that is.

"I don't know how to fix it," I confess sadly, because I've been mulling over this for weeks, and coming up short for ideas.

"Talk to him. You're both as stubborn as each other, but I think more than anything, Jasper is hurt."

Lucas and V are full of relationship wisdom. No wonder they never fight.

I know I've hurt Jasper. And now my bitterness is replaced with sorrow. I have to fix this—now. Jasper is working at the shelter tonight. I have to make this right.

Jumping up, I give Lucas a quick kiss on the cheek. "I can see why my friend is crazy about you." V looks up at me, smiling an 'I told you' smile.

"V, would it be okay…"

"Yes, go…Lucas can take me home." She knows where I need to be.

Giving her a quick hug, I bolt out of the bar like the devil is on my heels.

~

I've broken about fifty road laws to get home in record time to feed Oscar and change. If I'm going to see Jasper and beg for forgiveness, I don't want to look like a bird has taken up permanent residency in my hair. I'm a mess. Physically and emotionally.

I need to go home and collect myself. I need to shower and feel semi-normal before I do this. Running inside, I call out to Oscar. He's so cheeky, and I hope tonight isn't one of those nights where he has selective hearing.

Frantically running around my room, trying to decide on the most appropriate outfit to wear, I finally settle on jeans and a tight knitted sweater. I head back downstairs, calling out to Oscar, but he still hasn't arrived.

I shake the cat food container in the hopes that food will coax him home, but he's still nowhere to be seen. Just as I start to worry, I hear his little bell chime from across the road. As I walk through the kitchen to let him in, I suddenly hear the gut-wrenching sound of brakes squealing, and a horrible thud, followed by a car speeding off. My heart drops into my stomach and I can't open the door fast enough.

Leaping down the stairs, my mouth falls open in disbelief as I stare at Oscar lying in the middle of the road, motionless. I run as fast as I can, almost falling over in my grief. Tears are falling down my cheeks as I stop and fall to my knees to check if he's alive. His heart is beating so faintly, and I know I need to get him help now or he'll die.

Ripping off my sweater, I bundle him up and he lets out a pained meow. "I know, buddy, I'm sorry. You just hold on. Don't give up on me."

There's only one place I'm going.

Why does it feel like the words I just whispered to Oscar are also appropriate to the man I am running to?

Chapter 22
Second Chances

I break another fifty road laws, my tires squealing as I pull into the parking lot of the shelter. Running to the passenger seat, I gently pick up Oscar and cradle him to my chest. He looks dead, but thankfully, I see his little chest rising faintly. Leaving my car door open, I bolt to the entrance, the door chiming as I enter. I search frantically for Jasper, but he's nowhere in sight.

Shouldering the staff door open, I rush to the back where he usually hangs if it's a quiet night, and call out to him like a raving lunatic. Thankfully, I see his head peek around the end doorway, looking absolutely confused. He gasps as his startled eyes take in my disarrayed state. I know I look a mess with my black yoga pants, ripped tank top, and heavy tears mixed with Oscar's blood smears, but I don't care.

"Ava, what's wrong?" Jasper asks as he comes running down the hallway, hissing as he sees the limp form I'm holding out to him.

His eyes widen in alarm. "Shit. Take him into room three. I'll call the vet."

He rushes into the office while I place Oscar on the silver

gurney. My vision is blurred with my endless tears as I'm patting an unmoving Oscar. Jasper rushes in and starts to prep for the vet. He works quickly, his delicate hands preparing the devices that will save Oscar's life. I hope.

Breaking down, I place my head on the gurney, cooing to Oscar that it'll be all right, but I can't guarantee him that. Jasper stands beside me, apprehensively at first, but when he sees my shoulders shuddering in anguish, he gently rubs my back. His heady scent assails my nostrils, and I bite back a sob. I've missed him so much. He looks just as I remember, stunning, but I wish our reunion was under better terms.

"He'll be okay, Ava, I promise. He's a tough little guy." His words calm me somewhat, but as I look down at Oscar, I know he doesn't have long.

"How long till the vet gets here?" I snivel when Oscar lets out a little injured meow.

"Not long, only a couple more minutes. He was out on a house call. He'll be here soon, I promise." Jasper is stroking my back, trying to comfort me, but I'm a mess.

His blue eyes are assessing me with such tenderness and care, and the concern he feels for me is crystal clear.

Oh God, I was so stupid to let my insecurities ruin what we had. I don't deserve the compassion he's showing me, and a fresh set of tears fall down my cheeks.

He pulls me into his arms and kisses the side of my neck. "Let it out. I'm here for you. I promise you, I always will be."

True to Jasper's word, the vet arrives two minutes later.

Jasper tells me to wait in the lunchroom while he helps the vet attend to Oscar. I feel sick. If I had eaten, it would have been thrown up hours ago. What's taking so long? I pace the small lunch room for about the hundredth time, and as I'm about to rush into the surgery room, Jasper enters, looking exhausted.

Running up to him, I stare into his eyes for answers. "Is he okay? What happened? Oh my God, is he…dead?" I choke on the last question.

Jasper pulls me into a tight embrace and murmurs into my hair, "He's going to be fine, Ava. He had a few injuries, but the doc fixed him up. He'll need to stay here for a week, but he'll be okay. I'll personally make sure he's given the VIP treatment while he's in here."

The relief is overwhelming, and if I wasn't in Jasper's arms, I would have collapsed. "Here, sit down. Let me get you some water," Jasper says, placing me into a seat while going over to the water fountain.

Mesmerized by the way his muscles contract under his t-shirt as he bends down to pour me a glass of water, I know I was so stupid to compare my feelings for him to the way I felt for Harper. I've never felt this way for anyone, not even Harper, and that scares me.

Jasper hands me the water and takes a seat next to me. He looks at me cautiously, like I might break down at any second. "Are you okay? Can I get you anything?"

"Give me your hand," I whisper.

Jasper looks puzzled, raising his eyebrow, but entrusts me with his hand.

Slowly placing his palm over my heart, I look into his deep blue eyes, and exhale a brave breath before I confess, "What you make me feel in here, it scares me." I recite his words, hoping he can understand how I'm feeling.

"Your generosity, your convictions, and your heart, they astound me." I then place my hand over his heart.

We sit quietly with our hands on each other's rapidly beating chests, just staring at one another. He has an unreadable look on his face, but I don't care. I need him to know how I feel. No matter how late it is.

"Jasper White, you overwhelm me." And for once, I lean in to kiss his stunned lips.

At first he hesitates, but I quickly encourage him to open his mouth wider so I'm able to invade his warmth. He at last gives in with a soft sigh, crushing me to his chest. His heart beats frantically against mine, and I breathe heavily, drowning in everything Jasper. I need him more than my own breath.

As I run my hands through his tousled hair, which has grown since I last touched it, I can't stop myself, and grab a fistful of his luscious locks, pulling hard. My actions elicit a soft moan from him, and he bites my lip passionately.

Pressing my chest into his, I'm desperate to get lost in him because I want this man with my last breath. But sadly, as I feel him pulling away, I know I've lost him. I've left it too long to apologize for my stupidity, and my heart breaks with his withdrawal.

He gazes intently at me, resting his forehead on mine. "This doesn't change anything, you know that."

"I know." I sigh sorrowfully. "I'm sorry, Jasper. What I said to you, it was unforgiveable, and you have every right to hate me."

"I could never hate you, Ava, but I needed to hear that weeks ago." Jasper pulls away, his lips wet and inviting. I suffer a profound sadness that I may never kiss those lips ever again.

"Better late than never," I half heartedly joke, but he notices my discomfort.

"Thank you for being honest, but it's hard for me to forget. I've forgiven you, but I'll never forget the feeling of being told you may never be able to fall in love again. I would be stupid to accept anything but all of you, because that's what I want... I want to posses you, mind, body, and soul."

I have no one to blame but myself, and I drop my head, overwhelmed. "I'm sorry."

"Me too, but that doesn't mean we can't be friends. I've really missed you. I think we know how to be friends, it's just the other stuff we seem to suck at." More like *I* suck at.

Jasper gazes at me hopefully, chewing on his scar, and I'm transfixed on his mouth, but I look away quickly. I can't look at him, because if I was to be honest, I would argue with him, stamp my foot in protest that I don't want to be his friend—I want more. I'm ready now. It took this stupid time apart for me to realize that I'm ready.

But he doesn't want that, he's made that loud and clear. So if friendship is all he can offer me, then I'll take it. I prefer that than the alternative of not having him in my life at all.

Pushing down my heartache, I half smile. "Okay." I'll just have to live with the error of my ways.

Jasper looks satisfied, while I want to bawl my eyes out. "So, here's to Jasper and Ava's friendship, part two." He extends his hand.

I look at it cautiously because I don't want to shake it. I want it to be running down my face, in my hair, all over my body.

I take it gingerly, and smile. "Here's to second chances."

But inside my torrent of tears submerges my soul.

Chapter 23
Merry Christmas

Work is busier than it's been all year because it's a week before Christmas. I usually love Christmas, but this year I won't be standing under any mistletoe, because the person I want to kiss just wants to be friends.

Being Jasper's friend this second time around has been awful. How can I be friends with him when I know what it's like to be held in those arms? To know how he sets my lips alight with his kisses? I want to touch him freely, run my hands through his hair, but I can't—because we're just friends. That word, which should signify unity and happiness, makes me want to puke. How did I manage to mess things up with Jasper so badly? Oh yeah, that's right, by being an insecure cry baby, that's how.

I can blame Harper all I want, but deep down I know Jasper is right. I'm too afraid to give Jasper my all, just in case I get hurt again.

A little piece of me dies every time a glance between us lasts too long, or an accidental touch lingers. It's tearing me up inside because I know he feels it, too. But I have hurt him by being an idiot, and not committing to him completely, like he was with me.

Why am I so afraid of someone who has given me no reason to be? I have no choice but to go along with the charade, as not having Jasper in my life is not an option.

~

It's Christmas Eve, and I'm frantically trying to shop for everyone's gifts before everything shuts down for the holidays. I have everything for everyone, even a gift for Jasper, which I specially ordered. I know it's a little personal, but it reminded me of him.

As I'm loading up the car, I wonder what Jasper is up to for Christmas. Pulling out my iPhone as I take a seat behind the wheel, I decide to find out.

He's been very vague as to where he plans to spend his Christmas, and I have an inkling that's because he's staying home alone. I know he won't be going to Lucas', as V is meeting his parents for the first time tomorrow, so it's just family. Andy and Mariah are in Hawaii, and Jasper's other friends are with family.

Friends invite friends to Christmas dinner, right? I know my parents would never want a friend of mine to be alone on Christmas Day.

So, I text him before pulling out of the parking lot:

what U up 2 2mro?

Within two minutes, my phone dings, indicating a new message.

It's from Jasper.

sleepin' u?

Stopping at a red light, I quickly reply:

Lunch with parents. Sleeping?? But it's Christmas :(

Good time to catch up... zzzzz

Laughing, I type out a quick reply while waiting for the light to change:

U told me sleep is overrated

He texts back within ten seconds:

That was before I met you, U wear me out LOL

If only that were true.

I'm staring at the screen, trying to decode his message when I hear a honk alerting me that the light has changed to green. I quickly apologize to the driver behind me with an apologetic wave over my shoulder in hopes they see me.

Jasper's comment is playing on my mind, and I have to reply. I pull over this time and tap out:

After U catch up on UR beauty sleep, want 2 come over 4 Christmas dinner. U'd be doing me a fav.

He doesn't reply for a long while, and I start to get paranoid. Maybe I shouldn't have invited him. Have I overstepped some friendship boundary line?

As I am lugging my shopping into the house, I feel my phone vibrate in my jacket pocket. I quickly retrieve it and smile when I see it's from Jasper:

Okay :)

I happily leap down the stairs, singing a Christmas carol because it's Christmas, my favorite time of the year.

V is making coffee in her pajamas, and I grapple her into a

bear hug. "Merry Christmas, V!"

She laughs while trying to hug me and pour coffee at the same time.

"Merry Christmas, Ava. Gee, someone is pumped up on Christmas cheer. You get into the spiked eggnog early?" she jokes.

"What's not to love about the holidays? Eat, drink, be merry, and all that," I reply, sashaying across the kitchen to pour myself a cup of coffee while humming.

V raises a suspicious eyebrow. "You're spending today with Jasper, aren't you?"

I look remotely guilty as I gulp down my coffee.

"I'm not judging, he's snapped you out of your mood, so I'm happy. And it's good he's got someone to spend today with," V continues, sipping her coffee, leaning a hip against the kitchen counter.

"Well, that's what friends do. They invite one another to ones' Christmas dinners when they are alone," I reply, but there's no point trying to convince her.

"Ah ha." V frowns, totally unbelieving of my tale.

Sticking my tongue out playfully at her, I warn, "If you keep being such a Grinch, you won't get your Christmas presents."

V quickly blinds me with a big smile, and I laugh.

"Better." I giggle as we run into the living room to exchange gifts like little kids.

After we have waffles for breakfast and unwrap our Christmas presents, I run upstairs to get ready. I've decided to wear my red dress and little black cardigan as I love getting dressed up at Christmas, and don't do it often enough during the year.

I'm slipping on a beautiful pair of onyx earrings V got me for Christmas, singing away because nothing can dampen my mood today. As I hear my phone chirp, I wonder who it could be. Looking at myself in the mirror, I smile, and my reflection finally smiles back.

My phone chirps again, a reminder of the awaiting text message.

It's from Jasper.

He must be wishing me a Merry Christmas before I see him. However, rage flushes my cheeks when I open his message:

Merry Xmas. Can't come…Sorry xx

Oh, hell no!

~

I'm quite the delinquent behind the wheel these days as I make it in record time to Jasper's house.

Storming to the front door, I charge straight in, not bothering to knock. Jasper is lying on the sofa, his bare feet propped up on the recliner. He looks stunned at my abrupt entrance.

Storming over to him, I demand, "What the hell do you mean you can't come? You don't look like you have somewhere important to be."

He simply stares at me and mutes the TV, which pisses me off. When he doesn't answer my question, I prompt him, cocking an annoyed eyebrow at him. "Well?"

"What are you doing here? Don't you know how to knock?" he asks, sitting up and looking absolutely adorable with his ruffled bed hair.

But I won't let his good looks distract me. Well, I'll try not to.

His brief reply enrages me further. "Excuse me if my manners have taken a holiday."

He has the nerve to smile at me, biting his lip in amusement. "Why are you so mad?"

"Because…" I stammer. Yeah, Ava, why are you so mad?

"Because…?" he inquires, crossing his arms over his chest, awaiting my answer.

I steer my eyes away from his sculptured chest, as that can definitely be counted as a distraction. A BIG distraction.

"Because I told my parents you were coming, and my mother has prepared a feast to feed a hundred people. She'll be disappointed if I turn up alone." What a lame excuse, but it's all I can come up with.

"I'm sure your mother will be busy cooking, and be glad she has one less mouth to feed." He entwines his hands behind his head, stretching, and in the process, exposing a slither of his ripped stomach. I can feel my eyes drift there of their own accord. Damn him, he's doing this on purpose.

Closing my eyes, I take a calming breath. Once my hormones have subsided, I open my eyes and peer at Jasper, who looks mighty satisfied with himself.

"Why won't you come?" I ask.

Jasper shrugs, giving me an impassive look. Then a thought hits me, and I want to flee.

I assemble enough courage, and ask softly, "Would you prefer to spend Christmas alone, than with me?"

Oh God, that was it. Blanching at the scene I've made, I feel my breath catch in my throat.

"Ava, no, that's not it." Jasper quickly leaps up from his chair, grasping my arms and looking me in the eyes.

"Then what is it?" I ask, biting my lip in apprehension.

He sighs before replying. "Christmas has never been my favorite holiday. As a kid, it was the most depressing time of the year, not the best, like it should be for most kids. With a family like mine, I wished Santa would give me a new family for Christmas. It never happened."

Of course, I'm so stupid. I should have figured the holidays were never a good time for him. Ugh, I deserve a lump of coal in my Christmas stocking this year!

But I suddenly want to change that for him. I want this to be the best Christmas ever.

Hoping I'm not crossing some line, I whisper, "You're not a child anymore. I think it's time to change your opinion on the best holiday of the year. Don't let your family ruin Christmas for you as an adult." We're quiet for a moment as he looks deep in thought.

I continue. "And please don't let my stupidity get in the way of you having a good day with good people and good food." I want him to enjoy himself, just for today. Maybe he can forget what an idiot I am for hurting him.

As a ghost of a smile passes over his mouth, I think I've won him over.

"And my mom makes the best apple pie. The boring family traditions are well worth it just for a slice of her warm apple pie." I cringe when I realize my comment could be interrupted quite crudely.

Jasper laughs when he sees my reaction. "Well, in that case, how can I resist an offer like that?"

I knew he would come around. He just needed some coaxing, and bribing.

"Merry Christmas, Jasper," I whisper, and the words warm my heart.

As I peer up at him, his beauty astounds me and I really want to hug him. Well, I really want to throw my arms around his neck and fist his untidy hair, but I stop myself. Only just.

"Merry Christmas, Ava," he replies with a dimpled smile.

I'm fidgeting with my silver rings, hoping to keep my hands busy before I paw at him. He surprises me by opening his arms. I hesitate for only a second before I quickly step into his welcoming embrace. Burying my neck into his chest, I'm showered with his rich fragrance, and I can't help but think this is a nice way to spend Christmas morning.

Lost in all things Jasper, I suddenly remember. "I have your Christmas present in the car, but we're running late. Can I give it to you later?"

"You didn't have to get me anything," he murmurs into my hair.

"I know, but I wanted to." To make up for my idiocy, I silently add.

Still in his embrace, he sighs contentedly. "I've got all I want for Christmas."

Too afraid and confused to ask, I only nod and enjoy being in his arms on Christmas morning.

As we walk up my parents' driveway, Jasper looks slightly nervous. I look over at him as I ring the doorbell, and am surprised to see him wiping his hands on his jeans.

I'm actually surprised to see him so tense because there's no need to be. But then I remember his confession that Christmas hasn't been a happy one for him in the past. So I promise myself I'll change that, starting with today.

My mom answers the door, engulfing me into a huge hug. "Merry Christmas, honey."

I pat her back uncomfortably because Mom gets way too emotional at Christmas, and I'm afraid if I return her hug too enthusiastically, she'll cry.

"Thanks, Mom," I whisper, still trapped in her death grip. When she finally lets go, I point to Jasper. "This is my friend, Jasper."

"Hello, Mrs. Thompson. Merry Christmas. Thank you for inviting me." Jasper smiles politely, his cerulean eyes shining brightly.

Ten points for manners.

My mom looks at Jasper, and I can tell she's thinking what every hot blooded woman thinks when first meeting him. WOW!

She clears her throat and smiles. "That's okay, Jasper, please call me Maggie. Come in." I'm stunned that my mom is going to let one of my friends call her by her first name. This is certainly a Christmas for firsts.

Mom leads the way into the festively decorated living room, humming some random Christmas carol. I look over at Jasper, who still looks a little anxious.

Raising my eyebrow, I whisper, 'Please call me Maggie.' It's a lame impression of my mother, but I get the response I want as Jasper snorts back a chuckle.

Dad is talking to my Uncle Charlie. He beams when he sees me. "Merry Christmas, princess."

I run over and give my dad a big hug. "Merry Christmas, Dad. This is my friend, Jasper."

My dad raises a suspicious eyebrow.

Oh no, the last friend that was a boy I introduced to my parents was Harper, and look how that turned out. Sadly, Jasper's good looks haven't won my dad over, although, I would have been a little concerned if they did.

Dad shakes Jasper's hand suspiciously. "Merry Christmas, Mr. Thompson. Thank you for having me."

My dad nods with an apprehensive look. Before the scene can get any more uncomfortable, I cry out, "I'm starving. When is lunch ready?"

~

Christmas dinner is nearly over, and my parents haven't embarrassed me beyond belief—yet.

I'm helping my mom clear the table for desserts when Dad asks, "So Jasper, what kind of *friends* are you and my daughter?"

Oh God! I drop the plate I'm holding, resulting in peas rolling all over the table and floor.

"Dad!" I reprimand, glaring at him and shaking my head with a stiff upper lip, trying to transmit in code not to pursue this topic.

"What, princess? The last boy you brought over here that was a friend was that good for nothing Harper." Looks like my code signaling blows ass!

Can't I even escape his name on Christmas day?

Jasper smirks as I peer at him from the corner of my eye. "No, I agree with you, Mr. Thompson. Harper is a good for nothing SOB." My dad looks at Jasper, and a long, awkward silence passes.

I stare from Jasper, to my dad, and then back to Jasper. This is emotional ping pong!

All of a sudden, my dad laughs unexpectedly. "Well put, son, I'll drink to that!" and just like that, Jasper and my dad are best friends, saluting over my SOB ex!

The rest of the day progresses with no other embarrassing hiccups. After a banquet of delicious foods, I duck outside, as my family is happily chatting to Jasper.

Standing outside for a moment, the frosty breeze chills my cheeks, but it feels somewhat peaceful. I think about last Christmas, and how this one has been so much better. And that's because I'm with my family, and…a friend.

"Hey you," whispers my friend.

I must have been deep in thought as I didn't hear him approach.

"Hey yourself." I smile, lifting my face towards the heavens and closing my eyes, feeling fortunate to be alive.

I can almost pretend the light touches on my cheeks are Jasper's fingers, stroking me. He stands beside me silently, not wanting to disturb my moment of passivity.

After a while, he quietly reaches over and holds my hand, and we both stand there, not saying anything, just hands entwined. But we don't have to speak, the silence says enough.

"Bye, Mom, thank you so much for having us over," I whisper against her shoulder, in yet another bear hug.

"Oh honey, you're welcome. This is your home. You too, Jasper."

Wow, I look at my mom. She never said that to Harper. Kudos to Jasper.

As my dad happily shakes Jasper's hand, I actually think he likes him. The day has been a success.

Jasper looks at ease on the way home, his eyes closed with his head resting against the headrest. Seeing him this way, I know my mission to change Jasper's mind on Christmas has worked.

"Thank you for inviting me." He smirks with dimples on parade.

It never ceases to amaze me when he does that, it's like he can read my thoughts. "You're very welcome. Thank you," I reply.

"Thank me?" he asks, puzzled, arching his eyebrow.

"Yes, thank you for coming. It was the best Christmas I've had for a while," I explain, my eyes never leaving the road.

"Me too," he answers softly.

Pulling into his driveway, I reach into the backseat for his gift.

However, he stops my retreat with his hand on mine. "Come inside. I have something for you."

"You what?" I ask, confused.

He grins cheekily as he unbuckles his seatbelt. "Yeah, Santa told me you were a good girl this year."

Following him into his house, I try not to hyperventilate, because I wasn't expecting him to buy me anything.

"Take a seat, I'll be right back," Jasper says over his shoulder as he walks upstairs.

Sitting on the sofa, I nervously begin fiddling with anything I can find because I'm nervous. Jasper coming to Christmas dinner was all I wanted. To spend that time with him was invaluable. However, I'm curious to know what he bought me. But suddenly, I'm very apprehensive that my gift isn't good enough.

Before I can beat myself up further, Jasper bounces down the stairs smiling, sitting next to me. "Merry Christmas, Ava," he says, holding out a box in his outstretched palm.

Oh no, that box holds a very expensive present, a jewelry kind of present. I'm right, my gift cannot compare to whatever treasure this little velvet box has within.

I swallow nervously as I stare at it.

"It's not going to bite you, I promise," Jasper teases, sensing my apprehension.

My hands shake as I remove the beautiful silver ribbon, wrapped around the blue velvet box. I'm too afraid to open it, so I sit and stare at it in my hands.

Jasper places his warm hand on my trembling fingers and we open the box together. Tears descend down my cheeks when I see what lays on top of the silky white interior.

It's an elegant silver charm bracelet, with one charm dangling delicately from a link. I finger it gently, and the light catches the charm. It's a bird, midflight.

I'm sitting without a sound, staring at the beautifully crafted bird, feeling the ridges of its wings as I pass my finger back and forth over the charm. I'm too afraid to take it out of the box, as I know the moment I see it on my wrist, a flood of tears will fall.

Jasper reaches for the box and I hesitantly let it go. His elegant fingers unclasp the clip, and as he softly reaches for my wrist, fervor so hot burns me when he makes contact with my flesh. He tenderly repositions my open palm to rest on his thigh as he attaches the bracelet onto my wrist. Looking down, I realize he hasn't removed his grip from my wrist, and his thumb is tracing a soft line, backwards and forwards, relaxing me.

As I raise my eyes, Jasper whispers, "You once told me you wished you were a bird, that you could fly away, and never have to land. Well, I can't wish you into a bird, but I thought this could give you strength when things get too much." Tears begin falling down my face because this is the nicest thing anyone has ever done for me. "It was meant to make you smile, not cry," Jasper laughs, while wiping away my tears.

"They're happy tears. Thank you. I'll never take it off." I touch the charm and it gives me strength because it's from Jasper.

He nods happily. "I'm glad you like it."

"I love it," I quickly correct him.

We are silent for an eternity and I finally remember I haven't given him my gift. My present seems absolutely modest compared to his.

"I didn't know what to get you," I mumble nervously as I search in my bag for his gift.

"Whatever you give me is perfect."

As I timidly hand it to him, he sits gazing at it for the longest time, lost in thought. I shift uncomfortably as I want this to be like a band aid—quick and painless.

He slowly removes the light blue tissue paper and uncovers a leather bound journal with his initials carved on the bottom right hand corner. As he looks up at me, stunned, his hair falling into those big eyes, I can tell he likes it, and I exhale a relieved breath.

"Open it," I whisper as his fingers dance over the engraving.

He removes the leather bindings and imprinted in script on the front page is a Chinese proverb I found, which reminded me of us:

A bird does not sing because it has an answer. It sings because it has a song.

Inside is a pen with a blue sapphire diamond tip, it's not very masculine, but the sapphire pierces me like Jasper's eyes. He looks at it and then at me.

"I found that proverb, and it reminded me of you… and me. I thought you would like it. You can keep all your notes in it, or all your cures you're secretly working on," I joke, referring to our conversation in the coffee shop.

He looks flabbergasted, and I struggle to speak without buckling under his gaze. "It's your private haven. Whatever ideas you need to write down that may be trapped up here," I say, tapping his forehead, "you can write down in here, and maybe, they'll make more sense."

He's completely unresponsive, and I start to question if he actually likes it or not. As I doubt my decision and scold myself for a stupid gift choice, Jasper looks up, his long eyelashes wet, and a single tear slides down his cheek.

I'm taken aback, but I shakily wipe away his tear because for once, I'm the one consoling him.

I softly repeat his words while resting my palm against his cheek. "It was meant to make you smile, not cry."

He softly pulls me into his arms lovingly, and whispers, "They're happy tears."

Chapter 24
Happy New Year

On New Year's Eve, we're all headed to Little Sisters because Passengers of Ego are ending the current year and welcoming in the New Year with a bang. V and I are decked out in our best scandalous 'bring on the New Year' outfits.

I have made my New Year resolutions. My list, in no particular order:

1. I am going back to school. I have decided that I'm ready—I'm ready to get my life back and follow my dreams of becoming a chef; carpe diem!

2. I am going to give myself an emotional makeover. I may not be the broken, miserable girl that I once was, but I certainly am not fixed. I have a long way to go before I'm happy with the Ava Thompson looking back at me every time I glance into the mirror.

That leads me to resolution number 3. I have to get closure with Harper. If I'm to patch myself up, I need to get all this Harper baggage buried once and for all. I need him to be aware of the pain he caused me. How his selfish actions crushed my heart, my soul, and my spirit. But ironically enough, I want to thank him. If it wasn't for him dumping me, I would still be that pathetic girl with no direction in life. I would be a ghost of my former self, all because I thought I knew what love was.

But most notably, I need to thank Harper for letting me go. When we broke up, I thought I would be a prisoner to my grief forever, but now I know he set me free. He set me free to find myself, and more importantly, he set me free to find Jasper.

And that leads me to my final resolution.

My final resolution is simple... I'm going to make Jasper mine.

So on that note, no time like the present to make good on that resolution. I always smell Jasper before I see him. He has the most delicious fragrance. It is refined, oriental, and almost woody. He wraps his warm arms around me, my back pressed to his chiseled front as he kisses my neck playfully. Little does he know, I have just internally combusted at the contact. After spending Christmas with him, I feel like we may be on the road to recovery.

He strokes the charm around my wrist, kissing my shoulder, and then sweeps me around to face him to assess my attire. I'm wearing a gold sequin strapless dress with a black belt that sits high on my waist. It's a little short, but that's the point of spending a small fortune on this dress. I'm wearing it to impress only one person, and judging by the look on his face—mission accomplished.

He looks at my high stilettos and smiles. "Only a few more inches and you'll reach me, Shorty."

However, I know he likes what he sees, just as I do, because he looks exceptional. His usual black snug jeans ride low on his sinful hips, and his black combat boots are accompanied with a button up, blue checkered shirt. His hair has been recently cut, but his tousled locks still sit in perfect disorder. His eyes, as usual, are gorgeous. I want to drown in those eyes.

"Hey, you twoooo..." V smiles, interrupting our moment.

Clearing my head with a shake, I look over at my drunk friend.

"How much have you had to drink?" I ask, laughing at her intoxicated state.

V pinches her thumb and forefinger together. "Only this much."

"I think you've had more than that." I giggle, as I'm pretty certain my friend has underestimated her beverage intake.

"Okay, maybe this much," she says, widening her fingers a few inches.

Lucas hugs her from behind, laughing at her reply. "Baby, you've had a lot more than that. I was on my first drink, versus your third."

"That's not true. You're just a slow drinker." V pouts, while Lucas pulls her into a passionate kiss.

Jasper and I are standing uncomfortably, looking at our friends make out like it's the end of the world, not the end of the year.

My throat suddenly becomes very dry. "I need a drink."

"It's on me," Jasper offers. I think he's also eager to leave V and Lucas to their lip locking.

We reach the bar and the scantily dressed bartender runs to take Jasper's order.

"I'll have a Heineken, and a Tequila Sunrise?" He looks at me to make sure that's what I want.

I nod happily.

The bartender is totally eye-fucking Jasper, attempting to impress him with her *Cocktail* impression, but he seems oblivious. However, looking around the bar, I notice masses of girls looking at Jasper with lidded eyes, the look of craving on their face and lips. As usual Jasper is unaware, surprising me by stepping inches away from my face, while I'm giving unpleasant looks to all of his admirers.

"You look beautiful." He salutes my glass like his statement was, in fact, a toast.

I gulp, suddenly very nervous with that devilish look on his face. He licks his lips before he takes a swig of beer, all the while his eyes are locked with mine.

Holy crap, the look he's giving me leaves me breathless, and like a cat on a hot tin roof, I down the WHOLE drink and hold back a choke. I'm suddenly drowning in tequila… and Jasper.

"At this rate, you're going to be wasted before midnight."

I take a look at my empty glass and shrug. "That's okay, you're here to protect me if I'm someone tries to take advantage of me in my drunken stupor."

"What if I'm the one taking advantage?" he replies mischievously, winking at me.

Is Jasper *flirting* with me? Well, two can play that game. "It wouldn't be taking advantage if I was a willing participant."

Jasper nearly chokes on his beer while I grin stupidly.

Do friends do this, this playful flirting? I don't care what the 101 rules are of Friend Flirting, because this is driving me crazy.

Sadly our banter is interrupted by Shooter, telling Jasper that they're up in five minutes. I look at my watch, and realize it's already 11p.m.! One more hour until the New Year is here. Good fucking riddance, I say!

Jasper pulls me toward the stage, my hand snugly in his. Positioning me firmly in front of the podium, he spins me around to face him, and again I'm left breathless by his beauty.

"What are you doing?" I question cheekily, pursing my lips.

"How can I stop you from being taken advantage of if I can't see you? This way, I can keep an eye on you while I'm up here."

I concur quickly, 'cause who am I to turn down front row Rock God Jasper action!

As he gives me a chaste kiss on the cheek and heads backstage, I feel hot. Is it the alcohol I just inhaled, or is it Jasper White's innuendo of taking advantage of me?

I know the answer.

V joins me, drunk as all hell, and we share her gallon of strawberry margarita while waiting for Passengers of Ego.

By the time they hit the stage, I am somewhat intoxicated. The three boys start with a rocky tempo, revving up the crowd. This goes on for minutes because they know how to tempt the mob, but finally, Jasper saunters out, waving. The crowd erupts in cheers and wolf whistles while Jasper approaches the microphone stand.

"You guys ready to rock out into the New Year?"

"Hell yeah!" the crowd roars.

Jasper nods, smiling at his adoring fans and sends a wink my way. He looks at ease on stage, a born showman.

"1,2,3,4!" Jasper growls into the microphone and begins

singing.

Catching his eye on many occasions throughout the set, I feel a heat gather in my middle as I watch him get lost in the music. Totally spellbound in the performance, I wonder what time it is. Looking at the clock, I realize it's two minutes till midnight. All of a sudden I feel foolish, because who am I to share my customary midnight kiss with?

Looking at my friends, I see V readily applying lip gloss preparing for her smooch with Lucas, and Mariah seems just as eager. I really should have thought about this before standing alone in front of the crowd, like an idiot.

An overwhelming need to run and hide overcomes me, and I attempt to push through the mounds of people squashed shoulder to shoulder, but this is going to take freakin' ages.

With 'sorry' and 'excuse me' and 'pardon me can I get through' exchanged with happy-go-lucky patrons, I move forward about three inches when I hear the countdown:

10 shit
9 oh god
8 suffocating
7 hyperventilating
6 fuck
5 tears are forming
4 holding back a sob
3 wanting to die
2 kill me
1…

HAPPY NEW YEAR!!

The noise is deafening and I witness everyone kissing boyfriends, girlfriends, strangers, and staff, all but me, who is looking at the exit sign like it's my savior. I try to take another step toward the exit before I choke on despair, but suddenly, I feel a pair of strong hands take firm hold of my waist, spinning me around.

Stunned, I look up and see Jasper swoop down, capturing my lips in the inferno of all kisses. I'm surprised and not prepared for his kiss, but as his tongue pushes into me with such force and passion, I'm gasping and ready for his onslaught. He continues his assault on my mouth, working me until I am putty in his hands. He languidly kisses my neck and exhales an erotic breath as I sculpt my body to his. Whimpering, I frantically pull at his hair, forcing his lips back to mine and tilting his head assertively for a better angle. He slides one hand down my back and rests it lightly on my butt. Now I'm certain I am on fire. I don't care who is here, I want him stripped and naked, like now!

As always, I lose all sense of time and space when we kiss. However, coming back down to earth, our kiss slows and I unhappily pull away, pouting slightly.

Looking at the clock, I see that it is now 12:05a.m.

Smiling at Jasper, whose eyes are heated to the temperatures of hell, I whisper, "Happy New Year."

He tucks a stray lock of hair behind my ear, his eyes still full of wanting.

"What a fucking way to start it."

Chapter 25
Number 3

"Food expression is about art. Not being afraid to express yourself through your cooking."

I took that step I was so afraid of taking and I haven't looked back.

I've been back at CIA for a few weeks and it's been wonderful. When I spoke to my coordinator about the possibility of returning, he literally clapped his hands and shoved the paperwork under my nose. It was a nice feeling to be accepted back so readily.

After all the formalities were taken care of, I was able to re-enroll into my Culinary Arts Degree. It was like coming home. My teachers welcomed me back and gave me a pile of catch up notes, which I happily devoured.

Life is good, and finally, my smile isn't forced.

College is great and work at The Coffee Bean is steady, helping me pay for my astronomical school fees. I'm spending more time with my parents, and Oscar is back to being a normal outdoor cat, as his stint inside nearly sent us both to the loony bin.

And then there's Jasper. Things between us have been amazing since That Kiss.

We harmlessly flirt with one another, and V has commented the sexual tension between us is so heavy, she could smell the pheromones when she entered the room. But I don't care. I'll take what I can get.

I want more from Jasper, but I know he's happy with the way things are. Sometimes, I can sense he longs for more, but I know he's afraid of going down that road with me again. I can't blame him though, seeing as that road ended up a dead-end.

But whatever we're doing, it works. I remind myself on a daily basis that I'm the one to blame for us being stuck in the friend zone.

Class is over, and as usual, my thoughts have ended with Jasper White.

"Hey, are we going to the student bistro?" my classmate Ben asks.

Ben and I have been paired up for the rest of the term as cooking buddies, and I couldn't have asked for a better buddy. He's polite and seems to be into class as much as me.

"Yeah sure, let's see what the other classes have over us," I joke, grabbing my backpack.

The student bistro is a campus eatery where culinary students practice cooking in a restaurant environment, and the hospitality staff can practice waiting tables. Meals are cheap, and it's a sneaky way to snoop on how good the other classes are.

As we make our way out of class, Ben ducks into the bathroom, looking over his shoulder, implying he'll be a minute. I give him a courteous nod and decide to wait out in the courtyard. However, before I can take another step, I'm confronted with a pair of cerulean eyes, and my heart plunges into my stomach.

"Hello," I gulp, noticing a few heads turn when they see the hottie I'm talking to.

"Hello yourself. That look suits you." Jasper mockingly smiles, looking at my attire.

Looking down, confused, I quickly blush, as I've forgotten to take off my food splattered apron. I swiftly take it off and shove it in my bag.

"What are you doing here?" I ask, trying not to sound rude and conceal the fact I'm fist pumping to happy town within.

"To have lunch with you," he replies with poise, the sunlight reflecting off his milky smooth skin.

"Out of all the things you could do on your day off, you want to have lunch with me? Here? At school?" I ask to clarify my wires aren't crossed.

"Yeah, why not? This place is as good as any."

I smile at his impulsiveness as things between us are looking brighter every day.

He reaches for my backpack and places it over his shoulder—always the gentleman.

"Hey, Ava," Ben snarls, and I wince, as I completely forgot about us having lunch together.

However, I wince for another reason when I unexpectedly witness Jasper's shoulders hunch up tightly, and the air can suddenly be cut with a knife.

As Ben and Jasper glare at one another, I stare transfixed—do they know each other?

"Hi, Jasper," Ben sneers.

Okay, question answered, they *do* know one another.

Jasper ogles Ben, and if looks could kill, Ben would be a smoldering pile of ashes. What the hell is going on? I look at Jasper, giving him a 'care to explain' look, which he dismisses quickly.

"I'll catch you later, Ava," Jasper says, hurriedly kissing my forehead and exiting the building before I can question him.

I glance at Ben, who shrugs a shoulder, offering no explanation. *What* is going on? I am so confused, and curse myself for jinxing our reunion.

Needing to find out what's wrong, I give Ben a quick apologetic smile and run out after Jasper, who is a few yards ahead.

"JASPER!" I yell, chasing after him.

I'm not a runner, and with my little legs trying to keep up with Jasper's huge strides, I'm puffed.

"JASPER!" I shout again, and he finally slows down.

Out of breath, I catch up to him, hands on knees, attempting to steady my breathing.

"What the hell was that about?" I ask breathlessly.

"How do you know him?" he asks, narrowing his eyes.

"Who? Ben?" I ask, confused.

"Yes, Ben." He sneers his name like he's eaten something nasty.

"He's my cooking partner, why?"

This conversation is going nowhere, because I have no idea why Jasper is so mad. Judging by the murderous glare in his eye, I would say their connection is an unpleasant one.

"Because he's an asshole, that's why!" Jasper replies while attempting to storm off, but I grab his arm, stopping his retreat.

"Hey, hold up. What's going on? If he's an asshole, then you should tell me why. I'll be spending a lot of time with him over the next few months, and I'd like to know if my partner is a douche bag."

"Why?" He's seething, looking over my shoulder in case Ben decides to interrupt us.

"Um, because that's how it works. He's my partner and we cook, study, and so on together." Jasper's face tightens in frustration.

"What the hell, Jasper? Talk to me," I implore.

I'm starting to think Ben may be a serial killer judging by Jasper's reaction to my news.

He senses my concern, and after much deliberation, he finally answers, "He's Indie's boyfriend."

Okay, definitely not a serial killer, but *definitely* a douche bag. Boyfriend? When did she date? What are the odds I would be partnered up with the psycho bitch's new squeeze?

"How do you know that?" I question, raising an eyebrow, because I didn't think Indie and Jasper still kept in touch.

"I don't want you seeing him. Can you swap partners or something?"

I look at Jasper, offended by his request. I don't understand why Ben being Indie's boyfriend is an issue. Is he jealous? Does he still have feelings for her? Indie has been out of the picture for many glorious months, or so I thought. Is seeing Ben bringing back memories of Indie? Does he miss her?

Jasper is aware of my fears, as my face, no doubt, betrays me. "Don't go thinking stupid things, Ava, okay? I would still hate that jerk if he wasn't Indie's boyfriend."

I still can't wrap my head around the issue here. "He's her boyfriend, big deal. Why do you care?"

Jasper folds his arms across his chest and huffs. "I don't."

I throw him a skeptical look because I know he's lying.

When he doesn't elaborate, I chuckle sarcastically. "You obviously do, if we're standing outside my school, arguing about your ex and her current lay."

Jasper pulls at his hair, letting out a frustrated sigh. That makes two of us.

"I don't care, Ava. It's just…hard to explain." He tosses me an ambiguous look, and I roll my eyes.

No way is he getting out of this without an explanation. The last time Jasper lied to me about Indie, he ended up getting pulverized by Brandon.

"Try me," I simply state, crossing my arms.

Jasper bites his lip and averts his eyes, which certainly isn't a good start. "I know to others, Indie comes across as a heartless bitch." That's his only explanation? That explains nothing.

"That's because she is." It comes out before I can stop myself, and I realize I may have vocalized it a little louder than anticipated as a student zigzags to get out of my way with an uncomfortable look on her face.

But Jasper continues as if I hadn't spoken. "But I've known her since we were kids, and I'll always look out for her. So when I see her dating a jerk like Ben, I care. Just like I'm sure you'll always care about Harper."

His words infuriate me, and I literally see red.

What is it with Jasper's obsession with Harper and me? On almost every occasion we have discussed Harper, it has ended in a fight. Look what happened the last time we discussed Harper, for Pete's sake!

Needing to set Jasper straight on where my feelings for Harper lie once and for all, I step up toward his towering frame, poking my finger into his solid chest. "You've got to be joking. I couldn't care less if that bastard dropped off the face of this earth. He would be doing me and females all over the world a favor!"

My words have failed to convince Jasper, and I can tell by the determined look on his face this is going to turn into an argument.

"That's not true and you know it. You wouldn't be getting so angry if he still didn't get under your skin." His words hurt because there is some truth there.

But for the first time, it's not because I'm mourning our relationship, it's because I hate him. I hate the bitter, insecure person I become whenever I think about him. I hate him because he stopped me from being open to a new relationship with the person standing in front of me. I hate that he still has an affect on me.

But that's going to change.

"That's where you and I differ. You care for Indie. I hate Harper. I hate everything he did to me, and if I saw his current girlfriend, I would give her some money to buy a ticket to heartbreak hotel, because that's where she's headed, being involved with a sociopath like him!"

Wow, that felt good.

Jasper gives me a pained look. "Ava, you need to talk to him, or sort something out. You need to get over him so you can move on…" He leaves the sentence hanging because I know he means I should have sorted my shit out before I got involved with him.

However, I'm sick to death of hearing Harper's name, so I mockingly cry, "I'm quite happy where I'm situated right now, thank you very much."

Jasper blows his bangs in frustration. "Why are you getting so mad? I'm right, aren't I? You still love him."

Seriously, was our previous fight over Harper not enough for him? The fight that resulted in us not talking, and then reverting us back to being friends.

A million thoughts are zipping through my brain, and as I glance up at a deflated Jasper, I suddenly want to slap him. Why does he insist on bringing up my ex? And how is it Harper can still ruin my life, and he's not even in it anymore? And how did this conversation turn into being about me?

I've had enough, and it's time to put a stop to this chat, and also time to put a stop to Harper controlling my life.

"If you actually think I could still be in love with that pathetic excuse for a man, then we have nothing further to say to one another." I storm off, the breeze carrying Jasper's voice, calling out for me to stop. But I need to put as much distance between us before I chicken out with my decision.

How can Jasper think I still have feelings for Harper? I know the answer lies in my behavior on that fateful night. I really can't blame Jasper for being unsure of my feelings for Harper, because I've never sat down and explained myself.

But that can wait for another day, because right now, I don't give a darn about the rest of my classes, because there's one imperative mission I must complete.

New Year's resolution number 3: Contact Harper.

Chapter 26
Stronger

What's the appropriate terminology to address an email to your good for nothing, sonofabitch ex?

I sit, staring at my laptop, like it will give me the answers I so desperately seek. Slamming down the lid in frustration, I can't believe this so hard. I know what I should say, but actually conveying that into a sentence, it's all so daunting. I don't want to revisit all those memories—all those feelings. What if I reopen that door and I can't close it again? I can't do this. Then, I envision a pair of cerulean eyes, and the argument that prompted me here.

Blowing out a frustrated breath as I fire up my laptop, I decide to put on some music for inspiration. Searching through my playlists, one particular song title catches my eye, and I laugh at the irony of life. I listen to the lyrics over and over, on maximum volume, and what I want to say to Harper falls into my lap, musically.

What better way to express my feelings, than using one of my favorite songs, "Stronger" by Kelly Clarkson.

So, thank you to a strong, powerful woman, for summing up how I feel about my manipulative, devious ex.

My email is simple, heading the subject title with: "Thanks to you."

As I type out the lyrics, I sing along with enthusiasm, and when I'm done, I stare at the screen for a few minutes, but at no time do I doubt my email. Moving the cursor over the send button, I hesitate, but as the chorus of the song blares at me through my speakers, I press send and the relief I feel is instant.

Jumping up from my seat, I run around the room, singing loudly, as tears of happiness stream down my face. I'm laughing like a crazy woman, yelling at the top of the lungs, butchering this song, which will never remain the same for me. As I'm propped up on the couch, playing air guitar, V walks in and yells to be heard over the music and me.

"Don't get me wrong, I prefer this than the depressing stuff, but if you don't cease with your "singing," you will be imprisoned for your crimes against music."

Leaping off the couch and laughing, I latch onto V's hands and twirl her around, coaxing her to sing along with me, and even partake in some clapping. I feel on top of the world. Why didn't I do this sooner? Why was I so afraid? I now know the hole in my chest will eventually heal, and even though the scar tissue will always be there, whenever my thoughts pass to Harper, that scar tissue will be a reminder of a life lesson learned.

"Why are you in such a good mood? Did you and Jasper finally sort your shit out?" Even the mention of Jasper, who I'm still mad at, can't sour my mood.

"No, V. Nothing to do with him, directly. It's all me. Ava Thompson, this is your life, and I'm taking it back!"

V beams up at me. "Oh babe, I'm so happy for you. Whatever is going on, I like it. I haven't seen you smile like this in forever. Bring it on!"

I'm apprehensive to tell V the reason for my latest happiness, as I know she'll want to talk about it and analyze it. I just want to keep it for what it is: closure.

Deciding to steer things in a different direction, I ask, "Did you know Indie was dating someone?"

"As if I would. I didn't talk to that bitch when I was supposed to be nice to her. How did you find out?" V collapses onto the couch and pulls me down to sit near her.

Leaning my head on her shoulder, I reply, "Her boyfriend is in my class. And if that's not bad enough, he's my cooking partner." I curse the paradox of life.

"Oh my God! You're joking! Ava Thompson, what have you done in your previous life to warrant such bad luck?" V teases.

I chuckle, interlacing my fingers into praying hands. "I wish I knew. Whatever it was, I put it out there... I'M SORRY!"

"How did you find out?" V looks serious, and I exhale in frustration.

"Jasper."

That dampens my mood slightly, as we didn't really sort out why he was so upset about Indie dating Ben.

"Jasper?" V asks, clearly confused.

As I explain the story, V asks, "Why does he care who she's dating?" I shrug in response.

However, then a thought occurs to me. "Did you know he was still in contact with her?"

V nods guiltily, while chewing on her lip ring—never a good sign. "Yeah, Lucas mentioned it. I didn't think it was a big deal, so I never said anything. Are you okay with it?"

Deciding facing my demons is better than hiding from them, I reply, "Honestly, not really. Jasper and I had a huge argument about it, and he had the balls to say he would always care for Indie, just like I would Harper."

Even the thought leaves a sour taste in my mouth, which just confirms my decision to email Harper was the right one.

"And he's wrong?" V questions, genuinely curious.

So much for this not turning into Harper talk. What is it with people? Do they not get Harper ripped out my heart and left me for dead?

"Don't be getting that look on your face, Ava. I'm only speaking from experience, and I know you hate Harper, but as time goes on, that hate will fade. You'll always remember that feeling of your heart getting broken. I mean, he was your first love, and feelings like that may be buried, but never forgotten."

As I reflect on her words, my mouth has a mind of its own, and I unexpectedly blurt out, "I want Jasper."

My candid reply sets V off, and after a full minute of laughing, she wipes her tears away. "Okay, don't hold back or anything."

I smile, as I don't see the point of being aloof about it. "I want more with Jasper. I want him so bad, it hurts. He's my first thought in the morning, and the last at night. That's something, right? At the beginning, I thought it was only physical, but honestly, Jasper could be a pirate with a wooden leg, and my feelings wouldn't change. I want him. I was so stupid to let my insecurities get in the way."

V claps loudly, and I look at her, confused, as I'm afraid my insanity has finally rubbed off on her. "Fucking finally, now that you have admitted it to yourself, go tell him, and don't be stuffing it up this time around."

Insecurity has reared her ugly head. "But what if he doesn't feel the same way?"

Expressing my fears out loud seems all the more daunting. I know what I want. But what does Jasper want? He seems happy just being friends.

V startles me when she slams her palm onto the table to emphasis her point. "Honey, seriously, are you blind? People in Antarctica can see the chemistry between you two. Sadly, he's being a little bitch about it all. So you want that man, you gotta go get him!"

She's right, not about the little bitch part, but about the chemistry.

"Okay, you're right." I sigh.

"You know, I will never tire of hearing that." V giggles while I throw a pillow at her self-righteous ass as she gets up and heads upstairs to get changed.

My palms grow clammy at the thought of actually telling Jasper how I feel. I may have had a surge of confidence after emailing Harper, but that doesn't mean I'm confident enough to declare my feelings for Jasper right now, this second. I need time to prepare, and maybe rehearse a speech.

I cringe when I realize the next few nights will be sleepless, thinking about the appropriate etiquette on how to address this. I berate myself, this isn't a conference where I can prepare notes. Golly, I really need to stop thinking about this.

Luckily, there's a knock at the door to distract me from my thoughts. V bounces down the stairs to answer the door, and I head into the kitchen to start on dinner. I can hear her talking to someone, who I presume is an annoying salesperson.

Lost in thought and humming to myself, I open the fridge and gaze inside. A chicken and a few vegetables sit all by their lonesome on the bottom shelf, so I decide to make a chicken pot pie.

Bending down to retrieve the food and not using my knees, I'm glad I'm alone, as these yoga pants really don't leave much to the imagination. Anyone standing behind me would get a nice view of my butt.

"Hey you."

Holding onto the fridge door for support, I close my eyes, mortified. Maybe if I stay in here, he'll go away. Or, maybe he can't see me. I try to subtly shuffle forward to conceal myself.

"Are you hiding in the fridge? If so, I can see you."

Damn it!

I'm getting a slight case of hypothermia standing here in this compromising position, so I take a steady breath and face the music that is Jasper White.

V ducks her head around the corner, grinning. "Hey guys, I totally forgot I have to go to the…um, library to return a book, so, I'll see you soon." She runs out the front door.

V is a terrible liar. The fact she left in her pajamas really made her story of returning an alleged library book less believable.

Jasper walks into the kitchen, his heavy footsteps ricocheting on the tiled floor as he pulls up a seat and casually sits. With his elbows braced on the wooden back, he watches as I dance around the kitchen, placing the dinner ingredients on the counter. I can feel him watching my jumpy movements, but I can't stop fidgeting as he's making me nervous.

"Can you please stop doing whatever you're doing? I'm getting dizzy just watching you."

Damn him. I can hear the amusement in his tone, as he knows I'm nervous.

Dumping the carrots onto the counter, I lean against the corner, ankles and arms crossed. "What are you doing here?"

Flinching at my curtness, I realize that's not really a polite way to greet a guest, especially a guest, who only moments prior, I was going to proclaim my feelings for.

"I don't like how we left things," he replies, his eyes never leaving mine.

Peering at him nervously, I can clearly see he looks beaten and exhausted. Will this emotional rollercoaster between us ever come to an end?

Taking a deep breath, I push my insecurities down—deep down. "Me neither. I'm sorry for blowing up on you. I shouldn't have stormed off that way." I'm woman enough to admit I'm at fault for losing my temper.

As Jasper shakes his head, massaging his forehead, I almost feel sorry for him.

"I didn't give you much choice. I was being an asshole. I'm sorry for asking you to change cooking partners. That was wrong."

I was not expecting an apology, but I'll take it. "How about we forget today happened?"

Even though we haven't addressed the reason behind him hating Ben, I really don't want to argue with him anymore. If that argument never happened, I would have never emailed Harper. So it would be pointless holding a grudge.

"I'd really like that. Are you sure you're not going to do some chick thing and yell and call me out on being a jerk when I think things are okay?" He chuckles while I throw an apple at him, missing him by a long shot.

"You already know you're a jerk." I smugly shrug in response.

"Oh, you're going to pay for that," Jasper warns. He has me pinned before I can say how.

He has my arms restrained behind my back, holding me

prisoner against his upper body. Our chests are touching, and I feel giddy as his steady heart beats madly, racing alongside mine.

Staring up into his eyes, I know he's assessing me as closely as I him. Can I really do this again? Am I ready? As his warm breath puffs lightly against my face, and I inhale his heady fragrance, I know I have to do this.

This is it; I'm going to do it, no chickening out.

As Jasper rests his forehead against mine, I open my mouth, ready to declare my feelings for him once and for all.

But sadly, Jasper has other ideas as he whispers, "Friends?"

You've got to be kidding me!

I sigh, frustrated at myself. Come on, Ava, tell him. Then that niggling voice called doubt stops my confession because is that all he wants? Friendship?

Uncertainty plagues my mind because, what if V is right? What if what is buried may never be forgotten?

I'm such a chicken. I can't tell him how I feel and be rejected.

I don't know if I can do this again, but I reply with an unconvincing nod. "Friends."

Bwaaakkkkkkkkk!! Bock! Bock!

Chapter 27
Broken Harmonies

We never discuss Ben or Indie again.

It's difficult seeing Ben every day, because neither he, nor Jasper, will explain their mutual hatred for each other. But seeing Ben is not as difficult as seeing Jasper and his new 'friend,' Harmony.

Harmony is the epitome of beauty, and, I hate her. With her long auburn hair, innocent hazel eyes, and full pouty lips, I feel like the ugly duckling in her presence. She always looks stunning no matter what she wears, and she usually opts for a chic, bohemian look. Overall, she's a nice enough person, which makes it hard to hate her, but I manage.

Jasper and Harmony have been friends since she brought her puppy into the shelter one evening while he was working. Her puppy had swallowed some foreign object, and Jasper being the gentleman that he is, offered to monitor her dog personally. Her dog made a full recovery, and Harmony felt it was her duty to thank Jasper by jostling her breasts into his face every chance she got. He knew what she was doing, and he seemed to like it, which hurt, but more than anything, it pissed me off.

I've tried to ignore her obvious play for Jasper's affections, but it's hard when her double D's are bouncing off his smug face. It's uncomfortable for me to question Jasper about her without sounding like a jealous, crazy person. As much as I hated it, Jasper can have all the double D's he wants, because I still haven't told him how I feel. Therefore, I can't be mad or annoyed at Jasper, or even Harmony, because Jasper is fair game.

So, I throw myself into school and try to avoid any gatherings where Harmony will be. This meant I missed a few Passengers of Ego shows, but I couldn't stomach them together. His friendliness with her was just that, but I didn't want him to be friendly with anyone other than me. I knew I had no right to be so possessive, so I excluded myself, not wanting to make things awkward for everyone.

Jasper knows something is up, but no matter how many times he has asked, I have shrugged it off as nothing. This has caused a rift between Jasper and I. However, I have no doubt if I told Jasper about the situation, he would laugh it off the same carefree way he does most things, and put my mind and heart at ease. But I'm afraid to say anything, because what if he doesn't? What if he actually *likes* Harmony, and the flirting is mutual? I couldn't handle that, so I bury my head in the sand because denial is bliss.

It's been a busy day at work, and I've been on the go, nonstop. I'm wiping down a table when I hear a familiar voice.

"Hey you."

I know without looking it's Jasper, but as I see a pair of blue sandals through the glass table I'm cleaning, I know he's not alone. I squirm because I don't want to have this conversation today.

Mustering the biggest smile I can, I reply, "Hey... you two." Jasper looks at me puzzled, and then, there's that awkward silence.

I continue cleaning the spotless table, and wish Jasper and Harmony would just go away.

Harmony looks confused, sensing the apprehension between Jasper and I. "Hey, Jasper, I'll go grab us a table," she says and quickly excuses herself.

Even her damn voice is attractive. I can't stand here any longer and promise I won't pull out her lush brown hair. So as I'm about to walk off, Jasper catches my arm. "What's up? You don't write. You don't call. I'm not feeling the love."

We both shift uncomfortably with the L bomb slip. This uneasiness between us is new, and I don't like it. I know I have no one to blame but myself, but he doesn't have to flaunt his new friend and her assets in my place of work. These feelings I have for Jasper are going to leave me with a serious cause of the crazies if I don't stop obsessing.

"Nothing is up," I reply, tucking my pen into my bun. "I'm just busy with school." That sounded even less convincing out loud.

Jasper looks at me in disbelief. "I know you're lying, Ava. You've never been a good liar."

"Well, that's a good trait to have," I reply, trying to walk away from him, but he steps in front of me, blocking my path.

"I don't like you being dishonest with me. I thought we could talk about anything. That's what friends do," he says with a genuine smile, but that's the last thing I want to hear right now.

I've had it with Jasper and his friendship. He can shove his friendship, because today, I don't want to be his friend.

"Jasper, I'm fine. Everything is fine. You seem to have a new friend to occupy yourself with, anyway, so you better not keep her waiting." That was totally uncalled for, but I can't help it.

"Ava, what? Talk to me," Jasper says, probing my face, clearly puzzled by my random hostility.

I say the only thing I can, without revealing too much. "I'm done talking."

Jasper is still confused, and I can't help but think he's clueless to my feelings. Or maybe it's because he simply doesn't care anymore.

Either way, I don't want to stick around to find out. I excuse myself and head to the locker room where I shrink into the corner and cry.

What is it about Jasper White that breaks my heart time and time again?

I haven't seen Jasper for the past couple of weeks—I just can't. I've ignored his numerous texts and calls, and he even resorted to emailing me when his other forms of communication failed to elicit a response.

If I were to evaluate my actions, I know it's because I feel rejected and jealous. There has never been a right time to tell Jasper I have feelings for him, and that I want him to give me another chance. Every time I try to bring it up, I chicken out or choke up.

Maybe Jasper and I *are* just better off being friends. I'm so miserable and the only friend I like having at the moment is my treasured New York Super Fudge Chunk ice cream. But as I look into the empty tub, I heave a crushed sigh.

To stop myself from becoming a total depressive ball of negativity, I decide to go shopping. What a nice, expensive distraction.

I go to the mall and pay a visit to all my favorite shops, and unnecessarily buy four pairs of shoes I will probably never wear. I justified purchasing all four pairs because they all serve a different purpose.

My all time favorite are a pair of Jimmy Choo black, gladiator sandals. They have a very high heel and make my legs look endless. Definitely not everyday shoes, so that brings me to pair number two.

Yet another pair of Jimmy Choo shoes, but this time a little more conservative. They are champagne gold ballerina flats. They're also super comfortable, and can be worn for any occasion. I was content with my purchase and happy to leave, but then a pair of Christian Louboutin trademark red soled shoes caught my eye, and they became pair number three.

I quickly scurried out of the store before I could spend more of my college fund and was doing so well until I walked past my fourth and final pair of shoes. They worked for Carrie Bradshaw, and I knew they would work for me. A pair of Manolo Blahnik heels.

I know I'll regret this in the morning, but at the moment, I needed some retail therapy, and I must admit, after my splurge, I feel better. Well, that is until I hear a magical laugh, and I know who it belongs to.

Harmony.

Looking up, I see she and Jasper are headed straight toward me, but luckily, they haven't seen me yet. I dive into the first store I see and pretend to be perusing the numerous items on display. Just my luck, the shop I threw myself into is an outfitter store with a big display of hunting and survival gear.

Yeah, that doesn't look suspicious.

I'm faking interest in the new models of Swiss knives and their functions, when I see Jasper and Harmony's reflection in the mirrored wall in front of me. Even his mirrored image makes me go weak at the knees.

He's laughing happily with her, while she's offering him a sip of a bright orange beverage in her clear plastic cup. He shakes his head with a mocking look, and says something, which earns him a playful slap on the arm from her. He looks carefree and happy. I, however, want to stab myself with the limited edition Ranger Grip Swiss Army Knife.

They walk past swiftly, luckily not taking interest in Uncle Sam's. Bracing my hands on my knees, I take a relieved breath that they didn't see me. I'm thankful I'm no longer witness to their enjoyment, but I bite my lip and decide to do what every twenty-two year old girl would do in my position—I follow them.

I tail a good distance behind, but I can clearly see them walk down the crowded pathways, occasionally stopping at stores that garner their interest. I catch sight of Jasper looking over his shoulder as Harmony window shops and I spin around quickly, afraid he'll spot me. I take cover behind the closest vendor's cart while putting on a pair of red, heart-shaped glasses that I blindly grab in an attempts to disguise myself. The assistant looks at me with a puzzled, nervous look.

As Jasper turns back around, I let out a small sigh and they stroll off, oblivious to my stalking, while, I on the other hand, look like an older, crazier version of *Lolita*. The sales assistant clears his throat and I apologize quickly as I hand him his merchandise.

I continue my stalking and notice Jasper looks so relaxed, strolling casually in his hip-hugging blue jeans, navy Chucks, and black sweater. I miserably witness Harmony attempting to take hold of his hand on numerous occasions, which he avoids by pointing to something trivial, or rubbing the back of his neck. Now his hands are tucked into his sweater's front pockets, and I'm praying that's to stop Harmony's prying hands.

Totally lost in thought, I fail to notice them stopping at a cart selling scented candles and other items. As I obliviously continue walking, I bump into the back of some poor shopper and drop all my bags in the collision.

"Oh my God, sorry," I quickly apologize.

However, when I look up, my eyes meet an amused pair of cerulean orbs, and I turn a bright beet red. Jesus, I just ran into Jasper! This serves me right for thinking I can pull this off.

I'm quickly on my knees, collecting my goods and hiding my face while cursing life. Jasper is also on his knees, helping me gather my things, and I'm avoiding his eyes like the plague.

"Hi," he smugly says, and I hear a hint of hilarity behind his tone.

I bite the inside of my cheek to stop myself from cursing. This can't be happening. I'm a terrible liar, and if he asks what I'm doing here, I'll most likely blurt out I was partaking in my own James Bond movie.

"Hi," I mumble, still avoiding his gaze while fumbling around, assembling my bags.

Once I have heaped all my shopping bags onto one arm, I stand up, dusting my knees. However, as I notice I'm a bag short, I look over and see my goods are being held hostage by Jasper.

Slowly peering up at him, I take a steadying breath. I can feel my face is flustered, and I know Jasper can see my embarrassment—it's plastered all over my rosy cheeks.

Looking down at the bag, I point at it and smile. "Thanks." I extend my hand, expecting him to hand it over.

He, however, has other ideas.

"Fancy bumping into you." He grins, his dimples on display.

I nod with a stiff upper lip, trying to appear calm.

"A bit of retail therapy?" he asks, looking down at my bags.

"Yup." Oh God, please let this be over, and I promise I'll go to church every Sunday.

He peers into the bag he's holding and whistles as he reads the brand name. "Jimmy Choo, that's some therapy." I lunge for the bag, but he snatches his hand away defiantly.

"What do you need with," he makes a quick calculation, "with four pairs of shoes?"

To get over you, I internally scream, and I was doing a good job of it before you ruined it with your big, broad, handsome back.

"To wear," I answer blankly.

He looks at my plain, ripped at the knee, faded blue jeans, baggy sweater, and scuffed Chucks and smirks. "And where are you going to wear these four pairs of shoes to?"

"Out," I retort, nervously tucking a piece of hair behind my ear,

"Out where?" he questions, examining my face.

"I don't know, just out."

Peering around, I wonder where the hell Harmony is. This is the one and only time I want her to take Jasper away. There's an uncomfortable silence between us, and he notices my discomfort as I fidget with my hair.

"Why haven't you returned any of my calls? Or texts? Or emails? Have I done something wrong?" he asks nervously, running a hand through his coma-inducing hair.

Yes, you're driving me crazy, I ad-lib within.

"No, Jasper, I've just been busy," I reply, looking over his shoulder, searching for an escape route.

As he pulls in his bottom lip, looking unconvinced of my tale, the uncomfortable silence between us becomes even more intense.

The air is charged, and I know we can both feel the electricity.

"I miss you." I quickly snap my head up at his comment, but he immediately corrects, "I miss you helping me out at the shelter."

I try my damnedest not to pout, but I feel my bottom lip tremble slightly.

"Hi, Ava." My pouting stops.

"Hi, Harmony," I reply, plastering on a fake smile.

As I take in her beauty, I feel ill. Standing beside Jasper, they look like a Hollywood A-list power couple.

Ugh, I need to get out of here.

We're all looking at one another awkwardly, and out of habit, I begin twirling my silver charm bracelet, a nervous habit I recently developed. As Jasper's heated gaze focuses on my jumpy fingers, toying with the charm, I suddenly stop and lower my eyes, because the memories of when he gave me this bracelet overwhelm me, and those memories have me wishing we could go back to the past.

Harmony clears her throat, breaking the silence and the reminiscing. "Ava, did you want to join us for something to eat?"

Both mine and Jasper's eyes widen in alarm. I'd rather starve. "No, thank you, I better get going," I reply, trying my hardest to smile.

"Oh, okay. Are you sure?" she asks.

Looking at Jasper's uncomfortable face, I am more than sure. "Yes, I'm sure. Thanks again."

Jasper takes a relieved breath as us three having lunch together is definitely not a good idea.

I look down at my bag pointedly, wanting to get the hell away from this awkwardness.

"Oh, here you go," he says, handing me my shopping bag.

Our fingers brush each other's lightly, and I snatch my hand back like it's been burned.

Harmony is looking at us with a confused look, and I wonder if Jasper has told her about our past. Judging by her baffled look, I dare say she's clueless.

"Okay, see ya." I look at Harmony, nodding goodbye, and then turn my gaze to Jasper, who surprises me by stepping forward and giving me a tight hug.

My arms are hanging loosely by my sides because I know if I hug him back, I may never let go.

After a few clumsy moments, he lets me go and I sigh sadly. How did things get so weird between us?

"Bye, Jasper."

He nods unhappily. "See ya, ba—" but he stops at the accidental slip.

The look on his face kicks me in the guts, and I don't want to leave him. I want to throw my arms around his neck, and tell him once and for all how I feel, but I slap myself out of my daze and scurry away.

My head droops the whole walk to my car, and not even my four pairs of shoes offer me any comfort, because I know what I need to do.

I need to get over Jasper because my feelings for him are killing me. I need to move on and accept fact that maybe Jasper and I *are* just better off as friends.

Chapter 28
Dirty Dancing

"I can't believe first term is over," Casey says, beaming. Casey is a friend of Ben's, and he's also in our class. "We need to celebrate!"

I chuckle while we sit outside on a lunch break. "Isn't that a little premature? Shouldn't we be celebrating when we actually know we've passed all our subjects?"

"Oh, please, little Miss Smarty Pants! As if you have anything to worry about." Casey sniggers while bumping me with his shoulder.

Casey likes me. I'm not blind to his subtle flirty hints and unnecessary touches. The feeling is definitely not mutual, but I enjoy his company, so I'm happy with his flirting as long as it stays that way.

Ben agrees. "Yeah, fuck it, let's do it. I hear the new club downtown is the place to be. Cheap booze. Great tunes. What more could we ask for?" They both look at me, eagerly awaiting my answer.

I cave, as I was never any good at handling peer pressure.

I can see why Jasper hates Ben. Ben has turned out to be an officious know-it-all, but I've heard him give Indie a run for her money when he cusses her out on the phone, so Ben is my friend. As long as he doesn't bring that shit to the table when we're working together, I can deal with him. I can only imagine the sob stories Indie has been feeding Jasper. And I believe this is the reason why Jasper despises Ben as much as he does.

Anyhow, that's what leads me here, on a Friday night, throwing every garment out of my closet because I hate everything I own. What does one wear to a chic bar? I peer at the only garment hanging that I don't totally hate—it'll have to do.

Reaching for my version of the classic little black dress, I finger the soft material and am happy with my choice. This dress is a little risqué, but what the hell. It'll be nice to dress up and feel good after the miserable few weeks I've had. And I really need to wear one of the four pairs of shoes I blew hundreds of dollars on.

When I wear this dress, I know it always turns heads, and I feel like a little head turning tonight. It is a banded, formfitting dress, and the star of the show is the halter keyhole at the bust, exposing a whole lotta bust. It has hook-and-eye closures behind the neck and a long zip at the back, running down the whole length of the dress, which is not a lot. Yes, it is short, but not slutty short. It exposes half of my back—so no bra for me tonight.

Slipping on my black Christian Louboutin skyscrapers, I don't hate what I see in the mirror. My brown hair is pinned up in a messy chignon, with strands falling around my face. My makeup is light, some mascara, foundation and clear lip gloss.

Taking one last look in the mirror, I decide to grab a cardigan because with this much cleavage on show, I need a security blanket.

V is waiting for me downstairs. She begged to come out with us as she's dying to check out this club. I finally surrendered, as I knew she would just come, anyway. I told her there's one condition to her tagging along—no Jasper talk.

She agreed, so as the horn toots outside, I grab my clutch and we meet Lucas out front. Ben and Casey are meeting us at the club, so Lucas, V, and I head straight in.

V looks adorable in her Mary Janes, and her own little black dress, with a leopard print bolero. We are dressed to impress, and

I'm glad V is coming, as being alone with Casey and alcohol readily available, may not be such a good combination. My reflexes may drown in tequila and not be on high alert if Casey tries anything. I know I'm being paranoid, but I'm a cheap drunk.

Lucas parks his truck and we walk to the club. As we enter, the place is dreamy with soft lighting radiating from the chandeliers. The patrons are a mixture of rock and yuppie, which is a strange combination. V heads straight for the bar, while Lucas and I trail behind, laughing at her eagerness.

"Holy crap! These cocktails are twenty-five dollars. Each!" I shriek to V as I look over the drink menu.

V is studying each drink carefully, and merely shrugs. "With the amount of alcohol that's in them, we'll be on our asses after two!"

She's totally right.

We both order a Japanese Slipper, but not your standard cocktail, as this drink is on steroids! Taking a sip, I get an instant head rush, and I know this is going to be a messy night.

We sit at a table, drinking and chatting for about forty minutes when I finally see Ben and Casey arrive. Getting up on the step on my chair, I wave frantically. Yes, I'm a bit tipsy.

V sees the boys and nudges me with wide eyes. "Who's the blond Adonis?"

Following her line of sight, I realize she's referring to Casey. I'm not sure if it's the alcohol, but Casey *does* look good. His sandy hair is slicked back and he's wearing blue jeans with a white polo, which emphasizes his upper body. But he's not the one I want to be undressing with my eyes. I drown that thought with a gulp of my margarita, and as they reach our table, I start with the introductions.

V makes it more than obvious she thinks Casey is quite the eye candy, and as Lucas also notices her checking him out, he puts his arm protectively around, V staking his claim. I giggle, and V looks at me like I've lost my mind. At the moment, my mind is occupied, as it's swimming in alcohol.

"Do you want a drink, Ava?" Casey asks, dropping his not so

subtle gaze to my cleavage.

This dress has superpowers!

"No, I'm good for the moment," I reply, smiling shyly, as Casey is making it extremely obvious he's gaping at my bust.

Ben clears his throat and Casey lifts his eyes to mine. He seems undaunted that I'm aware of his ogling.

"Come on, Casanova," Ben teases as they head off to get their drinks.

V violently kicks me under the table within five seconds of them leaving.

"OUCH! What the hell, V?" I demand, rubbing my shin.

"You need to get into that man's pants." By *that* man, I know she's referring to Casey.

I only raise an eyebrow in annoyance. "No, he's my friend."

"Who cares what he is? He's hot! What are you waiting for?" I know the answer and so does she. I look down guiltily, and blow out a melodramatic breath.

"Ava, look, I know there's Jasper, but what's a little harmless flirting? It's not like you and Jasper are a thing." V is right, but I feel wrong even considering a little flirting with Casey, although it might help me get over Jasper.

Before I can ponder anything further, Casey and Ben return with drinks for everyone. I know I'll be paying for these cocktails with an awful hangover, but I'll deal with that tomorrow.

The alcohol unwinds us all, and before I know it, Lucas, Ben and V are chatting happily about their love for baseball, which leaves Casey and I to entertain one another. Casey shifts his barstool closer to mine, glass in hand, prepared for a salute. "Let's make a toast."

"Okay." I smile apprehensively. "What to?"

"To you." He doesn't go into detail, but he has that perverse look in his eye, and I catch his gaze slipping to my cleavage once again.

"To me?" I quiz.

"Yes, to you. You really don't know how extraordinary you are, do you?" I gulp nervously.

When Casey proposed a toast, this was not what I was expecting. Casey is cocky, but not obnoxious, he knows what he wants, and by the look in his eye, he wants me. A blush creeps up my neck in about three seconds, and I timidly salute his glass.

An hour passes with Casey and me chatting vividly of our passion for food. I never thought I would have so much fun with him, and question the reason why. That reason is eating a hole into stomach. Maybe Jasper and I *aren't* meant to be together. Maybe we *are* better off as friends.

Shaking Jasper thoughts aside, I grab Casey and drag him down to dance. I must be drunker than I thought, as I'm usually the first to shy away from bodies gyrating against each other on the dance floor.

Casey pulls me into his chest and wraps his arms around my waist, rocking me to the upbeat tempo. Looking at his handsome face with my hands resting lightly on his wide shoulders, I wonder if I could flirt with him, or maybe even attempt to kiss him. He's attractive, funny, and we have the same interests. He does tick all the right boxes. Judging by the way he's holding me, I wouldn't have to try very hard for that to happen.

He pulls me even closer and runs his lips over my neck slowly. I shiver at the sensation, but don't melt like I usually do with someone else. We dance this way for a few minutes, and all the while, I feel lightheaded. I'm not sure if it's the cocktails, or if it's being in someone's arms that aren't Jasper's.

As the next song starts, Casey motions he's going to get a drink and for me to stay put. He surprises me by leaning in and giving me a chaste kiss on the lips. My eyes widen in alarm and I attempt to pull back, but he holds my head in place with a firm grip. It's only a peck, but it feels wrong.

I touch my lips and feel my heart breaking as I stare at his retreating frame. I should be happy Casey is showing interest in me, but there's only one problem—he's not Jasper. He doesn't set me ablaze with one look, and he doesn't send my heart into a frenzy when I think about him. I'm screwed.

Deciding to drown my depressing thoughts in music, I begin

swaying to Lana Del Ray's "Blue Jeans," as I love this song. I'm surrounded by bodies, as the dance floor is crowded, but I strangely don't feel too self-conscious dancing on my own while waiting for Casey.

I'm totally lost in the music, because pathetically, this song reminds me of Jasper. Eyes closed and entranced by her dark voice, I'm startled when a pair of warm hands encircles my waist. That was quick. Casey must have pushed his way to the front.

Casey molds my back into his solid torso as he lazily caresses my waist and stomach with his hands. With my eyes still closed, my head falls back onto his muscular chest, allowing him to lead me. He's hard in all the right places, but he feels somewhat familiar. I inhale and a recognizable fragrance sends my sense of smell into a wild, riotous frenzy. I disregard it as my drunken brain playing tricks, and wishful thinking.

I let the music take me on this sensual journey with Casey, because for some unknown reason, it reminds me of being in Jasper's arms. That thought alone makes this dancing all the better, because I can pretend I'm with Jasper.

As his hands snake up my body, he boldly dips his fingertips into my exposed bust line, but they vanish before I have a chance to enjoy the feel of his fingers on my flesh. His confidence is unexpected, but what's even more surprising is my reaction to him. I feel like a forest fire has spread rapidly from the tip of my head to the bottom on my toes. I didn't feel this way before, and I feel a stab of guilt for enjoying this seductive expedition.

His hands slowly ascend to my neck, holding me closely. He isn't hurting me, but his grip is firm enough to leave me breathless. He uses his thumb and forefinger to gently extend my head back so it rests against his shoulder. As his lips graze my temple, I feel his hot breath brushing against my cheek.

I'm about to detonate under his skillful, erotic touch, and I want more, which surprises me. Feeling a surge of confidence overtake me, I turn to kiss him, but he holds me firmly in place. I let out a frustrated whimper, and I feel his hot breath stroke my ear as he lets out a soft chuckle. He slowly releases his hold on my neck and slides his hands to rest on my waist, while circling his groin against my ass.

Wow, this takes dirty dancing to a whole new level.

I'm completely under his spell, and don't know how much longer I can take this sexual tension, as he won't let me touch him. But if I was to be honest with myself, it's totally turning me on. I like this sexual aggression. It makes me feel wanted, and it makes me feel like a Goddess.

I feel improper dancing this way with Casey, but I can't help it. It just feels *right*. What kind of person does that make me? A horny one, my inner harlot screams.

My eyes are still closed, and I bite my cheek as he dips low and takes my earlobe between his teeth. His lips then trail down the shell of my ear, and as his warm breath tickles the side of my neck, I'm about to explode if I don't get some lip on lip action, like now. I attempt to turn around, but my knees buckle when I hear him speak.

"Looks like you've put those shoes to good use." My passion turns to panic, as that voice isn't Casey's, it's *Jasper's*.

I struggle to spin around, needing to confirm if it's him, but he holds me prisoner against his chest.

"I wouldn't want to ruin your fantasy by seeing it's *me* you're dancing with. Do you rub up against everybody this way? Or is your *friend* the only one who gets the privilege?"

Shocked at his crude words, I take a calming breath, needing to still my frenzied heart. Jasper's words are malicious, and I can taste the jealousy in them, but I want to face him so he can see the sincerity in my eyes when I tell him it was *him* I was thinking about. It was him I would have happily danced this way with, if he would man up and tell me that's what he wanted.

Finally his grip ceases, and I spin around to explain.

But that's a bad idea. He looks fucking hot! Livid, but hot. His hair has been yanked in every direction in disorder, his cerulean eyes have a hard, furious stare, and his sinful lips are pulled into a tight scowl.

I know he's mad at me, but I can't help myself as I need to

know why he's here. "Did you follow me here?"

He rolls his eyes and the tip of his tongue shoots out to lick his upper lip.

"No, Ava, get over yourself. I'm here with Harmony." Ugh, that's a name I don't want to hear right now.

What a way to ruin the mood.

He's looking at me in silent challenge. Does he want me to fight him? Well, if it's a fight he wants, then I'm ready to wage war.

"Well, does she know her date is fondling another woman?" I ask, looking at him smugly, while crossing my arms under my chest, very aware that my breasts are sitting perkily on display.

As I catch him sneak a peek, clench his jaw and exhale deeply, I literally have to stop myself from dancing on the spot in excitement, because even at each other's throat, he still wants me.

"Nope. Does *your* date know you're fondling another man?" he answers arrogantly.

Well, what a way to rain on my parade.

"No, he doesn't. And for the record, I thought it was MY date who was fondling me, not you," I throw back, infuriated.

I'm such a liar, but with that smug look on his face, I'll be damned if I tell him the truth.

His eye twitches, revealing my words have wounded him. But as he takes a composing breath, and his game face slips into place, I know its game on.

I'm not aware what song is playing, or how we are standing in the middle of the dance floor, hogging up prime space for patrons. But more importantly, I most definitely am not aware of where my *date* is, because I never had one. Casey was never my date.

"Oh, sorry to disappoint you!" he retorts, snapping me out of my thoughts.

The frustration I feel comes boiling to the surface, and I'm so wound up, I can literally feel the blood pumping through my veins.

"Are you fucking kidding me?"

Jasper takes a step toward me, his face inches away from mine. "No, I'm not, please enlighten me."

We're totally glaring daggers at each other when I feel myself explode. "Maybe if you grew some balls, and actually manned up, we would be doing A LOT more than dancing right now!"

There, I said it. This is not how I envisioned telling Jasper how I feel about him, but this was Jasper and I. Nothing goes to plan.

Jasper chuckles smugly and takes another step forward. He bends so we're pressed together, chest to chest, and whispers in my ear. "You didn't seem to mind my balls digging into you a few minutes ago. I'd even say you liked it. Or maybe you act that way with all the boys."

I'm appalled at his crudeness, and when I pull back to look at his self-satisfied face, a million emotions race over me at once. I feel possessed. I can't control myself and I do the first thing that feels natural, I slap him so hard it can be heard over the music.

He looks at me horrified, his palm resting over his reddening cheek. But what did he expect me to do, the arrogant ass! I shouldn't have slapped him, as nothing condones violence, especially with someone who grew up with an abusive dad. But I'm so mad at him for saying such an indecent thing about me, I lost sight of reason.

My hand instantly heats, and I know my slap had power behind it.

"What the fuck!" he asks, stunned, his hand still resting on his cheek.

I shouldn't have slapped him, but I'm not in control at the moment. I need to leave.

"Yeah, my thoughts exactly," I shout, referring to his sordid behavior.

Before I do something else I regret, I storm off and find the exit in a blur. I don't care that I don't have my bag. I don't care if Casey and V are looking for me. I don't care that it's freakin' pouring rain and I'm akin to a drowned rat. Raging through the streets, I hail a taxi and thankfully one picks up my sopping ass and transports me away from an argument I don't want to finish.

Chapter 29
Stars and Hearts

I run into the house to grab some money for the cabbie as I left my purse, jacket and patience back at the club.

Kicking off my shoes, they hit the wall with a thud, but being barefoot allows me to pace backward and forward freely, and I need to walk because I'm fuming. How dare he! Why is he treating me like some whore? It's none of his business if I want to dry hump my way around Los Angeles. He needn't know I wished it was him I was dry humping.

He's made it crystal clear that we're nothing more than friends, and I'm sick of these games. I don't have an on/off emotional switch, and his hot and cold behavior is confusing. It's pissing me off.

He wants me, he doesn't want me. He says we're friends, but then he sends me mixed signals. This guy is the most infuriating man I have ever met. I know I haven't declared my feelings, but I've always been civil towards him, and never insulted him on purpose.

I do the only thing I can do with my temper at boiling point, I fire up my laptop and put on Florence and the Machine. As the first song, appropriately named "Kiss with a Fist," comes blasting through my speakers, I begin pacing the house once again like a caged animal.

Totally lost in the music, I'm unaware I'm not alone until I turn around and am faced with a pair of enraged cerulean eyes.

How did he get in?

"What the fuck do you want, Jasper?" I yell at him, unsure I have the strength to continue with round two.

He quickly races over to me, pulling me into his wet arms, and just before crushing his lips to mine, he pants, "You."

Game. On.

Jasper pushes me up against the wall—hard. I bang my head on impact, but I don't care. I need to consume this man, like now.

Kissing with an urgency I can't keep up with, he holds my head in place with both hands to continue his passionate assault on my mouth. There's a desperate need to get these wet clothes off and be skin to skin. I then realize he is also wet. He must have chased me out of the club not that long after I stormed out.

Droplets of rain slip from his hair, splashing my cheeks, but I couldn't care less. I pull his soaked hair, hard, and he moans while I bite his lip, angrily. I'm so mad at him, but I can't get enough of him, and the more I kiss him, the more I want him.

His tongue is in my mouth, searching every part of me, and there's no tenderness in the action. He's rough and merciless, but I like it. I want more.

As I push him back forcefully, his eyes eat me up. They're filled with wanton frenzy. The look drives me crazy, and I surprise myself as I reach forward and rip his t-shirt in half.

Holy shit.

He's standing before me shirtless, with all those lean, ripped muscles on display, and he's dripping wet. As beads of water cascade down his chest, moving into the line of hair on his stomach, I'm envious of one little droplet which slips into his snail trail and gradually slithers into his pants.

Sensing my desire, he yanks me up so I'm straddling his narrow waist. He then walks us over to the sofa, never ceasing with his attack on my mouth. I fall back onto the cushions with him on top, but he in no way breaks contact with my lips.

His hand plunges under my dress and he roughly pulls aside my underwear so he can touch me in my entire naked splendor. I thought kissing Jasper could create an inferno, but this, will surely make me explode.

Raising my hips, I silently beg him to soothe my burn, and he takes the hint by slowly inserting one finger, testing how far he can go. It's been a while and the intrusion is painful, but as he leisurely works another finger into me, I am soaked.

I desperately try to get his pants off as I fumble with his zipper, but clumsy with eagerness, I fail. He, however, doesn't halt his sweet torment of me below, as he quickly unhooks the clasps on my dress, pulling it down, revealing my heated breasts. Hissing in a pained breath, he lowers his sinful mouth and latches onto a nipple, sucking with a long, wet pull.

I arch my back and cry out as he tugs on my right nipple before moving to the left. All the while, his fingers move back and forth inside me, increasing the speed as I moan in need.

My dress is pushed down, but I want it off. I want this so bad because I want nothing between us. I've wanted this from the moment I fell head over heels for him. His mouth is everywhere, and I'm about to explode.

When his fingers leave me to undo his belt, I cry out, missing his touch. I swiftly offer to help him with his offending garment as he sits up on his knees to unbutton his jeans. He looks down at me, and unexpectedly, he stops. His cheeks are flustered, his hair in disarray, his lips red and swollen, but he finally seems to take in what we're about to do.

"Are you sure you want to do this? This will change everything," he whispers, trembling slightly. "If you say yes, I won't be able to stop myself. I want you so much."

Reaching up, I touch his face. "I've never been more certain of anything in my life. Don't you *dare* stop."

Jasper rewards me with a heart stopping smile, but questions one last time. "Are you sure? I know once I start, I'll be lost in you."

I understand his apprehension, as the last time we were about to get physical, I freaked out. As I pull him into a kiss, a kiss that is filled with months of wanting him, the desire to give myself to him emotionally and physically, that answers all his doubts.

Off come his jeans and boxers, and I gasp when I see him in his glorious stripped state. He's ready for me and I swallow in concern, because how am I meant to accommodate him? He senses my anxiety, and softly brushes the hair off my face.

"We'll go slow, okay?" I bite my lip and nod quickly.

He slips my dress clean off, along with my underwear, and as he bends down to retrieve a condom from his jeans pocket; I know there's no turning back.

Peering down at myself, reality sinks in, and I realize that I am *really* naked right now. I shyly reach down to cover myself, but Jasper stops me with his hand.

He searches my face. "Don't ever feel ashamed. You, in this moment, looking at me, trusting me, it's just fucking beautiful."

And with that, he pushes into me quickly, moving me up the sofa with his forceful stroke. I choke back a sob of pleasure, and he stills for a moment, as my insides are stretched further than I thought possible. He slowly rocks into me, trying to make our connection as comfortable for me as he can, without driving into me too deeply, too quickly.

This is so foreign to me, and I feel like I'm about to implode.

"Are you okay? Am I hurting you?" Jasper whispers, his head resting in the crook of my neck, attempting to catch his breath.

I can't form a sentence because I feel so full, body and soul. But I nod, holding in a breath and biting my lip in blissful pain, hoping he'll understand that I'm more than okay.

Thankfully, he understands my actions and picks up the pace. He starts with measured, light, controlled strokes, and the sensitivity is heightened as he reaches down, rubbing my center lightly with his thumb. The noises coming out of me are primeval, but I can't stop myself. And Neko Case's "I Wish I was the Moon" is doing a poor job of concealing my cries of pleasure.

I nearly explode from the sweet torment, but I know he's not there yet, so I hold off until we're both well spent. He is staring at me, his eyes assessing my reaction to him moving so deeply within me, ensuring I'm not in pain.

This sensation is like nothing I've ever felt before. I close my eyes, basking in the pleasure of having Jasper buried deep inside of me. I'm heated all over. When he softly bites my chin, I exhale an untamed moan, which encourages him to increase his velocity and I buckle with the force.

I'm engulfed in his mouth-watering fragrance, and my senses in this moment are heightened tenfold. I can feel, see, and hear everything so clearly, the sensation is too much.

"Let go, baby, this is all for you," he pants, stroking me so deeply, I feel like I'm about to burst.

"No, not before you. Together," I barely manage to reply, his voice enough of a trigger for my close climax to almost erupt.

"I know how I can make you," he answers confidently as he pulls out of me fully then pushes himself back in slowly, caressing my center with skill.

Folding, I pant in pleasure, and in no way do I doubt his expertise. But I'm stubborn, and hold on—only just.

As I open my eyes, I see him gauging my reaction. I know he's stopping himself from totally letting go in fear of hurting me. But I want him to be enjoying this as much as me, so I raise my hips, encouraging him to go faster. He inhales a gulp of air through clenched teeth as we both glide into one another smoothly. The feeling is pure ecstasy, a feeling I never want to end.

Before I can stop myself, the harlot in me whispers, "Go faster," and I coax him with my feet, pressing into his firm behind.

As he lets out a load groan, his body undulating with the sensation, I know my mission has been accomplished.

"Holy shit! Are you trying to kill me?" he gasps, his damp hair sticking to his brow.

"What a way to go," I reply breathlessly, and clench my inner muscles around him tightly.

He closes his eyes in bliss. I can tell by his concentrated breathing and swiftness of his movements that he's close. I was done twenty minutes ago, but looking at his scorching, sultry body, moving above and within me with such passion, I'm glad I waited.

Running my fingernails down his firm stomach, I arch my back, making my intentions loud and clear, and that's all the encouragement he needs as he powers into me with a force so deep, it brings tears to my eyes. All the while, those cerulean eyes are searching mine, ensuring I'm okay.

The deep longing look in his blue eyes and the feel of him inside of me, it's all too much, and I let out a groan which Jasper captures into his mouth while pinning my hands above my head. He undoes me, and I let out a scream of pleasure, and so does he. We explode together—it's incredible.

Now I know why they say, once you've had the orgasm of your life, you see stars. As my breathing slows, with Jasper still inside me, all I can see is his beautiful eyes, and stars. But, maybe if I look close enough, those stars are really hearts in disguise.

Chapter 30
I Love You

The next morning I wake sore, but surprisingly, not hung over.

I'm in bed, and as I reach my arm out, I make a spine tingling connection with the man lying next to me. He's totally naked, the thin sheet twisting around his perfect body. My eyes devour him, and a heavy feeling forms in my chest because I think I'm in love with Jasper.

If I was to pinpoint the exact moment, I couldn't tell you. This isn't like those romance movies V and I used to watch when we were kids, where boy meets girls, they fall in love, and live happily ever after—this is real. This, with Jasper, has been one hell of a journey, and most of the time, it has driven me to the point of insanity, but was it worth it—fuck yes.

Being with Jasper the way we were last night, I never knew it was possible to experience such pleasure. I shiver at the memory of him moving inside me, touching me, bringing me over the edge, and I shamefully want more.

"Why are you thinking so early in the morning?" he asks sleepily, eyes closed.

I wonder how long he's been awake, and suddenly, I'm paranoid that he knows I've been watching him sleep, and contemplating doing all kinds of dirty things to his unconscious form. That's kind of creepy, so I hope not long.

"I'm not," I reply nervously.

He cracks open an eye and I gasp at the color. They're such a deep blue; I could happily drown in them.

"Don't lie. You've never been a very good liar," he replies, his voice hoarse. "Are you okay?" he asks when I remain quiet. "I didn't hurt you last night, did I?"

My cheeks flush at his comment, and he rolls toward me, brushing my hair off my brow.

"Sorry I was a little crazy, but I couldn't stop myself. Seeing you with that asshole, I lost control. I'm sorry, Ava. I shouldn't have spoken to you the way I did. You have every right to be angry at me. Please forgive me," he concludes.

I stare open mouthed because surely he isn't apologizing after blowing my mind with the best orgasm of my life.

"There's nothing to forgive you for, Jasper. If anyone should be apologizing, it should be me. I never should have slapped you, I was out of line. No actions ever condone that violent behavior. Regardless of you being an ass, that still gave me no right to hurt you."

He grins, agreeing with the asshole jab. "I tried to stop myself, but I just couldn't. I was running on auto pilot, and my jealousy got the better of me—again. When I saw that guy with his hands all over you, I lost it. You'll be the death of me," he confesses, running his fingers through his hair nervously.

I, on the other hand, am high fiving myself because this is progress. This honesty between us, it gives me hope that we'll be okay.

"For the record, it wasn't Casey I was thinking about when I was dancing with you," I sheepishly reply.

I completely understand why he reacted the way he did. If I saw him dirty dancing with some random girl, it would be murder on the dance floor.

I snuggle into his chest while he strokes my back and we're both quiet, deep in thought. "Let's just forget about it. Even his name is pissing me off," he spits, and I let out a laugh, liking this jealous side of Jasper.

"So, are you going to tell me what you were thinking?" he murmurs sleepily into my hair.

Taking a deep breath, I know it's now or never. "I was just thinking, does this change…things between us now?" His answer will crush me if it's the wrong one.

He doesn't answer for a long while, and the longer he waits, the louder my hearts beats.

"Of course it changes everything," he whispers. "Last night, baby, it was epic. I've never felt that with anyone before. Ever."

I'm shocked at his admission. Ever? This smile will never be wiped clean.

Jasper senses my happiness and continues. "We now know we rock it physically, as much as we do being friends, so there's only one answer." Please be the right one, please be the right one, I internally beg.

"And that is…" I prompt. A horrible thought weighs me down. What if he still wants to be friends, who occasionally have sex? Oh God, I feel sick. My heart just couldn't handle that.

I'm about to leap off the bed to hide in the bathroom when he grabs my chin. "Look at me." I hesitantly peer at him. "Ava, this changes *everything*. What we shared, it wasn't just sex, it was life changing. You make me feel like a better man. I want to better myself so I'm good enough for you."

I stare wide-eyed, rivaling a deer caught in headlights. "What do you mean *good enough* for me? You're more than good enough," I whisper, touching his cheek.

But he stubbornly shakes his head. "No, I want to be everything for you. When I'm with you, you make me forget about all the shitty stuff in my life. I feel like I've been given a second chance with you." I don't know what to say, and a tear slides down my cheek.

"That wasn't meant to make you cry," he says softly, the concern in his face clear, as he fears he may have said something wrong.

"They're happy tears," I reply, easing his worries by referring to our Christmas conversation.

He licks his lips before kissing me softly, and unlike last night, where we were devouring one another, this kiss is filled with worship for one another. This man plays my body like a finely tuned instrument made especially for him.

He begins his descent down my chest, kissing my breasts and then down my stomach, twirling his tongue in my bellybutton. As he heads further, I stop him, fisting his unruly morning hair, and he groans against my core as I suppress a shiver.

"Before you do…that. I just want to know, um, where we stand." I bite my lip, knowing I have the worst timing.

"You want to do this *now*?" Jasper teases, looking up at me from between my legs, and I nod, working my bottom lip with my teeth.

Still stretched out between my legs with his chin resting on my stomach, he looks up at me with his disheveled bedroom hair and I pat myself on the back that his bedroom hair is *my* doing.

"Ava, I want you, all of you. Not just your perfect body," he says, kissing my hip bones, "but *you*. I want to make you laugh every day, and I want to push you when you don't want to be challenged. I want to grow with you and discover where this crazy path leads us. I want to be the one responsible for your cries of passion every night, and I want to be there to wipe away your tears. I can't stay away from you. I've tried, but it doesn't work. I want to be with you always, baby."

I bite the inside of my cheek to stop myself from being an emotional ball of goo.

Jasper smiles when he sees his answer has soothed my concerns, and huskily asks, "Now, can I finish what I started?"

I nod, because who am I to stand in the way of a man on a mission?

And that's how Jasper and I became a couple. It was that simple. Why I didn't do this months ago remains a mystery. But there's no looking back because I'm so happy. We have spent almost every night together, and the nights we didn't, I missed him terribly. After his shift ended at the shelter, he would crawl into my bed, waking me up with kisses and whispering how much he missed me.

It's so surreal that a man who was so closed off could be this open about his affections. But not everything was smooth sailing. We still fought like crazy, but at least we could engage in a little make up sex after our heated arguments.

We have been 'official' for a little over a month, and it's been the best month of my life. It's been close to ten months since I arrived back home, and I feel like a different person than the one that stepped off that plane. I know I have Jasper to thank for that.

V is happy we've finally worked out our shit, saying it was about time. She and Lucas are also doing fantastic. Life seems to be going well for all of us.

It's Saturday night, and Passengers of Ego are halfway through their set at Little Sisters. Jasper is setting me on fire with his suggestive looks and I want him like always. So, two can play that game.

Sitting on a barstool to the left of the stage, I slowly put the tip of my finger into my mouth and circle it leisurely with my tongue. Jasper can see exactly what I'm doing, and is watching attentively for my next move. As I slip my finger halfway into my mouth, twirling it around suggestively, I see him visibly gulp. But as I place my whole finger into my mouth and suck, he lets out a muted groan, which he quickly covers up by cutting to the chorus of the song he's singing.

He smirks, giving me a sweltering look and I know he's received my message, loud and clear. I blow him a kiss, relishing in this open affection between us.

As they wrap up their set, I can't wait to throw my arms around my man. I'm sitting with V, tapping my foot impatiently, when Lucas walks over and grapples her into a big bear hug. I hear her giggle, but don't pay them too much attention as I'm looking around for Jasper. He's usually not too far from Lucas, but he's nowhere to be seen.

I'm about to interrupt Lucas and V's snogfest to question him on the whereabouts of Jasper, but then I catch sight of the reason for his delay. That reason slaps me in the face—it's Indie.

Why is she here? But more importantly, why is she barreling Jasper into a corner?

Before I can stop myself, I leap off my seat and walk over, purposely standing beside Jasper, staking my claim.

He places an arm around my waist and kisses my cheek. "Hey, baby."

"Hey you, nice show," I reply, leaning into his lips, feeling his stubble abrade my face.

"Nice show, yourself." He smirks, referring to my earlier sexual suggestions.

Indie clears her throat, obviously annoyed that Jasper isn't acknowledging her royal highness.

"Hi, Indie. What are you doing here?" I ask, as I see no point being evasive.

"Well, I'm here because Jasper's mom asked me to talk to him." I stare confused, and it takes a moment for me to process her sentence because I feel like she's just slapped me.

"About what?" I question, looking at them both after finding my voice.

Jasper shrugs while his hands are shoved deep into his pockets. "She's really sick."

Golly, now I feel like both cheeks have been slapped.

"I'm so sorry, Jasper. What happened?" I ask, concerned that the news is dire.

"This is something *private* between Jasper and me," Indie snarls, flicking back her mane.

I'm just about to bite the bitch's head off, but Jasper stops me. "Indie, enough. What you have to say to me now involves Ava, because she's my girlfriend."

Wow, now I feel like I have been KO'd! Girlfriend. He doesn't use that term often, and when he does, I always feel a little giddy. However, judging by the bitter look on Indie's face, giddy is nowhere near what she's feeling right now.

She ignores Jasper and snaps, "Fine, whatever. The doctor found a lump in your mom's breast, Jasper, and it's cancer. The good news is they caught it early so they can cut it out. They say she should be fine, but it looks like she'll lose her breast."

Jasper looks stunned, but not overly glum. I knew his relationship with his mom was strained, but I didn't realize how much so until I see his non-reaction. If I found out my mom had breast cancer, I would be an inconsolable mess on the floor right now.

Then another thought pops into my head—why does Indie know this? I know they grew up together, but seriously, she still keeps in touch with Jasper's mom after she knows what she did to him as a child? Another reason to hate this soulless bitch!

"Jasper, I know you and your mom haven't spoken in a while, but she's really sorry. She's changed. She's a different person now. She wants to rebuild your relationship. I think you owe her that."

Indie is standing all righteous like, with her hand propped on her hip, and I can't bite my tongue. "That doesn't make up for all the shit he had to put up with as a kid. She should have been a different person twenty years ago when her husband was beating up a defenseless child."

Indie glares at me with a death stare, laced with malevolence. "Just because he's currently fucking your brains out doesn't mean you know anything about him or his past."

Not able to stop myself, I angrily shrug off Jasper as he places his hand on my upper arm to stop me from exploding. "Oh, and you know him so well? You're okay being friends with his mom, who was too busy drowning in pills, than being a parent! That doesn't surprise me, though. I mean, I shouldn't expect much from an immoral whore!"

It's game on as Indie and I close the distance between us, ready to go to war. As luck would have it, "The Kill" by 30 Seconds to Mars is the background music for our smackdown.

Sadly, Jasper intervenes, stepping between us before I claw her eyes out. "Hey, enough—both of you! Indie, tell my mom it's going to take a lot more than crocodile tears to forget what a shitty parent she was. And you—" He chuckles at me, while I'm glaring daggers at Indie's stupid Botox face. "Calm the fuck down, Rocky. I'm taking you home before you do something you regret."

I snort. "Oh, believe me, if it has anything to do with taking that bitch down, it won't be something I regret. I'd rather enjoy it!"

Indie's nostrils are flaring in rage. "Try it, tramp. I dare you!"

That's it. I lunge forward because this bitch is going down! This has been a long time coming.

Jasper seizes my arm, all the while chuckling as he's hauling me off in the opposite direction. We glare at each other over Jasper's shoulder, so ready to engage in the biggest showdown with Jasper being our referee.

I attempt to make a mad dash forward, but Jasper is like a brick shithouse, and I'm pushed outside. He stands in front of the door, obstructing my path to retribution. I try desperately to shove past him, needing to slap that smug bitch in the mouth.

"Ava, seriously, stop it." He grins, his dimples revealing his amusement.

I'm glad he finds me entertaining, as I'm about to fly off the handle and smash that handle into Indie's plastic face!

After he finally stops laughing, he says, "Baby, listen to me. I appreciate you getting so fired up, but don't. Indie and my mom can both go to hell. Mom can say she's changed till she's black and blue in the face, but that won't change the fact she deserted us when we needed her the most. I'll never forget that, so you have nothing to worry about."

"I'm not worried, I'm livid. How can she just pretend nothing ever happened?" I yell, still trying to push past him to confront Indie.

He wraps me in his arms to calm me down. It works when I'm engulfed in his smell. "Because that's what she does. When reality is too hard, she copes by going into denial. Now that there's no escaping that reality, she wants to make amends. But it's too late." Jasper is so calm; I realize this is old news to him. This isn't the first time his mom has tried to pull the sympathy card.

"Why the hell does Indie still keep in contact with your mom?" I ask.

"They've always gotten along. Even if we weren't seeing each other at the time, she would keep in touch with Mom," Jasper replies, leaning forward and kissing my neck, no doubt in hopes of reassuring me everything will be okay.

"Just another way to keep her claws firmly embedded into you!" I snarl, shrugging him off.

"Are you jealous?" Jasper laughs.

Damn straight I am, but more so, I'm mad at those two conniving, scheming women. I only scrunch up my face, annoyed.

"Naw, baby, that's sweet," he teases, and I playfully punch him on the arm. "Okay, Bruce Lee, I think you've had enough for one night. I'm taking you home."

~

Jasper is in the bathroom getting ready for bed, but sleep is the last thing on my mind. I'm still fuming from my encounter with Indie, and thinking about Jasper's mom adds fuel to that inferno because deep down, I know Jasper will go see her. That's the kind of person he is, and it's the right thing to do. No matter what she did to him, she's still his mom.

Tearing off my jeans and t-shirt, I slip into bed in my underwear and bra. Jasper turns off the bathroom light and strolls into his bedroom, hands raised in surrender. "You calmed down yet?"

I'm glad someone finds this amusing.

Pulling back the covers, he slips in beside me. "Baby, don't be upset, because I'm not. That mom wound, it's been closed over for a long time." I calm down slightly as he strokes my face, searching my eyes. "But I'm going to go see her. I would be a shitty son if I didn't."

"You're what?" I knew it was coming, but that doesn't make it any easier to digest.

"Ava." He exhales noisily. "Two wrongs don't make a right. Just because she doesn't know the meaning of family doesn't mean I have to stoop to her level. You know I'm right." He is right, but I can't help the irritation brewing.

"I know." I sigh.

"That's it? No fight?" he asks, kissing my shoulder.

"You're right. I don't like it, but you're right. If anything was to happen to your mom, and you didn't go see her, you would never forgive yourself." Jasper pulls me into his chest, my head tucked under his chin.

Then I have an idea and berate myself for not thinking it earlier. "I'll come with you. Probably not the best way to meet your mom, but I can be there for you."

He replies quickly, "I appreciate the sentiment, but you've got school. You can't just take off for a few weeks, midterm."

He's right; I can't afford that much time away, especially with exams approaching.

"Now is probably not the best time to tell you…" he says. I pull out of his embrace, meeting his eyes.

"Just tell me." I sigh, because this night couldn't possibly get any worse.

"Well, Indie will probably be there," he confesses, biting his lip.

"What!" I take it back; my night has just gotten a whole lot worse.

Indie alone with Jasper, consoling him during his mom's recovery and using that as an excuse to offer her boobs as a sympathy pillow, well, there's never a good time for that!

"Ava, look at me." I turn to face him as he places both hands on my cheeks. "You have nothing to worry about, okay? Before you know it, I'll be crawling back into your bed after weeks of missing you like crazy. You won't even notice I'm gone."

"That's unlikely." I sulk against the headboard.

"I have to do this, baby, please tell me you understand," he pleads, his concerned eyes searching mine.

"I do, doesn't mean I have to like it. But I get it. Go see your mom, and I'll be here waiting for you when you get back."

"I won't be gone long, I promise. And besides, you might like being on your own," he teases, but we both know this is going to suck.

"I'm going to miss you," I whisper.

"I'm going to miss you, too. So, we better stop wasting precious time talking."

Jasper begins kissing my neck, trying to push me down, but I remain seated.

"Why? When are you leaving?"

"I was thinking tomorrow night, if I can organize a flight in time."

"Oh," I glumly reply. This conversation just gets more and more depressing.

Jasper senses my despair and kisses my forehead. "Think of it this way, the sooner I leave, the sooner I'll be back."

His positive spin on a shitty situation is really not making me feel any better. I can't help it, I just don't like this. He'll be surrounded by Indie and his mom, and even though I don't know his mom, I just have a feeling nothing good can come out of this. But she *is* his mom, and this is his decision to make, not mine. I'm his girlfriend, so I have to support him, even if I don't like it.

"Come here," he coos.

I shuffle into his lap, wrapping my arms around his neck and burying my nose into his neck. "I like that you're so upset I'm leaving. It means you care that I'll be gone."

"Of course I care. I care a lot," I confess.

Is this conversation going to involve the L Bomb? I don't think I'm ready for that just now.

"Well, I care a lot about you, too." He smiles. "And I know I'm going to be missing you, every hour of every day, until I'm pressed up against you."

Melting at his heartfelt words, I soon realize this will be the last time I'll have him in my bed. So with no time to waste, I press my lips to his and claim him.

Wrapping my legs tightly around his waist, I begin kissing his throat, feeling his pulse quicken under my lips. He groans as I move sensually against his bare chest, his deft fingers quickly reaching around to remove my bra. His hair tickles my chest as he dips low, his lips latching on and entrapping my nipple. How can this feel so new? Every time I'm with Jasper, he makes me feel like it's the first time we have explored each other.

He gently slips his hand between my legs and touches me over my underwear. This feeling is more intense than when there's no material separating us, and as he increases the tempo, I ride his fingers, begging for a release, but Jasper wants to take this slow. As he removes his hand, he laughs at my disappointment, but quickly flips me onto my back, peering up at me from his onslaught of kissing my breasts.

I raise my hips, giving him a silent plea of what I want, but he won't budge. I know it's not due to lack of excitement on his behalf, as his arousal is evident through his boxer shorts. But I can sense Jasper wants to savor this moment, as it'll be the last we'll have for a while.

His teeth lazily drag across my flesh, down my stomach, over my hips, and finally, he kisses me over my underwear. For the love of God, if he doesn't take off my undergarments, I'm going to rip them off!

Reading my frustration, he slips them off my hips and gradually kisses my core. His skillful mouth licks, blows, and sucks at me, and I'm riding an intense wave of pleasure. He adds to that bliss by inserting two fingers while his clever mouth is licking every part of me, up and down, tonguing my center, causing my hips to buck off the bed in pleasure. But he's taunting me, stopping just before I'm about to release.

But finally, with his exceptional mouth and fingers working me in just the right way, I explode, yelling out a string of incoherent curses. However, before I have time to return back to earth, Jasper replaces his hands and mouth with himself and slips into me gently. He waits for my muscles to accept him, as he embeds himself deeply within me. He kisses below my ear and begins his sweet, tortuous onslaught on my body.

"You're my world, Ava." He exhales against my cheek while moving steadily inside me.

I let out yet another pleasurable moan, and Jasper bends down to kiss the hollow in my neck.

He increases the tempo, assaulting my insides with unspeakable pleasure, and I know he's close.

"I'm going to miss you… so much," he says in between glides.

I nod, as I have no coherent words, as I'm on the brink of blacking out with him working me so vigorously.

"Being without you, it's going to kill me," he pants, his hair tickling my cheeks as he bends forward, kissing my neck.

"Me too," I manage to choke out.

"Ava, baby…" he whispers against my throat. "Ava…I love you."

I don't have time to freeze at his confession, because those three simple words have us both detonating in pleasure.

Convulsions overtake my body, and the aftershocks are felt long after Jasper withdraws from me. I don't know if it's his actions, or words that make my release the most powerful I've ever had.

Either way, I don't care, because Jasper White loves me.

Chapter 31
Don't Let Me Go

I awake, shivering in anticipation, as light butterfly kisses are fluttering across my bare back. I'm lying on my tummy, one arm braced by my head and the one buried beneath the pillow. My face is squished, turned to the side, and I can feel a hint of drool dribbling out of the corner of my mouth. How embarrassing.

I dare not open my eyes, as I know the sight before me will tear my heart in two. I vaguely heard Jasper early this morning, organizing a red eye flight, headed for Chicago tonight. If I keep my eyes shut, maybe I can pretend it was all a dream, and Jasper isn't really leaving me.

"Why are you sighing?" I hear Jasper whisper softly against my ear, kissing the outer shell.

Another shiver, this time in pleasure, ripples through me, and a slow smile spreads across my face. How can his voice alone have this affect on me?

His fingertips trace small circles over my arched neck, and then slowly slide down to my shoulder, where he places a light kiss. A breath hitches in my throat as I feel his short fingernails slither down my arm, his fingers sashaying across the crease in my elbow.

All the while, my eyes are still shut, anticipating the next move on his sensual journey of me. I hear him shifting and repositioning himself, and the experience of being blind to him, trusting him, is a heady one.

I wait with bated breath, and am rewarded when my pillow dips slightly. Jasper's scent overwhelms my senses, and I know he's lying near me, as I can feel his warm breath flutter against my cheeks. I will never tire of this feeling, nor will I ever tire from seeing Jasper's angelic face. I open my eyes, because I miss not looking at him. Yeah, this time apart is really going to suck.

As my eyes drink in the sight before me, my breath catches in my throat because Jasper has no shirt on, revealing his hard muscles and sharp contours. The crease between his collarbones is crying out for me to pay it some well deserved attention with my tongue. Peering lower, I lick my lips when I see his abs rippling under my scrutiny. I sigh, slightly disappointed that he's wearing pants.

Scanning back up to his face, I notice his hair looks damp, like he's showered, and I wonder what time it is. I strain my neck to look at the dresser over Jasper's shoulder and it reads 11:37a.m. Holy shit! I've been asleep for over ten hours.

Jasper can read my concern and chuckles. "I didn't want to wake you. You looked so peaceful, and your sleep talking was quite entertaining."

I hide my head in shame as I've been told I do sleep talk, a lot. Suddenly, I feel a blush paint my cheeks as I wonder what escaped my comatose lips.

Jasper reads me like a book and grins, holding his hand up in a scout salute. "I promise, it'll never leave this room."

Oh no, what did I say? Hopefully nothing too embarrassing or incriminating. Speaking of incriminating, Jasper told me he loved me last night. I don't know if it slipped out because he meant it, or because he was lost in the throes of passion. Either way, I can't just blurt it out now.

"I'd give a penny for your thoughts." He smirks as his left dimple is practically punching me in the face with its cuteness.

"Only a penny?" I reply, brushing wisps of hair off his face.

"Yeah, but with the amount of thoughts passing through that brain of yours, my pennies would amount to a small fortune."

He's right. I need to stop overthinking everything. Whether it was Jasper's hormones or heart talking, he still said it, unlike me. I wish I could, because I know I feel it, but… but what, Ava, I question myself.

Jasper's quiet laughter snaps me out of my head. "You're your own worst enemy. Stop overthinking, Ava, and just let life happen. You start dissecting everything, and life becomes pretty boring. So stop overthinking, and start living." Jasper is forever the scholar. I wish I had his confidence.

Before I can question anything further, my tummy belts out a huge, embarrassing grumble. My eyes widen in shock, and I bite my lip, mortified.

Jasper rewards me with a deep, throaty laugh. "*You* may keep me guessing, but your stomach certainly doesn't."

I bite back a giggle and Jasper jumps off the bed, leans down, and offers me his hand. "Come on, grumpy guts, I'll make you breakfast." He looks over at the clock and corrects. "Or should I say, lunch."

~

Breakfast/lunch is perfect. I can tell Jasper is apprehensive cooking for me, afraid I'll be critical of his skills in the kitchen. I dare not admit his cooking skills are the least of my concerns, as he stands barefoot and topless scrambling my eggs. My hunger lies elsewhere, and my scrambled eggs aren't it.

After a pleasant breakfast, I shower and feel a million times better. I left a few girly items at Jasper's, which has come in handy for days like today. Jasper mentioned over breakfast that he's catching a flight later this evening. I try not to pout and behave immaturely, but fail miserably.

Jasper suggests we go on a drive before he leaves, but he won't let me in on where we're going. I'm curious, and I'm also grateful for the distraction. We're heading out of suburbia and deeper into the valley.

Staring out the window and taking in the wilderness, I think about my life, and how I've changed. Is that change for the better? I'd like to think so. I'm trying my hardest to be open in my new relationship, because I owe that to Jasper. The time spent apart taught me a valuable lesson, and I never want to feel that again. Jasper accepts me, flaws and all, and he doesn't push. When he once told me he's my passenger and will follow my lead, he has stuck true to his word. How did I get so lucky?

As his truck tires crunch over gravel, I know we've reached our destination. He has taken me to a beautiful winery, where the vineyards can be seen for miles. Jasper turns to me, sunlight kissing his face, making him appear ethereal. I take a visible breath as he leaves me breathless.

As I notice him fiddling with an unlit cigarette, I ask, "What's wrong?"

He toys with his bottom lip as he replies, "The way you look at me." I mentally slap myself. Was I drooling while undressing him with my eyes?

"I'm sorry?"

He clarifies quickly. "The way you look at me, I've never had anyone look at me that way."

"Are you blind?" I scoff. "Are you totally oblivious to the heads you turn just by walking into a room?"

Jasper shrugs, looking out the window. He's quiet for a long while, and just when I think he's not going to respond, he confesses, "They mean nothing to me, but you do." He pauses before he confesses, "I love you, Ava."

I sit, dumbfounded and incoherent. His words are beautiful and instantly bring tears to my eyes. But I still can't bring myself to replicate his sentiment. What is wrong with me? Am I an emotional mute? I know I feel the same way, so why can't I say it?

Jasper sighs softly. "It's okay, Ava. You'll say it when you're ready, or when you mean it." I attempt to retort, tell him I *do* love him, but actually saying it makes it all the more real. And I'm still scared of getting hurt.

He runs his hands through his messy hair and down his face. "I want you to tell me when it feels right for you. I won't push you. I know Harper hurt you, but trust me. I haven't given you reason not to."

His words unleash a waterfall of unshed tears. How is it he knows me better than myself?

Chapter 32
Gone But Never Forgotten

After a teary goodbye, well, teary on my behalf, I watch Jasper board his place while I gnaw on the inside of my cheek to stop myself from crumbling into an emotional mess. When I can no longer see him, it's only then that I allow myself to break down.

Airports have caused me nothing but heartache, and I decide the next time I'm here to pick up Jasper, I will end that sentiment and associate airports with new discoveries. We don't mention Jasper's declaration of love, and I don't say it back, as I don't want to return something so important just because he said it first.

Jasper assures me before he leaves that time will fly, and he'll be back in my arms before I know it. But I somehow doubt that. If the drive home is any indication of our separation, it's going to be a long, depressing, lonely one. I can't bear going home without him, so I sneak into his house with the spare key he has given me, and spend the night in his bed, comforted by his smell.

~

The next day, I quickly stop by home, collecting my school

books and work clothes.

V is home from work and gives me a comforting hug when she sees me. "You look like you needed that. He'll be back before you know it, and you can pick up where you guys left off."

Her comment saddens me. "I'm really going to miss him. He told me he loved me last night."

V beams at me. "Oh, Ava, I'm so happy for you guys. It's been a rocky road, one I admit I had my doubts about, but seeing you two together, I'm almost jealous."

"Jealous? You and Lucas are meant for one another," I reply, startled by her revelations.

"I know, but what you and Jasper have, that runs deep. Not everyone is blessed with having that kind of connection with another person."

"I don't feel blessed all the time," I joke.

But V goes on. "Everyone has their ups and downs in a relationship, but when you two have your ups, it's like no one else exists. You two are perfect for each other. You're a yin to his yang."

This conversation is not helping the ache in my chest. "I've never felt this way about anyone else, not even Harper. Feelings like this, I think only ever comes once in a lifetime."

V has tears in her eyes. "That's just beautiful. Just remember who stuck by you when you're deciding on baby names."

That strikes a chord with me. Will Jasper and I ever have children? I remember he told me his future with Indie didn't end with a white picket fences and kids. Was he referring to a future with her, or all future relationships? This is something we'll have to discuss. However, before I start planning our wedding and future kids' names, I need to get over this time apart.

Ben and I are currently studying Asian cuisines. This part of the course is a component level to Asian dishes, and I love it. It incorporates serving and evaluating traditional regional dishes of Asia, and the fact I once lived in Singapore, lets me feel like I have an upper hand over my classmates. Although, I wish I knew about their food traditions before I lived there. Of course Harper convinced me not to bother with school, declaring I would never have to work a day with him supporting me.

School is the perfect distraction I desperately need. With all the new subjects we're learning, the Jasper ache has dulled slightly, but never gone.

Today we're learning how to serve up traditional Chinese, when Ben whispers, "You okay about Indie and Jasper going back home together?"

"Yeah, fine," I lie.

"Well, I'm not." Great, this conversation is not one I want to be having with Indie's boyfriend, especially while trying to perfect Peking duck.

"Why not?" I finally give in.

"Because Indie has been distant and seems preoccupied. She was packing a month's worth of clothes, and some were a little *inappropriate* for the occasion."

His comment stops my heart. "What do you mean *inappropriate*?"

"I'm probably just reading into things, but she was packing all this fancy underwear and nightwear. Am I just over-reacting?"

I feel sick because I know Ben is not over-reacting. Indie *is* up to something, and that something is not good.

I merely shrug. "I'm sure you're just overreacting, Ben. You have to trust her."

Ben snorts. "I don't."

"Then why the hell are you with her?" I snap.

"Because deep down, under that tough façade, I know she's a scared, lonely girl, waiting for someone to love her." I stare at him. Is he blind?

When I look at Indie, I most definitely do not see that. I see the queen bitch, ordering her male minions around to please her. I just hope Jasper can see that, too.

Work is a daze, and I have fluffed through my shift with universal replies and greetings to customers without giving away where my mind was. No points guessing where, what, and whom. What was Indie trying to achieve by packing all those barely there garments? Was she hoping a little grief would lead Jasper to cheat on me? I know him better than that, I criticize myself. He told me he loves me, for Pete's sake. That means something, right?

But it's *her* I don't trust. I'm not there to stop her from flaunting her lady parts in his face, and that thought scares me. I need to speak with him to put my silly, overactive mind at ease.

Finally my shift ends and I drive back home, depressed. By 8:30p.m., I have showered, eaten, and attempted to study, but I still haven't heard from Jasper. I'd be a liar if I didn't admit that worries me. I would have called him the second I landed, but I push those insecurities out of my mind and remind myself why he's there. His mom is sick, and he also hasn't seen her in years—they're probably catching up.

Peering at the clock perched on my bedside table, I realize this is normally around the time I would be heading down to the shelter. God, I miss him. V is right, we do have a special connection, and we're damn lucky to have experienced such intensity in our lifetime. The spark was instant and has only grown, as have our affections for one another. I'm miserable and lonely, and decide the only way to get over the next few weeks is to sleep through the majority of it.

My phone startles me out of my daydream, and I answer it without looking who it is.

"Baby, I've missed you."

Goose bumps spread across my body in a matter of seconds as I hear his voice. Because I'm so happy, I trip over the debris littering my bedroom floor as I jump up from the edge of my bed in excitement.

"Hi, how are you? How was your flight? What's the weather

like? I miss you, too." It's so good to hear him laughing at my obvious enthusiasm. How is it possible that that sound disentangles my bitter mood?

"I'm good. The flight was boring, I couldn't wait to land. The weather is typical—windy. How are you?"

"I'm all right, work was boring, but school was fun. We learned a modern twist on the traditional Peking duck in my Asian Food studies, which was cool." Enough with verbal diarrhea, I scold myself, ask him what's important. "How's your mom?"

Jasper is quiet and I hear him sigh quietly. "I'd rather talk about you, and how much you're missing me," he teases, evading my question.

"That bad?" I reply.

Again he sighs. "No, it's not bad, it's just…awkward. I haven't seen her for three years, and she wants to be the perfect family. That just doesn't sit right with me."

I understand his anxiety, as it's going to take a lot for his mom to win him back—if ever. I know this isn't the right time to mention Indie, but it's eating at me. "Where are you staying? Is, um…Indie there?"

"I'm staying at a hotel. Mom wanted me to stay with her and Ross, but I just can't. Indie is here, she's at her mom's."

That's it, he doesn't elaborate. I don't want to make this time about her, but I can't help it. "Will she be with you when your mom goes in for surgery?"

Jasper huffs in exhaustion, or frustration. "I'm not sure, baby. Don't worry about her, okay? I'm just counting down the days till I'm back home, snuggled against that warm, naked body of yours. I miss you so much, and it's only been a day. I'm not sure how I'm going to last another few weeks."

I beam, as it's nice knowing he feels it, too. "I know what you mean. It feels like a piece of me is missing with you gone."

"I know the feeling," he whispers. "But I'll be back soon, and we'll go back to driving one other crazy." I laugh because it's true. Our love is passionate and capricious at the best of times.

"Okay. I wish you were here to kiss me goodnight." I sigh,

fingering my lips.

"Me too… I really didn't anticipate this to be so tough. Ava, I meant what I said…I love you."

There is a lingering silence between us, and declaring my love for him for the first time, over the phone, with him being thousands of miles away, to console his sick mom, was not how I envisioned it, so I stupidly don't say anything at all.

Jasper quickly recovers. "Anyway, I better go and unpack."

I realize my lack of a reply may seem like the feeling is not reciprocal, so I try to make up for my lack of response. "Jasper…"

He cuts me off. "Don't worry about it, Ava, I'm tired. I'll talk to you tomorrow. Miss you." The phone goes dead.

What the hell is wrong with me? Why didn't I just tell him I loved him, too?

Chapter 33
I Miss You

The next few days elapse painfully, and Jasper has called me every day, but we never mention the L bomb. I have tried to subtly drop hints about how I feel, but the time is never right to just blurt out, I love you. When we speak, it's mainly about his mom. She's had the surgery and is doing fine. However, the doctors can't put a timeframe on her recovery period.

Jasper fails to mention when he'll return, and I'm too afraid to ask. So I throw myself into school, trying to ignore a nagging, sinking feeling in the pit of my stomach. Something is off, and I know when I discover what, it'll break me in two. I'm a pessimist by nature, so I disregard this feeling as an overactive imagination.

Ben has constantly asked if I've heard from Jasper, as he hasn't heard a single word from Indie since she left. I don't know what that means, but it makes me apprehensive.

As if my week couldn't get any worse, I'm called into the course coordinator's office for a chat. I have no idea what this is regarding, and I really don't like surprises.

He clears his throat. "Ava, you must be wondering what you're doing here."

"Yes, sir. I hope I haven't done anything wrong."

"Oh no, quite the opposite." I scrunch up my face in confusion. "Judging by the baffled look on your face, it seems you have no idea what this is all about." I only shake my head and shrug my shoulders.

"Ava, your teachers have been very impressed with you since your return. You have a certain flare we look for in a student, and one with exceptional talents like yours are not overlooked. Your teachers are aware of your excellence, and above average grades in your Cuisines of Asia studies. Every year, our school gets given the exciting opportunity for a student exchange. We would like to offer you a scholarship to study at our Singapore campus for a year. In return, a student from their campus will replace you, and vice versa. This is a huge opportunity for you to study and work alongside the best chefs in Asia. We really think you'd do CIA proud, and I hope you'll consider this offer seriously."

I am gobsmacked. This most *definitely* was not the reason I thought I would be sitting opposite Dean Chamberlin today.

Singapore? That place holds so many bad memories for me. Can it really provide me with a new, positive start?

"I know this is a lot to take in, but you have a month to decide. I'll leave all the info with you, and please don't hesitate to contact any of your teachers with questions you may have."

That felt like a dismissal so I stand shakily. "Thank you very much, Mr. Chamberlin, for this wonderful opportunity, which I will think earnestly about."

"Don't take too long, Ava. This is an opportunity of a lifetime. This will promote your name in the culinary world, and provide you with a head start to advance in this tricky, selective industry." He's right, but it's just too much to take in and make an instant decision.

"I know, Mr. Chamberlin, and I'm honored to be considered for such a life changing opportunity. I'll have to read through the information and be in touch." He nods, and I let myself out.

I walk back to class in a state of bewilderment. Is *this* what that bleak feeling was? This fantastic, life altering opportunity? I should be jumping for joy and packing my bags this instant, but I can't. There are so many reasons—my friends, my family, work, Oscar, but most importantly, where does this leave Jasper and I? I can't expect him to uproot to Singapore with me. I made that mistake once, and I won't subject Jasper to the same fate.

Class passes by in a haze, and I can't imagine having to deal with taking mindless coffee orders with this huge decision weighing on me, so I call work, making up some excuse about why I have to miss my shift, and head home in robot mode.

How can something I should be so overjoyed about, make me feel so sick inside? This is something I've been working towards. This is why I enrolled at CIA, to succeed and become a world class chef. But now, that doesn't seem as important to me. My priorities have changed, and I'm afraid to admit that Jasper is the main reason. It would madden him if he knew I was passing up this opportunity because of him. But achieving this without him, it just isn't worth it.

But what if I did accept the offer? What would that mean for Jasper and I? Would he contemplate coming with me? Could I ask that of him? His whole life is here, he's made Los Angeles his home. A real home, where he feels safe. A home away from his horrible childhood memories. I can't expect him to follow me halfway across the globe to chase *my* dreams. I would never do that to him, because I know how that feels, first hand. But could I even return to Singapore without bad memories overwhelming me? I doubt I could succeed in a city that stole a piece of me, as the memories are too cruel. But this *is* my dream, presented to me on the proverbial Singapore platter.

It's my twenty-third birthday in a week's time, and this is the last thing I thought I would be considering before my birthday. I sit on my bed to check my emails. On occasion, Jasper has sent me endearing animated cards, declaring how much I am missed. I could do with one of those today.

My inbox chimes, indicating I have mail. I open it cheerfully, thinking it's from Jasper. I am wrong. I am very, very wrong.

My heart drops, and I feel all the blood rushing from my face.

If I wasn't sitting, I would have fallen into a heap. Clicking the email open, which has no title in the subject line, I read the three little words that shatter my reality into a million tiny fragments.

I MISS YOU...

The sender being the one, and only…Harper Holden.

Chapter 34
I Was the One Worth Leaving

I sit, staring at the screen for an hour.

How did this happen? How did my semi-perfect life go to being a fucked up mess in the span of a week? What does his email mean? He misses me? He's just realized this after all this time apart? Too bad he didn't miss me when he shattered my heart into a million pieces. Too bad he didn't miss me when I had to piece myself back together again. Too bad he didn't miss me when I thought there was no light at the end of the tunnel.

I know Harper, and this email was sent to cause a reaction. So, when I jump up, throwing all the contents of my dresser onto the floor, shattering my perfume bottles and scattering my makeup everywhere. And when I rip all the blankets off my bed, screaming at the top of my lungs, I think it's fair to say this is a normal reaction to receiving such an email from your two-faced ex.

I feel sick inside, and suddenly realize that I'm actually going to be sick. I run to the bathroom, barely making it in time. The feelings of despair and anguish are overwhelming me, and I don't want to go back to the place I was at ten months ago. I've come so far and I can't go back, because I know I won't survive. But I *won't* allow myself to go back there. My Harper story has finished—there will be no sequel.

After splashing some water on my face, I feel less apprehensive, but my stomach is still in knots. My phone jolts me out of my stupor and I run to answer it.

"Hello," I answer breathlessly.

"Hi, baby." I cringe as I hear Jasper's voice.

This isn't the best time to speak to him as my brain is fried, and I really am not prepared to have the Harper conversation with him just yet. *I* can't even wrap my head around it.

"Hello?" he questions as I haven't uttered a word.

"Oh, hey, Jasper," is all I can muster.

That sounded cold, even to my ears. He's going to know something's up, so I try my best to put on a happy voice. "Sorry, you just caught me in the shower." Lame, lame, lame!

"Oh really, so you're all wet and soapy right now, huh?"

I force out a laugh. "Yeah, something like that. What's up?"

Jasper senses my aloofness. "You sure everything's okay? You sound weird. Something happen at school?" Oh yeah, you could say that.

"Nah, just the usual stuff, learning how to fry and chop, you know." Oh my God, I need to stop talking now.

Jasper remains silent, and before I can make amends, he says, "So, V told you?"

A feeling of dread hits me in the guts. "V told me what?" I ask quickly, as I haven't seen V today.

"Oh. I thought you knew, because I figured she had spoken to Lucas."

"No, I haven't spoken to V today. What's going on, Jasper?" My palms are sweating, and I feel another bout of nausea steadily approaching.

He takes a deep breath and there is a long pause before he finally replies, "I'm going to be staying in Chicago… for longer than I expected."

I stare at the debris lining my bedroom from my earlier outburst. I have nothing left to destroy luckily, as Jasper's words have charred my soul.

"Ava, I'm sorry," he says quietly.

"How long?" I ask on a mere whisper.

"I don't know," he replies.

"You don't know?" I question, as that doesn't make any sense. "A month? Two months? Six?" I press, but he remains quiet because he obviously doesn't know the answer.

What the hell has just happened to my life? I feel helpless, like I'm looking at a stranger wearing my face.

"Ava, are you okay? I'm really sorry, baby. Things with Mom, they've been decent, and I feel like we're making progress. I can't leave, not yet. But I *will* be coming home to you, I just don't know when." I'm mute as Jasper continues. "I'm sorry I didn't tell you first. The only reason Lucas found out was he wanted to know if he could book a show, and I had to tell him I'd probably still be in Chicago."

"When's the show?" I ask, rubbing my temples.

"In six weeks," he confesses.

Six weeks? What about his life here? What about me?

"Baby, please say something," Jasper begs.

In reality, I don't know what to say. I have no words to explain how I feel. There is no phrase in any language that could express what I'm feeling.

So, I say the only thing I can without falling apart.

"Okay."

"Okay?" Jasper queries. "You're not okay."

What does he expect me to say? I could jump up and down like a raving lunatic, demanding he return to me like he promised. I could scream at him that being away means missing my birthday. And most importantly, I could cry my heart out that he made such an important decision without talking to me about it first.

I know he'll stay in Chicago for as long as it takes, until he reconciles with his mom. No matter how long that takes, he'll stay with her, and most likely, Indie.

I need to get off the phone, so I spit out quickly, "Jasper, I'm happy things are going well between you and your mom."

"Really? You're okay with this?" Jasper asks me, disbelief in his tone.

When I remain quiet, he replies, "I'll make it up to you, I promise. I just have to do this, it feels important."

I know I'm being selfish. He has every right to do this, but what about us? Am I just supposed to wait for him? What about me and my decisions?

"I understand. You'll be back soon, right?" I whisper.

Jasper is silent, and I don't need any further confirmation that he doesn't know when, or *if* he'll be back.

"Ava, I..." he starts, but I cut him off because I disintegrate into a messy heap.

"I gotta go, sorry. I'm standing in a towel, dripping wet all over the floor. I'll chat later, okay? Bye." I quickly hung up.

I don't give him a chance to explain further, because I'm about to fall to pieces. I crumble to the floor in a heap and sob a cry so profound it hurts my chest. I lie with my cheek pressed to the cold floor, and weep until my tears run dry.

Jasper has made a decision easily enough without talking it over with me first. What does that say about our future together? He was the first thing I thought about when offered my scholarship. But it seems I was the last thing he thought about when he made his decision to stay. It hurts to know that when he made his choice, I was the one worth leaving.

Chapter 35
Happy Birthday to Me

It's my birthday today, but celebrating is the furthest thing from my mind.

Jasper hasn't returned, and since our phone call a week ago, we've been drifting apart. We've spoken about futile topics, and I could feel it was strained on his end, as much as it was on mine. And to make matters worse, I'm no closer to making a decision regarding my scholarship.

So, when V bounces into my room, arms filled with birthday gifts and a birthday cake, I want to throw them out the window.

"Oh, don't look so glum, you're the birthday girl," V says, sitting on the edge of my bed.

"It's my party, and I'll cry if I want to," I chide.

"Oh, quit it. What sort of best friend would I be if I didn't treat my friend to cocktails?"

"You would be the best. V, I'm serious, I'm not going anywhere." I've succeeded in moping around the house for the whole day, as V was supposed to work. She tried, but failed to reschedule her clients. I'm more than happy to lie in my misery and sulk all day.

I haven't replied to Harper, but this morning, I received a

Happy Birthday email from him. I had to rub my eyes, twice, just to make sure my sleep deprivation hadn't clouded my vision. But there it was, bright as day, my ex-boyfriend wishing me a happy birthday, while my current boyfriend has remained unheard from.

I haven't told V about my scholarship, or Harper emailing me. She thinks I'm in such a snooty mood because Jasper isn't here. That's only one of the reasons why.

V shakes me out of my depressing haze by throwing a present at my head. "Ouch!" I yell. "What the hell was that for?"

"To snap you out of this foul mood. I get it, Ava, I really do. What Jasper has done is really shitty, but it's not like he has gone on holiday. He's done this to better himself, to better himself for you. To become a better person and have a happy future with you. He needs to do this for himself."

"I know." I sigh, annoyed.

"Then stop with the sulking, get your ass out of bed, and come party like it's your birthday!" I know this is a losing battle so I throw my hands up in defeat.

V shrieks in excitement. "Were going to have so much fun!" She finally leaves me alone.

Fun. I doubt I even know the meaning of that word anymore. Getting out of bed, I stand in front of the mirror and attempt to brush my hair. I give up after fruitlessly trying to do anything with an untamable beast.

After twenty minutes of blindly dressing, I once again look in the mirror and cringe as I see my sunken eyes, which have shed millions of tears over the past week. The girl whose reflection was on the way to being put back together again has been blown apart. All the kings' horses and all the kings' men couldn't put Ava together again.

With that depressing thought my mantra for the evening, I decide to do something foolish. I open up my laptop and hit reply:

"Thanks, Harper. How are you?"

This is the first form of contact I've had with him for over ten months. What the fuck am I doing?

～

The night is grating on me. V tries everything to make my birthday memorable, but the only memorable thing about tonight will be me not killing someone.

V has invited the boys and a few classmates. It's a small gathering at Little Sisters, but it may as well have been empty, because I'm not paying attention to anyone.

There are a million thoughts going through my head. Should I accept the scholarship? What would that mean for Jasper and I? Is Jasper ever going to come home? Why the hell did I email Harper?

V is trying her best to keep the party going, attributing my unsociable mood to PMS, but I don't care what excuse she comes up with. I'm too tired to care. I'm heartbroken and lost. I excuse myself to go to the bathroom and ignore V when she offers to come with. I feel awful, but I can't fake a smile, not even for my best friend.

As I walk into the bathroom, the air whooshes out of my lungs in astonishment because the last person I expected to see is standing in front of me, applying lipstick in the bathroom mirror.

What the fuck is *she* doing here?

As I stand and stare, dumbfounded, she turns mid-stoke and sneers, "Happy Birthday, Skank."

I'm speechless. We glare at each other in the tiny, suffocating bathroom, and I take a calming breath before I explode. "What the fuck are you doing here?" I snarl between clenched teeth.

Indie laughs. "Currently, I'm applying my favorite shade of lipstick."

"I meant *here*, at my birthday party. I'm pretty sure you weren't on the guest list," I reply angrily.

"What kind of person would I be to miss your birthday celebrations?" Her comment slaps me hard with her obvious implication to Jasper's absence.

I stand horrified. And even worse, I have nothing crass to say. "Well, you're not welcome here. Leave."

Indie tsks me. "Oh, Ava, are you angry because Jasper isn't here? Or are you angry because Jasper chose to stay in Chicago, on your birthday, because he couldn't face you after we fucked like rabbits while he was supposedly tending to his mom?"

The wind rushes from my lungs and I take a deep breath before I pass out. "What?" I utter murderously.

"Oh, you heard me. You're so pathetic. Did you seriously think he was staying in Chicago to try and reconcile with his mom? Surely you're not that stupid. Jasper and I fucked every night, and not once did he think about you. You're old news, babe. I warned you, Jasper will NEVER leave me for you."

I'm dying inside, and I feel my insides curl over and shrivel in despair. I just want to run away and never look back. I just don't understand how Jasper can see any good in her. But I guess there are a lot of things about Jasper I don't understand.

"Oh, poor little lamb," Indie consoles sarcastically. "You didn't really believe he loved you, did you? You're nothing to him. You were just a warm body for him to fuck until he got bored and came running back to me. Came back to a real woman who knows how to satisfy her man. Not some sad, weak loser who couldn't please a man to save her life. You seem to forget, I was Jasper's first. I know *exactly* what he likes, and *how* he likes it."

I have no control over my body, as I walk up to Indie and punch her in the face. I shake my hand, as the pain I feel is blinding, but it's so worth it as I see Indie drop to the floor like a sack of potatoes. Her lip is busted open and blood is pouring out of the wound while she's tonguing it, her eyes wide open in shock. How does she like her favorite shade of lipstick now?

She looks up at me with such hatred, but the feeling is more than mutual. "Shut your filthy mouth. You two deserve one another." I storm out before I kick her while she's down.

I see nothing in my path but the exit. I need to get the fuck out of here before I suffocate. V chases after me, but I don't listen when she yells desperately for me to stop. I break into a fast pace, tears blinding me. I need to get away from everyone.

I hail a cab and direct him home, where I go back into the bathroom and start round two.

~

Once inside, I kick off my shoes and head into the sanctuary of my room. My phone is beeping, indicating I have a text message. Looking at the screen, I see seven missed calls, a voicemail, and numerous text messages from Jasper. I listen to the voicemail of his futile apology for why he hasn't contacted me sooner, and he'll call me later. Fuck later, I fume, and dial his number.

"Hey, baby, happy..."

Before he can continue, I yell, "Did you fuck Indie?"

I can hear the horror in his voice. "What? NO! Of course I didn't. Why would you ask me that?"

"Because I just had an interesting conversation with her. She told me the real reason you're still in Chicago."

"She did? Please explain, as I'm pretty certain this is news to me," Jasper asks me calmly.

"Oh, stop with the act, Jasper! She told me how you guys fucked like rabbits when she was in Chicago. She was your first sexual experience, so of course she knows all about your sexual preferences, which she not so subtly threw in my face. That's the real reason you're not here, isn't it?" I'm out of control and my temper is flaring.

"Are you serious, Ava? You *believe* her?" Jasper now has an edge to his voice. He sounds horrified that I would trust her.

"Well, what am I supposed to believe?" I ask, dropping to the floor in defeat, because somehow, I know he's telling me the truth.

"You're meant to believe me because I'm telling you the truth. Nothing happened between us. Period. How could you believe her? I've told you there's nothing between us, and never will be ever again."

I question myself, why *do* I believe her? She has never been honest in the past, so why should I believe a single word that comes out of her deceitful mouth?

I know the answer. Deep down, I *want* that to be the reason why Jasper isn't here. Not because he chose to stay with his mom. Not because he made a decision that resulted in me being second best.

Indie is right, I am pathetic. I've let another male rule my life. I've lost myself once again for love. And for what? This pain hurts even worse the second time around. When will I stop being second best?

Suddenly, a revelation hits me like I'm the one being punched in the face. I'm going to accept the scholarship. I'm going to put myself first, because no one else will.

"Jasper, I'm going back to Singapore. I've been offered a scholarship at the CIA Singapore Campus. I leave in a month." I feel like a boulder has been lifted off my shoulders, and I can finally breathe for the first time in forever.

"What?" he asks, clearly confused by my bi-polar.

"I have accepted a scholarship. I leave for Singapore on the fifteenth of next month." He doesn't need to know the details aren't quite cemented, because there's no turning back.

"For how long?" he asks.

"A year," I reply, and I hear him suck in a mouthful of air.

"A year? Singapore? When were you going to tell me this?" Jasper is surprised, and I know right about now, he's pulling his hair into disarray, like he usually does when shaken.

"When you decided to come home." I know it's a low blow, as the circumstances why he's away are dire, but I can't help it.

I believe nothing happened between Indie and him. I would know if he was lying to me, but that doesn't change my decision. This wasn't about Indie and Jasper, or even about Jasper and I. This was all about me. I needed something like this to happen for me to finally make a decision.

"You're going back to…him, aren't you?" he says sadly. I dare not tell him I've heard from Harper, because he has nothing to do with my decision.

"Don't be ridiculous. This is for me, Jasper. This is an

opportunity I can't pass up. This is my future."

"I thought I was your future," he says, and I bite my cheek to stop my tears.

"Well, I thought I was your future too, but then you decided to stay in Chicago."

"I am not *staying* in Chicago. I'm coming home to you. I'm doing this, all of this, for you. I'm trying to fix my fucked up past so I can move forward, onto a better, happy future…with you. I never knew what it was like to be in a normal relationship, but then I met you, and all of a sudden I have all these feelings trapped in my chest, and it's hard to breathe. I don't know how to deal with all these emotions, Ava. Forgive me for doing you wrong."

It takes all my willpower not to break down, because I know he's spilling his heart out to me, to explain why he chose to stay in Chicago. But it's not going to change my mind.

"It's too late. I've made my decision."

"So, you're leaving me because I wanted to reconcile with my mom? You're punishing me by moving to another country? Am I that horrible to want that with my mom?" I can hear the break in his voice.

"I'm not leaving because you wanted to make things right with your mom. I'm leaving because just like you, I have to do this to better myself. I can't move forward if I'm stuck in the past. I am so tired of being weak and scared all the time. Don't you see? I'm doing the same thing I did with Harper. I'm relying on you to complete me. I'm so lost, and I need to find out who I am."

"Then let me be your compass," he whispers. "Please don't leave me."

My heart breaks and I hold back my tears. "I'm not leaving you. You could come with me…" Even as I say the words, I know the answer.

"And what, follow you to another country like a lost puppy dog? That didn't seem to work out that well for you. How could you ask that of me?" He's right, I'm being a big, fat hypocrite, but I can't take back my decision, because for once, it feels like the right one.

"I know, Jasper. I just… I have to do this. I understood why you chose to stay in Chicago, so now please, try to understand mine."

"Circumstances are a lot different, Ava. I'm not moving away to another country for a fucking year!"

"I'm sorry." It's the best I can come up with without breaking apart.

Jasper has every right to be angry at me, but I have to do this for myself, just like he did what he had to for himself.

"So, this is it? This is over between us? After everything we've gone through, you're just going to throw it away? This is fucking bullshit! I'm coming home right now!"

"NO!" I yell. I know if I see him, I'll change my mind. I'll look into those eyes and I won't leave.

"You don't want me to come?" he asks apprehensively.

After a long pause, I whisper, "No…This is for the best, Jasper. We always knew this was headed for tragedy."

"Bull fucking shit! You're just afraid. You're so afraid of being hurt again, to love again. You can't even tell me you love me. *Do* you love me?"

I feel my mouth dry up.

"Answer me."

"It's not that simple," I reply quietly.

"Yes, it is. You're the one who told me relationships are black and white."

"Well, you're the one who told me they aren't," I retort quickly, referring to the conversation we had all those months ago in my living room.

"That was before I met you. I want you, Ava, with all my heart. Can you say the same thing about me? Be honest with me, but more importantly, be honest with yourself. Why are you so afraid of allowing yourself to love me? I'm prepared to fight for you, for us… are you?" He questions me without hope.

I ponder the question, am I? Can I really risk everything for this turbulent relationship? But Jasper is wrong, I'm not afraid of loving him, I'm afraid of loving him *too* much, and losing myself like I did with Harper.

"Tell me you love me, please." But I don't answer him, I can't.

"Fine. You know what? Fuck it. You can't even tell me you love me, and you're not prepared to fight for us, so why the hell am I wasting my time? Happy fucking birthday! Goodbye, Ava." The line goes dead, along with my heart.

The sob I've been holding onto bursts out of me and I cry a mass of tears. How can a decision I should be celebrating all of a sudden feel so wrong?

Chapter 36
Don't Call Me Bunny

After our phone call, I lock my door and don't emerge for three days. I leave the curtains drawn, turn off my phone, and welcome sleep.

V knocks incessantly, yells at me, curses me out using some creative language, threatens and bribes me, but eventually, she understands—I'm not coming out. She leaves meals by my bedroom door and sits and talks to me through the walls. But I never talk back because I'm in and out of consciousness. I'm drowning in regrets, asleep *or* awake.

Finally after three days I surface, and when I glance at my reflection, I burst into tears. I shower and dress in mismatching clothes, not even aware of the time. The curtains that are still drawn have made my world permanently night, a reflection of how I'm feeling.

As I stomp down the stairs, V drops her phone when she sees me. I must look like hell to cause a reaction like that. Good to know my appearance matches my mood. V quickly retrieves her phone, while I peer into the fridge for something to tweak my appetite. Nothing does, so I settle on cereal.

I sit at the kitchen counter while I listen to V apologizing to whoever she was chatting with, then she hangs up. I can feel her eyes watching me closely, like I'll flee if she says the wrong things. We sit silently for a few minutes, and I robotically stuff my face, not wanting to talk. Every spoonful I take is readily replaced by two more, and I'm gagging on cereal and grief by the time V quickly runs over to me, pushing the bowl away from me before I choke.

"Ava, stop. Sssh. Sssh," she coos, while I burst into tears.

I can barely breathe. V guides me to the sink where I throw up. She holds back my hair while I vomit till I have nothing left to give. I'm shaking in despair, and a flood of tears break the flood gates. V lets me cry till shudders vibrate throughout my body and I nearly collapse onto the floor.

"Ava, stop this. Please talk to me. You're making yourself sick." I can hear the fear in her voice.

Wiping my runny nose on my sleeve, I take a few calming breaths. I brace myself over the sink, afraid I'm going to be sick again.

"We broke up," I whisper, feeling my stomach drop yet again.

"Oh, honey, why? What happened?"

"It's all my fault, V. What is wrong with me? How do I keep fucking it up?" A sob breaks free and I lean my head against the edge of the sink.

"Can't you just call him? Talk things through?"

"No, I hurt him…again. He'll never forgive me." I can scarcely breathe.

"What did you say that's so bad?"

Looking at her, I shake my head slowly. "I can't take back the words I never said." I sob hysterically.

V gets it. She understands my insecurities have gotten the better of me—again.

"Oh, Ava, you'll sort it out." V is trying her best to console me, but I'm inconsolable.

"No, we really won't."

The realization hits me hard, and the thought of never seeing Jasper ever again, never touching him, never telling him that I love him, drags me down, and the last thing I remember before my limp body hits the floor are his heartbroken words.

"Tell me you love me, please."

~

"I'm so pleased you've accepted, Ms. Thompson." Mr. Chamberlin smiles at me.

"Thank you, Mr. Chamberlin, for such an exciting opportunity. I'm honored, and hope to do CIA proud," I say, reciting my practiced speech. I feel like a phony. When I made this decision, it felt like the right one. Now, I'm not so sure.

I haven't spoken to Jasper since our heated argument, and I can't gather the courage to contact him. I wish I could take it all back, but I know I can't. Jasper deserves better than me. I'm emotionally damaged goods forever.

I leave in three weeks, which suits me just fine, as the sooner, the better. But I haven't even told my parents yet. Or V. When did my life get so complicated? I decide there's no time like the present and drive to my parents' house.

As I walk up the driveway of my childhood home, I realize, this will probably be the last time in a long time I'll be here.

My mom opens the doors. "Oh, Ava. What a lovely surprise! Come in." I walk into her arms and rest my cheek on her shoulder. "Honey? What's wrong?" It's obviously a mother's intuition to know when her offspring is a crumbling mess.

Walking inside, I collapse on the sofa and confess, "I'm going back to Singapore, Mom. CIA has offered me a one year scholarship, and I accepted. I leave in three weeks." That wasn't so bad after I eventually got it out.

"Oh, honey, this is fantastic news!" She must see my depressed reaction, because she asks, "Isn't it?"

"Yes, Mom, it's a great opportunity," I say, tears stinging my eyes.

"It's Jasper, isn't it?" she asks, but she knows the answer.

The mere mention of his name depresses me further, and I

begin to cry.

"We broke up, Mom, and all because I'm too afraid of being hurt again. He wants to fight for us, but I don't know what I want. But if I don't go, Mom, I'll never forgive myself, and I don't want Jasper to be the reason I pass up this opportunity. Because I know if I do, I'll end up resenting him—but without him, it just feels pointless."

My mom sits down next to me, pulling me into her arms.

"Honey, you really love him, don't you?"

I nod. "I really do, but I can't even tell him. I'm so afraid of losing myself in another relationship. I won't do that to myself again."

My mother concurs, like she knew all along that Harper and I were destined for disaster. "What do I do?" I plead like I'm five years old again.

"Honey, you're a smart, intelligent, beautiful girl, far wiser than a twenty-three-year-old should be. Listen to your heart, honey, because in the end, if your heart isn't 100% committed to your decision, you'll come to regret it." She makes it sound so simple: Listen to my heart.

My heart at the moment isn't telling me anything, as it's in denial, not wanting to be held liable for any decision it has to make. My heart has retired, and is beyond repair. But is that because Jasper and I have broken up, or is it because I know the decision I have made, although painful, is the right one?

I'm so confused. I feel adrift. I need a beacon of light to guide me through this dark tunnel of uncertainty.

"You'll figure it out. I know you'll make the right choice. Whatever that may be, your father and I support you all the way. We're so proud of you, Ava. You've got a big heart, use it to steer yourself in the right direction."

How can I possibly have more tears? Then I understand. Tears of surrender. As I lay my head in my mother's lap, I know I've made my choice.

I just hope it's the right one.

After talking to Mom about Singapore, I feel better. I feel a little more settled that the choice I've made is the right one. It's right for me, and that's important.

In a slightly better mood, I head upstairs to check my emails. My mood spoils when I see a new email from Harper sitting in my inbox.

I open it:

> *Hi bunny, I'm so happy you replied. I know I don't deserve your forgiveness, nor would I expect it from you. I was such an idiot for letting you go. You can't imagine how I wish I could take that back. Every day I mourn you. I miss you. I want you back, Ava, and I'll do anything to make things right between us. Please give me a second chance. I'm sorry.*
> *Yours forever, Harper xx*

What the hell? I check through the email for fear that I've misread it, but it reads the same every time.

I was not expecting this. He wants me back? I must be living in a parallel universe, because this Harper, this apologizing Harper, is not the Harper I know. What does this mean? I can't overthink things. I've decided to be impulsive and courageous, so I reply without a second thought.

> *Harper,*
> *I'm not your 'bunny' anymore. You gave up the right to call me such endearments when you broke up with me so tactfully (not)... I'm not the same person I was 11 months ago, Harper. I've changed, and*

> that change is for the better. I'm not the lost, voiceless Ava I once was, and I have you to thank. I'm not sorry you broke it off, I'm grateful because I found myself, the real me. As for second chances, I doubt that'll happen in this lifetime, but I can try for friendship. I have been offered a scholarship to CIA Singapore, which I have accepted. I leave in 3 weeks. Maybe I'll catch you around sometime.
> A

So, this is what closure feels like. Why do I still feel so numb?

~

Over the next few days, Harper and I exchange emails. It isn't as awkward as I once imagined it would be. We obviously can be civil to one another, on the basis however, that he understands nothing romantic will *ever* happen between us ever again. I have made that fact quite clear during our correspondence, and surprisingly, he's accepting my terms.

Maybe there is such a thing as turning over a new leaf. Either way, new leaf, tree, or forest, I'm keeping my wits about Harper, as I know he has the ability to sweet talk the devil!

We keep things light, old friends catching up. Harper has been promoted by his company to manage a smaller firm just outside the Singapore CBD—looks like he's achieving his dreams of working his way up the corporate ladder. He has moved to a bigger condo, which he gave me directions to, just in case I wanted to catch up when I get there. I write them out onto a scrap piece of paper and hide it in my CIA Singapore information folder out of sight from V's prying eyes, who is still in the dark about me moving. I don't know if I'll ever go see Harper, but I write down the details, anyway.

He has a dog named Charlie to keep him company, which I'm

presuming is to make up for no girlfriend, as there's no mention of one. I tell him about my life, school, work at The Bean Bag, but I never divulge I have fallen head over heels in love, which recently ended in a fiery ball of pain.

Speaking of the fiery ball, I still haven't heard from him. It's been over two weeks, and this hollowness is still as brutal as ever. I ask V not so subtly if Lucas has heard from Jasper. She said Jasper called Lucas to let him know he doesn't know when, or if he'll return to L.A. I know the reason for his indecision: me.

As the days drag on, my ache to contact Jasper becomes excruciating. I attempt to call him at least a dozen times, but chicken out. How do I make him understand how sorry I am? How I fucked up? I want to beg him to give me another chance. But how can I ask that, when I'm leaving in a week's time?

I know what I have to do, because I don't want it to be goodbye, I want it to be hello. Hello to a new beginning for us… together. I don't know if he would even consider a long distance relationship, but I have to try. It's better than the alternative.

I'm not naïve, and I know it's harder for the person staying behind than the one leaving, but I have to tell him. I was wrong not to fight for Jasper. He has given me everything, and I've done nothing but give him a half-assed attempt at love. This time apart, no matter how angry I've been, has shown me that I want Jasper in my life.

Jasper offered to be my compass when I was lost, and now I want to be his—directly to me. I'll tell him everything once and for all. My doubts, fears, hesitations, everything he needs to hear to give me a second, or rather, third chance.

But most importantly, I'll tell him what I should have told him a long time ago, that I love him. That he helped me heal when I thought I would never mend. That he showed me what strength and commitment was between two people. That he is everything to me, and I can't bear to go on if we don't give this another chance.

No holding back this time, we're in this together: mind, heart, body and soul.

~

I have to go to the mall to get a few things for my trip, which is a good distraction to keep me busy. While out shopping, I bump into Ben.

"Hey, Ava. Did you want to grab a coffee? Be good to catch up before you leave your partner for bigger and better things," he jokes.

I haven't spoken to Ben outside of class after I punched Indie, but he doesn't seem to hold any grudges, so I agree. We grab our coffees and head to a booth.

"So, you got much shopping left to do?" Ben asks, nodding to my shopping bags.

"Nope, all done. I seem to forget there will be shops where I'm going." I laugh nervously, as you could cut the tension with a knife. Suddenly, I'm ready to do the cutting. "Ben, I'm sorry I hit your girlfriend, but she totally deserved it."

There, I have addressed the big elephant in the room, or in Indie's case, the big cow.

Ben lets out a relieved breath. "Thank fuck you said something. I was too chicken, and didn't know how to bring it up. I know she deserved it, Ava. Indie is a heartless bitch. I'm glad you smacked her one, as I don't believe in hitting girls."

This is news to me. "Then why are you with her?"

"I'm not. We broke up after she came back from Chicago."

"Why?" I'm going to regret this answer.

"Because she's in love with somebody else." He looks at me sadly.

"Yeah, herself," I retort angrily.

Ben chuckles. "That, too. I'm better than being second best, or in Indie's case, third best. I'll never be him."

By him, I know he's referring to Jasper. "You're better off without her, Ben. Indie is a resentful, selfish person, who will end up a lonely, bitter old lady when her looks fade."

"You're right. I'm sorry about you and Jasper."

"How do you know about that?" He doesn't need to answer, I know the how is actually a *who*. That bitch needs to leave Jasper alone. I get they're childhood friends, but it's about time he gets new ones.

It's nice to clear the air between Ben and myself and I'm actually having a pleasant afternoon, well, that is until my phone chimes with a new text message.

It's from V.

I stare at her message confused. It's a photo of the piece of paper I wrote Harper's address on. Under the photo reads the caption:

CARE TO EXPLAIN?!?

Why does V have that?

As I search frantically through my bag, my fears are confirmed. The piece of paper must have fallen out of my bag accidentally.

Fuck!

Chapter 37
Love Isn't Enough

I speed home because I desperately need to talk to V. This isn't the way I wanted to break the news to her, but I have no choice. Running up the front stair, I barge into the living room and see her sitting on the sofa. She holds the corner of the paper between her thumb and forefinger, like it's an offensive object.

"Talk!" is all she says.

I sit down near her, turning my body so I'm facing her. "I'm sorry, V. I was going to tell you, I promise, I just didn't know how." I'm beyond ashamed. Not knowing how to tell my best friend, practically sister, life alerting news is inexcusable.

"Are you fucking serious, Ava? How 'bout, hey V, guess what? I got offered a scholarship to Singapore." I then realize the piece of paper with Harper's directions had my Singapore schedule on it also. I'm a shitty friend. How have I fucked up with so many people I love?

"I know, you're right. I'm sorry. It sounds so simple, but it wasn't an easy decision to make. I wanted to be sure it was the right one before I told you."

"But it was okay to tell Harper before your best friend?" Oh crap, I should have seen that coming.

"No, it wasn't like that." Wasn't it, though? I had no difficulty letting my ex-boyfriend know about the scholarship. I didn't even think twice about it. But with V, I avoided the topic like an outbreak of cholera.

"Ava, talk to me! What the hell is going on with you? Ever since Jasper left for Chicago, you've become a shadow of your former self. Now that you two have broken up, you're a ghost. You're here, but you may as well not be. I don't even know what exactly happened between you and Jasper. You're both moping, sad sacks of shit. I don't understand why the hell you don't talk to one another!"

I cock my head and ask, "How do you know Jasper is moping?"

V looks at me, puzzled. "Because I saw him the other day, being all sulky."

"He's back in L.A.? When?" I demand softly. My heart crumbles.

"You didn't know?" V questions. I shake my head. "Oh shit. I'm sorry, I really didn't know. I thought you knew. He's been back like, three days."

Three days, I whisper to myself, that's a long time for him to be home without telling me. I feel lifeless and frozen inside. So, it really is over. If he wanted to work something out with me, he would have contacted me, but he hasn't. My futile attempt at maybe patching things up with him is crushed. I have no reason to try anymore, as it seems he doesn't want to talk to me. I've really fucked up this time.

"Ava, look at me. Talk to me, please." I look up at V, my lip trembling in anguish.

"I fucked up with Jasper. I thought I could make things right, but I don't think he'll ever forgive me."

"What did you do that's so bad? What did you say to him?" V begs for an explanation.

"It's what I *didn't* say, V. He's been honest and given himself to me completely, but I haven't done the same. I don't deserve him. He says he wants to better his relationship with his mom to better himself for me, but he's so wrong. I have to better *myself* to become a better woman for *him*. I overreacted when he told me he was staying in Chicago, I just felt like he wasn't thinking of me when he made his decision. The decision to go to Singapore was made easier because of that, but that's not the main reason. The main reason is because I'm so scared. The feelings I have for Jasper, I can't—" I sob. "I can't get my heart broken again. It's safer not to feel anything, than the pain of losing him."

"Why do you think you'll lose him? He's crazy about you. Anyone can see that," V says, encouraging me.

"I thought I'd never lose Harper, and look how that turned out. My heart got broken beyond repair, and I couldn't bear to live through that with Jasper. I can't stand another heartbreak. I'm scared if I give him a real chance, he'll leave me, or we'll fuck it up like we have in the past."

"Jasper is not Harper, Ava. Give him some credit. He loves you. He really loves you."

"V, sometimes, love isn't enough," I reply, disheartened.

"So that's it? You're just going to run away to Singapore? To Harper?"

"I'm not running to Harper! Harper and I may be living in the same city, but we may as well be living universes apart. There's only person that will hold my heart, and I'm too afraid to give him ALL of it. He deserves better than that."

"Tell Jasper how you feel. He needs to know. Let him be the one to make that choice, don't make it for him."

But I can't face Jasper, now or ever. I'm going to Singapore, and this will all be over with.

I can cry myself to sleep in a new city.

~

Time speeds up closer to my departure, and I can't believe it's my last day in L.A. I've had a going away dinner with my parents and am looking forward to some well-deserved rest before my grueling flight tomorrow.

Ever since my talk with V, she has laid off about the whole Jasper thing, but keeps dropping not so subtle suggestions that I should contact him. As always, my answer is no.

I have accepted that this is for the best. A long distance relationship would never work. Jasper is a physical person, and I think the distance without sex would kill him. And that's only the physical side of things. Emotionally, we can't even function when we live in the same state, let alone a different country.

I'm all packed and V has promised me a movie night with ice cream and lots of chocolate. I'm going to miss her like crazy, but we promise to visit to each other, and I'll be back for the holidays.

V and I are sitting on the sofa, deciding what to watch. It's between two soppy, cry your heart out movies, and I like both. This way, I can blame the storyline for my sudden emotional meltdown, not a certain cerulean-eyed boy.

V is in the kitchen preparing the popcorn when my phone beeps, indicating a new text message. It must be from one of my classmates wishing me luck. I reach for my glass and iPhone off the coffee table in front of me.

My heart almost bursts from my chest when I find out who the text message is from. I begin trembling uncontrollably. I drop my glass, it shatters into a million tiny fragments, along with my heart.

V comes running into the living room when she hears the commotion. "Ava, are you all right?" She's at my side in seconds, trying to make sense of my catatonic state. "Ava…what?" she asks when I don't respond.

My hand is over my mouth and my eyes are huge. I shakily hand her my phone so she can read the cause for my reaction. She looks at the message, confused.

All it says is:

I surrender.

The sender is Jasper.

Chapter 38
One More Step Toward Regret

"What the hell does 'I surrender' mean?" V asks, waving the phone in my face.

Still semi-catatonic, I reply, "I don't know. He's said it once before, I thought it had a double meaning then, but now... I have no idea."

"Go to him," V says.

"What? Now? I can't just go there."

"Why not?"

"Because he doesn't want to see me, V," I explain.

"Judging by that message, it sounds like he very much wants to see you."

I'm not so sure, as Jasper is being ambiguous, like always. What does he mean by 'he surrenders?' Surrenders to what? This is so typical. I shouldn't expect anything less than a vague goodbye message. Biting my lip apprehensively, I wonder, should I go? Is V right?

All of a sudden, I'm sick of being afraid. I'm sick of what ifs. I need to know, once and for all, if this is really the end for us. If it is, then it'll kill me every day for the rest of my life, but at least I'll know.

Jumping up, I grab my bag and smile bravely at V. "Fuck it! I've got nothing left to lose."

~

The car ride is agonizing. I can't sit still.

I'm getting every red light, and I randomly notice I have mismatched socks, with no shoes on. I was in such a hurry, I just bolted out the door, without any thought to my attire. I must remember to take off my socks before I confront Jasper, as having a discussion with one red sock and one pink sock may look like I've totally lost it—not that I'm far off.

As I pull into his driveway, I quickly switch my headlights off, as I don't want him to know I'm here just yet. I need to prepare myself for whatever Jasper and I say to one another. I practice every speech I have ever rehearsed suitable for this situation. And even though I've practiced them a million times in my head, now they just sound lame.

Collecting all the courage I have left in me, I get out of the car and then quickly jump back in, shutting and locking the door behind me. The locked door provides zero comfort and won't avert the inevitable.

Telling myself to stop being such a coward, I muster all the guts I can and walk to his front door. With my hand braced ready to knock, I suddenly hear heated voices coming from inside. I stop to listen and overhear muffled talking, but can't make out what's being said.

One voice is definitely Jasper's, the other is a female, but I'm not certain who. If I stand around the side and peer in, I can see who Jasper is talking to, so I quietly walk to the window, trying my hardest not to feel like a peeping tom, but failing. I'm too short to see in, so I step up on my tippy toes, hoping to get a clearer picture.

Jasper is talking animatedly to someone, and my breath hitches in my throat when I see him. After not seeing him for so long, he looks like an angelic vision sent straight from hell with his sexy, devilish looks. He's wearing his usual snug black jeans, combat boots and a grey t-shirt, which he's cut the sleeves off, displaying his impressive arms.

I can't see the other person, as she's obscured by the bookcase, so I wait anxiously to see if the mystery woman will make an appearance. Finally when she does, I really wish I hadn't been so eager to find out.

As a curtain of long blonde comes into view, I know who this is, but when she turns around, my stomach drops. It's Indie. I can't make out what they're saying, but I can see she's pouting and closing the distance between them. Jasper is holding his hands up—in defeat? Is this what he meant by I surrender? I watch anxiously, my palms sweating profusely as the scene plays out.

Indie stops inches away from Jasper, who looks torn as he turns his head to the side, away from her malevolent lips. But she stops his retreat by securing his chin firmly, and slowly licks her lips before kissing him violently. I can't watch anymore and pull away from the window, nauseous as I stumble backwards.

I have to get out of here. This was a big mistake, and I was SO stupid to think Jasper wanted to reunite. He only wants to reunite with Indie's genitals!

I storm off as silently as I can. Considering what I just witnessed, I'm surprised I'm not burning down the neighborhood.

With angry tears brimming over my lashes, I rip the bracelet Jasper gave me for Christmas off my wrist and throw it into the dirt, where he and it belong.

~

As I explode into my house, V jumps up, startled. Looking at my muddy socks, tear-stained face and frenzied hair, she runs over to me. "What happened?"

"Indie happened!" I seethe, feeling like I need a shower to wash this feeling of despair off my body.

"Again with this bitch! I'm so sick of this tramp!" V snaps, throwing the remote on the sofa and standing up in a frenzy.

"You and me both! Too bad Jasper can't keep his lips off her filthy mouth!" I yell.

"He didn't?" V asks, mortified.

"Yeah, he did. I sadly witnessed the debacle with my own two eyes!"

V looks sympathetic and mad. "What the hell is wrong with him?"

"I have no idea, but that's not my problem anymore. Goodbye, L.A. Hello, Singapore! I can't get out of this city fast enough!"

V gives me a half smile. "I'm sorry, this is my fault. I shouldn't have encouraged you to go over there."

"Please, I'm glad I did! It was exactly what I needed to get over that jerk. If I never see Jasper White ever again, it'll be too soon!" I yell loud enough for the whole neighborhood to hear.

As the doorbell chimes, V and I look at each other, confused. Neither of us are expecting any visitors. Storming over to the door, I curse the irony of the world—it's Jasper.

Chapter 39
Set Me Free

"I'm sorry to disappoint you," he says, lowering his eyes.

I instantly slam the door in his face and run up the stairs to my room, locking the door. This will keep him out; however, it sadly won't keep my tears under lock and key.

Sobbing into my pillow, I can hear his heavy footsteps ascend the stairs. Go away. Go away, I beg silently.

"Ava, I'm sorry," he whispers, the ache in his voice clearly evident.

But I can't reply. I'm too scared I'll either cry or scream.

"I know you were at my house. I saw your bracelet on the ground when I threw Indie out on her ass."

"Was that before, or *after* you fucked her ass?" I spit in rage.

"I'm so sick of having this conversation with you. You know I would never do that." His voice is muffled through the door, but I can hear his anguish.

"Do I?" I roar.

"Yes, you do. If you had stayed around long enough, you would have seen me tell her to get the fuck out of my house," Jasper replies, clearly beaten. He sounds how I feel. "Please, just open the door. I need to talk to you, face to face."

"No."

"Please, Ava," he begs. "I need to talk to you."

"Then start talking!" I shout.

He didn't seem too desperate to talk to me when he got back from Chicago. I sit up on my bed so I can hear him clearer. However, when I'm only confronted with silence, I fear he may have gone.

After a moment of pause, I hear a sliding down my door, and a, thump…thump… thump.

I believe Jasper has slid down the door, sitting on the floor, banging his head in defeat against my door. Shuffling up on my knees, I look at the thin door separating me from the love of my life.

"Ava…I'm sorry. I'm sorry for everything. If I could take everything back, everything that has happened between us, I would. I promised to be a better man for you, but I have done nothing but fuck everything up." I listen with care to his crushed words.

"I should never have stayed in Chicago without talking to you first. I was just grateful that my mom and I were talking. It was selfish of me. I never considered how that would make you feel, and for that, I'm sorry. I'm sorry for confusing you with my erratic behavior, that wasn't fair on you. I just… I just have never felt this way about anyone. I know you're scared, Ava, but I am, too. I have never felt this connection with anyone, and I don't know how to react. What I feel for you, it's burning me with an ache so deep. And you leaving me, I don't know if this feeling in my chest is ever going to go away. The thought of never being able to see you smile, hear you laugh, smell you, touch you… I'm dying inside."

I'm openly weeping. My actions are involuntary as I crawl off my bed, walking across the floor on my knees. Placing my hand where I think his head is resting just outside my door, I instantly feel invisible sparks fly between us, and Jasper surprises me as he inhales deeply.

"I can feel you, Ava. Please open the door."

Hesitating only a moment, I slowly unlock it and see Jasper sitting defeated, head hung low. But as the door opens, he quickly turns around so we're facing each other. He stalls for a second, then slowly rises to his knees, until we're both kneeling in front of one another.

I stare at him, taking in his appearance, tears stinging my eyes at what I see.

His messy, chaotic hair, which is wild, is sticking out like it's been pulled to the point of being painful. His sad mouth droops into a slight frown, and heavy stubble caresses his face like he hasn't shaved in days. His eyes, usually clear and bright, are now heavy, sunken in, and bloodshot like he hasn't slept for days. The light has dimmed, he looks beaten and bruised. He looks like shit. He looks just like I do.

Reaching out, he shakily caresses my cheek, and I sigh into his touch because it's been so long since I've felt his hands on me. I close my eyes as his warm hand engulfs my tear-stained cheek, and I feel the tremble in his touch as another tear rolls down my cheek. His thumb wipes it away, but his attempt is futile, as another just follows in its path.

"Baby, I'm sorry," he whispers, and as he pulls me into him, I drown in all things Jasper.

Resting my head in the corner of his neck, I feel his pulse against my face, and that pulse is giving him away because it's beating like a drum. He's obviously as deeply affected by me, as I am him. Suddenly, everything we've been fighting about fades, and everything seems so... trivial.

Pulling away, I place my hand over his heart, my eyes never leaving his.

"I love you."

A lone tear rolls down his cheek at my confession, and *this* is how I envisioned our first time to be. Not over the phone, or not because he said it first. I wanted to say it when it was right, when I meant it with my heart and soul.

"I love you so much. I surrender everything I am to you, Ava Thompson. All the good, all the bad, I give to you. I surrender myself to you. Do what you wish with me. I submit to you, I am yours. Whatever choice you make, I accept it. I support you, and I will love you forever and a day."

A howl rips through me, and I can't breathe because I'm sobbing uncontrollably. This is tearing me in half. Jasper embraces me and I weep harder, harder than I ever have before.

After I regain some control, I pull away as I have to explain myself to him. "Jasper…" God, is that really my voice that sounds so croaky? "You *are* a good man. I've never met a more honest, extraordinary, amazing person than you. You saved me, Jasper. You saved me when I was drowning. You were my life raft because you pulled me out of my misery. Without you, I would be dead inside. So, don't you dare think you're not good enough for me, because if anything, I'm not good enough for *you*."

He opens his mouth to reply, but I silence him with my finger. "You worshipped me every single day we were together. You were always there, holding my hand when I needed you, no questions asked. I am the selfish one. I should never have behaved the way I did about you staying in Chicago. You had every right, she's your mom. I'm the one who should be saying sorry, not you. Forgive me. Forgive me for doing you wrong." I sob, sending my apology back at him.

We're openly hugging each other, still on our knees, me a weeping mess, with Jasper stroking my back.

I finally pull myself together and sigh.

"I know," he answers like he can read my mind. "I know you still have to go. But I'll be here when you come back."

I sniff sadly. "Don't make promises you can't keep. I'll come back home, fighting for your affections."

Jasper ducks his head down to look at me seriously. "I mean it, Ava. There is no competition. You are, and will always be, the only contender for my heart. I love you with everything I am. No one compares to you because I have loved you from the first moment I saw you."

I close my eyes at his beautiful words. "I don't deserve you. But I want you, so I have to do this. I have to go on this journey, so I'm worthy of your love. I have to do this to become a better woman… for you."

Jasper strokes my hair, resting his cheek on my head. "Wishes do come true."

"What do you mean?" I ask, confused.

"When you told me you wished you were a bird, that you wanted to fly away and never have to land…Well, you got your wish. You can fly away from here and discover new places, and if you don't like where you land, you can always come home, and I'll always be here, waiting for you. Whenever you decide to come to rest, even if its two years, ten years, twenty years or fifty years from now… I promise, I'll be here, waiting to catch you when you're ready to land."

I'm a mess, my eyes are raw from crying so profoundly and my chest feels heavy. I don't want to leave him, but I need to do this to find myself. Jasper looks at me with tears in his eyes, and I know this is the right choice. I have to fly away, and like a bird every season, I'll come home to him. He is, and always will be, my home.

"Make love to me," I whisper, smiling through my tears, as the word *love* has taken on a whole different meaning to us now.

Jasper slowly closes the distance between us, and the moment I feel his mouth on mine, a need of being with him, in him, overwhelms me and I lose control. His luscious lips taste like tears, mine and his, sculpted together to become one, and nothing has ever felt so right.

Jasper slowly lowers himself so he's sitting, and pulls me into his lap so I'm straddling him. My fingers instantly curl in his hair, which is so much longer than when I saw him last. And I can't help myself as I pull, loving the feel of the glossy strands between my fingers.

"Baby, I need you," Jasper whispers against my lips, and his pressing arousal against my leg is a sure sign he's telling the truth.

The proper thing to do would be go into my room, close the door, and have our way with one another in private, but I don't think I can wait. And judging by the way Jasper's fingers are quickly unfastening my jeans, neither can he.

"I can't wait," he hisses, reading my thoughts, his fingers slipping into my pants, bypassing my underwear and going straight for my center.

I groan the moment he makes contact. He doesn't have to prep me, because I'm so ready. Bucking against his hand, I'm about to come undone, but I calm myself down. When I explode, I want it to be together.

Fumbling between us, I finally get his jeans undone, and he quickly removes his hands from my pants so he can strip me of mine. As he drags them down my hips, he quickly slips on a condom, angles himself, and enters me with swift precision.

"Holy shit," he curses, stilling so he can catch his breath.

My eyes roll into the back of my head, as I've almost forgotten how good he feels, but as he begins moving, the pleasurable memories come flooding back, and I'm determined to make more.

Wrapping my arms around his neck, I use his body as leverage and begin rocking against him, taking him as deep as he will go.

"Baby, oh fuck," he growls. His pleasure gives me the courage to ride him a little faster.

Being in control this way, I feel so alive, and my release is close because every stroke is hitting me in just the right way. Throwing my head back and arching my neck, Jasper leans forward and sucks on my flesh, which drives me wild. A sex demon overtakes me, and I ride him harder, and faster, and before long, we're both panting and grunting, and crying out each other's names.

"I can't, oh…God!" I whimper, coming so loudly I almost cry with the release.

A second later, Jasper groans, his hips pumping into me furiously and I know he's also spent. That was…wow.

Slumping in his arms, I doubt I'll feel my legs any time soon, but the paralysis is so worth it.

"You okay?" Jasper mumbles into my neck.

I grunt in response, and he laughs.

We stay this way for minutes, and I'm almost asleep, but V's timid voice, calling out to me from downstairs rouses my sleepy state.

"Is it safe to come up? I really need to use the bathroom."

My cheeks instantly heat as she no doubt heard our very PDA, but I can't help the sinister smile which spreads from cheek to cheek.

"You ready for round two, lover?" I whisper as I meet his curious eyes.

"I'm always ready for you, baby," he replies, nudging his hips forward, and I can tell it is indeed true. Moaning at the contact, V groans from downstairs when she hears my whimpers of pleasure.

"Again?" she yells.

"Think…of this… as…payback," I manage to reply, as Jasper drives into me, deliciously slow.

Payback has never tasted this good.

Chapter 40
Forever and a Day

I'm on my way to the airport, and I'm trying my hardest to keep the tears away after V and I said an extremely teary goodbye. I miss her already.

Jasper is silent behind the wheel, as we're both deep in thought. If someone told me a year ago, to the day, I would be heading back to a place that held so many bad memories; I would have laughed, calling them a fool. But it looks like I'm the fool.

It's been exactly a year since I touched down at LAX, a broken, battered lost girl. But now, as I look at myself in the mirror, I no longer see that reflection. I see a girl, who is still broken, but whose scars are healing. And about being lost, well, we're all lost souls, waiting for someone to be our guide. I found my light, but I'm flying in the other direction towards the dark—towards the unknown.

Yes, I'm scared, but I'm also at peace, because I know when I return, I'll return a better woman. If Jasper is still waiting for me, then all of this will be worth it. We need to repair ourselves before we can begin a future with one another. If I'd met Jasper two years in the future, would I still feel the same? Would I still be crazy in love with the devoted man next to me? Is all this worth it? I can't answer that.

Life takes us on unexpected voyages, in which we ultimately have to decide which crossroad we'll take. If I had to go through all the hardships in my life to get to Jasper, then yes, it was worth it, and so much more.

As I check in, I can feel the tears creeping up on me. Jasper squeezes my hand tightly, sensing my emotional breakdown. Taking a steady, calming breath, I close my eyes. I can do this. We sit in the lounge, waiting for my boarding call. We wait in silence, but the silence is deafening. I can tell by the slump of his shoulders, disheveled hair and steady frown that he feels everything I feel.

The announcement over the loud speaker indicates boarding for my flight to Singapore has begun. All of a sudden, I feel panic rising as my bottom lip trembles uncontrollably. "I can't go," I state, jumping up and pacing frantically.

Jasper grabs my hand, ceasing my movements. "Yes, you can."

"No, I really can't. I don't want to say goodbye," I say, on the verge of tears.

"We're not saying goodbye," Jasper replies with a sad smile.

"Yes, we are. When I get on that plane, you'll be gone." I look up at him sadly, biting my lip to stop the tears

"I'll never be gone, Ava. I'll always be here, waiting for you. I promise."

His words open the floodgates, and I begin weeping uncontrollably.

I'm on the verge of hyperventilating, my breath catching in my throat. "You say that now, but you'll leave me when it gets too hard." I know I need to shut up, but I can't help it as my insecurities make an unwelcome appearance.

"Baby, listen to me," he says, standing up and holding me an arm's length away, his eyes searching mine. "I'll never leave you. I am yours, forever. Losing you is not an option."

"But…" I choke.

"No buts." He puts his finger over my lips to silence me. "I'm nothing without you. Everything in my life has led to this moment—me meeting you. Me loving you. And me letting you go. I know you've loved me the best you could, and I feel like a better man being loved by you. Every breath I've taken, every step I've taken, it has led me to you."

Looking into his bright, clear eyes, I memorize his face, which is filled with unconditional love. I bite my lip to stop the avalanche of tears, but it doesn't work.

"I was stupid to think I could leave you." And here come the tears.

Jasper grins, that boyish, carefree smile he has rewarded me with so many times. He reaches into his backpack and pulls out the leather journal I gave him for Christmas. He sits down and pulls out the beautiful pen with its sapphire tip that reminds me so much of his stunning eyes. Scribbling something quickly, he rips out the page, folds it, and puts it into my back pocket. He rests his hands on my waist, looking down at me as he stands.

"You read that whenever you need it."

"What is it?" I question, trying to pull it out of my pocket, but Jasper stops me.

"You read it when you feel lost. When you're flying on your journey, and if you ever feel like you're flying in the wrong direction, you read that, okay?" he says, brushing away a tear. "You read that, and it'll set you right."

Sobbing uncontrollably, I throw my arms around his neck and take in his smell, his warmth, everything that is Jasper, and I store that in my memory bank for when I miss him and feel lost.

As the second boarding call is announced, I know I have to go.

Jasper pulls me in for a long, tender kiss, and our mouths are prisoner to our sorrow. We can't stop kissing, and crying, our tears mixed together, and I taste our salty sadness.

Jasper reluctantly pulls away, those blue eyes assessing me, taking in every corner of my face, as he too, is storing me into his memory bank.

He smiles sadly, kissing my forehead. "Remember that night, when you asked if I was happy?"

I nod in response, a sob catching in my throat.

"Well, I am now. I am perfectly happy because I know I have your affections and you love me. Thank you for making me feel like I'm someone worth loving. I'll never forget this feeling, the feeling of being loved by you. I love you, baby." With that he pulls away, tears running down his face as he turns to leave.

Crying uncontrollably, I watch his retreating form until I can no longer see him.

"I love you, too," I whisper, as I walk down the tarmac a broken woman.

***

"Ladies and gentlemen, the captain has turned off the Fasten Seat Belt sign so you may now move around the cabin.

"In a few moments, the flight attendants will be passing around the cabin to offer you hot or cold beverages. Now, sit back, relax, and enjoy the flight. Thank you."

So, here I sit, once again, glancing at the reflection staring back at me from the window. I wonder, is this how others see me? A girl whose eyes are too big for her melancholy face. A girl whose frame is so small, her feet barely reach the sticky floor. A girl who laughs at everyone's jokes, even when she doesn't see the point of laughing at mindless nothingness. A girl whose heart has been crushed, chewed on, spat out, set on fire—and put on repeat, just for fun.

But this girl has had her heart healed by a wonderful person. A person who has made her laugh, made her cry, and made the pain fade just by loving her entirely with his big heart. The reflection staring back at me is of a stronger woman, a whole year older than she was when she last made this journey.

I hear a throat clearing. "Ah, Miss, can I get you anything?" I look up at the air hostess. Why does she look so familiar? Oh, the paradox of life. This air hostess was on this journey with me a year ago, and her eyes also look as if they've seen a year's worth of pain, happiness, and sorrow, just like mine.

I smile at her, in better spirits than the last time I was on her flight. "No, I'm okay, thank you." She nods and smiles, moving onto the next passenger.

Rearranging myself, I rest my head against the glass and look out at the vast nothingness of being so high up above the clouds. I put in my earbuds and select "Miles" by Christina Perri, as I feel this song is the soundtrack to my life.

As I get lost in the words, I remember Jasper's note in my pocket. I reach for it with such care, like it might detonate, and pull it out, staring at the folded piece of paper. It takes all my willpower not to breakdown.

Jasper White has taught me so many life lessons, and I will turn my back on the dark. I will follow my white knight into the light when I'm ready.

Trembling as I open up the note, I stare at his elegant, left hand script writing, and without a word, Jasper has left me speechless once again.

> *If you love something, set it free. If it comes back, it's yours. If it doesn't, it was never meant to be.*

A tear streaks the page, as I read his words over and over again.
Jasper White, I'll be yours, forever and a day.
I'm coming back home to you…I promise.

Acknowledgments

Mum and dad, you have been a constant support throughout my life, and have encouraged me through thick and thin- I thank you!

Fran, Matt and my two beautiful nieces, Samantha and Amelia, you make me forever smile and I'm so lucky to have you in my life.

Louise and Jaz- you put the awesome in, well... awesome.

Lisa Edward, thank you, thank you for allowing me to bounce ideas off of you, and listening to me talk on and on and on...and on

Roger Rothfield- we did it!! Thank you so much for your help and advice.

Jo Dorn- Thank you for all your advice, and the laughs!

Karli Roderick- You are the only person who gets my craziness. I thank you for being crazy with me!

My amazing editor, Toni Rakestraw. You truly are a genius. Without you, this wouldn't be possible. I am forever indebted to you.

Emily Tippetts, I'm sorry for the endless questions! You did a brilliant job!

To all my friends and family who have shown constant support throughout this crazy ride thank you... that means YOU!

To Daniel, Buckwheat, Dacca, Mitch, Jag and Ninja, you are the reason why families exist- I LOVE YOU!

Oh, and thank you to YOU... for giving me inspiration whether good...or bad...to finish what I started.

About the Author

Monica James spent her youth devouring the works of Anne Rice, William Shakespeare and Emily Dickinson.

When she is not writing, Monica is busy running her own business, but she always finds a balance between the two.

She enjoys writing honest, heartfelt and turbulent stories, hoping to leave an imprint on her readers, and her inspiration comes from everyday life. She is an Amazon Bestselling Author in the US, Canada and the UK.

Monica James resides in Melbourne, Australia, with her wonderful family, and menagerie of animals.

She is slightly obsessed with cats, chucks and lip gloss, and secretly wishes she was a ninja on the weekends.

This paperback interior was designed and formatted by

E.M. TIPPETTS BOOK DESIGNS

www.emtippettsbookdesigns.com

Artisan interiors for discerning authors and publishers.

Made in United States
Orlando, FL
17 November 2023